REFLECTIONS

Jena Baxter

Table of Contents

ACKNOWLEDGEMENTS

A hearty thank you to Barbara Kuntz, who spent hours plotting this story out with me, and Chris Drew, who went over my work, almost on a daily basis. Thanks to Rachael Adams for her editing skill, Susan Stuckey, Helen Aveling, and all the people on Scribophile who critiqued and corrected my chapters, as well as checking the historical validity of my work. Last, a big thanks to my husband who has the patience of a saint.

Chapter 1

"Have a heart that never hardens, and a temper that never tires, and a touch that never hurts." Charles Dickens.

London, England. 1807

Juliette shut the front door behind her, and slowly climbed down the stairs of her home, cringing at every creek of the steps. She walked down the paved road, back straight and chin up, until the house was out of view. She looked around, pulled off her bonnet, and ran all the way to the beach.

Stopping to catch her breath, she scanned the riverbank until she spotted Emily, gazing into the clouds above the Thames. It was a gray and dreary day, but a fisherman stood in the water trying to entice the fish, and a few people were scattered along the shoreline. Sea birds flew back and forth, seeking a tasty morsel. Juliette joined Emily, and sat in the scrub.

"It took you a long time to get here," Emily said, smiling.

"Sorry, it's my birthday and mother is hosting a party tonight. I had to sneak out of the house, but no one saw me. Then I ran all the way here."

Emily shrugged. "Doesn't matter." She held out her arm, and opened her hand. "I made this for you."

Juliette took the hair pin with a tattered yellow ribbon tied in a bow attached to it.

Emily's cheeks colored. "Sorry it's not new."

Juliette hugged her. "It's wonderful. Thank you. I have to go back now, before they notice me gone," she said, pushing the pin carefully into her hair.

"Okay, I'll go with you. How old are you today?"

Juliette smiled. "I'm six years old," she said, as they made their way back to the road. "How old are you?"

"Seven, since last month." She ran dirty hands down her tattered and stained black dress.

"Look!" Juliette stopped, and pointed toward the water.

Emily followed the direction of her finger. "Oh! What a beautiful chestnut horse."

9

Juliette shook her head, ringlets blowing in the wind. "No, it's not a horse. It's a unicorn sighting for my birthday." She continued walking toward the road.

"But unicorns aren't real," Emily said, looking back at the animal.

"How do you know they aren't real? That horse has a black horn. Trust me, that's a unicorn."

They stepped onto the dirt road.

"I'll race you there!" Juliette yelled.

Laughing, they ran until they found Mrs. Barrows waiting at the front door of Juliette's home. Juliette went silent and ran to her mother. Emily stopped in the road.

"Where have you been? Look at your hair, it's a mess… and what is that ugly thing sticking out of it?"

Mrs. Barrows swiped the pin off Juliette's head. She winced as strands of her hair fell with the ribbon to the ground.

Juliette followed her mother's eyes as she glared at Emily, standing on the road.

"What have I told you about spending your time with people like that, Juliette? That girl has no business talking to you, and you have no business playing with our domestic help."

"But she's not our domestic help, Mother."

"The girl is as good as employed by this household with her aunt Zylphia, working here."

"I don't want to see you with her again. Do you understand me? What if someone saw you?" Mrs. Barrows shrieked. "You embarrass the entire family associating with people like that, Juliette. Get in the house!"

Juliette jumped when the door slammed shut behind her.

Juliette picked up a glass of punch and sat with the children attending the party. She watched her mother laugh and sip tea with her guests. The children chattered beside her, she ignored them. Her mother had made it clear that the only reason she hadn't received a strapping was so she could sit down at the party. Juliette struggled with the sting of tears, holding them back, but just barely.

Margaret sashayed over, and stood with her hands on her hips. *She always has something to say about everything.* Juliette frowned, waiting. All of the children stared at her.

"I heard you were playing with a servant girl today. Robert Beale said he saw you running and laughing on the road like it was the most normal thing in the world. You're liable to get a disease spending your time with something like that."

"It's not your business, Margaret. I'll spend time with whomever I want."

"Suit yourself, but I don't want any part of that, or you." Margaret lifted her chin and joined the other children.

Juliette turned to see her mother, who had been just out of view. Her knuckles white as the dish she held.

"Go to your room, Juliette."

Tears spilled down Juliette's cheeks. She tried to think of something to say, but couldn't. She ran to her room.

Minutes later the razor-strap slammed into her bare buttocks. The humiliation of knowing the party heard her screams was part of her punishment. When the governess finished, she had been instructed to return Juliette to the party where she remained until the last guest departed.

Her mother turned to her. "Get to your room. I don't want to see your face again tonight."

Juliette obeyed moving much slower than before. Her bottom and the back of her legs stung with welts. She crawled onto the bed, and wept into her pillow.

Ten Years Later

Juliette grunted, eyebrows narrowed as Emily tightened the laces on her corset, pulling her breasts straight and high. She slipped the heavily embroidered bodice on each arm, then smoothed the fabric with her hands. When she was finished, she bowed her head, and backed out of the room.

Juliette moved right and left, twisting at the waist to admire herself in the mirror. She was wearing her favorite dress, white embroidered muslin, with a gathered bust, tiers of ruffles at the bottom, and long sleeves with small puffy shoulders.

"I'll be ready to go in five minutes, Emily," Juliette called, from her bedroom door. "Be sure to get a basket from the kitchen."

That girl always has her head in the clouds. Let's see, all I need now is... she fumbled through a small grey hatbox on the bureau... *a head dress.* Juliette turned back to the mirror, pushing the comb through her hair to hold the head dress in place. When her ensemble was finished she smiled. *Perfect.* She looked good, but the sun was streaming through her bedroom window and the layers of the shift and petticoat were already making her hot.

Rushing down the stairs, underskirts rustling with every movement, the wooden planks creaked with every step. She called for Emily, and found her at the bottom, putting on her plain white bonnet. The picnic basket sat on the floor beside her scuffed black shoes. Juliette's mother stood at a table near the hearth, brown ringlet curls hanging perfectly down her back, her deceptively warm brown eyes belying the severity of her anger. She threw some coins into a small purse. Ignoring Emily, Juliette went straight to her mother, and held out her hand. Mrs. Barrows dropped the beaded, pink and yellow purse into it.

"It is absolutely absurd," Mrs. Barrows said louder than she needed to. "That I should have to send my own daughter to buy what is needed because of dishonest servants. My husband pays a generous wage. You have no reason to steal from us or anyone else. All of your salaries will be fined a farthing. Not just this time, but every time I send Juliette to the market."

She turned back to Juliette. "Don't be late, darling. The dressmaker needs to take some measurements for a new dress," Mrs. Barrows said, fingering some of the new materials she had purchased, sitting on the back of a pink and white sofa.

Juliette grinned as her mother kissed her cheeks.

"Don't worry, Mother. I won't be long."

Juliette walked out the door with Emily trailing behind her.

Juliette closed her eyes at the bright morning sunshine. She crinkled her nose and opened them again at the smell of fresh baked bread. There were vendors with carts selling household goods and colorful linens, and a cobbler had a table set up along the street. A woman with chubby cheeks and braided corn silk hair, sold flowers of every color, and across the road a young boy knelt, breeches tight, as he shined the shoes of a man in a brown suit and hat. A black carriage drove through the village square, horse hooves clip clopping on grey and brown cobblestones.

Emily cried out and crashed into Juliette. Juliette pushed her away, then slapped her without a thought. A thin young man with dark hair, brown eyes, and the longest eyelashes Juliette had ever seen jumped in front of Emily. Emily's hand rested on the angry red mark forming on her right cheek, and she was weeping. Juliette smoothed her skirt mumbling under her breath. *I am going to kill her when we get home. The stupid little sheep.*

"Please excuse us, Jonathan, this fool of a girl—"

Jonathan's hands waved back and forth. "No, Miss Barrows. Please, I am sorry. The fault was my own, not the servant girl's."

Juliette smiled. "This one is inept and bumbling at times."

Jonathan reached into his bag and pulled out a muslin pouch. He held the contents in front of Juliette. "Turkish Delight. Would you like one? A small offering to make up for the trouble I caused."

Juliette's smile lit up her face. "Yes, thank you." She chose a red square powdered with sugar from the pouch.

Jonathan held the bag out to Emily. Juliette's eyes flashed. *What is he doing? Why is he even speaking to her? She's a servant!* Emily shook her head back and forth, then looked away. Jonathan held them closer.

"Please, I insist."

With a trembling hand, Emily took one, but before she could eat the sweet, Juliette pointed to the basket.

"We need to go. I have an appointment this afternoon." The courtesy was a show for Jonathan's sake. She would take care of Emily at home. "If you'll excuse us Jonathan, we really must be on our way. Thank you for the sweetmeats."

Juliette purchased the potatoes and carrots Cook required, the dirty-faced farmer extended his thanks, and she turned to see Jonathan smiling at Emily. The girl looked away, but not before her cheeks colored. Juliette had had enough. She grabbed Emily's arm.

"Good day, Jonathan."

Juliette had never been so embarrassed in her life. *A servant girl! And one that was stumbling all over the place. What was he thinking? No! What was she thinking?*

Juliette stormed up wooden steps and through the door without waiting for Emily to open it. "Mother!"

Emily wept openly.

"Emily was flirting with Mrs. Walsh's son. She even received a gift from him."

Mrs. Barrow's porcelain face darkened, and her fingers clutched the folds of her dress as Juliette recounted the story. Moments later, Juliette's mother grabbed Emily's arm and pulled her to the Governess' room. A heavyset woman in a plain black dress and long white apron, her brown hair tucked beneath her bonnet, sat at an old oak desk looking grim. The room was modest, with only a narrow bed, and a plain wooden bureau against the opposite wall. The only color was a handmade quilt the woman had made for herself, and a full-length blue dress hanging in a tiny closet.

Agnes stood when Mrs. Barrows entered the room, and stared at Emily, blue eyes icy cold. The Governess opened a drawer, and pulled out the razor strap used for disciplining the household.

Emily's sobs grew louder, her eyes wide. She grimaced, shaking her head frantically.

"No," Emily whined, looking at the thick leather with three long flexible straps. "No, please." Her sobs grew louder still as the Governess dragged her out the door to a wooden shed.

Juliette's mother smiled as Emily began to scream incoherently. Standing by the new material, they heard the whack of leather meeting the flesh of Emily's bare backside.

Juliette fingered the soft new pink and yellow fabrics, frowning. *I'm not fond of yellow. Mother knows that.*

"Emily will be indisposed for a while, Mother. Could you send Bessie up, please? I really need to freshen up before we leave."

"Of course, dear."

Juliette bustled up the stairs, hands clutching her skirt, listening to Emily scream. *That's too bad. She won't be flirting or accepting treats from boys above her station anymore.* But she shivered inwardly. Juliette knew well what it meant to be on the receiving

14

end of that strap. She had been beaten for spending time with Emily when they were girls. Juliette was younger then, and hadn't understood how important it was not to entertain people below her station. She knew better now. Emily wouldn't be able to sit for a week. Perhaps then she would learn her lesson and not entertain people above her station.

Juliette entered her room, letting the door shut behind her, and took off her head dress.

Bessie entered the bedroom, picked up the brush and pulled it through Juliette's curls. Her hands trembled and she winced at every thwack of the strap on, Emily's, bared flesh. At one point she wiped a tear from her eye. Juliette smiled, and ignored her.

Zylphia dusted a lampshade trimmed with burgundy roses. She had already gone over the end tables and swept the floors. She tucked runaway strands of brown hair under her already loose bun, and saw something smeared on the wall. Emily walked in, concealing her face, and staring at the floor.

Zylphia motioned with her hands as she spoke. "Emily, go get me a cleaning cloth for the wall. Bessie will get one for you. They're in the kitchen."

Emily nodded her acknowledgement to the floor, stiffly leaving the room. Zylphia stared after her. *What is wrong with her today?* Emily had always been a shy girl. She was quiet, but that was expected of a domestic servant. You did what you were told, bowed and backed out of the room as quiet as you could, hoping that no one would hear you. These things had never been a problem for her niece. That was why Zylphia had brought her here. She got along with everyone, was quiet, kept her own counsel, and took her work seriously.

Emily returned with the cloth. Zylphia watched her shuffle across the room.

"Why are you walking like that? Come here."

Emily's speed picked up. She whined and winced, until she slowed down. She gave Zylphia the towel.

"What is wrong with you? Look at me when I talk to you, girl!"

15

Emily looked up. Zylphia saw chocolate brown eyes, similar to her own, except they were red, sad, and swollen. Her brown hair was a tangled mess. She took Emily's hand.

"Come with me."

Emily obeyed, but wept all the way to, Zylphia's, bedroom. Zylphia removed Emily's white apron, and black uniform dress. Zylphia gasped, fire red welts blistered, and covered Emily's buttocks and the back of her legs.

"Who did this to you?"

Emily told Zylphia about the boy at the marketplace, the candy, and Juliette's anger. "I tried to say no, but he insisted." Tears fell down already swollen cheeks. "I t-tried to s-s-say no. I didn' know what t-to do."

Heat flushed through Zylphia. She pulled a jar of ointment from under her mattress, and slathered it over Emily's welts. The response was immediate. Zylphia couldn't take away the welts, that would have been too obvious, but the swelling went down, and the redness faded. Emily shuddered, then sighed with relief.

"It's over now." *And I'm going to make certain it won't happen again.* "Go back to work. It's alright."

"What are you going to do? Please don't curse her Aunt Zylphia. We were friends once. She even gave me a doll when we were small."

"Juliette isn't the person you used to know, child. She's grown to be callous, and cruel. Trust me to know what to do. She needs to pay for what she's done. You need to help in the kitchen. Now go."

Emily looked skeptical, but did what she was told.

"Why can't I take Bessie?" Juliette demanded. "I don't want that insolent girl anywhere near me."

"I'm sure you don't, darling, but Bessie has chores to do for your father. The only other servant I can send with you right now is Zylphia."

"I don't want Zylphia." Juliette stomped her foot. "She's not normal." *That one hardly knows her station, and the way she looks at me is frightening sometimes. I don't trust her.* "Mother!"

"That's enough, Juliette. Take both if you choose, but Bessie cannot go."

"Emily! Zylphia! Get down here. Now!"

Moments later, Emily and Zylphia entered the room.

Chapter 2

"There's none so blind as those who will not see." Jonathan Swift.

London, England

Juliette strolled through the marketplace. She had no appointments today, and her mood was just foul. The complaints of the birds, and chatter in the square only made it worse. She caught sight of Jonathan, escorting his mother toward a vendor and looking her way, but acted like she hadn't noticed. *That is the least he deserves for flirting with a servant girl.* She stood a little taller.

She looked up again to see Jonathan gazing at Emily. Juliette's lips parted, and she glanced at Emily, who was looking the other way, trembling. Juliette lifted her chin. *Well then, the beating did some good after all.*

An old woman, with white hair and a plain old fashioned white dress, slipped twisting her ankle, and caught Juliette's shoulder to keep from falling. Juliette twisted, dropping the woman to the cobblestones. She heard the crunch of snapping bone. Trembling, the woman reached out.

"Please, Lady. Won't you help me up?

Zylphia can help the woman. Juliette looked around. *Where is she? Maybe I should have her beaten this time.*

"Don't touch me, old woman. Surely someone will stop for you. I haven't the time." Quickly, Juliette moved away.

It wasn't long until she saw a couple of men helping the woman. When the woman was upright the gentlemen left, and the woman caught her eyes.

Juliette shivered, cold to her bones. She blinked, the air shimmered like glitter. The woman never moved, and Juliette hadn't looked away, but suddenly, she was gone.

Juliette stood in her nightdress in front of the full length mirror her father brought from Italy. Hand-carved cherry wood displayed intricate carvings of vines and roses. Juliette ran her

18

fingers over them, then ran her hand down its clear and flawless surface. Truly, her finest gift and the possession she loved most.

She picked up her watch, and attached it to a small concealed pocket sewn to the inside of her clothing. Another gift from father that mother insisted she keep on her person. The watch was gold, its band simple with a few carefully placed roses, much like the ones on her mirror.

Where is Emily?

Two knocks on the door and her mother came into the room. She reached for the brush in Juliette's hand.

"Emily is helping Cook clean the kitchen floor since Bessie dropped what was left of the roast and gravy. I've been wanting to speak with you about a few things so I thought now might be a good time."

She moved Juliette's chair from the vanity to the full length mirror, and motioned for her to sit down. Wondering what her mother might want to discuss with her, Juliette sat. Her mother ran her fingers to the front of her hair, gingerly smoothing it as she pulled it back from her neck to brush. Juliette took a deep breath, enjoying the feel of her mother's light fingers on her skin. She gently ran the brush through her hair.

"Your Father and I have been speaking. You're sixteen years old now." She ran her hand along her jawline, an affectionate playful glint in her eyes.

"You're a beautiful young girl. We've decided it's time for you to have a home of your own to manage." She ran the brush through the length of Juliette's hair again. "It's time to find you a husband. I can arrange tea parties and socials. Surely there is no suitor that could resist these soft ringlet curls and those big innocent brown eyes." She bent to Juliette's neck, smiling at her in the mirror.

Juliette giggled.

"Your waist, while not as small as mine, is smaller than most girls of your age."

You had to add that to ruin the moment, didn't you Mother?

"And your breasts will certainly turn a young man's eye."

Mrs. Barrows stood up right and resumed brushing. "Is there a suitor that's caught your eye?"

Juliette's cheeks warmed. "Jonathan Walsh. I've always thought him to be an extraordinary boy."

19

Mrs. Barrows shook her head. "No. You might think so now, but he isn't what you want. Any man that is smiling at the servant girls will not be faithful."

Juliette's smile faltered. A knock at the door, and Emily entered the room. Mrs. Barrows handed her the brush.

"Well, Emily will finish up here. We'll talk more about this tomorrow."

Juliette heard the sound of music, and stopped to listen. "What is that music?"

Mrs. Barrows looked at Juliette, frowning. "The house is quiet, darling. There's no music."

Emily ran the brush through Juliette's hair, and Mrs. Barrows, moved to the door.

"Think more about what I said, Juliette. There must be others."

She left the room and Juliette to her thoughts.

Juliette remained silent as Emily worked the brush through her curls. *This was such a difficult day, and now this. First those ridiculous piano lessons mother insisted on. Even my teacher winced when I played. It isn't my fault the piano sounded like a strangled cat each time I tried a sonata. And now those dreadful violin lessons too. Marriage I can deal with, but my heart belongs to Jonathan.*

She heard music again, but louder this time. She looked at Emily's reflection in the mirror.

"There it is again. You must have heard that."

"I'm sorry, Ma'am. I didn't hear anything."

The sound stopped. Juliette scanned the room. "I'm sure it was nothing, I'm just tired."

Juliette waved her out of the room. She headed for bed, and blew out the candle.

A gurgling sound near the mirror and light flashed. *What was that?* She scrambled into the bed holding the blanket against her pounding heart. Another flash of light. Juliette shrank further, cowering until only her eyes showed.

"Emily? Is that you?"

Taking shallow breaths, Juliette tried to control her breathing. She hated the dark. She yawned trying to make no sound. *This is silly, a trick of my eyes. None of this is possible. I just need to go to sleep.* She covered her head, and closed her eyes.

A waltz played in the background. Her eyes flew open, her breathing shallow. *What is that?* A woman hummed softly to the music. Juliette froze.

Where is it coming from? She carefully stuck her head out from under the covers, and the sound grew louder. She hadn't heard that tune before. The humming grew louder, and more off key. Then came a voice.

"It's time for recompense, Miss Juliette."

Juliette yelped. *Recompense? For what?*

"You're a spoiled, rich chit! You punish those that displease you, sniff at the poor, ignore the lame, and beat those who have done nothing to you."

Well of course I do. They're servants. Father pays their wages.

The music stopped, the temperature dropped, and Juliette shivered. The mirror made a crackling sound, and Juliette found herself staring at Emily, shaking her head, but it wasn't Emily because she could see through her. *What is going on?* Everywhere she turned, the vision was the same. *I need to get out of here.*

"No. No, please." Emily's voice echoed, her eyes were red and swollen as she struggled uselessly to free herself from the governess' grip.

The vision blurred until Emily stood with her dress and petticoats falling to the floor. Her buttocks and legs were black and blue.

Juliette saw the faces of beaten servants, and heard the echoed thwack of the strap against flesh. Screams and begging of those who were beaten became shadows on the off-white walls of her room.

The vision stretched into taller, slender, Bessie. Strands of brown hair stuck to her face. She lay on her belly, infection covering blisters on her backside. Juliette had her beaten for disappearing the day before Emily's whipping.

Everything in Juliette's room was gone, the bed, the mirror, the door, even the room itself. Nothing was as it should be. The room spun. *Help me!* She whined.

Her former governess, Min, stood before her father, head bowed.

"I only meant to pull the child out from under the bed when she failed to arrive for lessons."

"The child has a name," her father demanded.

"Yes, Sir." Her hands cupped her mouth as she wept. A younger Juliette stood smiling as father dismissed her.

Again, the vision blurred. Min's body lay still on a hill overlooking the Thames, strands of auburn hair blowing in the wind. Her dress was torn, and her arms were bone thin. Her face gaunt and haunted eyes stared into emptiness. *How could I have known that would happen?*

The lame woman from the marketplace reached out to her, calling for help, but when she blinked, Zylphia, stared up at her.

Another blur, and Ben, their coach driver, lay on the side of a cobblestone road. Juliette heard the dead man's voice. She closed her eyes and tried not to see, but nothing enabled her to escape the madness. Covering her ears she cried out.

"But sir, I cannot control the surface of the roads. I assure you, it was not my intention to jostle your daughter so."

Father's chilled voice. "You're dismissed without reference."

"But Mr. Barrows, I won't be able to find work without a reference. What will I do?"

Her father picked up a quill, scratching black ink onto a piece of paper. He didn't look up.

"Dismissed."

Gripping his black hat in shaking hands, his lower lip trembling, Ben left the room.

Zylphia's voice shattered the vision. "With no reference, he was unable to find another situation."

The sudden silence was deafening. Juliette trembled.

Silvery blue light filled the room, deepening shadows crawling on walls. Juliette's eyes opened wide, and she shot upright as Zylphia stepped out of the mirror, metallic color twisting and melding around her body. Juliette blinked and the metal cloak fell to the floor.

Juliette clutched her blankets. "H-how did you do that?" *'Always show the servants that you are the one in control,'* mother always said. *'No matter what the situation is'.* "What are you doing in my room Zylphia? I'll have you strapped for this, now get out." Juliette dropped the covers and forced herself to point toward the door. She wanted to cower under her blankets. "I said get out!"

Zylphia didn't move. Fear clutched at Juliette's heart. The light increased, melted silver tinged with blue. Juliette shivered, there wasn't a candle lit in the room so where was that strange light coming from?

"I'll have you dismissed for this, Zylphia. Get out of here now, and I'll allow you to keep your job. I'll scream, and you'll be lucky if my father doesn't give you to the magistrates. Go!"

I just need to calm down. Show her she will not get the best of me. Get rid of her now, and see she's dismissed in the morning. Father will not tolerate such behavior.

"Scream," Zylphia said. "You won't be heard. But I might remove that pretty voice you're so proud of anyway."

Juliette recoiled.

"I've watched you grow up from a baby, Miss Juliette. I rocked you to sleep. Watched over you when you were sick, even put you to bed at night. You're sixteen years old now, and one of the most terrible people I have met. What happened to you?"

Juliette's eyebrows furrowed, and she opened her mouth.

"Silence! You had an innocent girl beaten because you were jealous."

Juliette tried to speak, but her voice wouldn't come. Lightning filled the room, striking everywhere. Juliette covered her eyes and screamed as an unseen force slammed her. She heard the sound of shattered glass and felt shards slicing her body. She was stuck in a place without time or end. The air was gray and fluid, but she was able to breathe.

She screamed until she landed as if falling from the sky on green grass blanketing hard earth, somewhere other than her room. The strange blue light, tinted with silver permeated and covered everything. Juliette tried to regain equilibrium. *What am I doing outside? And why does everything look so strange? Is she going to kill me? Dear God.* Her heart beat faster.

Groaning, Juliette stood, and looked at her body. *There's no blood.*

"Where am I?" No one responded. "Zylphia, where are you?"

"Recompense."

The voice chilled Juliette to the bone. *What does that mean?* "Zylphia?"

"This is your new home, Juliette. You will remain here until you find compassion in your heart for another human being, sacrificing yourself for someone else's welfare."

23

Juliette fell to her knees shaking her head. "No, you can't leave me here."

"In return, they will be required to sacrifice something for you, but only if you are worthy of their kindness. People like you have been abusing power for centuries."

"You can't do this." Juliette's heart banged at her chest. She tried to swallow the lump in her throat, but couldn't. *Oh, God. Help me.*

"Only when you've met my terms will the curse be broken. If anything happens to me, my death will seal your fate."

"Zylphia—"Juliette covered her ears. *This can't be happening.* "No, Zylphia!"

"You will be permitted to leave this land and walk the earth the first night of the full moon. Make good use of your time. The doorway will remain open from moonrise until the beginning of dawn."

Juliette circled, spotting a wall enclosure hiding all but the slate roof of what looked like a cottage. There was no other dwelling she could see, only land.

"The doorway? Where is this doorway?" *If I can find a door I can find my way home.*

"If you do not return, you will not be permitted to leave for the turning of two seasons. Do you understand?"

"You still haven't told me where this doorway is."

"In the cottage, of course. It's the back of the mirror."

A chill ran up Juliette's spine. "The mirror?"

"There is a doorway between the worlds where you stand, but it has closed. Your door is the mirror in the cottage."

"You can't do this," Juliette pleaded. "You witch!" she shrieked. "Zylphia, stop this right now!"

There was no answer. *I don't even know where I am. What am I going to do?* Juliette crumbled to the ground, hands covering her head. Zylphia was gone.

Chapter 3

"Some men see things as they are and ask why. Others dream things that never were and ask why not." George Bernard Shaw.

The Mirror World

Juliette hoped to wake and find it all a dream, but it wasn't. It was a nightmare. She sat at the edge of a meadow, surrounded by brown and green mountains, the tallest of which were snowcapped. The sun burned red in a silvery blue sky, shining upon the meadow of green grass. *At least that's normal.* Pink and yellow wildflowers danced with the breeze, surrendering their sweet aroma to the wind. Juliette could vaguely see a house or cottage in the distance.

A chill pierced Juliette's heart. "I have to find my way out of this place," she mumbled.

"There is no way to leave here," a deep, temperate voice said, from behind her.

Juliette's head whipped around, her hand clutching her chest. She cowered from a towering white unicorn that stood taller and larger than any horse she had ever seen. It was an exquisite creature with a long silky black mane and tail that sparkled. The unicorn's body was sleek with hard, muscled haunches. The horn was black as pitch, tapering to a sharp point with a thin band of gold spiraling around it.

"You're in the Land of Mirrors. Only the witch can release you."

The unicorn moved closer. Juliette screamed, scooting away. *It talks!*

"Keep away from me!" Eyeing the sharp horn, Juliette groped for something to throw.

The unicorn stopped, but made no move to leave.

What do I have to do to make it go? Her hand met rock, fingers curled around a hard jagged stone almost as big as her hand, and she hurled it. Blood trickled down the elegant white coat. The

25

unicorn reared, and snorted sharply. Juliette found another rock, then another.

"Get out of here," she screamed, her voice shrill.

After hitting it with the third rock, the unicorn bolted.

Juliette stood with her arms crossed, hugging herself, and looking at the cottage at the end of the valley. It was going to be quite a walk and she had no shoes. Every muscle ached with tension, but the soft grass tickled her feet.

If there's anyone here that can help me, they will most likely be found there. I need to find help, even if I will be shamed by being in my nightdress. Father will pay for their trouble. Besides, that creature might come back.

Juliette sighed, and began the long walk to the cottage.

Juliette knelt beside a pond that looked curiously like a moat with sparkling blue water. Her feet hurt and it was hot out. She cupped her hands and drank, then sighed, enjoying the cool liquid. She dipped her hand for more, yelped, and jerked her hand out. Blood trickled from a row of puncture wounds. She inspected the water, and a school of two foot long ivory fish with big eyes and whiskers, swam back and forth, frenzied. One of the fish broke the surface and snapped as though it saw a fly. Thin inch long teeth glistened in the sunlight. Juliette backed away, sucking on the wound that had pierced all the way through her finger.

She followed a trail that led around a tall stone wall until she arrived at the cottage. The structure was made of pink-hued stones and mortar, with a dark brown slate roof. The stone wall surrounding it supported a stable, and flower gardens grew around the buildings. Juliette walked to the opposite side and found a shed near a well-made of darker stones, covered by an open wooden enclosure with an old fishing rod and spear leaning against it. A dry bucket hung from the wooden structure's roof.

Juliette straightened her back and walked to the front door. She knocked and waited. She tried again, but no one answered. With a trembling hand, Juliette twisted the latch, and the door creaked open. Entering, she saw a hearth on one side of the room with blackened logs. They looked cold. A wooden table with leather chairs sat by a wall covered in windows. The glass was cut into small panes creating three large oval designs. Juliette cleared her throat, but her voice was small as a child's.

"Hello? Is anyone here? I need help." Juliette stepped forward and faltered. There was a kitchen to her left with a small preparation table, and an empty pot resting on a wood burning stove. An open fire pit was built into one wall with a kettle lodged inside it. Everything was clean. Not even a speck of dust anywhere, except the stone-tiled floor. Emptiness screamed through the cottage's rooms, and hallway. She tried calling again.

"Hello? I'm lost, and I need to find my way home."

Moving down the hall, Juliette found a bedchamber. She peered into the room, and saw a mirror similar in size to the one on her bedroom wall. It was fancier than hers, with a gold frame with strange creatures carved into an intricate, spiral pattern. One of the creatures was a unicorn, holding his head up with pride. Another was an odd creature Juliette had never seen before. It looked like a man, rugged and handsome with bearish features. The fish from the pond were carved into the four corners, and there were groups of centaurs mixed randomly amongst the unicorns, making it difficult to tell them apart. There was another face carved in at random. She moved closer and gasped. It was her face, and the long flowing ringlets of her hair.

Juliette saw a silvery flash and movement in the mirror. It had to be a trick of her eye. She shivered, remembering being thrown into her own mirror. *"Your door is the mirror in the cottage,"* Zylphia had said. Juliette sat on the bed, and stared in amazement at her mother sitting on the bed in her own bedroom.

"Well her bed's been slept in. Someone should know where she's gone," Mrs. Barrows demanded.

Emily picked up the clothes Juliette left on the bureau the night before and started to shuffle out of the room. Juliette's mother grabbed her arm.

"What do you know about this, Emily? You trail after her day after day. I've already contacted the magistrates."

Emily shook her head. "Nothing ma'am. I haven't seen her."

Mrs. Barrows waved her hand dismissively. "Go then, and tell the rest of the staff I want to see every one of them up here."

Emily paled as she bowed and scurried out of the room. Mrs. Barrows sat on the bed, waiting.

Juliette stood and moved to the mirror. "I'm here mother, in the mirror. Help me!" She banged on the surface. "Mother, please. I'm here!"

Mrs. Barrows gave no reaction.

The governess entered the room. "You wanted to see me?"

"Yes. Juliette is missing. Have you seen her?"

"Why, no ma'am. Maybe she's out for a morning stroll, or gone to market."

"She wouldn't have gone without telling me first," Mrs. Barrows snapped. "Very well. Back to your duties then."

The governess left the room, with a great deal less subservience than Emily had shown before her.

Juliette pushed at the mirror. *Maybe if I can get behind it.* Light flashed, catapulting her across the room. Her body slammed into the wall. Aching and rubbing the new bump on her head, she crawled onto the bed, and watched as one by one every servant came into her room. Her breath caught when Zylphia walked in and looked straight into the mirror. Juliette ran to her.

"Zylphia. Please, don't do this."

Zylphia turned to Mrs. Barrows.

"You can't leave me here! You servants are always acting like you don't hear. Listen to me."

Mrs. Barrows sighed. "I want to know everything you know about my daughter's disappearance."

"I've not seen her since the day we went to market, ma'am."

"If you hear or see anything, you are to tell me immediately. Now you may go."

Zylphia looked in the mirror, and smiled. "Recompense."

Juliette shrank back and shuddered, her hand resting against her throat.

"What did you say?" Mrs. Barrows asked.

"Nothing ma'am, I'm sorry to have disturbed your thoughts." Zylphia's voice echoed slightly. Juliette's mother didn't notice.

Mrs. Barrows mumbled something Juliette couldn't hear as Zylphia bowed her way out of the room.

Juliette's hands slid down the face of the mirror. She could touch it, but couldn't push or pull. She wrapped her arms around her chest. Her mother got up and fluffed her hair in the mirror.

She was so close that Juliette felt like she could touch her, but her hand only met the cold, glassy surface.

"Mother," she whimpered.

Mrs. Barrows left. Juliette threw herself on the bed, pulled a wool blanket close around her, and wept.

London, England

At the end of the day Zylphia found Emily waiting in her room. She pulled the metal pins from her hair allowing it to fall against her shoulders, and ran sore fingers through it.

"Emily?"

Emily bit her trembling lower lip, and took a deep breath. "Please Zylphia. Let her go."

Zylphia shook her head. "That's not possible, child. What's done is done," she said, turning to the small mirror on her wall. "You go, and forget about it. Am I understood?"

Emily nodded, her eyes desperate.

Zylphia put a hand on her shoulder and pushed her toward the door. "Good, then go to bed."

Chapter 4

"My mind is troubled like a fountain stirred; and I myself see not the bottom of it." William Shakespeare.

The Mirror World

Juliette opened her eyes, and glanced at her watch, a gift from father, to find it past noon. *How long has it been since I've eaten?* She covered her face with one hand and fought the tears that stung her eyes. *Crying will accomplish nothing. I need to find food, light for the night, and whether or not there are any other people here. I have to find a way home, and when I do, Emily and Zylphia better watch out. I'm not only going to whip them, I'm going to kill them.*

Moving through the hallway, Juliette saw two other bedchambers, but apart from a bed and lamp, they were empty. All the rooms were spacious for a cottage, giving it a small castle feeling. She found her way back to the kitchen and opened the cupboard. A loaf of bread, wrapped in a linen cloth, sat on the shelf. Juliette grabbed it and frowned. It was hard as the wood of her Stradivarius violin. *Well, I can wet it with water and eat it if I must. That's what they did in the stories I read when I was a girl.*

She returned the bread to the shelf and saw a piece of fruit toward the back. She snatched it up. *It looks fresh.* She pierced the skin and tasted the juice on her finger. *Delicious.* She took a bite, moaned with pleasure, then closed her eyes and chewed.

Opening her eyes again, she flipped the fruit around and saw a wriggling worm inside. She spewed the fruit onto the floor, and ran to the well to rinse her mouth. It was too late when she realized the water might be stagnant, but it tasted fine. Returning to the kitchen, she picked up the fruit and smashed the wriggling worm on the table.

Juliette sat down. *There was a fishing pole, and spear by the well, but where would I use them?* Her stomach churned. Juliette got up and headed for the door. *There has to be something to eat in this place. That fruit came from somewhere.* Not that she wanted to eat it again just now.

Out in the sunshine, Juliette grabbed the fishing pole and spear. It was good to be doing something to keep her mind off of hunger and frustration. The meadow sprawled out before her. She didn't remember the faintest hint of water there. She wasn't going near the fish in the pond again.

Juliette turned around and went the other way, and found a brook off a trail leading through the forest behind the cottage. She decided to follow it. After about a mile walk, she rounded a bend and stopped to gaze at a lake that stretched as far as her eyes could see. It was bordered by forest in some places, and meadows in others. Juliette was hot, and the water inviting, but she wasn't going to get any body parts near the water again.

She looked at her rod, and sighed. She wasn't exactly sure how this was done, but there were always fisherman at the beach. They put a worm or other kinds of food on a hook and placed it in the water. That didn't sound so hard. She debated going back for the fruit. Maybe the fish would bite that. She looked for a place where the trees and shrubs were especially green, found a stick and dug in the dirt. She loved playing in the dirt as a child when mother couldn't see her. She wished it gave her joy now. It didn't, but her efforts were rewarded with a long brown, wiggly worm. She stabbed it with the hook numerous times before it stuck, put the line in the water and waited.

Juliette inspected the area around her. It was so different than home. That blue, silvery color tinted everything, and the red sun made a gorgeous purple hue when it kissed the water. Colors were richer, the flowers brighter, the lake was royal blue. *I hope it doesn't flavor the fish…or poison it.* Twigs crackled and an almost imperceptible growl sounded behind her. The line on the pole went taut. She ignored the fish and turned around. A white lion with bright blue eyes and a huge white mane, stared at her with its fangs exposed and lips pulled back in a snarl. Eight feet of fur and muscle poised to spring.

The lion roared, the sound deafening. Juliette threw her hands in front of her face, and fell to the ground as it sprung. Before the cat landed, a brown blur crashed into it with the speed of a cannon. The two animals rolled and fought in a snarling mass of fur. Juliette swiftly scooted away, then managed to get to her feet, but her legs wouldn't move.

31

With a terrible roar, and a swipe of its claws, the lion turned and ran. Juliette finally managed to flee. She ran for the cottage, but it was too far. The muscles in her legs burned. She couldn't breathe, and tripped over a log, crying out when she landed on a bed of rocks in the creek. Pain seared her hands and knees. Juliette held her breath against the pain. The huge dark animal that fought the lion splashed into the water. Long claws attached to a human hand tugged at her. Juliette fainted.

When Juliette woke her entire body screeched with pain. She wiggled stiff fingers and toes.

"Are you alright?"

It was a male voice, soothing, and calm with a rumble in his throat. Juliette turned toward the direction of the sound. A man stood at the edge of the forest, but he wasn't a man. The top half was a bearded man, with thick black hair covering his bare chest as well as his head. The bottom half had legs like a bear. Though his feet were human, his fingers were claws. Juliette's heart lodged in her throat. Juliette managed a slight nod. The creature came toward her, and she backed away. He stopped and placed her fishing rod, with the fish still attached, at her feet. Something rustled in the forest, and a different beast stood at the tree line, staring. Juliette read about this beast in her lessons as a child, but the centaurs were a myth.

This centaur was certainly real. _Jesus, Mary, and Joseph._ She stood six feet tall with her back straight, and long red hair that matched the silky sheen of her equine body. She stared at Juliette with eyes as dark as the grass of the meadow if it were clothed with the chill of morning frost. Her breasts were covered with green cloth cascading down her belly in a V shape. Her red lips pressed together in obvious displeasure. Juliette fought the urge to back away. The centaur turned her attention to the other creature, her voice as cold as her eyes.

Juliette struggled to claim her voice. "Who are you? I need to find a way home. If you help me, my father will pay." _My father will pay? Do creatures like this need shillings? The centaur is no more than a horse and who knows what that other thing is._

The centaur ignored her. "This is the woman that hurt Colovere, Tolor! And you risk your life to save her?" Her legs shifted, hooves scraping dirt and rustling grass. "She threw rocks at him!"

Tolor shrugged. "It would not have been right to let her die, Selene." His voice was gentle, yet firm. He moved toward the centaur, hard muscles tightening with every step.

"I didn't mean to hurt him. He scared me, and he wouldn't go away," Juliette said.

Selene's cold eyes fixed on Juliette. Tolor ran his hand gently down Selene's hair, her neck, and along her back. She shivered.

"Let us go now, Tolor. This woman is no concern of ours," Selene said softly.

Tolor smiled and brushed her cheek with his lips. "Of course."

Juliette watched them disappear into the woods. *One fish, that's all I have for dinner. It's better than nothing I suppose.* If Zylphia was going to leave her in this place, the least she could have done was provide protection and servants to care for her needs. Juliette didn't even know how to cook the fish.

She heard the sound of hooves, and scanned the tree line wondering if Tolor and Selene returned, but that wasn't where the sound came from. She turned to see Colovere walking away, a knotted twine bag lying near the fish. *Maybe I was meaner than I needed to be.* Juliette wondered what was in the bag.

She stared at the brook, gazing at the rock, and running her fingers through the soft green grass. Today, someone risked his own life to save hers. She would have been dead by now if that bear-creature hadn't come. No one had ever done anything like that before. She frowned. *No one has ever done anything for me unless they were paid.* Guilt filled her. *Except for Emily's bow.* She stiffly rose to her feet. It was going to be a slow walk home, and she needed to find firewood along the way.

Chapter 5

"It takes two flints to make a fire." Louisa May Alcott.

The Mirror World

Juliette was hungry. Her hands already sore from the fish bite and falling onto the rocks in the brook, hurt worse after trying to make a fire. She sat on the floor by the fire pit with her head in her hands. *I must have a fire to cook the fish. I need matches.* She remembered watching the servants build fires when she was a girl. Most of the time they used coal but they had used wood and kindling a couple of times, so she picked up twigs for kindling, and a couple of small logs for burning. They also used paper, but she didn't have that so she used dead grass and fallen leaves, hoping it would work. Juliette wondered how to start a fire without matches. *It's not as if I can go find a matchgirl to buy them.*

Juliette opened the bag Colovere left her. A couple of carrots, various fruits, and a sweet scented baked bread. Juliette pulled out the bread, took a bite and moaned with pleasure, it had a gritty fruit inside that reminded her of the figs back home. She stuffed the rest of the roll into her mouth. *Mother would be appalled if she saw me do such a thing.* Scooting to sit against the stone wall, Juliette took a deep breath and relaxed. She was still hungry, but she felt a trifle better.

She pushed herself up off the floor, and scoured the cupboards for matches, then looked around the fireplace in the main hall to no avail. *Well, there's only one more place to look.* Juliette headed for the bedchamber, but there weren't any around there either. She glanced at the mirror, it was dark and empty. *I want to go home!*

Juliette walked back to the kitchen, picked up the twine bag, and sat down. It was a shame to toss the fish, but she didn't know what else to do. She pulled out the carrots and fruits, and saw something shift on the bottom. Smiling she pulled out two matches. Relieved, Juliette chuckled. *One for the kitchen, and one for the fireplace in my bedchamber.* Then came the reality that she had

34

absolutely no idea how to cook a fish or carrots. *How hard can it be?*

First things first. She knelt on the floor in front of the fire pit and struck her first match, laughing at her good fortune when it flamed. She quickly moved her hand to the kindling. The match went out. She pressed her lips together in determination and grabbed the other match, striking it closer to the wood. The flame came close to burning her fingers and the kindling still wasn't lit.

"No," she pleaded. She saw the other partially burned match stick, and relit it. Just before her fingers got singed, she dropped the match, and the kindling smoked. Leaves curled and crackled and the twigs finally caught, making little popping sounds. Juliette didn't move, for fear of it burning out. When she felt confident the fire was big enough, she stood, added a log to the fire, picked up the stick she'd brought from outside and skewered the fish. Then she held it over the fire until it almost fell off the stick. She pulled it back so fast that pieces fell to the floor. She ate it anyway, savoring every bite.

Dinner wasn't anything like Cook would have made. The carrots and fish were black but she could have eaten the carrots raw if she had thought about it. It didn't matter, it was the best meal Juliette had ever eaten. *Well, that's done.* She rubbed her hands together to clean them. It was odd, but she felt proud of herself. She left her mess in the kitchen, and went to her bedchamber.

Standing in front of the mirror, Juliette ran her fingers down its sides, and then across its surface. There was nothing to be seen in her old bedroom. When the room was dark she could see her reflection like any other mirror. She set her hands on the surface, and pushed. Light flared in the room and Juliette hurled backwards. She grunted as she slammed into the hard stone wall. *Well that didn't go too well. I need to put pillows on that wall.* Juliette picked herself up from the floor, bit her lip and ran, ramming into it, but found herself again, hitting the back wall. Grimacing, she stayed on the floor, and stared at the mirror.

While Juliette sat watching, her mother strode into her old bedroom. She looked around as if she thought Juliette might be

35

hiding, sat on the bed and bit down on her trembling lower lip. Juliette approached the mirror and frowned, tears stinging her own eyes.

"No, mother, don't cry. I'm here. I'm in the mirror!" Juliette stomped one foot on the ground and screamed when her bare foot hit the floor. She hopped on one leg to the bed, sucking air through her teeth, whimpering at her pulsating toes.

Mrs. Barrows stared into the mirror so long Juliette wondered if she could see her. When she said nothing, Juliette knew that wasn't true. She placed her hand on the mirror, able to touch it without harm when she wasn't trying to get through it. There had to be a way to get around it.

"Why can't you hear me?"

The door opened, and Zylphia quietly entered the room, handing a piece of parchment to Mrs. Barrows.

"Emily found this on Miss Juliette's bed sheets, Ma'am."

Mrs. Barrow's read the note, then stood up, her fist clenching the paper. "When did Emily find this?"

"Only this afternoon. She can't read, Ma'am. She didn't know it was important and she was afraid to disturb you. Miss Juliette often wrote after she retired to bed."

Mrs. Barrows sat back down on the bed. "Juliette says she's not coming home." Mrs. Barrows stared at the wall. "She's run away with a boy, to be married."

"No," Juliette breathed, her face ashen. "No. I'm here Mother." Her breathing was heavy. "Don't listen to her. She's lying! I didn't run away. I'm right here! You let me out of here right now, Zylphia!"

"It doesn't matter what it says, anything from my daughter is to be given to me immediately." Mrs. Barrows trembled. "Don't you ever let this happen again, Zylphia. Do I make myself clear?"

"Yes, Ma'am" Zylphia bowed her head, backing out of the room. When she was almost past the mirror, she looked up into Juliette's eyes. Juliette held her breath until Zylphia was gone.

Juliette swallowed hard. Her mother sat on the edge of her bed and wept.

She watched her mother wipe her nose, pat her eyes and smooth her skirt before leaving the room.

Pain and loneliness filled Juliette to the deepest part of her soul. Despair over the loss of the life she knew consumed her. What would happen to her now? She had to find a way to go home. The bedchamber was dark, and she'd never looked for candles. She tried to remember if she had seen any, but if she had, she wouldn't have forgotten. Unable to do anything else, Juliette wrapped herself in a patchwork quilt and went to sleep.

Howls broke through the solitude of night. Juliette sat up. *What is that?* The sound came again. *Wolves?* Her heart beat faster. *Surely they can't get in here. I'm just being silly. They aren't even close.* But her body trembled and it wasn't from the cold. A wolf howled again. This time it was close. She got out of bed, wrapped the quilt around her, and tried to peer out the window. She couldn't see past the wall. She pulled a wooden box out of the corner, stepped onto it, then covered her mouth and gaped.

The first thing she saw was two moons, side by side, emitting blue into the constant gray light. Then she noticed that the pond around the cottage no longer had an opening. It was completely enclosed leaving no entry. *A moat? But that's not possible.*

On the other side of the moat, eight blue wolves were jumping and whining, trying to find their way across. They were bigger than any wolf Juliette had seen. Everything seemed oversized in this world. The biggest wolf splashed into the moat and yelped drawing his paws back. It sniffed at the air and looked toward her window. Juliette shrank back. The wolf threw its head back and howled.

Moonlight reflected off the glistening ivory bodies of the moats fish. They were jumping and snapping everywhere. *There are so many. How do they all fit in there?* It didn't matter, they were not allowing the wolves to come nearer. Agitated, the wolves snapped at the jumping fish, but they couldn't find a way to cross. The moat would be another problem Juliette would have to figure out in the morning, but it would keep her safe for tonight.

Juliette took a deep breath. Her breathing calmed, and her heartbeat slowed. She watched the wolves trying to get into the water, biting at the fish with snapping teeth, whining, jumping, and yelping.

Stepping off the box, she shoved it back into the corner. Then she placed the blanket and went back to bed. She listened to the yelps, yips, and whining most of the night, wondering if Colovere, Tolor, and Selene were alright. Not that she cared, but Tolor had saved her life.

Chapter 6

"The possible's slow fuse is lit by the imagination." Emily Dickinson.

The Mirror World

Stretching her arms overhead, Juliette took a deep breath, groaned, and glanced at the mirror. It was dark and quiet. Lying back down, she closed her eyes. *The wolves!* She got out of bed and ran to the window. *It looks like they're gone, but what if they come back?* Juliette stared at the moat. *It's no longer closed, a pond again? How is that possible?*

Bewildered, Juliette dressed, went to the kitchen table, and ate the last of the fruit. Then she scouted along the stone wall with a knife, jumping at every sound, in case any of the wolves managed to get inside. When she was confident they hadn't, she retrieved the bag Colovere gave her and walked out into the morning sunshine. Gazing across the meadow's green grasses, she admired the pink and yellow wildflowers. Colovere's herd of unicorns grazed in the distance. *Colovere's been friendly, maybe they will be too.* She walked around the edge of the meadow leaving plenty of distance between them.

Juliette wasn't sure what she was looking for, anything edible and preferably tasty. She wasn't ready to brave the lake after her encounter with the lion. After a few hours searching, there were only a few plump blackberries in the bucket. Then Juliette saw what looked like an apple tree in the distance. Clapping, she ran toward the tree, heavy with bright red, bell-shaped fruit.

Juliette stood under the tree, chewing her lower lip. The fruit on the tree were out of her reach, and the ones on the ground were half eaten, or rotten. She laid her bag down, and reached out trying to shake the tree. Neither trunk nor branches budged. *How do I get to them?* She gingerly picked up a half-eaten fruit and threw it at one of the branches hoping something would fall from the tree. Only a few leaves floated to the ground. An old memory came to mind.

39

She stood below a peach tree laden with fruit, only a girl of seven or eight. She licked her lips fantasizing about the sweet, juicy nectar and firm tender flesh. She couldn't reach it, but that never stopped her before. She picked up a stick, and threw it at the largest peach. The stick hit her mark, but the fruit didn't fall.

Jonathan and his friend, Robert, came down the road toward her, fishing poles resting on their shoulders and buckets of fish in their hands. Jonathan smiled, and Robert laughed.

"Can't get one down, huh?" Robert taunted. "That's because you're a lady, and ladies can't do things like that."

"Can too," Juliette countered, wondering how to prove him wrong.

She stared at the tree with a bigger purpose. Jonathan rested his fishing pole and bucket on the side of the road, smiling at her.

"I'll get it. Ladies are more fragile than men are, and they aren't supposed to mess up their dresses," Jonathan said.

"I'm not fragile."

"Yes you are," Robert said. "All ladies are. Father says so."

Juliette scowled. Jonathan ignored her and climbed the tree, fast as a squirrel. He was down in less than a minute with three blemish-free orange and yellow fruits. He held the biggest one out to Juliette.

"Here," he said smiling.

Juliette took the fruit, her cheeks warm. "Thank you, Jonathan."

Robert huffed. "Come on, Jon, let's go."

Jonathan threw a peach to Robert, picked up his fishing rod and bucket, and followed his friend down the road.

Juliette smiled at the memory. Jonathan had been attractive even as a boy. *Irrelevant, I need to focus.* Tilting her head, she chewed on her upper lip. *He made it look easy. How hard can it be?* She placed one foot on the tree, and then the other. Two steps up, and her feet slid, scraping all the way down. Juliette held her breath, stiff, until the stinging on her legs subsided.

Crossing her arms, she huffed. *I need clothes, food, servants, and shoes. Did Zylphia mean to kill me by sending me here?*

Juliette turned at the sound of Colovere's hoof beats and watched him coming toward her. She picked up her bag and waited until he moved beside her.

Colovere dipped his head in greeting.

"Maiden."

Juliette wasn't sure what to say. "Colovere." She nodded. That had to be the proper greeting. It was the way he greeted her.

"My herd has eaten all the apples on the ground. We pull the fruit down one at a time by combining two of our horns above them and pulling." He kicked at the dirt with one hoof. "Maybe we can help each other, young maiden."

Juliette lifted her chin and met Colovere's gaze. "What did you have in mind?"

"If you climb onto my back, you will be able to reach the fruit. We could divide them. Half for my herd, and the rest for you."

Juliette's lips parted with surprise. *Climb on his back? And how am I supposed to keep from falling off? What if he runs away with me?*

Colovere waited.

If I don't do it I might not eat today. Maybe I should take my chances at getting another fish. She looked Colovere over. "And how am I going to get on your back?"

Colovere knelt for Juliette to climb onto his back, and waited.

"But, but there's no saddle."

"A unicorn doesn't wear a saddle. This is your choice, young maiden."

"Stop calling me that. My name is Juliette. Miss Juliette to you."

"Yes, young maiden. Climb on my back, and hold onto my mane."

Juliette narrowed her eyes, but climbed onto the stallion's back, struggling for balance.

"Now hold on." Colovere rose.

Juliette squealed, her fists wrapped in his thick dark mane, but Colovere's movement was grace in motion. When he reached the apples, she gingerly stood, lifted her arm and tugged at the fruit, tossing them to the ground. She lost her balance, yelped, and grabbed a branch to keep from falling, then gave Colovere instructions and he shifted until she sat upright again. When the last of the fruit fell, Juliette re-wrapped her hands in his mane.

"Okay, you can put me down now."

Colovere obeyed. One of Juliette's hands loosened. She tried to rewrap it but the movement caused her to wobble. Screaming, she fell on her back with a thump. Colovere neighed as her fingers pulled out a chunk of his hair. Juliette lay on the grass, staring at the few apples that remained on the tree. Then got up, her face red as the fruit.

"You did that on purpose! I knew I shouldn't trust you. I should keep all the apples for that," Juliette said.

"Then how would you get to the apples next time?" Juliette lifted her chin. "What do you mean?"

"Do not think, if you do not keep your part of the bargain, that I will ever lift you up to the apples again."

Juliette huffed, and turned to find half the apples already separated into two neat piles and half of one pile already being eaten. In her anger she hadn't noticed the unicorn separating them with her horn. Juliette stayed close to Colovere.

"Miss Juliette, this is Meneme, a mare in my herd."

Meneme's rich auburn coat shone in the sunlight as she dipped her head once. Juliette returned the gesture, half-heartedly. The mare wasn't as tall as Colovere, or as muscular, but was every bit as elegant. Her horn was brown, and shorter than Colovere's. Juliette watched her finish separating the apples, and trot away. Juliette took the apples from one of the piles, and placed them in her bag.

"What is this place, Colovere? Why are you here? How did you get here, and how do I get home?"

"This land and the cottage in which you are living, belongs to the witch. I told you the day you arrived there is no way to leave. This world is separate from any other. Few ever leave, and when they do, it's for less than a day."

"Then how did you come here? Do you expect me to believe Zylphia moved you and your entire herd?"

"I do not care what you believe."

Colovere nodded twice to someone behind Juliette, and she turned to see the herd moving toward the apples. Juliette jumped away, giving them a wide berth. Colovere turned to enjoy eating the apples with his herd.

Since Colovere was ignoring her, Juliette turned to leave. At about fifty paces, Colovere shouted behind her. "Remember, young maiden, you must be back before sunrise."

"Sunrise?" Juliette spun around. "What is this you're speaking of, horse?"

Colovere neighed and reared, his herd fussing uneasily in the grass. Juliette took a few steps back.

"Mind your tongue. I am not a horse."

Juliette folded her arms. "You were saying? The sunrise?"

"This is the night of the full moons, you will be able to leave at moonrise, but you must return before the sun."

Juliette cleared her throat. "And if I don't return by sunrise?"

Colovere snorted. "Everything has a consequence, young maiden." Already finished with their half of the apples, Colovere and his herd galloped through the meadow.

Juliette looked at the stripped tree. *I wonder how Jonathan managed.* She picked up her bag, and made her way back to the cottage to find a cool place to store the apples, and think about what Colovere said.

When she arrived at the door, another bag hung on the handle. It was unfortunate there were no matches this time, but her mouth watered at the rich smell of cooked meat, and sweet bread. Juliette looked around, but didn't see anyone. She smiled and went in to eat her cold dinner.

Chapter 7

"There is no part of my life, upon which I can look back without pain."
Florence Nightingale.

London, England

Juliette sat in front of the mirror watching for any kind of signal. She was getting out of here tonight, and she wasn't ever coming back to this place again. When she told Mother and Father what Zylphia had done, they would punish her severely. The hours to moonrise seemed long, but eventually the daylight faded away. She heard the wolves howling in the distance. They were earlier tonight.

The moment Juliette saw the moon, the surface swirled with the same melted metal appearance. Juliette slowly raised her hand to the surface. It slid through like butter. Juliette laughed, *I'm finally going home*. She stepped through the mirror and rough calloused hands clamped onto her arms. Juliette screamed.

It took only a moment for Juliette to realize she wasn't in her room, but in somebody's wine cellar. She writhed and kicked, trying to detach herself from the man holding onto her.

"Miss Juliette Barrows." Zylphia's voice startled Juliette out of her struggle.

"Let me go!"

"Don't worry, Miss Juliette, he will when I'm done. Surely you understand that I can't allow you to come through the mirror into your bedroom. I had to sneak it out while your mother napped. It was easier than I expected, although I did have to use a spell to make the servants forget they saw me and old Grover here. I'll have to return it in the morning, but that should be easy enough."

Grover smiled. His breath stank and he was missing half his teeth. Juliette retched until she managed to control herself.

"You won't get close to your family home. I've placed magical wards around the area of your home that work like a fence. They will make you burn if you try to pass them."

"Why are you doing this? You can't hold me. The magistrates will catch you."

Zylphia laughed. "You would die before I got caught, but you're welcome to test my wards. The farther you walk, the more you'll burn. I'm amazed you even have to ask why. I told you the night I cursed you. Recompense for Emily, and those you've abused before her. But there is more. You see, your great great grandfather, killed my mate. He was one of the few true witches burned at the stake and one of the last. We built the world I keep you in together. It was meant to be our home. Now it's your prison."

Juliette stared, hardly able to breathe. "But I've done nothing to you."

"And he did nothing to your great great grandfather. He burned at the stake for saving your great grandmother's life. She would have died at birth, else. He helped her breathe when she couldn't catch a breath. Your forefather said, *only a witch could do such a thing.* It was a time when people feared what they couldn't understand, even when it was good. They put a wet cloak on top of him so he would have more time to repent of his sins." Zylphia trembled. "I've taken or killed one of your family in each new generation."

Juliette's breath caught. "Aunt Margaret."

Zylphia nodded. "I helped raise you, so I've been lenient in a sense. I didn't kill you because I still have a fondness for the little girl I once knew, but it's not likely you'll be coming out of that world before your family is gone." She shrugged. "If you do, I'll kill another."

Juliette's face was ashen. "You're mad."

"No, I'm quite clear, and I won't allow you to grow up to be like your ancestors. So let's move on. I don't have time for little girls tonight."

"I am not a little girl!"

"Once again, here are the rules. You have until sunrise to obtain what you want or need, and you may not go anywhere near your family home."

"But I have no money. And what will I be able to find at this hour?"

Zylphia handed Juliette a shilling. "This will have to do. I took it from where it lay hidden in your room. If you wish to

45

make a purchase most business owners will open for you if you knock on their doors early enough."

"How will I return?"

Zylphia pointed to the mirror. "Really, dear. Isn't that obvious?"

Juliette lifted her chin. "And if I don't?"

Zylphia put her gloves on. "You'll wake up the next morning transported back to the mirror world by the nearest portal to where you are. Some of those portals are only meant to be used in emergencies. You don't want to be transported by one of those. I advise you to return at the proper time." She glanced at Grover. "You can release her."

Grover's vice grip fell away. Juliette rubbed her wrists as Zylphia walked out the door. "You would do well to obey me," she called. "I own you now."

Juliette shivered. *How can I shop in my night clothes? They're filthy.*

Juliette moved through the city cautiously, not wanting to be seen unless she could find a magistrate. The more people she passed, the hotter her cheeks became. Her hands became fists. She stopped. *Zylphia is not going to get away with this. I'm going home.*

Chapter 8

London, England

A Matchgirl stood on the side of the road, with twine tied around her neck, holding her product in a box resting against her chest. Her hair was tied back with a ratty old ribbon, her grey dress dirty. She stood alone, shifting bare feet as if they were tired. Juliette bought two packages for a half penny to the young girl's delight. *Just in case I wind up needing them.*

Juliette's growling stomach urged her to find the way home. She had always been transported by coach, except for the occasional trip to market when Mother was certain the servants were stealing from them. The market was close enough to walk. Juliette had been a good daughter and did as her mother bade her. The servants might have been lazy at times, but she believed them to be honest. *Emily would never steal from anyone and when did Bessie or cook ever have the time? The governess maybe, but who would ever accuse the house disciplinarian?*

She passed a tavern that smelled of stewed meat and headed for the door before realizing what she was doing, then caught herself. Taverns were not an acceptable place for a well-bred young lady. She sighed, the truth was simply that she still wore her bedclothes. *I have to find something to wear. If I had asked, would Zylphia have given me something? There is no way I'll ever ask her for anything.*

Juliette followed the road, crept into an alley and found what she sought. Dresses, bodices, and skirts hanging on makeshift lines. Rubbish scraped the ground by her feet. A rat scurried around one of the buildings. Juliette jumped back. She couldn't steal anything, her mother had taught her better. But she needed clothes. She turned back to the road and went in the direction she thought would lead her home.

The night was chill, but Juliette felt warm. At first she didn't think anything of it, but soon wondered if she was ill. Stopping,

47

she clutched her stomach and bent over. *I am not going through that mirror again.* Still, she needed to get away from the burning Zylphia warned her about. Her physical reaction told her she was going the right direction. She turned down a familiar street and the burning sensation lifted. Soon she found herself at the dressmaker's shoppe. Peeking through a window, she saw two women straightening dresses and hanging new ones. She waited until only the proprietor remained, and banged on the door. After the third try Mrs. Baker opened it, first scowling, and then incredulous.

"Miss Juliette? Miss Juliette, what's happened to you?"

Juliette sighed in relief. "Mrs. Baker. You have to help me. I've been taken from my home and held hostage by a servant. She's a witch. She keeps me in a mirror and only—"

"Are you alright, Miss Barrows?"

"Of course I am," Juliette snapped. "I'm telling you the truth."

"I don't like getting involved in the way people live their lives, Miss Barrows. But I would have thought you stopped playing such games when you were a girl. If someone was holding you hostage you wouldn't be here. Your mother raised you a proper lady, Miss Barrows. Why, she would be ashamed if she heard you talking like that."

"I'm telling the truth! Listen to me." Juliette stomped her foot.

Mrs. Baker winced and walked toward the back of the store. "I do have those dresses you were fitted for. I wondered when you'd be coming for them."

Juliette clenched her teeth. "Yes, Mrs. Baker. I should like to have them now."

Mrs. Baker handed them to her.

"What do I owe you?"

"Not a thing. Your mother paid before the dresses were made. That's my policy you know."

Finally a bit of good fortune. "Yes, I had forgotten that. Is there a place I might find someone with a coach at this hour?"

Mrs. Baker scratched her head. "The tavern most likely. That's where I'd go if I needed a coach at this hour."

After changing, Juliette hurried back to the tavern. If she was going to go into such a place, she might as well have a hot

48

meal. Taking a table in the corner, she asked for a bowl of whatever they were serving. The curly haired tavern girl eyed her warily.

"You got the farthing to pay for it?"

Juliette's eyebrows furrowed. "Of course I do. Now bring my meal before I report you to the master of this establishment."

"Yes, Miss." The barmaid scurried away, returning in minutes with a steaming bowl of stew.

Juliette looked around the room, grimacing. *Well that went poorly. First, Mrs. Baker, and now this dreadful girl. Who here would I ask about a coach?* She could ask the man behind the bar, but with his thick eyebrows furrowed and the way he was scanning the room, he didn't look too friendly. *Oh, alright, I'll have to ask the girl, once I've eaten. At least it's better than dealing with a brute.* She ate her meal with such vigor people turned and stared. Then, paying for the meal, she asked the barmaid if anyone had a coach for hire.

The warm satisfaction of a hot meal in Juliette's stomach didn't last long. At first she was excited and determined to go home. Until she became so hot, she was in danger of losing her meal. Moment by moment, the rock in her belly grew bigger as the temperature increased. Her breathing quickened. She rose, swaying with the motion of the coach, and pulled a rope to alert the driver, but he didn't stop. She pulled harder, still no response. She threw the door open. The driver cried out, pulling on the reins so hard, Juliette nearly lost her grip on the door frame.

"What are you doing?" The driver climbed down from the coach.

Unable to speak, Juliette threw herself onto the road. Scampering to her feet, she tried walking back the way they came. The driver yelled after her.

"I'll take you back if you've changed your mind, Miss."

Juliette ignored him, she couldn't get back into the coach, much less endure the ride, but the man rushed to her side and helped her back in. Juliette, too sick to protest, allowed him to guide her. As the coach travelled the way they had come, the burning subsided. The coachman helped her out when they reached the tavern. He tried to help her inside. She pushed him away.

"No," she cried. "No." She collapsed in the street, and wept. She didn't return through the mirror. She crawled into an alley and hid behind some crates, and cried herself to sleep, leaning against a wooden door.

The Mirror World

Juliette opened her eyes to the sound of a low growl. Her heart wedged in her throat. She turned to find a large, blue wolf standing ten paces away, ready to spring. Its fangs were bared, and she could smell its musty scent mixed with bad breath. Other wolves came out of the bushes. *Oh no. What do I do now?* A moment before the wolf launched itself, Juliette sprang to her feet and ran.

She didn't take more than a couple paces before a wolf caught her leg.

She cried out as sharp teeth punctured her delicate skin. Another bit her arm. Her arms lifted to shield her face. Two wolves dragged her across the grass with their teeth. Juliette fought, kicked, screamed, and tried to fling herself away from them only to tear more skin. Pain wracked her body with new puncture wounds. She didn't know how long she could fight. A wolf sprang for her throat. She closed her eyes tight and screamed.

The sound of hooves, a lot of hooves. Wolves yelping, baying, and biting. Juliette opened her eyes, but she couldn't focus. It looked like there were pinpoints of light surrounding her. The noise was awful, then everything became quiet. Juliette hated the silence. She hated her life, she hated the wolves, and most of all, she hated Zylphia. Her body lay shaking, in pain on the grass and a ring of unicorns formed a barrier around her.

"Go get Tolor. Or Selene if you cannot find him," Colovere said.

The sound of galloping horses calmed her. She wondered why. And then a large mass of mane and hair lay down beside her and Colovere used his horn to lift her head, and wedge his nose underneath it. Juliette welcomed the comfort and warmth, safe with his body touching hers. She knew in her heart he wouldn't let anything harm her. She turned her head and squinted at a faint light. Colovere's horn was shining.

Tolor and the unicorn were back in minutes. Juliette was just coherent enough to wonder how they got there so fast. Tolor checked her wounds with one hand and covered his nose with the other to lessen his reaction to the blood. She winced at his touch, but tried to remain still, watching him. Blood seeped into her green dress, leaving it torn and damaged.

"Her wounds are bleeding sluggish now. Why did you not heal her?"

Colovere gently nudged his muzzle from under her head. Tolor caught her so she didn't slam into the ground.

"I can heal poison, but I cannot heal open wounds."

"She's lost a lot of blood. You killed all these wolves?"

"I wasn't alone. I had help."

"Will you carry her if I place her on your back?"

"Yes."

When Juliette regained consciousness she was in the cottage, her wounds clean and bandaged. Tolor sat in a chair near the window. He looked uncomfortable. Her matches rested on the table beside him. Tolor saw her watching him and chuckled.

"You were not going to let go of those for anyone. I retrieved them when you passed out."

Tears rolled down Juliette's cheeks. "Was this the punishment for not returning through the mirror, Tolor?"

Tolor shook his head. "The witch is rarely so cruel. The wolves were a matter of you arriving through a portal near their den while they were returning from the night's hunt. Not that they wouldn't have hunted you, given the chance, but that was not what happened."

"Then Zylphia was bluffing? There is no punishment for not returning?" Juliette hoped it was a bluff, because if it was, she was probably bluffing about other things too. "Tolor, when does this nightmare end?"

"There are some things we can't control. You're alive. Be grateful for that."

Right now Juliette didn't feel grateful for anything.

A unicorn neighed from the yard. Tolor laughed.

"Colovere is impatient to know how you are doing. He told me to tell you he wants more apples."

Juliette laughed.

"I'll let you get some sleep. Selene will be looking for me when she wakes."

Juliette looked at Tolor in surprise. "Isn't she well?"

"Yes, she is, but she remained awake awaiting my return last night."

"You get to go out too?"

"Yes. Though I would defer the honor to Selene if I could. Selene comes from a magical family, so she is required to remain in this world."

"Why? What did you and Selene do to be sent here?"

Tolor looked at her as if she had sprouted horns. "We did nothing. The witch of this world prefers to keep a few exotic creatures she finds unique. Selene cannot leave because the witch fears she will escape. If she catches her going through a portal, she will kill her. You shouldn't think poorly of people you hardly know."

"What is the punishment for not returning?" Juliette's blood turned cold, but she needed to know. "Do you know?"

Tolor glanced out the window. "I can only assume that yours will be the same as mine."

"And what is yours?"

"I am forbidden to leave again until the world turns two seasons."

Juliette lay back, relieved. It wasn't exactly pleasant, but she had been afraid Zylphia would use her lack of obedience to do something worse.

"I really must go. I see you bought no supplies. I'll see if there is anything to spare."

Tolor left before Juliette could say another word. Even Colovere wasn't that fast. Juliette laid thinking for a long time, and then she slept.

Chapter 9

"And ill doth her days employ who lets life pass without love's joy."
Guillaume de Lorris, Romance of the Rose.

London, England

Emily wiped an arm across her forehead, then stood to empty a bucket of dirty water. She turned to see that the kitchen floor sparkled, and heard a rustling sound.

"Aunt Zylphia." Emily dipped her head, never sure how to respond to the older woman. They were related, but they weren't the same.

"Put the bucket away and come with me."

Emily shoved the bucket under the sink, and followed her aunt out the door to the road. "Where are we going?"

"It's time to find out if you have the spark."

The spark? "I don't understand."

"It's been many generations since anyone in our family has had the ability to be trained. I was the last. It's time to test you for the magical power that would enable you to walk among the blessed, joining with witches and sorcerers."

"But I don't want to be a witch."

"Nonsense, girl. The power to control your own destiny would enable you to repay those who seek to harm you. Your life as a servant would be left behind unless chosen. My power will continue on long after I am gone. It would be foolish to shun the spark."

"No one would ever choose to be a servant."

At the end of the road, Zylphia helped her into a small carriage, shutting the door after climbing in behind her.

Zylphia sighed. "People do things for all sorts of reasons, Emily. Life has a way of moving you in directions you would have never thought to go. Have you forgotten that I am a servant because I choose to be?"

"No," Emily murmured. "But I've never understood why."

"Because your uncle was a good man, skilled with herbs and a natural healer. He never turned anyone away when they needed help. He loved everyone. He was kind to the beggar, a friend to the blind, and an anchor for the poor, when people were treated worse than they are today. I'll be a servant to the Barrows, until their line ceases, or I do. With Juliette imprisoned, this may very well be the end of their line."

Emily shrank away, grateful that Zylphia was looking out the window. Would she leave Juliette in the mirror forever? *What will it take for her to put me in that mirror world too? Or Jonathan, if she ever catches us together?* She swallowed hard. "Are we almost there, Aunt Zylphia?"

They had been riding through the woods for some time. Between fear and the motion of the coach, Emily's last meal battled to remain in her stomach.

The coach stopped in the forest by a small cottage with a dark roof and what appeared to be grey stone and wood. It was dark and everything was visible only by moonlight, or cast in shadow. She shivered at being alone with Zylphia in what felt like a faraway place. Her aunt ushered her out of the black carriage towards the cottage. Emily glanced back to find that there was no driver. The horse that pulled them stared off into the distance.

They entered the cottage and Zylphia raised her hand to the fireplace. White fire fell from the chimney like lightening into preset logs. Emily trembled as it crackled and popped.

Zylphia glanced at her. "There's nothing to be afraid of Emby, stop shaking."

Emily took a deep breath comforted a little by the use of her Aunt's childhood pet name for her. She scanned the room. The cottage was circular. One large room and the top where the wall met the ceiling was encircled with windows. There were sets of small windows lower, but they were the size of stained glass, thick enough that light could shine through but no one could see in to impinge on their privacy. Herbs and other botanicals were hung on wooden pegs to dry, giving the air a sweet musk scent, blended with sage that sat partially burned on a wooden table against one of the walls. A staircase led up to a loft with a large bed.

"Emily, pay attention!"

Emily jumped and turned her attention back to her aunt, her cheeks warm. "Sorry, Zylphia."

Zylphia ignored the apology, picked up a vase full of wilting flowers and placed it on the floor. "This is painless. It won't take long. I want you to raise your hand to the vase and will it to shatter."

Will it to shatter? I will a lot of things to happen and they never do. Why would this be any different?

Emily raised her hand and watched the vase. Nothing happened.

"Concentrate," Zylphia snapped.

Emily inhaled and focused her attention on the vase causing everything else in the room to disappear. She focused again, still nothing happened.

"Try harder."

Emily concentrated, there was nothing existed but the vase with flowers. Sweat trickled down her forehead. Zylphia picked up the vase, and placed it back on the table.

"So the magic has skipped another generation. It may be that only a child of my own would have carried the power." Zylphia stared at the wilted flowers, and one by one they coiled around themselves, and turned the color of crisp dead leaves. "I lost my baby when they killed my Merek. There will be no more. I had hoped that you would carry the family legacy, but it wasn't to be."

Zylphia picked up a metal plate with cold chicken, potatoes and greens. Emily's stomach rumbled and her mouth watered. The plate moved over the fire. When it was hot Zylphia set it on the table by Emily. "Eat. The concentration for magic depletes our energy leaving us famished until we're used to it. Testing for the spark is no different."

Even when Emily's mother couldn't provide food for two days, Emily hadn't felt as hungry as this. She tore into the food with ferocity, even eating the greens when she had no clue what they were. When she was finished, she was tired.

"Is there no more testing then, Aunt Zylphia?"

Zylphia shook her head. "If you can't do the simplest of magic, you won't be able to do anything else. We're finished here."

When they exited the cottage, the driverless carriage awaited them.

Chapter 10

"Friendship is unnecessary, like philosophy, like art...it has no survival value; rather it is one of those things that give value to survival." C. S. Lewis.

The Mirror World

After two days in bed feeling sorry for herself, Juliette rose and put on her ruined dress. Her nightdress needed to be washed, even if she wasn't exactly sure how to do it. She ate another apple. *I'm so dreadfully tired of these, maybe I should try for another fish.* She went to the shed and grabbed her fishing pole.

Outside the walls, Colovere's herd frolicked in the meadow. Juliette turned around and headed toward the lake. The hot sun caused strands of hair to stick to her face, but the breeze felt good. Clutching her pole to use as a makeshift weapon, Juliette watched for the lion. At length the lake came into view. The red sun beating on the water created a purple cast that rippled with the wind on its surface. Juliette sat for what seemed like hours without a bite. The comforting sound of Colovere's hooves came from behind her, and she twisted toward the sound. He dipped his head to greet her.

"It is good to see you well, young maiden."

"Colovere."

"Follow me." Colovere walked into the forest.

Juliette didn't move. He turned and waited. She shook her head.

"There are wild things in there. Lions and wolves, and who knows what else. I'm not going into the forest."

"I won't allow anything to harm you."

"You don't know that? You can't protect me from everything."

"I was the one that protected you from the wolves, maiden! Now follow." He moved into the forest.

Juliette stared at the trees as if they were giants that might stomp on her. Colovere stopped ahead. Juliette presumed he was

57

waiting. Clenching her teeth, she picked up her fishing pole, pushed the branches of a wayward pine out of her way, and entered the forest.

Juliette shivered, staring at the spring green mosses, rotted branches, and mottled salmon. Yellow and brown leaves littered the forest floor, and the air smelled woodsy and clean.

Oh! I left my nightdress in the river! She closed her eyes and slowed her breathing. She was tired of being afraid and panicking all the time. *The nightclothes should be safe for awhile. Who is here to steal it?*

"Where are we going, Colovere? These twigs are hurting my feet."

"You should have used your time more wisely, when you were able to cross worlds in the moonlight. Now it will be a year before—"

"A year? What do you mean a year? Tolor said two seasons. That is only half of a year."

"That would be true in your own world. It is not true here."

"Then tell me what *is* true."

"What is true is that you live in a world where you have to take care of yourself. You cannot expect others to do it for you. You will not be permitted to leave for one year. You were warned, yet you foolishly wasted your time on something else. Humans cannot live on apples. You need to learn how to survive."

Juliette stopped walking. Her eyes filled with tears, but she fought them back. "How dare you speak to me in such a fashion, horse!"

"I dare because it's true. Soon it will be winter, the ground will be white, and the trees will be bare. What have you stored for the days ahead? There is only a short time to prepare, or you will not survive. Now walk faster, we need to get there before dark."

Before dark? What about my nightdress, and the fish I need for supper? Juliette opened her mouth to argue, and heard twigs breaking. She realized she could smell smoke and something else in the wind. Something that made her mouth water. Juliette closed her eyes and inhaled, jumping when Tolor broke through the trees.

"Maiden, Colovere," he nodded in greeting. "I expected you yesterday."

58

Colovere shifted his sleek body. "The maiden hid in the cottage these last two days."

"Uh! I wasn't hiding anywhere."

Colovere snorted, and Tolor laughed.

"I haven't." Juliette stomped her foot for emphasis, her bottom lip in a pout.

"I'm glad you're both here. Come on," Tolor said, leading them further into the forest.

After climbing a hill the alluring smell of seared meat became stronger. Juliette's mouth watered. They passed through green shrubs, into a clearing. Selene came out of what appeared to be a large, covered stable, but house-like. The walls of its sleeping area rose more than half way to the roof, and everything was painted yellow and decorated with white trim. She greeted them, nodding slightly at Juliette.

"I'll have dinner ready shortly, Colovere. Tolor has cooked meat for himself and the girl." She returned to the house.

Juliette enjoyed the smell of wood smoke from the chimney. The familiarity comforted her. Colovere nudged her arm with his nose.

"Over here. This is what I want to show you."

What would Colovere want to show me?

Tolor followed them to a corner of the clearing where a vegetable garden was growing. It was a garden unlike anything Juliette had seen. Thick green stalks held the longest beans she could have imagined. Corn grew in tight rows, their flaxen silk shimmering in the afternoon sunlight. There were carrots, yellow and green squashes, and red and yellow peppers. A line of spindly plants grew in the corner. Juliette wondered what they were.

"Do you like them?" Tolor asked. "These are Selene's pride and joy. Pineapples that are white on the inside. I got them for her when I crossed worlds a few seasons ago." He smiled, placing a hand on her shoulder. Juliette shivered as one of the claws touched her skin. "I see you are not familiar with it. You can taste one tonight and see what you think."

Juliette nodded and looked at a patch to the right with cantaloupes and watermelons.

"Is this what you meant to show me, Colovere?"

59

Colovere nodded.

"Why?"

"I already gave you the answer, young maiden. We are about to go into winter and you have no food," Colovere said.

"What are you suggesting? You want me to put my hands in the dirt? Are you mad?"

"Tolor and Selene have stored for themselves all summer, with the exception of the meat Tolor eats. We have an abundance of rabbits and deer, so he is able to hunt during winter. He prefers his meat fresh, and it makes his bloodlust more managable."

Colovere snorted and Tolor laughed.

"They have grown greens for Selene and hay for my herd. In return, we have kept the grasses down around their home and shown them where wild herbs and berries are growing. We also accompany them to farther places where they have foraged nuts and other fruits we enjoy. We help carry them back.

"Tolor has left you small packages of food, but he may not always be able to do so. Next year you can contribute, and we will share all we have, but this year it isn't possible for you to contribute," Colovere said.

"When the witch made this world, she meant to live here," Tolor added, picking a large red pepper. "The land has been enchanted to produce much faster than the soil in your world, with fewer insects to attack the plants. I can show you how it's done, but Selene has forbidden me to do it for you. I can share my hunts with you. The rest you must do for yourself, and in the winter, the lake will be frozen."

Juliette smirked. "You would think she would at least have left the lake alone."

"She likes to walk on it with odd round shoes," Tolor said. "These are your choices maiden. Will you prepare and live, or die in the winter?"

Juliette turned to see Selene behind them, her eyebrows narrowed, and lips in a tight line. Her arms were folded across her chest.

"They are beating around the bush. Stop this foolishness. You have done nothing to help any of us prepare, or stock food for the winter. You wasted your night of freedom when you should have collected supplies."

"I helped you get apples," Juliette stammered.

"Only because you had no other way to get them for yourself," Selene shouted.

Tolor took Selene's arm. Sidling, she shrugged him off.

"Selene," Tolor pleaded.

Selene turned her attention back to Juliette. "You do what you need to, or you die in the winter. Do you understand me, girl?"

Juliette nodded.

Selene glanced at Tolor. "Good then. Dinner is ready."

Juliette stared at the dirt, whimpering. She could almost hear her mother, *ladies do not play in the dirt.* She had bruised Juliette's arm pulling her away from the mud pies she made. Covered in mud, mother sent her to the governess for what she called *"a good whipping."* After the governess was through with her, she could hardly sit for the next week. She remembered how much it hurt and crying all day.

Shaking off the memory, Juliette heard Emily's cries, as she too begged the governess to stop. Juliette lifted her chin and sniffed. *That was her own fault, she deserved to be beaten.* Juliette stared at the dirt. *Maybe I was a bit harsh. She did have it coming, but it didn't have to be so extreme.* Juliette heard Colovere and turned to greet him. *I don't remember leaving the gates open.* Then she saw Selene and Tolor.

"So, you haven't gotten anything done?" Selene smirked. "I'm not surprised."

Juliette's eyebrows narrowed and she looked away. *I can do this.* "I'm getting to it."

Selene laughed.

"Here." Tolor handed Juliette a bag.

"What's this?"

"Let's see. There are matches… candles… and you can't plant without seeds." After showing her the items, he took the bag and set it on a nearby bench. "Do you remember how I showed you to do this?"

"Yes. You took your claws and dug holes until the ground was soft all over."

Tolor smiled wide. "An excellent student. Now let me see you dig."

Juliette bent down to the dirt, grimacing as if it were a rotten fish. She glanced at Tolor. He nodded, holding up his clawed hands, encouraging her to move forward. Juliette put her hands in the dirt, and scraped at it hard. Pieces of clumped soil embedded under her fingernails.

"Owww."

Tolor shook his head. Selene huffed and shifted her hooves. "What's the matter?" Tolor asked.

"That hurt."

Colovere neighed. "I guess she'll have to hit the ground with a metal stick, like other humans do."

Tolor sighed. "This would have been so much easier if you had claws. Do you have metal sticks, young maiden?"

"Sticks? What do I need a stick for?"

"Look in here," Colovere said, kicking at the shed.

Selene opened a latched door, moved a few things around, and pulled out a shovel. She handed it to Juliette. "Of course you couldn't dig like a bear, but I had fun watching them encouraging you to try, and you did it. Amazing." Selene laughed. "Take this, and push it into the dirt with your foot, and then pull up. That's all you need to do."

Juliette's shoulders were stiff, but she put the shovel to the ground and pushed. The dirt came up easily. Everyone laughed, pleased with themselves. Everyone except Juliette.

Tolor bent down hovering over the freshly turned dirt. "Now watch me." He took a claw and dug small holes about six inches apart. He threw a couple of seeds in each hole, smoothed the dirt, and stood slapping the dirt off his hands. "Do you see how easy it is?"

Juliette huffed, but it didn't take long to sow the seeds. Selene ran home while she planted and returned with a pineapple plant. Juliette tried not to smile with pleasure, but she loved the juicy fruit filled with tangy sweetness. She thanked Selene, and found a place for it in the garden.

Selene watched Juliette plant the last pineapple, and Tolor help her up. *He always has to be the gentleman.* Selene shook her head, but remained silent, tired of fighting and bickering over the way he coddled the girl. Juliette would have learned nothing without her intervention. *We might all have starved trying to feed her.* She watched Juliette brush the dirt off that terrible ripped up dress. *Well, that isn't exactly her fault. Of course it was. What am I thinking?*

"I made some tea with the peppermint Tolor brought me. Would you like to come in for a while and have some?" Juliette asked.

Selene didn't want to go anywhere near the cottage. It belonged to the witch and she didn't like the current occupant any better. "Sure." *Why did I just say that?* Selene always felt guilty about the way she treated the girl and that made her angrier.

Selene followed Tolor into the cottage. The room reeked of rotting fish, rancid meat, and moldy vegetables mixed with wood smoke. She stopped inside the door, holding her breath, and trying not to gag. There were dirty dishes, leftover food rotting in bowls. It didn't look like the hearth had been cleaned since Juliette arrived. Dust covered everything. Juliette walked around her as if everything smelled like roses. She turned toward them, her face blank.

"Why are you all stopping at the door?"

Everyone fidgeted. *This is insane. What is wrong with this girl?* She hated all the time and attention Tolor spent on Juliette, but he was right about one thing, without him, the girl probably would have died.

"What is that smell?" Selene asked. "Look at this mess!"

Juliette cringed. "Zylphia never sent any servants to do the cooking, mending, and cleaning. I figured I would ask her about that when I see her next."

Selene almost choked. Tolor coughed. Selene faced them, and pointed at the door. "Both of you. Out!"

Colovere and Tolor looked relieved to go out the door, although Tolor gave her that 'be nice' look he always gave her when he didn't like what she was going to do.

"Why did you tell them to leave Selene? They haven't had their tea."

"They'll survive. You might not. Start a fire and put a kettle of water on. I would have had Tolor do it but it is past time you learned to stop acting like a spoiled frilly strumpet and learned to

63

fend for yourself. This is not London, and no one is going to be sending you any servants. Move!"

Tears fell from Juliette's eyes, and her hands fisted at her sides. "I am not a strumpet!"

Selene took a step forward and Juliette stepped back. "I don't care what you are. It's time you learned to take care of yourself. You can start by separating the trash."

Juliette cringed, but she started putting dishes, spoiling vegetables, and trash all in their own piles.

Selene had Tolor and Colovere bring their meals. Juliette did all the work as Selene gave instructions and guided. Selene asked herself numerous times why she even bothered to do this. She didn't go home for a week, but when she left, the cottage and its grounds were clean.

It only took a month for the vegetables and fruits to mature. Tolor found a cellar door in the kitchen that Juliette had been afraid to explore because it went underground. She was pleased to find that it was a large storage space with barrels filled with wine and water by one wall, and a keg of ale against another. There were shelves with a few wrapped cheeses on the second shelf, and onions in a small basket on the top. It was bare of any other vegetation, but they found salted pork, wrapped and covered in a rusty metal container on the dirt floor. It was cool, and large enough to store all her greens.

A metal tin sat by the cheeses. Juliette picked it up and opened it. She pulled out a piece of paper with her name on it, and read it out loud.

Juliette,

What you see here combined with what you find in this world should sustain you until your first outing. It's time for you to learn to take care of yourself.

Zylphia

Tolor grinned. "Well, it looks like you had food here, after all. Your fears were unfounded. If you had asked, I would have looked to see what was behind the door for you."

Juliette's cheeks colored. *It Looks like I'll be able to contribute after all.* She pulled out a small bottle of ink and a small stack of paper as well. "It might have helped if she left this somewhere upstairs."

"We should get back upstairs. Selene and Colovere will be waiting."

At least I can write again. Tolor grabbed the oil lamp, and Juliette followed him back to the kitchen.

When the weather turned cold, Tolor, Selene and Juliette went fishing. Selene didn't help for long. She didn't like the cold water on her hooves. After Selene left to make dinner, Tolor and Juliette caught a barrel of fish, Tolor using his claws, and Juliette using both her and Selene's poles. They spread them out on the ground and dug a hole while they waited for them to freeze. When the fish were frozen, they cleaned, wrapped and buried them. The ground was so hard that Tolor broke a claw in the process.

Selene asked Tolor to bring honey and flour when he returned from the other world, and when he did, she made sweet cakes. As long as Juliette shared with them, they shared with her. Tolor brought her pieces of deer she kept frozen until deciding to use it. Selene and Tolor, even taught her to cook and Selene insisted she learn how to clean.

Juliette didn't watch her room very often during these busy times. One day, she saw something white from the corner of her eye and turned to find that the maids had covered all her furniture. After that, no one ever entered her room.

Chapter 11

"Love works a different way in different minds, the fool it enlightens and the wise it blinds." John Dryden.

The Mirror world 1818

"No. Watch me do this." Selene snatched the crochet needle from Juliette, showing her how to turn the stitch and begin the next row.

I could finish the row if she would just turn it for me. Selene handed the wool back. Juliette pulled the needle through, and then let the sweater fall into her lap.

"Selene?"

Selene took a deep breath. "Yes?"

"Why are you doing this?"

"Because you wouldn't have lasted a month without help. I've never seen anyone so ignorant."

Juliette's hands balled into fists. She tucked them under the sweater to hide her frustration. "What I meant is that it's obvious you don't like me. But you've taught me to cook, and to clean, and a myriad of other things. Why?"

Selene put her own project down. "Teaching you how to clean is debatable, but I have tried. I don't understand why it's so important to Colovere and Tolor to keep you safe." Her face reddened as Juliette's paled.

"You came storming into this land like a prancing little mare. You've been rude and arrogant, and you don't care who you hurt! You spend all your time with Tolor, thinking he'll make everything right for you." Selene moved closer, looming over Juliette. "You hit Colovere with rocks. Did you ever apologize for that? No, you didn't. And he was trying to help you."

Juliette fought back tears. Her lips worked but she didn't know what to say.

"Tolor has shown too much interest in you from the first moment he saw you. Stay away from him!"

Selene stormed from the parlor and out of the cottage.

She despises me. Juliette's lips trembled, she pressed them tightly together. *I'm sick of crying* and yet her heart hurt. *What should I do? Will she ever talk to me again? I shouldn't have thrown the rocks. And I haven't apologized.* Juliette had never apologized to anyone.

She ran to her room and threw herself on the bed. "I'm a horrible, dreadful woman." She covered her face with her hands. *Colovere is probably my best friend. Maybe my only friend and I hurt him. But why should I stay away from Tolor? I haven't done anything. I can't fix things with Selene, but I can apologize to Colovere.*

Juliette blew her nose and dried her tears. A movement in the mirror caught her eye. *Good, I need a distraction.* Approaching the mirror she placed her hand on its smooth surface, and watched servants removing her things from drawers and placing them into a trunk. Juliette's heart ached. *They probably don't expect me to ever come home.* She rested a warm cheek against the cool glass. *I'm beginning to think they may be right.*

Wishing she could at least have some of her things, Juliette watched until the room was cleared and the servants left. More than a year had passed with only a damaged skirt, her bodice, and a nightdress. It was like walking around half-naked all the time. No one in the mirror world noticed or cared, or they never said anything. Juliette started to lay down when her old bedroom door opened and closed softly.

She returned to the mirror. *Who is that?*

A young man with wavy brown hair falling just below his collar, walked silently into the room, tugging a dark haired servant behind him. He turned away from the mirror, and leaned the servant against the drawers. Juliette couldn't see their faces.

What are they doing in my room? He's obviously a man of property. I can tell that by the suit he's wearing. What is he doing in our home? He pulled the woman into his arms, running his hand up and down her back. Juliette heard a familiar voice.

"You shouldn't be here. If we get caught—"

The young man placed his fingers over her lips. "We won't." He kissed her.

Juliette gasped. "Emily. That strumpet!"

The kiss was long and passionate. Juliette watched with curiosity. When he let go, Emily didn't speak for a moment. She wavered on her feet, winded.

"You must go."

"Run away with me. I won't allow that awful girl to beat you ever again."

"How dare you to talk about me like that!"

"I can't, you have to stop this. You must find a woman suitable to your station."

"I don't want a woman suitable to my station. Marry me. We'll run away tonight." He waited. "Tell me you don't love me."

Emily met his eyes. "I don't..." She looked away.

He ran his hand down her cheek, and then drew her close. "Meet me in the stable when the lights are out."

Emily shifted and the young man turned. Juliette's breath caught. His hair grew longer and he stood taller, but she had fantasized over this boy for years. It was Jonathan.

"But you liked me first," Juliette whispered.

Juliette heard a loud neigh outside, hooves dancing on the turf. She glanced out the window to see Colovere.

"Come out, young maiden."

Juliette turned back to the mirror. Jonathan and Emily were peeking out the door. They slipped out of the room.

Juliette's blood boiled, but she couldn't deal with them now. She went to greet Colovere.

"I was visiting Tolor when Selene came home," Colovere said. "I wanted to make sure you were alright."

"I'm fine. I asked her why she didn't like me. I knew it wasn't going to be a pleasant conversation."

Colovere blew the air out of his muzzle. "Then why did you?"

Juliette shrugged, and looked away. "I needed to know, but I never believed she hated me so much."

"Selene doesn't hate you. She's just angry."

Juliette chuckled ruefully. "She made that quite clear."

"Come on, let us sit for a while," Colovere said, lying down in the shade of a tall, white birch tree. Juliette sat beside him.

"Selene isn't angry at you. She stopped being angry when you pulled the first pepper out of your garden."

Colovere neighed with pleasure. Juliette smiled and became serious again.

"Well, that isn't what she said."

"Of course not. It's hard for Selene. She wants to go home, but she cannot. She loves and misses her family and she feels guilty about that. If she goes home to be with her family, she will break Tolor's heart. If she stays with Tolor, she can no longer be with her family. She doesn't have the freedom to go, and so she stays, but Tolor knows she would go if that door ever opened and they both must live with that."

"Why doesn't Tolor go home with her?"

"Because the beran, and the centaur are natural enemies. The centaurs would kill both of them. The witch put Selene in danger when she added Tolor to her collection."

"I had no idea."

"There is nothing you can do. Nothing any of us can."

Juliette nodded, and ran her hand over Colovere's back. "Something is still wrong. I can sense it."

Juliette shrugged. "There is, but you wouldn't understand."

"When have I not understood you?"

"Never, but I don't think you can this time."

The silence drew out between them. "Alright, I'll tell you my troubles." She settled back and told her story. She didn't really care about Jonathan anymore, there were other things to worry about. Why did Emily's lack of propriety bother her so much? Was it still because Jonathan had liked her better? *It isn't like we were rivals. Weren't we though? She has Jonathan and I'm living in a land away from my home, and yet I see my room, day after day.* Juliette swallowed hard.

"I cannot help you with such things as men. It is against my nature to do so. But I think I can help with your other problem. Climb onto my back and hold my mane."

Juliette did as instructed. It had been over a year since the day they picked apples together. Now she loved to ride. Colovere made her feel safe. She had grown fond of the red sun, the blue moons, the pink and yellow flowers of the meadow, and the silvery cast over everything. She had grown warm towards her friends too, and took pride in her new garden, but she still wanted to go home.

"Colovere?"

"Yes, Juliette?"

"I'm sorry."

Colovere stopped. "What are you sorry for, young maiden?"

"For throwing rocks at you."

Colovere didn't say anything for a few minutes. The whistle of the wind through the top of the trees seemed loud.

"It was forgotten long ago."

Colovere proceeded deeper into the forest moving slower than usual. He seemed somber. Juliette kept quiet and enjoyed the lovely day. He followed the water to the edge of the forest, and turned in a direction that Juliette had never gone. This part of the forest had wider spaces, and giant trees with trunks as wide as a coach. The bark was red. The air smelled of pine, and except for a few roots growing up from the ground, pinecones and needles, the forest was clear of debris. After walking for what seemed a lifetime, Colovere entered a small clearing, where the red of the sun descended through green leaves to the forest floor. He knelt so Juliette could climb down.

"What is this place, Colovere?"

"This is my home and the place I come to when I want to be alone. Few have been here."

"It's lovely."

Colovere approached a tree, placed his horn against its bark, and pushed. The trunk of the tree shimmered and glowed yellow. A door opened and Juliette's mouth dropped. Colovere stuck his head inside and came out carrying something black in his teeth. Juliette closed her mouth just before he dropped it into her hand and looked at him, confused.

"I don't understand. What is this?"

"It is the Horn of Ophelia, Queen of Unicorns, and my mate."

"But, I thought you were the only unicorn to have a black horn."

"I am the champion of unicorns. Similar to your king. Ophelia's horn turned black when we promised ourselves to each other. She received the golden spiral after we mated.

"Where is she?"

70

"Zylphia used her to lure me here. She told me Ophelia would be waiting. Before we arrived, she escaped. The witch was enraged. No one had ever managed to escape her world. She went after Ophelia, and when she found her, removed her horn and killed her."

"The magic in Ophelia's horn wouldn't work for the witch. She tossed it away. I found it in the meadow, and retrieved it. The horn will not work for someone who is stealing its powers, but a trickle of magic still resides in it."

Juliette twisted it, studying its shape and the golden spiral that matched Colovere's.

"My mate and I were the only unicorns living that had a black horn, but all unicorn horns turn black when we die. It makes them less recognizable so our magic will not fall into evil hands. When the magic is gone, it will eventually disappear."

"What should I do with it?"

"I cannot help you escape. The witch's magic is too strong. But I can send you to your home for a short time. Once you go through the portal you will have to work quickly. Hold the point against whatever you want to send here, envision where you want it to go and it will be transported. You mustn't try to escape or stay. If you do, Zylphia will kill me and my herd for helping you."

Juliette bit her lower lip. "Okay, when can we do this?"

"You can go tonight."

Juliette's heart fluttered with excitement.

Chapter 12

"When you're safe at home you wish you were having an adventure; when you're having an adventure you wish you were safe at home." Thornton Wilder.

The Mirror World

Using his teeth, Colovere grazed Ophelia's horn across the mirror. The mirror glowed for an instant, crackled like an electrical current, and turned into the liquid silver consistency that indicated it was safe to cross. He nudged Juliette's arm.

"I do not know how long the way will remain open. Go quickly and remember the things I have told you. It may be that the witch can sense one of her doorways has been tampered with. Do not let her find you on the other side of the mirror."

Colovere stepped back, and Juliette entered the mirror.

Thick, liquid silver enveloped her. She tried to scream, but didn't have air for it. Her lungs grew heavy. She fought to move forward. *Oh God, I'm going to die here.* Grasping the mirror's frame and heaving with all of her strength, she escaped out of the silvery muck that held her.

Juliette fell to her knees, her hands on her chest. Breathing heavy, she calmed herself, amazed to see that her clothes were dry, and the viscid substance hadn't left the smallest stain. Tears sprang to her eyes. She was home, and she wasn't going back.

London, England

Juliette opened the door trying not to make a sound. She wouldn't wake the house until locating Zylphia. She crept through the hall and stopped when she heard someone moaning. Juliette followed it to a small room at the end of the hall that Bessie shared with Emily. The servants used to live in the attic, but her mother thought they were hiding things and made them move downstairs. Juliette peeked into the room through a slit of the open door, and saw legs intertwined on Bessie's bed, the

72

coverlet lying in a heap on the floor. Readjusting herself to see who it was, she covered her mouth and gasped, finally understanding her father's need for Bessie.

She moved to see who was in the opposite bed. Emily lay wide-eyed, watching them. Juliette backed into the wall. *Does mother know about this?* She remembered the day Zylphia cursed her. *'Why can't I take Bessie?'* she had demanded. *'I don't want that insolent girl anywhere near me.'* And then her mother's angry reply. *"I'm sure you don't darling, but Bessie has chores to do for your father."* She straggled down the hallway and with a pounding heart, and trembling hand, reached for her mother's bedroom door.

The room was quiet except for the soft sounds of her mother's breathing. She could have wakened her, but no, not when her father shared another woman's bed, especially the bed of a servant. *Why does that excuse him anyway? He should be sent to the governess to be strapped. Although Bess didn't seem displeased. Well, at least Emily won't be running off with Jonathan tonight.* Her mother's breathing calmed her.

Colovere neighed a warning echo in the back of her mind. Footsteps came down the hall. Juliette glanced through the slit where the door was bracketed to the wall and saw her father coming down the hallway toward her. She backed against the wall. Her father swung the door, and it slammed into her. He grunted, and got into bed, pulling the red coverlet over himself and lay with his back to the door. Juliette took a step forward and heard Colovere's warning again, and then his words. *'You mustn't try to escape or stay. If you do, Zylphia will kill me and my herd for helping you.'* Juliette frowned, and left the room.

When Juliette was back in her room again, she realized the trunk was gone.

Looking through the house, Juliette heard the rustling of a skirt. She hid behind the couch in the parlor and watched Emily run out the front door. Juliette followed.

In minutes she was close enough to the stable to see Jonathan holding a glowing lamp, squinting to see who was there. He sighed in relief when Emily came into view. Juliette hid behind a tree trunk, hoping the darkness would cover what the tree missed in the moonlit night. Emily ran into Jonathan's arms. Juliette straightened her back, preparing to step out from behind the tree.

"Where are you going, Emily?" Zylphia asked.

Juliette's hand covered her mouth and barely managed to cover her squeal. Emily and Jonathan broke apart so fast Jonathan struggled not to drop the lamp. Zylphia was on the other side of the lawn, unable to see Juliette from where she stood. Zylphia left the shadows, walking towards Emily, who shook her head vigorously.

"Nowhere, Zylphia. We were just—"

Emily was shaking, and for the first time, Juliette felt sorry for her.

"Don't lie to me, girl. Who is this boy?"

Jonathan's shoulders stiffened and he lifted his head high. Juliette thought she had never seen anything so beautiful.

"My name is Jonathan Walsh and I will not be spoken to in that tone by a servant."

Zylphia folded her arms on her chest and laughed ruefully. "Yes Sir, then you won't mind my waking the lady and her husband to tell them a wealthy neighbor has come calling on one of their servant girls?"

Jonathan's shoulders dropped. "I'll give you a shilling to remain silent."

Zylphia shook her head. "I am not for sale, boy. Don't think for one minute that I can't get the information I want from you. I know how to deal with your kind. Where were you going?"

Jonathan remained silent. Zylphia muttered something under her breath. Emily yipped.

"No, Auntie. Please, we weren't doing anything wrong."

Zylphia lifted her arms in the air, her mutter became louder. Juliette could hear her chanting, but not in any language she had heard before.

"Zylphia, please," Emily begged.

Jonathan backed away, wide-eyed. "For the love of God, what's going on here?"

"We were running away to be married," Emily stammered. "Please Auntie, no."

Zylphia stopped chanting. Jonathan stared at Emily, lips pressed together. Zylphia pondered.

"Where were you running away to?"

"Gretna Green," Jonathan said, a little too quickly. "In Scotland."

74

Zylphia nodded. "Where do you plan on living after the wedding?"

Jonathan's chin lifted. "Not that it's any concern of yours, but I have my own home."

"When you return, meet me here at sundown. I'll watch for you."

"Why would we do such a thing?" Jonathan asked, shifting his feet.

"You will do as I say," Zylphia demanded. "And I can help you." She turned and walked away, leaving Jonathan, Emily, and Juliette confused.

"Come," Jonathan said, pulling on Emily's arm. "I brought a carriage."

Emily followed him into the night. Juliette waited until she heard the clip clopping of the horses' hooves fading into the distance. When she felt certain Zylphia wasn't coming back, she ran for the shed, hoping that was where her trunk would be.

The squeal of the old shed door was loud in the silence of the night. Juliette listened for a few minutes, but heard no one. She shut the door as quietly as possible. There was no light and she couldn't see anything. With trembling hands, Juliette pulled the horn from her pocket and it began to glow. It was only soft light, but it was enough. A spider busily spun a web in the corner. Juliette shrank away from it, hands on her chest.

The trunk rested against the back wall. Juliette carefully approached and knelt before it, rubbing her hands on the smooth surface. She hadn't realized until that moment that she was going back. That hadn't been her plan, but if she stayed, it would put everyone she cared about in danger. There was no question Zylphia would kill Colovere and his herd, and possibly Selene and Tolor too, and what about herself, and her family? *No, I can't stay.* Juliette placed the tip of the horn against the trunk. It glowed brighter. Soon the trunk faded until it disappeared. The horn radiated warmth in her hands. Juliette smiled. *Maybe I'll stop by the kitchen on my way back.*

She returned to the house and went to the kitchen, picking up a basket, and using only what light the horn gave her. A pie rested on the ledge. She licked her lips and grabbed it, lifted it to

75

her nose and breathed deep. *Oh! Raspberry.* She smiled wide as she placed it in the basket. Fresh bread sat on the table and candies filled a crystal clear dish. There was a bag of walnuts in a drawer, and a turkey sat dressed on the counter, but she left the meat. *Cook can replace the rest and no one will be the wiser.* She opened a drawer finding a nutcracker for the walnuts, and a burgundy tablecloth for color in her dining area. Unable to fit the pots because the basket was full, she touched the tip of the horn to the basket, and again followed the hall toward her room. On the way there, the horn's light went out.

Bessie still had a candle burning in her room. Juliette grimaced. *Candles, that's what I forgot.* Bessie walked into the hallway, and Juliette stumbled into the shadows. Zylphia came through the front door, and glanced down the hallway. Juliette held her breath until Zylphia turned towards the kitchen. The witch hadn't seen her. Juliette looked longingly the way she had come, but she couldn't go back for candles now. She ran to her room, careful not to knock into anything.

Juliette scanned her bedroom and frowned. Someday she hoped she could really come home, but she wouldn't let her friends pay with their lives for helping her. An oil lamp sat on the nightstand, Juliette grabbed it. *One of the servants must have used it when they cleared my room out.* It would stink when it burned, but Tolor would share the fat from his kills, and that would give her more light than a single candle. In a way, it was better than candles. Finally, she turned to the mirror, touched it with the horn, and nothing happened.

Chapter 13

"It is never too late to become what you might have been." George Eliot.

London, England.

Juliette kept grazing the horn across the surface of the mirror. It created a low keening sound, but nothing else happened. Her hands began to tremble. The horn dropped to the floor with a loud thump. There were footsteps coming down the hallway. Covering her mouth Juliette tried to conceal an involuntary cry. She lay down on the floor on the opposite side of the door and held her breath. Her eyes widened realizing the horn was on the floor where it fell.

What do I do? Please God, don't let them see the horn. Juliette prayed and stared at the horn as if she could make it roll to her by the sheer force of her will.

The door opened and an imposing shadow colored the wall beside her. Juliette recoiled, closer to the bed. Someone walked into the room, looked around, and slowly backed out. Juliette's heart beat like a hammer. She expelled the breath she'd been holding, and waited for the sound of footsteps to fade.

She retrieved the horn and returned to the mirror. Colovere neighed on the opposite side. *Why didn't mother ever hear me?* She tried everything she could think of, rolling the horn, skimming the edges of the mirror with it, touching the opposite end to the glass, but nothing worked. Engrossed, Juliette didn't hear the footsteps coming down the hall until it was too late. She looked frantically around the room. The door knob turned and Colovere screamed.

"Now!" He hit the mirror with his own horn. Light flashed.

"What's going on in here?" an angry female voice demanded.

Juliette jumped into the liquid-like substance, fighting to get to the other side, and watching helplessly as Colovere slammed into the back wall. Lightning seemed to cover him. When she

77

managed to get farther in, the mirror spit her out to the other side. She ran to Colovere.

"Don't touch me."

Juliette's hand froze inches from the hair of his mane. She dropped back, covering her face with her hands.

"I'm sorry." Tears stung Juliette's cheeks as Colovere started convulsing. Juliette watched until the light burned out and Colovere lay still.

When the light had extinguished, Juliette tentatively laid her hand on Colovere's neck. Nothing happened. She stroked and petted.

"I'm so sorry, Colovere."

She looked him over. He was breathing and there were no open wounds. *I don't know anything about magic. What if there's something I can't see?* She leaned close to his ear.

"I'm going to get Tolor. He'll know what to do."

Juliette left the cottage gate to find Meneme waiting, Colovere's herd stood pawing the turf behind her.

"Where is he, young maiden?"

Juliette stopped. "Colovere is in my room. He's hurt, I need to find Tolor."

The mare shifted. "I knew you were bad news the first time I saw you."

Juliette bit her lower lip. *If Meneme attacks, I'm minced meat. I don't have time for this.*

"I need to go, Meneme. Whatever you think of me needs to wait until we know Colovere is safe."

Meneme pawed at the turf with one large hoof. "If he is not safe, young maiden, I will kill you."

Juliette took a deep breath as the rest of the herd hovered around her. She pushed her way through them, and ran for the forest.

The Mirror World

Juliette didn't knock, but ran directly into Selene and Tolor's home, where she found Tolor lying under Selene's legs with one arm around her waist. Awakened so brusquely, he flew at her.

78

Juliette screamed and fell to the floor, barely escaping his long sharp claws.

"It's me, Tolor. Juliette." She was still breathing heavy from running the entire way there. Tolor stopped, but with his claws exposed, and furrowed brows, Juliette knew he was still angry.

"What makes you think—"

"Colovere. He's hurt. I didn't know what else to do."

Tolor's features softened. Selene stared, arms across her chest, eyes furrowed.

"He has no wounds. But crackling light covered him and he convulsed, and—"

"What did you do?" Selene demanded, her voice cold.

Juliette shook her head in denial, but this was her fault. "He helped me to cross worlds. I couldn't get back, so he ran his horn into the mirror."

Selene's eyes were wide. "Against Zylphia's magic? What in the name of Orion were you thinking, girl?"

Juliette wondered why Selene thought it was her fault.

"Can you help us?"

Selene shook her head. "Where is he?"

"My room, in the cottage."

"Is there any more magic you could see?"

"No."

"The portal, is it lit up?"

Juliette shook her head.

Selene put on a coat. "We should hurry. Bring what medicines we have, Tolor."

Tolor picked up a wooden box and they hurried back to the cottage.

Colovere was breathing heavy and snorting in his sleep when Juliette returned. Selene said he wasn't asleep, but too weak to open his eyes. By nightfall he was having breathing fits and chills. There was nothing they could do except wait.

Selene and Tolor stayed with Juliette for the next three nights. When they woke up on the fourth day, Zylphia hovered over Colovere.

Shaking her head, she chuckled ruefully. "So you found someone to help you escape, Miss Juliette. I could have told you it wouldn't work. It was all for naught. You would have awakened here in the morning. But you had to try, didn't you? And look what you've done."

Juliette's hands rested on her throat, it felt like something huge lodged there. There was nothing she could say. If Zylphia thought she made it to the other side, she would kill Colovere without question. Tolor broke the stifling silence.

"You can heal him, Lady Zylphia." It wasn't a plea or demand, only a simple fact.

Zylphia shook her head. "For what he's done, punishment is in order. I will not have my creatures challenging my wards."

"But he's done you no harm," Tolor said.

"That is irrelevant, Beran."

Tolor frowned.

"But he wasn't successful." Juliette hoped Zylphia, wouldn't catch the lie. "So no harm has been done, to you, or your wards."

Zylphia gave Juliette a knowing look, they both knew the harm that could have been done, and it would have, if Juliette hadn't been afraid for Colovere's life. Here they were now, his life in jeopardy anyway, and it was still Juliette's fault. If she had just done what Colovere told her, she would have gotten back while Zylphia remained outside, and this wouldn't be happening.

"Punishment. I believe I'll remove his horn."

"But he'll die, a unicorn cannot live without its horn," Tolor said.

"He should have thought about that before he defied me, and you're wrong, not all unicorns die when their horns are removed."

Colovere opened his eyes to slits, his breathing labored, and his body trembled. Zylphia took hold of his horn and a sickening whine filled the air.

"No! Stop, please. We won't ever do it again. Just, let him go… please." Juliette's arms were folded against her chest.

Zylphia released the horn, and Colovere's cry calmed, until it ceased. Juliette closed her eyes against a sense of relief, but the moment of calm was short lived. Zylphia walked toward her.

"Maybe I'm punishing the wrong person. It was you he tried to free, wasn't it?"

Juliette's nodded, her heart beating hard against her chest. Zylphia would not get the best of her. Zylphia ran her fingers through Juliette's hair. Juliette stood still, her chin elevated.

"Okay Miss Juliette, I'll make a deal with you. You forfeit all trips through the mirror for the next ten years."

"What will that do?" Juliette said. "We were unsuccessful." She set her lips in a tight line.

"Decide," Zylphia said.

"What? What do you mean?"

"You'll forfeit your trips to your world, or Colovere's horn. Which is it?"

Zylphia returned to Colovere and again took hold of his horn. "Last chance."

"Alright," Juliette stammered. "Ten years."

Zylphia smiled. "Very well then. I guess my business is done here. Be sure to watch the mirror. There are surprises that will soon be found there."

Juliette shivered. Zylphia stepped through the mirror, into her own world.

Chapter 14

"A fool flatters himself, a wise man flatters the fool." Edward G. Bulwer-lytton.

London, England.

Zylphia rode through the woods on a chestnut unicorn's back. She knew the unicorn didn't like carrying her, but it reaffirmed her control over the animal. One thing Zylphia would not tolerate was disobedience from her magical creatures. When they did as she expected, they lived a good life. When they didn't, they would suffer the consequences. In Ophelia's case it would mean the death of a family member so she had become quite compliant. In the distance she could see the lights of the Dancing Frog Tavern. They arrived a few minutes later and Zylphia dismounted. The mare would come to her call when she returned.

She entered the tavern and shed her coat, hanging it on a peg to dry. A fire burned in the hearth, its crackling and popping logs filling the room with warmth. Zylphia sighed at its pleasant contrast to the chill outside. A bard sat near the hearth playing a ballad forgotten by most. Witches and sorcerers loved to hear stories of days gone by, and often, of the days of their youth. She sat at the bar and a bartender with long blonde hair and strong brown eyes approached her. His eyes pulsed red and Zylphia shivered with pleasure. I would love to add a dragon to my collection, but he would kill anyone who tried to harness him. She watched him almost seductively as he placed a damp towel on the wooden bar.

"Whiskey and water, please."

The dragon gave her a look of contempt. She ignored him. It was no secret that she liked to collect magical creatures. *At least I have my beran. One of these days I'll work on a way to capture the dragon too.*

She drank down her whiskey, and set the glass on the bar. The room was full of sorcerers and witches. Why else would one find a bar in the middle of nowhere? She doubted a human had ever stepped inside these walls. A tall thin man with greasy brown hair and a top hat that made him look even thinner sat down beside her.

"Zylphia." He bowed. "To what do I owe the honor of this meeting?"

The bartender placed a whiskey in front of Donder. He slammed it down and the dragon poured another.

"I heard you talking about seeing a phoenix awhile back. I wish to obtain one for my own collection, Zylphia said."

"A phoenix. It's almost impossible to catch a phoenix. They self-destruct when someone tries to take them captive," Donder said.

"I'm certain you can find a way to make it happen. I freed you from servitude when Merek died, but I can call you back into my service. That was the agreement you made with Merek, when you were an impoverished boy who wanted to learn medicine."

Donder shivered. "Yes, lady. I will do my best to find a way to acquire your phoenix."

Zylphia threw a coin on the bar. "Good then."

She stood and the bartender stared at her.

"Keep the change." She grabbed her coat and returned to the cold night.

Chapter 15

"The pain of parting is nothing to the joy of meeting again." Charles
Dickens.

The Mirror World

Juliette handed a cup of tea to Selene, and sat down by
Colovere on her bedchamber floor. Most of the food had been
eaten, but she still possessed the oil lamp, linens, and the other
household items. Three days had passed since Zylphia left, and
Colovere slept most of that time. Juliette placed his head on her
lap and stroked his neck. Selene and Tolor, were cordial, but they
remained angry with her. Meneme waited outside, neighing and
snorting in restless irritation. Numerous whinnies and hooves
working the soil indicated more unicorns had joined her.
Colovere had never allowed any of the herd to enter the cottage
and Juliette hoped they would remain obedient to his command.

Colovere opened his eyes and sat up. He shook his head
and looked at everyone, then tucked his legs beneath him, and
rolled to his stomach. His whinny was weak, but he looked
better.

Tolor smiled warmly. "What were you thinking, Colovere?
The witch almost killed you."

Colovere looked away for a moment, then began to rise. He
moved stiffly at first, legs trembling, but slowly he moved
forward until he went out the cottage door. Juliette, Selene, and
Tolor followed. The herd greeted him with joyful whinnies, and
playful rearing. The younger unicorns galloped through the
meadow while Meneme walked beside him. Colovere didn't look
back. Juliette bit her lower lip, and wondered if she had lost her
best friend. Tolor and Selene said nothing when they left behind
him.

Exhausted, Juliette closed the cottage door and went back
to her bedchamber. Her long black trunk lay in the corner.
Zylphia hadn't seen it because she never went to that side of the

room. Selene had been standing there, her equine body taking much of the floor space, and obscuring the witch's view. Juliette yawned. *I'm too tired to deal with it now.* The truth was that the loss of her friends overwhelmed her and she couldn't bring herself to face that.

The mirror flashed with light and the room lurched. Juliette sat up in her bed so fast her head hurt. *Is Zylphia returning?* The surface didn't present the liquid consistency. *No, Zylphia isn't crossing. What is that?* A myriad of rainbow colors swirled. The room moved violently back and forth. *It feels like an earthquake. What is going on?* When the colors stopped and the room quit swaying, Juliette heard… *was that Emily's voice?*

"It's such a nice mirror. Here, hang it right here."

A screeching sound set Juliette's teeth on edge and the room jolted again. She covered her ears. When it stopped, Juliette saw Zylphia, and her heart stopped. *That's me!* And Jonathan stood beside her. Juliette couldn't breathe. Jonathan kissed the woman's cheek. Her face brightened, and she smiled. *What are they doing? Who is that woman? And what have they done with my mirror? Where's my room?*

"How's that?" Jonathan asked, looking directly into the glass.

He seemed so close, Juliette stepped back. *Does he know I'm here?* An older woman came into view, wearing a long blue skirt with a matching bodice. If she wore a corset, it wasn't doing anything for her. Jonathan kissed her on each cheek. The fake, was wearing a rich burgundy dress with a cameo broach, and a black and burgundy headdress with blue feathers on one side. Jonathan was in a black suit.

"Mother."

What is my mirror doing at Jonathan's home?

"I just stopped in to see how things are going. When your father and I lived here I so loved this house, it was nice to be out of the hustle and bustle of the city you know. How are things with you, Juliette? You look absolutely exhausted. I wish you had waited and married here rather than eloping."

Juliette's hands covered her mouth. Squinting, she looked at the imposture. *She looks just like me, but if I look closely, I can see Emily through the masquerade. Why can't the others?*

85

"Or should I call you Mrs. Walsh? Of course I should, I just love—"

Jonathan moved between them, putting his arm around the senior Mrs. Walsh, and turning her toward the door. "Mother, thank you for stopping by, but we are completely exhausted."

"Oh, well alright, dear. I'll stop in another time." She turned around and waved. "Goodbye, Juliette, and please let me know if you need anything at all."

"Of course she will, Mother. It was good to see you." He led her outside, shutting the door behind him.

Zylphia followed Mrs. Walsh out. Emily bit her lower lip, hardly stifling a giggle. Jonathan returned.

"I would say that went well. I was amazed this afternoon when Aunt Zylphia disguised you. It was utterly fascinating. I wouldn't have known you weren't Juliette myself."

Juliette's hands rested on her throat. *Neither would I.*

"Still, I have to say I wasn't disappointed when Juliette's mother refused to see you." He pulled her into his arms, and held her close.

My mother refused to see me?

"You can rest easy now. With Juliette disowned, even when the magic wears off, there is no one to say you aren't her. How did Aunt Zylphia do it? Do you know? Well, now all we have left to do is have the dressmaker make some proper dresses, and no one will ever connect you to a missing servant girl. If you remove the disguise a little at a time mother will never notice." He kissed her, and smiled. "Welcome home, Mrs. Walsh."

Emily's eyes sparkled. Juliette frowned. She had fallen right into Zylphia's hand. *In ten years, Emily will be established in her new life and home. And I will still be disowned.* Tears pricked her eyes, but she wiped them away. All the tears in the world wouldn't make this go away.

Juliette looked for Colovere every day, but he never roamed in the meadow. He was avoiding her. Juliette wondered if she might find him at the clearing in the forest, but that was his private home. *It wouldn't be appropriate to disturb him there.*

She wept when the full moon passed. The mirror didn't allow her passage.

Juliette needed to store food for the winter and would have to do it alone this time. That meant no apples unless she could find another tree, with lower branches, which wasn't likely. She did find some berries and a pear tree. Afraid to go near the water because of the lions in the forest, she stayed near the forest edge and the meadow. Juliette bit her lip. *I hope I have enough food to last this winter, because most of what I preserve is going to have to come from my garden.*

Colovere broke from the forest in front of her. Juliette stopped, and waited until he nudged her hand with his muzzle. She petted his silky hair, running her fingers through the strands of his coal colored mane. She threw her arms around his neck.

"I'm sorry. I've been so worried."

Colovere let her weep, and when she let him go, he nudged her hand again. Juliette smiled.

"I am well. I needed to be alone to heal."

"I still have Ophelia's, horn."

"You can return it after we collect apples." Colovere's neigh sounded like a chuckle.

After picking all the apples Juliette managed to reach, they sat on the grass by the pond and ate a few of them. Juliette laid her head on Colovere's side.

"Did you feel the earthquake this morning?" Juliette asked.

"Earthquake? No, young maiden. That was not the earth moving. Someone is tampering with the portals."

"Tampering with the portals?"

"Yes. They are moving or trying to shift them."

"The earth moved because they moved my mirror?"

"Someone moved your mirror?"

"Zylphia, this morning."

"Then yes, that would be the cause. This world reflects the portals, and sometimes what is beyond them. If a portal moves, our world will move with it."

Juliette finished her apple remembering the light and movement in the mirror. *I hope they don't move it often.* She turned her attention back to Colovere.

"Colovere, what happened that night? Why didn't the horn work? It worked on everything else. It even glowed to give me light."

"Power fades over time, you used up what little power it had to offer. It may be that a small amount will renew itself, but you used up what was available. I didn't think you planned on coming back."

Juliette stared incredulously. "Then why did you do it?"

"What is friendship without trust, or sacrifice?"

Tears stung Juliette's eyes. She fought them back and nodded.

"You came back, by your own choice. Look."

Juliette turned the direction Colovere was watching. Tolor, walked toward them with Selene beside him and she was limping.

Chapter 16

The Mirror World.

Selene's limp grew more prominent as she and Tolor moved closer. Her face was pale and her eyes had dark circles underneath them. Her beautiful red locks were a tangled mess. She wore a wrinkled shirt, ignored Juliette, and turned to Colovere.

"Why do you tolerate this girl, Colovere? She almost killed you, and you still follow her like a foal follows its dam."

Tolor reddened, glanced at Juliette, and then the ground.

"No, Selene, she was trying to return, and the mirror locked her out. Regardless of Juliette's actions, I am a male unicorn. Our nature drives us to maidens, to care for and to protect them. So even if she wasn't trying to return, I would still be here beside her now."

Selene scowled. Tolor looked at Juliette, and interrupted. "Selene is hurt."

"I don't want her touching me," Selene said, sidling and grimacing with pain in a struggle to regain her footing.

Tolor held his hand up, and Selene fell silent. "You said you would. I cannot fight the infection without removing the stone." He turned back to Juliette. "My claws." He held his hands in front of him as if seeing them for the first time. "I can't pull it out without driving it deeper and slicing her hoof. The stone is very thin, I've only managed to push it in deeper."

Juliette had never cut into a horse's hoof before. *There is no one else able to do it.* "Let me get a knife."

Selene flinched holding her hoof off the ground, her face ashen.

When Juliette returned she told Selene to lie down. Selene clenched her teeth, but did as she was told. Tolor held her. She cried out, clawed, and bit while Juliette worked at the stone.

"You don't have to remove the entire hoof," Selene yelled, through clenched teeth.

"I'm sorry. I've never done this before. The stone is embedded deeply." Juliette ran an arm across her forehead to remove the sweat accumulating there, then she took a couple of deep breaths, picked up the hoof and started again.

Selene groaned while Tolor gently ran his claws down her back and through her hair.

"Can you go any faster Juliette? Better a minute of intense pain than an hour prolonged," Selene said.

Juliette shook her head. "I can't see the bottom. Go into the kitchen Tolor, and bring me a clean, wet cloth."

Hesitantly, he went. When he returned, Juliette finished digging out the stone and cleaned out the infection and blood.

"You can stay here for a night or two so you don't have to walk on it," Juliette told Selene.

"Thank you," Tolor replied.

Juliette sighed and led them into the house, Selene leaning heavily on Tolor's strong frame.

"Do you have a blanket and pillows?" he asked, Juliette.

"In the extra rooms."

Tolor glanced at Colovere and the unicorn moved into Tolor's place to steady Selene.

After the blankets and pillows were spread and Selene lay down, Juliette went to heat soup for dinner. Tolor stopped her.

"Here, let me. I killed a small rabbit on the way here. After Selene's dinner is doled out, I'll add it to the soup."

Juliette smiled. She hadn't eaten meat since her last trip through the mirror.

Juliette sat down with her soup. Everyone had finished eating except for herself and Tolor. The room was quiet, the atmosphere calm. Juliette took a deep breath and let it out. Everyone turned to look at her.

"What is it Juliette?" Tolor asked.

"There has to be a way to break the curses placed on us."

"My family and I have been looking for a way to break it since the day I became imprisoned," Selene said. "The spell is solid. There is no way to break it."

90

Juliette put her bowl on the table. "There has to be something we can try."

"Not without the consequence of one or more of us dying when the curse recoils. Every time the mirror throws you against the wall, the curse becomes stronger. That's why the witch doesn't care that you're doing it. There is no way to break it Juliette. You would most likely harm yourself trying. Don't forget what happened to Colovere."

How could I ever forget? It was the worse day of my life. It seemed strange that something other than the night she was thrown into this place was her worst day, but it was true.

"But you will keep trying?" Juliette asked.

Selene nodded. "Of course we will, but you are not magical. Learn from what happened to Colovere and leave us to do the searching."

Juliette nodded hesitantly. "Alright." She finished her soup. "Would anyone like dessert? I made a berry cobbler."

Tolor growled with pleasure and Selene laughed. Even Colovere seemed to be smiling.

"Four cobblers to celebrate hope of an escape."

Selene shook her head and the room became somber.

Chapter 17

"It is only through labor and painful effort, by grim energy and resolute courage, that we move on to better things." Theodore Roosevelt.

The Mirror World

Kneeling in front of her trunk, Juliette inserted her key and unlatched the buckles. She pushed the top upward. It looked like all her things were here. *Who would've thought my entire life would fit in a trunk? If my parents disowned me, does anybody know I'm gone, or am I forgotten?* She glanced at the mirror; she knew the answer to that every time she saw Emily with Jonathan. They kissed a lot, laughed, and he always held her. Juliette had dreamed of being that girl.

She turned back to the contents of the trunk, and pulled out the lavender dress that lay on top. Clutching it in her fingers, Juliette inhaled the scent and closed her eyes. Rosewood and lavender, the scent she had always worn. Juliette laid the dress aside and began emptying the trunk.

She pulled out a corset. *I'm not going to begin wearing that again.* She hadn't even thought about how freeing it would be to not wear a corset. It was simply something she had always done. The dresses would be next to impossible to clothe herself in, but the slips and other undergarments would be useful. Selene made her men's breeches and the pretty triangular shirts she wore. At first Juliette felt immodest wearing them, but with time and encouragement, she came to prefer them for comfort and mobility.

Light shifted in the mirror. *It seems like there are always activities through the mirror these days. Why do I watch them? My life is completely over. Even who I am has been stolen.* She clung to the mirror now, for sanity and self-preservation. Juliette got up and went to sit in front of the mirror. *It's my only connection to the world outside.*

Emily was dancing around in a pretty pink dress, brown curls framing her face under a matching pink bonnet, when Jonathan came through the door wearing his favorite black suit.

His hair was ruffled from the wind, his cheeks and lips pink. He placed his hand on Emily's waist and kissed her cheek softly.

"Do I smell duck?"

Emily nodded, and laughed.

"To what do I owe the honor?"

"To Bessie's good mood." Emily giggled, and Jonathan picked her up by the waist and swung her around. Emily laughed with delight.

Bessie? What is Bessie doing there? Did Zylphia steal our servants too?

"Don't be impertinent with me, wife," Jonathan said. He grinned running his finger along the edge of her full pink lips. "You are beautiful when you smile that way."

Emily's cheeks colored. "In what way?" she asked.

"In that way that tells me you're glad I'm home." He pulled her closer. "That you missed me," he said, running his fingers along her side, outlining her petite body. Emily leaned into him.

"And that you can't wait to be in my arms." Jonathan ran one hand lightly over her hip, dragged his fingers back up to her waist, brushing her breast with his thumb before intertwining his hands in her hair, causing a pin and decorative comb to fall out.

"You're going to mess up my curls," Emily murmured.

"I couldn't care less about your curls." This time he kissed her deeply.

When he finished the kiss, Emily laid her head on his chest until she caught her breath, then reached up on her toes and whispered something in his ear. Juliette frowned, frustrated she couldn't hear.

Jonathan laughed, and hugged Emily so tight she squealed.

"A baby?" Jonathan yelled. "That's wonderful news. I guess we'd better eat our dinner now then… since you're eating for two." He kissed her on the forehead and they left the room.

Juliette presumed they were in the dining room. *At least the disguise wore off and she doesn't look like me anymore.* She was surprised to find herself happy for them. Marriages were arranged by station, and dowries. It was fortunate for a woman to find a good man who would come to care for her in time. It was what every woman hoped for, and dreamed of, the happenstance of love. Emily had it all. Juliette was still jealous, but she didn't hate her anymore. She was still a touch angry with Jonathan though, and hated Zylphia, for taking her life away from her. *There is nothing left for me now. The witch should have killed me.*

Something scurried in the bushes, and a bird screamed flying from a tree where Juliette stood. Her hands jerked to her chest. *Stop being such a child Juliette Barrows. You've walked through these woods with Colovere, countless times.* Her breathing slowed to a more normal pace. She looked all around her. *But that lion is still in these woods somewhere. Well this is what I get for saying I'm a big girl, and I could walk myself.* She straightened her back, and raised her chin. *I am a big girl, a grown woman.* She sniffed, and moved forward. A mouse scurried across the path before her. Juliette cried out.

Breathing heavy, she saw Selene and Tolor's stable-like home ahead. *Oh thank goodness.* Tolor came out to greet her. Placing his hand on the doorway, he looked her over from head to toe.

"You were supposed to be here when the sun touched the far side of the meadow. What on earth happened to you?"

"Nothing. A woman should always be fashionably late you know."

Tolor smirked. "Right." He grabbed a bag sitting on a home-made wooden table, high enough for Selene to eat off of. "Come on little coward."

Juliette stopped. "I am not a little coward."

"Juliette, I can smell your fear." He reached an arm towards her. "You better hurry up or you'll be left behind."

Tolor rounded a bend. They were eating at Colovere's clearing tonight, and Juliette hadn't been sure she knew how to get there alone. *Selene must be there already.*

A small bird landed on Juliette's shoulder and pecked at her hair. She squealed and chased after Tolor, almost crashing into him.

He laughed. "What is wrong with you?"

"A bird landed, and tried to bite me."

"Kamar is a finch. You've seen him before. And he was grooming you, not biting."

He narrowed his eyebrows, but Juliette saw his lips twitch. They walked in silence for awhile.

"How are things?" Tolor asked. "We haven't seen you for a few days."

Juliette told him about Emily and Jonathan's new baby.

"How many does that make since they decided to be celibate to avoid more children?"

Juliette smiled, "three."

Tolor laughed, One every—

Without warning the bushes rustled, twigs snapped, and the white lion sprang onto Tolor's back from a branch above them. Juliette screamed. Tolor flung himself back and forth, trying to throw the beast off him. Blood covered the ground, but Juliette couldn't tell who it belonged to.

"Stop screaming, Juliette. It's... not... helping!"

Juliette put her hand over her mouth, and whimpered as Tolor clawed at the lion. She heard the sound of Selene's hooves a moment before they struck. The lion roared, turning on her. Colovere's hooves landed in its chest as it lunged. Juliette ran for Tolor, but before she got to him, he sprang to his feet, slashing the lion with long thick claws. Colovere reared and backed away. Tolor screamed in a way Juliette had never heard before, raising the hair on her arms and neck. His hair became thick, black fur. A snout formed in place of his nose. His head grew rounder, larger, and his claws lengthened. The seams of his clothing split, his clothes turning to rags. Juliette watched wide eyed as the lion turned and launched itself at a tremendous bear.

"Colovere, use your horn," Selene yelled.

"I cannot without endangering Tolor."

The lion lashed out and bit. Tolor moved like the wind, slashing and biting. The lion was slowing down, but so was Tolor. Juliette found a large rock, picked it up with both hands and propelled it at the lion's head. It only grazed the lion's shoulder, but it was enough. With an angry roar it catapulted into the forest. Juliette fell to the ground, shaking.

The bear ran deeper into the woods. Selene bit her lower lip and helped Juliette up.

"We need to go back to Colovere's clearing," Selene said.

"But Tolor," Juliette said.

"He will return soon. We need to be out of his way until he is able to be near us without causing harm. Let's go."

Colovere knelt. "I will carry you."

Selene helped Juliette onto Colovere's back and they found their way back to Colovere's clearing where Selene packaged the food.

"I don't think Tolor will eat the lion. He will be famished when he returns if he finds no meat." She turned and led the way back to her home.

Juliette bit into a cold chicken leg Tolor had prepared for them earlier. He'd brought eggs into their world two seasons ago hoping they would be fertile. Now he and Selene had a small chicken farm. Selene didn't eat meat, but she understood Tolor's primal instincts, withholding judgment of his need for it.

Tolor snarled as Selene pulled a needle through his skin, stitching up his deepest wounds.

"Stop acting like a centaur colt. I'm almost done."

Tolor clenched his teeth. "I am not acting like a colt!"

"Alright then, a bear cub!"

"Come on you two, this has been a difficult day for all of us," Colovere said.

Tolor growled under his breath, but said nothing more. Selene knotted the thread and put the needle away.

"You're done."

Tolor pulled her down to him, and kissed her. "Thank you."

Juliette's heart stuttered. His voice was so gentle, so loving and grateful. Jonathan was like that with Emily. She was beginning to understand, or she thought she did, that Jonathan and Emily were meant to be together. Without each other they would have been miserable all their lives. Juliette wanted that for herself. She felt the sting of tears and fought them back. Then she swallowed the lump in her throat and finished her dinner.

Chapter 18

"We turn not older with years, but newer every day." Emily Dickinson.

The Mirror World, 1828

Juliette opened her eyes and leapt from the bed. Nothing ever changed in the world of the mirror, but she had spent ten years watching the change of seasons and Emily and Jonathan living their lives, having children, and coming and going as they chose. Tonight, she would walk that world too. There were things to say to Jonathan and Emily. She wasn't angry about the relationship anymore, that would be unreasonable. But Emily was still using Juliette's name and that made her furious.

It wasn't entirely true that nothing changed. Tolor had brought in some fruit trees they planted. Mangos, pears, cherries and plums. Juliette had never seen mangos before, now they were her favorite fruit. The gardens were bigger too and Juliette had planted flower beds and a herb garden for medicinal purposes.

Juliette was a little thinner now and Tolor a little thicker, but the only changes were the ones they had made themselves. Everything else remained untouched by time, including the animals and Juliette.

Selene watched the stars and seasons, so she knew when Tolor could leave. This time she informed Juliette too.

Juliette could hardly wait for moonrise. Selene would help her dress so she didn't have to walk the city in her nightdress or undergarments again. Women in London didn't wear the breeches that Selene made for her to wear in the mirror world. She had studied a pair of Tolor's breeches to learn how to make them. Juliette stuffed some coins in the secret pocket of her petticoat. Even though the centaur woman had a hot temper, she'd accepted Juliette after she pulled the stone from her hoof, and they had grown quite fond of each other over the years.

Colovere whinnied. Juliette found him pacing in front of the cottage. Light flew out of his nostrils. *What is that? It must be something that happens when he is worried.*

"Colovere, stop!"

He trotted over to her, and snorted. "I do not think you should go. You have not been away for ten years. What if the witch waits for you?"

Juliette stroked his nose. "Stop worrying. If Zylphia wanted to harm me, she would have done so before now. I'll be fine." She kissed his cheek, and he nickered.

"Let's run," Colovere said. "Galloping always calms my heart."

Juliette couldn't help but smile. "All right, but just for a short while."

Colovere knelt so Juliette could climb on his back. "Hold on," he yelled.

Juliette shrieked as he sprang into a sprint. She leaned into his neck trying to get a better grip, but couldn't. She gave up and soon found herself at ease, her hair trailing in the wind.

London, England

With silvery blue moonlight falling over the land, Juliette stood by the mirror, awaiting her moment of departure with a belly full of dragonflies. When the mirror changed to that familiar pool of liquid silver, Juliette took a deep breath and stepped through into Emily's hallway.

Emily kept lit candles on sconces throughout the house in case the children woke during the night. Glancing in the nursery, Juliette could hear their steady breathing. A light burned in Emily and Jonathan's room. That was going to be her first stop.

Juliette peeked around the doorframe. Jonathan sat against the wooden headboard of an intricately carved canopy bed with an olive green curtain displaying a red and ivory design. The curtains were tied back allowing her to see him. He was still gorgeous, wearing a white nightshirt and reading a book, while Emily lay in a blue nightgown, using his legs for a pillow. Juliette stepped into the doorway, and waited until he saw her.

Jonathan jumped dropping Emily's head out of his lap. He didn't recognize Juliette at first, but even with the sleep in her eyes, Emily did. Jonathan catapulted from the bed and had Juliette's wrists held behind her back in seconds. Emily backed to the wall, her hands grasping the nightgown at her throat. Juliette struggled in a feeble attempt at freeing herself.

"Miss Juliette?" Emily stammered. "H-how did you get in here?" Emily's voice was breathy.

"Let me go!" Juliette demanded.

Jonathan let her go, put on a robe, and positioned himself between the two women. Juliette's hands curled into fists.

"How could you Emily? My mother employed and trusted you when your family was starving!" She turned to Jonathan. "And you! Running off with a servant girl, and thinking you could use my good name? How dare you?"

"He didn't."

Juliette spun at the sound of Zylphia's voice. *Has she been there this entire time?*

"I did."

"You had been gone for a year," Jonathan interrupted. "Even your parents didn't expect your return. We did no harm. Now that you're back, Emily will simply use her own name. I'll tell Mother she prefers to be called by her middle name. She'll be none the wiser. Where have—"

Zylphia grabbed Juliette by the shoulder, and dragged her from the room.

"How dare you, Zylphia. Let me go."

Zylphia did, but blocked Juliette's path.

"You took me from my home, cast a curse you knew I couldn't break if I wanted to, and you've done everything you could to ruin my life ever since." Juliette trembled, fists clenching the folds of her dress.

"You've received considerably less punishment and pain than you doled out in your sixteen years."

Juliette flinched, guilt riddling through her. "Then why don't you just kill me and be done with it?"

Zylphia laughed. "I've told you before. That was never my goal. Now, you will never return to this home again. Do you understand?"

Juliette stiffened her back. "And if I do?"

"I'll take that mirror and put it in a place where you'll never find your way home again."

"What about the night of the full moon? This is where the mirror leads."

99

"You come through the mirror, and go straight through that door." Zylphia pointed to the door across the hall. "Understood?"

Juliette stared.

"Am I understood?" Every syllable articulated clearly.

Juliette nodded.

"Good then. If you break this rule I'll know because I have a room here." Zylphia left her and returned with a coat shortly thereafter. Juliette could hear Jonathan and Emily bickering in their room. "Come now," Zylphia said. "We have business to attend to."

Juliette jostled against Zylphia in a coach traveling bumpy roads, her arms folded across her chest.

"Where are we going, Zylphia?"

Zylphia glanced at her, and Juliette shuddered. *What was that look? Is she going to try to hurt me despite what she said?* Juliette tried to ignore the sense of foreboding that sat like a rock in her stomach. She raised her chin.

"There are things I need. Supplies I want to purchase." She stopped, refusing to beg. Zylphia wouldn't care anyway.

Zylphia sighed. "You're going home."

Juliette's heart leapt, tears stinging her eyes. "Home?"

Zylphia nodded. *What is going on? Zylphia has never relented on anything she's ever said to me.*

"You said I couldn't go home."

Zylphia looked at Juliette, her face blank. The silence dragged until Juliette thought the tension would drive her mad.

"Your mother and father died two years ago, Miss Juliette."

Juliette's eyes widened, and heat filled her. She launched herself at Zylphia and crashed into an invisible wall. "You killed my parents?"

"Hold your feathers, little chicken. I had nothing to do with their deaths. Cholera killed them."

Juliette remained silent the rest of the trip, unable to think, but trying to accept that her parents were now dead.

The house was dark and empty. The silence loud. Juliette had already gone through every room in the house, except one. She clutched the doorknob, twisted, and entered her parent's room.

The furniture was covered with dust sheets, but when she removed them, everything remained the same. The bed was made up with her mother's familiar red bedspread, now musty, and sprinkled with dust. Juliette pulled her mother's jewelry box from the chest of drawers, fingering a pink and ivory cameo necklace that lay in its top shelf. Juliette didn't look up as she spoke.

"Why did you bring me here?" Juliette asked, her voice low and strained.

"You are your parents' only heir. They disowned you, but your father never thought to change his will." Juliette gave Zylphia a look filled with hatred. "Since you are of age, according to law, you may inherit his property. I had the paperwork done on your behalf."

"Why save this when you gave everything else to Emily?"

"I'm a witch Miss Juliette, not a thief. Emily has taken nothing from you. She uses your name because I insisted she do so. Should you meet the terms of the curse, your identity will be returned to you."

"And my parents' finances?"

Zylphia moved a couple of trunks and dresses in the closet, exposing a back wall. She placed her hand to the left, and pushed on the wall. A compartment filled with money was exposed.

"It should be safe for the time being, or you can take it with you, if you prefer."

Juliette grabbed a handful of bills and placed them in one of her mother's purses that sat in a pile on a shelf. Zylphia put the wall back in place, while Juliette turned for the door. She wanted to see what might be useful from the kitchen. When she looked back to speak, the witch had disappeared.

"Ah!" Juliette complained. "I told you I need to purchase supplies. I hate when you do that. How am I supposed to arrive back in time?" Still no answer.

Juliette looked outside. The horse and carriage were still there. *But if the coach is here, where did the driver go?* She didn't know how to drive a carriage, but she could certainly ride a horse.

Something glinted in the moonlight. Juliette squinted. A horn, the horse was a chestnut unicorn.

The unicorn stood with her head held high, her tawny coat shining in the moonlight. The mane, like Colovere's, was dark. But Juliette couldn't tell if it was black or brown by the cover of night. She slowly approached the unicorn to avoid startling her. She knew it was a mare because it was small compared to most other unicorns she had seen. Mares didn't grow as large as stallions. Most people would look at her and see a large chestnut horse but Juliette could see the horn. The mare backed away.

"Please, I've no intention to hurt you. I've never seen a domesticated unicorn before."

"You're a witch. Else you would not be able to see what I am."

"No, I'm not a witch. I didn't know I wasn't supposed to be able to see you. Maybe the witch's magic is fading?" Juliette's heart leapt. *I could go home. But what do I have to go home to now? My parents are gone.* Tears stung her eyes. *No, this is not a time to weep. There will be time enough for that later. Right now I need to find a way back to the mirror.*

The unicorn snorted. "If you think the witch's magic fades, you are as much ignorant as you are a liar."

"I'm not a liar, and it's rude for you to say so." *This isn't going well, and I don't know how much time I have left.* "How did you come to be here?"

Juliette waited, but the mare acted as though she hadn't heard her. She asked again, still the mare didn't respond. Juliette took a deep breath. "Look, I simply must get through the mirror at Jonathan's and Emily's home as quickly as possible. Will you take me there? Please."

The mare had that faraway look Colovere had when he was thoughtful. "I'll take you there, if you agree to ask no more questions."

"Why?"

"That is the deal, young witch."

Juliette's cheeks heated. "I am not…" She bit her lower lip. "Alright, we have a deal."

"Enter the carriage."

It was the bumpiest ride of Juliette's life, but the mare delivered her to the doorstep in record time. Juliette thanked her, and looked for a way into the house. Every entrance had been locked. If she didn't get inside she would wake up in the mirror when morning came, and she wouldn't be able to leave for a year. After being unable to purchase the things she needed this night, waiting a year would be torture.

Something touched her shoulder. Juliette startled. "How did you—?"

The mare walked towards the door, hooves making no sound. She touched the tip of her horn to the doorknob and the door silently opened. The mare turned and disappeared into the darkness.

"Thank you," Juliette called under her breath, relieved she was going to make it on time. She ran for the mirror.

Emily stood at her bedroom door. "Miss Juliette, what are you doing?"

Juliette turned, and looked at Emily sadly. *She can't help me.* She smiled ruefully, and stepped into the mirror.

When Juliette entered her room she sat on the bed and watched Emily stare at the mirror for a long time. Juliette didn't know why, but she no longer believed she had a part in her curse. That thread of knowledge healed something inside her.

Chapter 19

"Into our deep, dear silence." Elizabeth Barrett Browning.

The Mirror World

Juliette entered her bedchamber, picked up a paper and quill pen from the nightstand, and a jar of ink.

"Where are you going?"

Juliette whipped around to see Emily through the mirror, standing at the end of the hallway. The silhouette of a woman and child stood in the open doorway, rays of sunshine infiltrating the room. Juliette would have known that silhouette anywhere.

"We won't be long," Zylphia said. "I'm going to test Amy Rose for the power."

Emily's hand moved to her chest. "The power? But I don't want my daughter to grow up to be a witch, Aunt Zylphia."

"Don't be foolish, girl. You don't have a choice. She either has the power, or she doesn't. I need to test her so she can be trained if she has the spark. We will return when I am done."

Zylphia left, the room darkening behind her. Emily watched the door as minutes ticked by, then turned on her heel with a look of determination. She went to the bedroom, and shut the door. Juliette, took a deep breath, and shuddered. *All the world needs is a little Zylphia growing to be the next witch in the family. Poor Emily. But there isn't a thing I can do about it.* Juliette took her writing supplies and went to sit at the kitchen table.

London, England

Donder sat at the bar of The Dancing Frog, shooting whiskey as the tavern erupted with song. The tune was The Widow With Violet Eyes, one of Donder's favorites, but it gave him no pleasure. Today he had been summoned to meet with Zylphia and even his favorite song failed to cheer him. He watched as she came through the door, heedless of the raucous and laughter surrounding him. Her long skirt and petticoats rustled as she sat down. The bartender slammed a glass to the bar, and poured her a drink. *He hates her as much as I do.* Zylphia ignored him.

"So, have you obtained my phoenix yet? I've not added anything to my world since the girl I cursed."

Donder shivered.

Zylphia smiled without warmth. "Yes, you should be nervous."

"My apologies Lady Zylphia, but I've been so busy creating remedies for people that I've not been able to search for it." Donder looked up and motioned toward his empty glass. The bartender moved his hand and a bottle of whiskey tilted filling the two glasses.

"I have to say," Donder continued. "It's so annoying to only be able to give my elixir to a select few when I could heal everybody. You know what they say though. People are afraid of what they don't know." *I'm babbling.* His hands clung to his glass, resting on the bar to keep them from shaking.

Zylphia downed her whiskey. "Why should I care about the people who killed Merek? They can all die." She stood to leave. "I set you free after Merek, died. And I got rid of the man who would have thrown you into the poor house. I don't care who's dying. You owe me Donder. Don't fail me again."

Donder twisted his hands in his lap. "I'll have the phoenix next time we meet, Lady Zylphia." But he knew there wouldn't be a next time.

Zylphia smiled and turned for the exit. A man by the door shoved his hand forward and a string of fire moved like lightning, slamming Zylphia in the gut. Her eyes widened with shock as she struggled for air. Donder watched as she raised her arms to return that killing power, a blue glowing ball formed in her hands, and her face flushed red with unbridled rage. But before she could move another man stood from the bar and rammed a second searing bolt at her side. Zylphia screamed as it burned its way through skin and into vital organs. The ball disappeared with a hiss as she doubled over and fell to the floor.

The man at the bar approached Donder.

"If you ever think to touch my phoenix again, I will kill you. Do you understand?"

Donder swallowed hard. "Yes, Sir."

The man nodded and stepped over Zylphia's body with little more than a glance as he went out the door.

Donder stood frozen. He knew why the man at the bar was at the tavern. Drist had been waiting for Zylphia to arrive. *But why was the hit man here? Did Drist hire him?* He finally allowed himself to breathe. Like everyone else in the tavern, he was staring at Zylphia, half expecting her to rise. It wasn't easy to kill an immortal. They were slow to die and usually found help before their last breath, but Drist had done his job. Zylphia didn't move.

The bartender walked around the bar and picked Zylphia up, taking the body outside. Donder saw fire in the clearing through the tavern's small windows.

The bartender returned with red eyes, breathing smoke from his nose and looked at the ashen face of the musician in the corner. "Play," he demanded. "That's all there is to see folks. Body's gone and the battle is over." His voice was deep and thick with the edge of an echo.

Everyone returned to their festivities and a few minutes later, Zylphia was forgotten. Donder picked up his jacket and walked through the door into the night. It was good to be free of his former mistress. She had become cruel since the loss of her husband. He wouldn't grieve for the woman slain this night, but he would mourn the kind and gentle woman his mistress used to be.

Chapter 20

"True friendship is a plant of slow growth, and must undergo and withstand the shocks of adversity before it is entitled to the appellation." George Washington.

The Mirror World, 1849

    Juliette sat in front of the cottage on a thick red and ivory striped blanket Selene made her for Christmas. She'd been in this strange land more than twenty years now, and still nothing and no one had changed. They still hoped for freedom as the seasons passed. Juliette wondered if she would ever go home. Knowing she brought this on herself had only made things worse. Now she tried to make the best of a bad situation. Things weren't all bad, she had her friends. No one had seen Zylphia since the day she left with Amy Rose.

    Juliette had spent many moonlit nights at her parent's home over the years, remembering her childhood, and days of her freedom. It felt strange moving through the house, sifting through her parents things. It was almost as if her childhood didn't exist and this world was the alternate dimension.

    A flock of large white birds with yellow plumes on their heads flew by, chirping in the breeze, their feathers tinted pink by the warm mid-day sun. Colovere ran through the meadow, the shiny black mane flowing in the wind, and his muscles bunching and releasing in full gallop. Juliette squinted looking at him, it almost looked like he was encased in light. She shook her head to clear it.

    She had seen the chestnut unicorn in her own world numerous times, but she couldn't get her to give a name or tell anything about herself. When Juliette asked the mare trotted away. Colovere was curious about her, but being trapped in an alternate realm, he couldn't do anything to get her away from the witch.

    When Juliette wasn't with her friends, she was usually in front of the mirror watching Emily's children grow. She almost felt like she'd attended her first daughter's wedding. They had used the mirror to smooth Amy Rose's dress and touch up her make-up. At the wedding there were so many people they spilled into the hallway.

Things seemed to be going well in Jonathan and Emily's home. Jonathan's son-in-law's family owned a cotton factory, and Frederick did well providing for himself and his bride. Juliette frowned wistfully, wondering again if a day would ever come when she could be a wife and mother. She had been raised and groomed for it, but she wasn't the same girl that entered the mirror. She had lived alone so long it might be difficult to sit in pretty dresses, doing nothing more than throwing parties and being cared for by servants. *No, I suppose I'll be a spinster all my life and die an old maid.* By society's standards, she was too old for child bearing even though she didn't look a day older than she was when she arrived in Zylphia's world.

Movement in the hallway caught Juliette's attention. Emily had her youngest daughter by the hand and the child looked pale. Emily took her to the nursery. The girl's name was Margaret, after Jonathan's mother. Not long afterward someone knocked on the front door. The butler answered the door with Jonathan on his heels. He invited a heavyset man with thinning brown hair into the house, and the butler took his hat and coat.

"Right this way, Doctor," Jonathan said, leading him to Margaret's room.

Juliette groaned, unable to see or hear what was going on. The doctor wasn't in the room long though. Emily shut Margaret's door softly. Juliette wished for the hundredth time that the mirror was somewhere other than the hall.

"What is it, Doctor? Do you know?"

"I'd say influenza. This is my eighth case this week. My colleagues are saying they are seeing a lot of this too." The Doctor bit his lower lip, crinkling his chin. "I hope this isn't the beginning of another outbreak."

He left without another word.

Learning how to make her own breeches, Juliette pulled a needle through brown linen fabric. The needle impaling her finger, she jerked it to her mouth sucking at the wound and bounced on her chair. Selene's look was scathing.

"If you paid closer attention to what you were doing that would not have happened!"

"I am paying attention, Selene."

"No you're not, you're distracted. Look at your stitches, they are crooked. Take them out and start over."

Grumbling, Juliette cut a thread with a knife and began tugging at the stitches.

"You're still pouting that we aren't letting you go through the portal tonight, aren't you?"

"No. Yes." She put the breeches down. "It's just that I get so little time in my own world."

Selene sighed and looked away.

"I'm sorry Selene. It was unkind of me to say that when you are never permitted to leave."

"It's alright." The sadness in her voice didn't match the words she spoke.

"I know you don't want me in the house because of the influenza, and I know I agreed. But I am going to go through the mirror. I promise you I'll be back in minutes."

"In minutes? What do you intend to do?"

Juliette bit her lip. "I saw someone walk toward the kitchen with a newspaper. I know it isn't right, but I have no other way to get one. Jonathan didn't take it to his room so he's probably done with it anyway."

"You're going to steal it."

"Yes. Sort of."

"Sort of?"

It's hardly stealing if they consider it rubbish."

Selene sighed and pointed at the breeches. "Let's get this done. I have to split wood today."

Glad it was Selene's turn to split the wood, Juliette went back to pulling out threads while Selene watched.

When Selene left Juliette sat down to eat the cold chicken Tolor had sent her. She didn't like eating meat in front of Selene and there was still some time before moonrise. When she finished eating she cleaned the kitchen and tried her new breeches on.

Not bothering to change, she went through the mirror at moonrise, and found the newspaper on the kitchen table. She grabbed it and quickly returned to her room.

Chapter 21

"Am I not destroying my enemies when I make friends of them?" Abraham Lincoln.

London, England

The illness swept through Jonathan and Emily's home, and on the third day, Juliette watched Emily faint. *She must be completely exhausted.* Jonathan wasn't home, so a servant called for the butler, who helped Emily to her room. Juliette watched with her hand on her throat, barely breathing. She couldn't see much but she heard someone say they sent a message to Jonathan's office, but by the time he came home, Emily was in the bedroom with her children again. Jonathan pulled her out of the room.

"You can't care for anyone, if you don't care for yourself, Em."

Emily struggled against his arms, but Jonathan wouldn't let her go. She began to weep and he pulled her close.

"Things are going to be alright. Jane will care for the children while you rest."

"But they need me," Emily sobbed.

Jonathan kissed her forehead. "I need you, too. You have to rest so you don't become ill yourself."

He led her into their room, but the following day, Emily came out as soon as Jonathan was gone. Juliette watched her as she leant against her bedroom door. Her face was pale as the powdered make-up their ancestors wore, her hair was an unraveled mess, and her body thin.

Why haven't I noticed that before?

Emily checked on her children, and then did something Juliette would never have expected. She knelt in front of the mirror, resting her hand against the glass.

Juliette's lips parted, and she stared at Emily. She was more surprised when Emily spoke.

"Juliette, are you there?"

Juliette shook her head, but didn't answer.

111

"Can you hear me?" Her voice was thin, and cracked. "I never meant... to hurt you. And, I never hated you." She looked away.

Juliette placed her hand against Emily's. When Emily looked at the mirror again, there were tears running down her cheeks.

"I wouldn't give up my years with Jonathan for anything in all the world. But I wanted you to know that.

"Zylphia enchanted Jonathan. He doesn't remember the night we saw you. He thinks I'm crazy, but I always knew the truth, and it's given me nightmares. I know you're there. I can feel the warmth of your hand on the cool glass. I'm so sorry, Juliette." She opened her hand and swallowed hard, tears filling her eyes.

Juliette stared at a hairpin with a tattered yellow bow tied onto it. Her eyes stung with unshed tears for shameful years of pain and loss, and for her own part in their friendship's demise. After all these years she could see Emily standing on the beach, waiting for her.

"It took you a long time to get here," Emily said smiling.

"Sorry, it's my birthday and mother is hosting a party tonight. I had to sneak out of the house, but no one saw me. Then I ran all the way here."

Emily shrugged. "Doesn't matter." She held out her arm, and opened her hand. "I made this for you."

Juliette took the hairpin with a tattered yellow ribbon tied in a bow attached to it.

Emily's cheeks colored. "Sorry it's not new."

Juliette hugged her. "It's wonderful. Thank you. I have to go back now, before they notice me gone," she said pushing the pin carefully into her hair.

"Okay, I'll go with you. How old are you today?"

Juliette smiled. "I'm six years old," she said as they trudged through the sand to the road.

And then came the moment that would change the destiny of both their lives.

"Where have you been? Look at your hair, it's a mess... and what is that ugly thing sticking out of it?"

Mrs. Barrows swiped the pin off Juliette's head. Juliette winced as strands of her hair fell with the ribbon to the ground.

Juliette followed her mother's eyes as she glared at Emily, standing on the road.

"What have I told you about spending your time with people like that, Juliette?

Juliette wondered what her mother would say if she knew the fruit produced on that day, and the cost of it.

Looking exhausted, Emily rested against the wall. Juliette stood on her knees so she could see her underneath the mirror. She shook her head.

"No. Get up Emily, please! We can be friends again. The past doesn't matter."

Jane came down the hall and yelled. Emily's hand fell from the mirror. She sat down hard on the floor. Jane helped Emily up and into her room to lie down. Juliette wondered if she would ever leave that room alive again.

"Not now, God. Please." Juliette fisted her hands in her hair, and wept for what was lost.

London, England

Emily tossed and turned in her bed, sweat falling from her forehead to the pillow. Jolting awake, she opened her eyes and gaped at Juliette, standing in the corner of her room. Big brown eyes stared back at her, filled with accusation.

"I didn't mean to," Emily said, watching her wide-eyed and trembling with fear. "Didn't mean to," she mumbled.

The door opened and Jonathan sat on the bed beside her. He ran his hand down her arm. The same love she felt when she first laid eyes on him as a girl filled Emily. He took her hand.

"Sweetheart, Darling, what is it? Jane is caring for the children. All is well."

He kissed the hand he held.

"She accuses me," Emily cried, tearing her eyes away from Juliette, searching for comfort in her husband's eyes.

"Who, darling? Who is accusing you? You've done nothing to bring harm to anyone."

"I should have done more. She was my friend. Surely she…" She swallowed the lump in her throat, and tears fell from her eyes. "She was my friend." She looked back to the corner. The apparition was gone.

"Sweetheart, there is no one there."

113

"She was there Jon, I swear she was."

Jonathan readjusted her pillow and tucked the blankets around her. Emily grimaced at the fear in his eyes. Had she put it there? He smoothed wet strands of hair from her face.

"Sleep, darling. All will be well when you have rested." His voice broke.

Emily tried to smile, to gather her courage. She knew he was wrong, and he knew it too. What would her knight do without her? Who would look after him and the children? She rolled to her side, unable to look at him any longer. He continued smoothing her hair and Emily's heart broke with every move of his warm hands. Living, shattered, pulsating pieces filled her chest. She closed her eyes.

"That's it darling," he soothed. "Sleep." He kissed her hairline. "I need to go out for a bit, but I'll return shortly."

Emily said nothing. She waited for the click of the front door closing, then rose from the bed and slowly made her way to the desk. For the first time she was grateful Jonathan insisted she learn how to read and write. He had been a kind and patient teacher. She pulled a sheet of paper from the drawer and drew the quill from the ink pot.

When she was finished, she folded the letter and placed it into a tin Jonathan had given her on their anniversary. The irony was what it had held... Turkish delight. She folded the letter and placed it inside the tin, opening another drawer and pulling out the faded yellow hair pin she had given Juliette on her sixth birthday. She set it on top of the letter, and put the top back in place. Then she set it on the nightstand by her bed and collapsed into the soft mattress, too weak to even crawl back under the covers.

Jonathan closed the front door silently behind him, removing his shoes. He hung his jacket and his hat on the coat rack and made his way down the hall trying not to wake anyone. He stared at the mirror and wondered. Emily had insisted Juliette was in the mirror, cursed by Zylphia. He never believed that but he knew she did. Zylphia always seemed to have some kind of hold on Emily. Odd as it seemed, her room remained as it always had been, even though they hadn't seen her in some time.

114

Jonathan frowned, beginning to wonder if they were the ones that were cursed. He heard the muffled sounds of somebody weeping, and stopped in front of Margaret's door.

Jane sat in a chair by the bed, Bessie on the floor with her arms around her. She turned her tear streaked face to the door and saw Jonathan. Margaret lay in the bed, her body ashen, and she wasn't breathing. Jonathan backed away, his hand covering his mouth. When his back met the wall, he crumbled to the floor.

He didn't know how long he sat there, but he remembered he still had Emily to attend to. He took a deep breath and wiped the tears from his eyes with a handkerchief, then shut Margaret's bedroom door, smoothed his clothing and went to see his wife.

Emily lay on top of the bed, her breathing broken and shallow, sleeping. Her skin was pale, her eyelids were dark and sunken, and she had lost a good deal of weight. He doubted she would make it through the night, and when she took her last breath, she would take his heart with her. There would be nothing left for him now that Amy Rose was settled into her own life. At least that was as it should be because nothing else was. Tears streaked down his face. *So much for being strong.* Emily opened her eyes and looked up at him. She tried to smile, but even that was weak. He sat on the bed beside her, planting a kiss on her forehead.

"Hello," he said, rubbing her arm. "How are you feeling?"

"Tired."

"I'll pull up a chair and do some reading. You should get more sleep." *Maybe if she sleeps.* He couldn't finish the thought.

He stood, but Emily's arm caught his hand before he could walk away.

"Yes, love?" he asked.

"I need you to do something."

She began to cough. Jonathan sat her up.

"Here," he said placing her pillow behind her. "Lay back and rest. We can talk later."

Emily shook her head weakly, and swallowed. "We need to talk now."

She tried to pick up the tin with one hand, but she couldn't get a hold of it. Jonathan picked it up for her.

"What is it Em? Do you want something sweet?"

Even when it was weak, her smile warmed his heart.

"No, I'm fine. I want you to make me a promise."

"All right, what is it that you want?"

"This." She pushed it toward him. "Put it by the mirror for me."

Jonathan's eyebrows narrowed. "Why would you want the tin by the mirror, Em?" *Is she delirious?*

"Doesn't matter. On the floor by the mirror, and leave it. Promise me."

"Emily—"

Emily started to weep. He could see her struggle to breathe already. It was part of the reason he hadn't told her about Margaret.

"Please Jonathan. Promise me."

Jonathan took the tin. "All right. I'll put it there right now. You can watch me." He opened the door and moved into the hall toward the mirror. She wouldn't be able to see him so he dropped it to the wooden floor with a thump so she could hear it fall. Then he returned to the room.

"Promise me you'll leave it there, Jonathan."

"I'll leave it."

"Promise."

"You have my word."

Emily squeezed his hand, laid back and fell asleep. Jonathan sat in a chair by the bed with a book in his hands, but he spent most of his time watching her sleep. An hour later her breathing stilled and her chest stopped moving. Jonathan jumped out of his chair, grabbing her.

"Emily. Emily, wake up." He shook her body. "Wake up Em, please wake up." Emily didn't stir. He pulled her close to his chest, rocking her body, and wailed.

Chapter 22

"A friend is someone who knows the song in your heart and can sing it back to you when you have forgotten the words." Unknown.

The Mirror World.

Juliette waited days for Emily to come out of her room, hoping against hope, she prayed. She couldn't see when it happened, but she knew the moment Emily died. She could hear Jonathan's grief from where she sat at the mirror.

She watched as a servant stopped the clocks, and turned them to face the walls. A dark wreath was taken outside to place on the door. Another servant closed the windows and covered them with black fabric. The last thing Juliette saw before someone covered the mirror with crepe, were two caskets. A black one for Emily and a small white one for a little child. *Margaret didn't make it either then.* A servant picked up a tin from the floor below the mirror, but Juliette had never seen it before and she had no idea why it was there.

She sat on the floor and wept for the life Emily shouldn't have lost, and for Jonathan's broken heart. She wept for Emily's children, who no longer had a mother, and for her grandchildren who would never know her, and for a child who would never see the prime of her life.

Juliette didn't own anything black but she lit a candle in Emily's memory and wore her darkest clothing, a brown pair of breeches, and a dark green top, until the drape on the mirror was removed. She couldn't pay her respects, but in her heart she mourned.

With Juliette's parents gone, Emily had been the closest thing to family she had left, absurd as it seemed. Colovere, Tolor, and Selene were her family now. They had been for many years.

She could see into their world again, but even with sunshine pouring through the windows, the Walsh residence was devoid of

117

cheer. Juliette wished she could see those windows, and not just the diffused light that made it to the hallway.

Soon it would be the full moon, and she could visit Emily's grave.

Emily's two small boys and the servants were wearing black as custom required. Jonathan wore a black band around his hat and a black tailored suit to honor his wife, with black gloves to indicate the loss of a child. He spent most of his time in his study or bedroom alone except when Amy Rose came to visit. They rarely spoke in the hallway so Juliette couldn't hear them, until one day she walked into her bedchamber to find them standing in front of the mirror, as if they could see in.

"Why are you giving us all of your things?" Amy Rose glanced at her father suspiciously.

"I thought you liked the mirror."

Amy Rose gave a hint of a smile. "I do. But this mirror was important to Mother, and to you. It makes no sense for you to dispose of it now."

"It makes all the sense in the world, darling. The cost to ship it to America would be atrocious if I were to send it later. Besides, you'll need furniture when you depart the ship."

Amy Rose hugged him. "Thank you, Father."

"You're welcome." His response was quiet, and distant. "So, when do you leave?"

"In just a couple of months. Frederick will have the actual date in a few days."

"He really thinks he'll strike Gold?" Jonathan shook his head. "That's certainly beyond my imagination."

"Peter Thomas told him all he has to do is reach down and pick up the nuggets."

"And you believe him?"

Amy Rose frowned. "It doesn't matter what I think, Father. Frederick's parents have done all they could to stop him, including disinheriting him and leaving the factory to his brothers. If he doesn't find gold we're leaving luxury for poverty with little recourse if things don't turn out well."

Juliette stood speechless as they left the hall. *Leaving England for America, and taking the mirror? Where in America? Jonathan said something about a boat.* Her breathing quickened. *I don't want to leave*

England. What about my home? Oh dear, two months? When is the next full moon?

The front door slammed shut, and Amy Rose was gone. Jonathan stared at the mirror before he returned to his room. Juliette scurried to find her friends.

Juliette searched the meadow for Colovere. *Today would have to be the day he isn't here.* She found him lying near some bushes growing along the forest's edge.

"Colovere."

He didn't respond. Juliette was almost beside him. She spoke louder. Meneme ran toward them.

"Colovere?"

He groaned, his body twitching and convulsing. Juliette reached out, but he coughed, and light spilled out of his nostrils like vomit. He retched. She placed a hand on his back and Meneme roughly flipped it off with her horn, causing Juliette to jump back. The mare moved between Juliette and Colovere.

"Don't touch him."

"Why? What's wrong with him?"

Colovere breathed hard, snorting, groaning, and spewing that odd light. *I don't have time for this.* Juliette turned and ran to find Tolor.

Tolor arrived with Juliette and Selene close behind. Meneme reared when he started to pass her.

"I'm not going to hurt him, Meneme. We need to see what's wrong with him."

Meneme's neigh sounded like a scream, her body shuddered. She moved out of the way and Tolor ran to Colovere's side. His breathing was heavy, his body twitched, and an unnatural groan emanated from his throat. Tolor looked him over.

"There are no cuts or bruises. Nothing to give any indication of what's wrong." He glanced at Meneme. "Have you tried to heal him?"

"What kind of question is that? Of course we have, but we had to wait until he collapsed to get near him."

"Do you know what's wrong?"

"He's not using his magic."

119

Tolor's eyebrows furrowed. "Colovere has never used his magic. Why is that a problem now?"

"Because the few magical creatures that draw magic to themselves have a built-in capacity to drain it. A unicorn cannot. He requires a unicorn of equal power to drain it from him."

"So you're saying he has more magic than his body can contain?"

"It's burning him from the inside out." Meneme neighed. "It will kill him if we are unable to drain it."

"Why doesn't he just use it?" Juliette yelled.

"You of all people should know why. The witch will kill him if she believes he is trying to go free. She almost killed him last time he used his power helping you!"

Juliette took a deep, broken breath, and bit her tongue to avoid responding.

"Save your petty squabbles for another day! How do we help him, Meneme?" Tolor asked.

Meneme's hooves dug up the turf with her anxious movement. "You can't help him. Only another stallion can."

"What?" Tolor scowled and looked at Selene.

Selene shook her head. "I can't help him. I know nothing of this."

"Can you try to drain him?"

Selene knelt on the ground, placing her hands on Colovere's head where his horn met flesh. A rush of light encased her. She jumped back, crying out and falling in her haste. Tolor ran to her.

"Don't touch me," Selene said. "I'll be fine. Give me a minute." She shook her head. "So much power, I don't know how he stands it. I can't help him, it would kill me to try."

"When will the moon be full?" Tolor asked.

Selene spoke through deep breaths. "In three days."

Colovere was quiet now. Tolor stroked his neck.

"You must have lessened his pain," Tolor said. "Forgive me Selene. I had no idea I was putting you at risk." He moved to hug her.

Selene threw up a hand to halt him. "Too much magic. It will kill you. I am not angry with you. I knew what might happen."

Tolor frowned, his eyes tearing. "Then why can I touch Colovere?"

120

"Smaller bits of magic are being released. I drained too much, too fast. It will dissipate in a while. I can continue draining him in bits to bring comfort until we can find help, but no more than that."

"Not if it could kill you. We know better now."

"Stop acting like a protective oaf! I know what I'm dealing with now."

Tolor didn't look convinced but he turned away. "Meneme, where can we find another unicorn stallion?" he asked.

Meneme's head swung back and forth. "We've been in this world for so many seasons we no longer know. We rarely run in herds. A free unicorn is always on the move unless he has given himself to a maiden's care. Colovere cares for Juliette, but his herd still comes first."

Juliette wasn't sure Meneme was right about that, but that was how it should be.

Crouching with his fist on his chin, Tolor glanced at Juliette. "That unicorn that helped you, do you think you can find her?"

"I didn't see her the last time I was out. It may be that Zylphia went back for her."

"We need to find her and see if she can help us. If we don't, Colovere will die."

Juliette nodded. "Okay." Her voice was quiet, and tears pricked her eyes. "We'll look for her."

Chapter 23

"Coming together is a beginning; keeping together is progress; working together is success." Henry Ford.

The Mirror World

Tolor showed Juliette the list of supplies Selene had given him. Looking it over, she shook her head.

"I haven't the slightest idea of where to buy such things as these. Most of them I can't even pronounce."

Tolor sighed, "I was afraid of that. Alright, we'll have to make do until the next full moon. We have plenty of food. At least I'll have a lighter load to carry back."

Juliette smiled demurely.

Tolor's mouth opened, a glint of distrust in his eyes. "What am I carrying back?"

She shrugged. "You'll see."

A few minutes later, the mirror transformed into the familiar liquid that told them they could pass. "Are you ready?" Juliette asked.

Tolor raised his arm to the mirror. "Ladies first," he said, smiling.

They landed together in the hallway barely making a sound. Jonathan snored in the bedroom beside them. Juliette listened, but everything else seemed quiet. She pointed to the front door and quietly they made their way through the hall, and slipped out into the moonlit night.

London, England

Juliette decided to try the stables first. She opened the door, and sprang back as hooves slashed the air. The unicorn screamed, and Tolor stood against a wall, a brown foot-long horn pressed against his heart. The mare's chest heaved from the exertion.

"I helped you maiden, and this is how you repay me? Bringing this filthy killer into my home? I should kill you when I'm done with him."

"No," Juliette cried. "Tolor isn't a killer. He's my friend!" Tolor stood frozen, his hands in the air.

"He lives in the other side of the mirror too. His lady is a centaur, and he lives in peace with the unicorns of our world. He is a dear and trusted friend. We came to find you and ask for your help."

"Why do you think I would help you?"

Juliette lifted her chin. "Because the help we seek isn't for ourselves, but for a unicorn named Colovere."

The mare moved back an inch. "Colovere," she whispered. "What of Colovere?"

"Do you know him?" Juliette asked, confused.

"Whether I know him or not is irrelevant. What is he in need of?"

"He's dying. We need to find a stallion to drain some of his power. Do you know where we can find one?"

"I do. I'll take you to him, but the beran stays here."

Juliette's cheeks reddened. "I will not leave Tolor behind. Colovere is as important to him as anyone else in our world."

"Maybe you don't know the beran as well as you think."

"Tolor would never hurt anyone."

"He is a hunter by nature. A natural born killer. Are you truly so foolish?"

"Colovere trusts him. Will you help us or not?" Juliette had no idea what she would do if the chestnut said no and her horn was still holding Tolor hostage.

Tolor was hardly breathing. The chestnut lifted her head and took a step back. Tolor sighed in relief.

"I mean harm to no one," Tolor said. "I promise your safety lady unicorn."

"For Colovere, I will help you." The chestnut snorted rudely. "Get on."

"Excuse me?"

"I said, get on. If you must be back by sunrise, we need to hurry."

"Only if Tolor comes too."

123

"I don't have to join you," Tolor said. "As long as you can get the help we need."

"I'll carry him too. But be warned beran, that if you get close, Petaire will kill you."

"Understood," Tolor replied, and helped Juliette onto the mares back."

"About being in a hurry," Juliette said.

"We'll talk about that later," Tolor said, climbing on behind her.

Juliette clung to the mare's mane in fear for her life. She never dreamed anything could move so fast. The chestnut ran faster than Colovere ever had, but like Colovere, she was grace in motion. Juliette's heart pumped hard with fear for her friend and exhilaration in the freedom she felt riding such an exquisite creature. Tolor had to cling to her waist to stay on, and had to do it carefully because of his claws.

It was late when the mare stopped. Juliette would have fallen off if Tolor didn't have a hold on her. He helped her down.

Not far away Juliette could see the outline of a unicorn as large as Colovere. His horn and coat was dark, shining with an almost imperceptible blue cast. He had a tan strip on his face, and sprinkled in his mane and tail. He stood tall and proud as if he weren't even breathing, and could easily have been missed by someone passing him unaware in the darkness.

"You will remain here," the mare said, still ignoring Tolor.

"But—"

"There is no but. Petaire will kill the beran if he comes near him without warning. Do as I say."

Juliette looked at Tolor, and the mare trotted off.

The black stallion reared, and the mare backed away for an instant, but she didn't back down. She moved forward as soon as she could, without being thrashed by the stallion's lashing hooves.

After what seemed like a lifetime, the mare turned to them. "The maiden may come, the beran may not. I will carry him back to my stable where he can enter your world through the mirror. The stallion will carry you, and he will be faster."

Juliette turned pale. *Faster?* Tolor gently pushed her forward.

Misunderstanding Juliette's fear the mare soothed. "It's alright. A male unicorn will not hurt a maiden unless she is threatening someone in his care. Go with him."

Juliette approached the stallion with slow even steps, and he knelt so she could climb onto his back.

The stallion Juliette rode didn't turn back to London. Her heart pounded with fear.

"Stop! We need to go back to London to try and take you through the mirror."

Petaire snorted. "I am a magical creature maiden. I don't need your mirror to enter your world. I can sense the reflective magic of its portals."

"I didn't know there were other portals."

"Do you and the beran always leave together?"

"No."

"Then you should have known. How did you think he was leaving your world?"

Juliette bit her lower lip. "Will you be able to help him Petaire?"

"If I cannot help him, there is no one who can."

"Why is that?"

"I have the strongest bond with him. I'm his brother."

Juliette's breath caught. Colovere never mentioned he had a brother. *That's a mystery to look at another day. Now we just need to make Colovere well.*

They arrived to find him lying on his side, struggling for breath. He wasn't jerking as often, but he was still trembling. Petaire lay down beside him, and eased his horn into Colovere's mouth. The light Colovere had been vomiting poured out like liquid, saturating Petaire's horn until it looked like a burning brand. Colovere's body calmed. His now feeble groans, stopped. Soon the glow covered Petaire's body, until even his tail burned with light. Colovere fell asleep. Petaire rose and began to walk away.

"But don't you want to see him?" Juliette asked.

"Colovere will sleep for days. I cannot wait for him to awaken, and take a chance of the witch finding me here. I must go now."

"Might I go with you? Please, there's still something I must do tonight. Can you help me?"

"After the length you went through to save my brother, yes."

Juliette turned to Tolor. "Wait by the mirror, and you can cross to carry my things over when I return."

"This is the 'about that' from earlier? You wanted me to carry something you can't?"

Juliette grinned and nodded. Tolor's smile held a fondness that made Juliette's heart stutter.

"Alright," he said irritably. "But don't make a habit of it."

"Of course not."

"What are you smiling about?" He crossed his arms. "I'm telling Selene you're being an itch under my fur."

"You do that. See if it helps you."

Tolor groaned, and Juliette laughed. She didn't miss the grin on his face as he watched her climb onto Petaire's back.

Arriving at Juliette's home, she opened the door and allowed Petaire to enter. If she was going to be able to make any purchases in America, she would need the finances to do so. She shifted the wall where the money was hidden, took the bills and coins, and placed them in a bag. She struggled to pick it up, but Petaire moved her aside with his horn, touching the tip to the bag. As it disappeared with a flash. Juliette's breath caught. "No!"

"It will await you when you arrive at your home."

Juliette remembered Ophelia's horn, and how she had transferred her things to the mirror world by touching the tip of the horn to the object. Petaire's touch was much stronger. Her trunk had taken a few seconds to fade. The air crackled with power when Petaire's horn had touched the bag. When they were finished she locked the door to her parent's home and hugged him.

"Thank you, for everything."

Petaire nickered, and touched the tip of his horn to Juliette's arm. It tingled, and Juliette screamed, her body falling through an invisible tunnel. She jolted as the strange feelings subsided, and looked wide-eyed at the meadow surrounding her. She sprang to her feet and ran to find Colovere.

Chapter 24

The Mirror World

Not even waking up for food, Colovere slept for three days just like Petaire predicted. Meneme wouldn't let anyone near him during that time, to Tolor's frustration, and Juliette's dismay. On the fourth day Juliette woke to Colovere's neighs from the cottage lawn. She stepped into a pair of slippers and ran to greet him.

He danced on the turf as though he were a colt again. Juliette laughed.

"I'm so glad to see you," she said, wrapping her arms around his neck.

Colovere nickered, leaning his head on top of hers. "Thank you. Meneme told me what you and Tolor did, and about Petaire. She told me about her part too, not letting anyone near me until she was outnumbered. I would punish her, but how does one punish loyalty?"

Juliette was reminded of Emily as a teenager, and the many times and ways she had punished her, and still she'd remained loyal. Juliette let go of Colovere's neck. "There is no need to."

"I'm curious. How did you know where to find Petaire?"

"It was the chestnut that found him."

Colovere took a few steps back. "Now I am more curious than ever. I need to know who this mare is."

"Her agreement with me is always the same, Colovere. Ask no questions."

Colovere shook his mane, and threw his great head back in frustration.

"You're healed, Colovere. Why is it so important now?"

"Because only someone related to us could have found us."

127

There should be two full moons before the mirror left for America. Juliette didn't know how much it would affect her friends, but she let them know when changes were taking place that might create problems with movement, cooking, or things falling off shelves.

When the full moon came and the portal opened, Juliette was ready to step through it.

Only the sound of deep breathing, gentle snores, and the ticking of the clock broke the silence of Jonathan's home. Juliette found sweet rolls in the kitchen. Chewing on her lower lip, she wrapped one in a napkin, and placed it into a pocket sewn on the inside of her skirt. She hadn't brought a bag and it was the only pocket she had. She went out the front door, and found the chestnut mare waiting for her.

"I thought you might like a ride."

Juliette nodded. The mare knelt and Juliette climbed onto her back.

The streets were silent, the trees edged in the silver lining of moonlight. Juliette wondered if this would be the last time she rode through the streets of London, or saw her home. She wished it was lighter so more of her surroundings would be visible. Arriving at her home, Juliette thanked the mare and invited her in.

"I'll remain out here, thank you."

Juliette was grateful at the mares decline. She wanted to be alone. She spent most of the evening sitting in her old room, looking out the window and gazing at the moon. It seemed strange that the world she lived in now seemed more real to her than her own.

She could still hear her mother's voice in her head, her father's rumbling laughter, the ringing of her mother's bell, and the swishing of the governess's skirts, and the clunk of her shoes on the wooden floor. She saw Cook in the kitchen and Bessie cleaning the kitchen floor. She could almost smell cook's sweet cherry pie. There were visions of Emily brushing her hair, cleaning the floor, and her screams the day Juliette had her beaten. As tears fell down her cheeks, Juliette remembered two happy little girls with their entire lives before them. One was destined for poverty, the other for riches, and how the tables had turned.

Will I ever see this place again? The house and its contents was the last of what belonged to her in the real world. The only thing left was the money and Juliette considered herself fortunate to have that. *I hope I'll be able to use it there.*

When Juliette arrived back at Jonathan's house, she explained to the chestnut that she would be leaving with the mirror, and thanked her for all her help. Again, she asked her name, the mare turned and walked away.

The Mirror World

Juliette, Tolor, Selene, and Colovere spent their last couple of weeks gathering as much food and supplies for the winter as they could. No one knew how this move would affect their world. Colovere and Tolor thought Zylphia would stop it. Juliette and Selene didn't agree because they hadn't seen her in so long. Why would she show up now? They debated and argued about it often, wondering what might happen to their world, and if Zylphia was testing them.

After a long day of fishing, Juliette placed a walleye on a stick, and held it over an open fire in the kitchen. She had better ways of cooking now, but she was too tired to deal with digging out pots and pans, and cleaning them afterwards. She ate the fish grateful Zylphia stocked the lake with some tasty varieties, and went to bed.

She heard a door click shut and then a tapping noise and sat up to see Jonathan, dressed in his black suit, standing in front of the mirror. He drank from a flask and ran his hand down its smooth surface. He wavered, and placed his hand on the wall to right himself. *Is he drunk?*

"Well, I'll be glad ta get rid of those nightmares," he slurred. He rubbed his nose and then laughed.

"Are you in there Juliette? Hahaha, I think not. Emily always thought you in there. She might've become a little crazy." He frowned and took another drink. "But," he raised his finger as if to make a point. "But I loved her. I love her." He swayed running his hand through his hair, leaned his back against the wall and wept. "I can't do this. I go to sleep, and she's not there. I wake up reaching for her, but she's gone. I can't function without her. She was the sunshine of my day, and the light of my world. The lovely rose in my garden. Everything is darkness without her. The world is empty. He stood on his feet and raised his flask. If I'm wrong, and you're in there somewhere, it's been an honor knowing you, Juliette. I can't do this anymore. I jus' wanted to say goodbye to somebody."

That last part sounded almost clear. I wanted to say goodbye to somebody... but where is he going? I jus' wanted to... Oh my God!

Juliette flew from the bed and banged on the mirror. The mirror slammed her against the wall. She screeched and banged again. "Jonathan. Jonathan, No!" She hit the wall again with a grunt. "No." She banged harder. "Jonathan." When she slid to the floor this time something trickled down the back of her head. Juliette ignored it. Placing her fingers on the cool glass. "Jonathan!"

Jonathan retreated to his room and returned with a gun in his hand. Juliette whimpered and screamed louder. He turned toward the nursery, stared for a moment, then wavered and grimaced. Juliette watched in horror as he left, the front door slamming shut behind him.

"No... Jonathan. Oh God." Trembling and crying, Juliette lay on the floor against the mirror. She woke to the incoherent screams of a servant the next morning, still lying on the floor by the mirror. Jonathan was dead. Once again, Juliette watched the servants stop the clocks and face them to the walls. The windows were closed and draped with black crepe, and candles were lit for the dead. The mirror was covered with black cloth once more.

London, England

Juliette stood with the chestnut mare in a garden cemetery. Jonathan and Emily had been buried in a mausoleum made of cement and stone, with a wooden door sealing the entrance. She hadn't been able to attend their funeral processions, but she wanted to honor them somehow. There was little she could do, but she came to say goodbye.

"They buried him near midnight."

130

Juliette turned at the mare's voice. "Near midnight?"

"I followed as close as I dared in the darkness, and hid by a large tree. I heard a man say it was the result of suicide. The man spoke of shame, but Jonathan's parents were heartsick. They have spent many nights grieving. They come at night because their son was buried at night. His mother often talks to him. I heard her tell him so. She thinks she bares the blame, and begs for forgiveness. The child rests here as well."

"Where are the surviving children?"

"With his parents. Frederick refused to raise them. He feels more people will know of the family's shame if he takes them in."

"Jonathan deserved better. He wasn't insane," Juliette murmured. She placed one hand on the door, kissed three roses and rested them in front of the mausoleum, and then whispered goodbye, and mounted the mare to return to the mirror.

With no one in the house Juliette was able to browse through the rooms she had never seen. The living room was larger than any she had seen before. Its furniture covered with white sheets. The kitchen looked cold and empty. Going back to the hallway, she stepped into the children's room. Jonathan's mother must have had the furniture moved to her home because the room was completely empty.

The last room Juliette explored was Jonathan and Emily's. The furniture had been covered here, but there was still an oil lamp by the bed, with a photo beside it. Juliette reached for it. Jonathan sat in a chair with Emily standing almost behind him, her hand on his shoulder. She had been posed to be life like, but Juliette could tell by the eyes and pale skin that she was already dead. Another photo was lying on the floor. Juliette grabbed it. It was Emily, lying in the bed as if sleeping. She took the photos with her when she turned for the hallway. A tin of some sort was lying beside the bed. She stooped to pick it up. *No. I've been invasive enough.* She stepped into the hallway.

Juliette stood in front of the mirror, her own image staring back at her. *It's so strange not to be able to see the other side. I wonder...*

She gripped the mirror with both hands and pulled. Light flashed and Juliette flew down the hall. *Maybe if I could move it back and forth to loosen the nail.* Again, she catapulted down the hall.

Brushing off her bruised knees, she stepped through the mirror into her bedchamber.

The Mirror World

Juliette guiltily wondered if Jonathan's suicide would change their timeline for moving. It didn't. Two months passed, and soon the mirror was covered with linens. Juliette, Selene, Tolor and Colovere watched as their world trembled and shook when the mirror moved. Dishes and candles crashed to the floor as the mirror was placed on what they presumed to be a cart. Their world trembled while they travelled cobblestone and dirt roads, and shook again when they arrived at the ship. Soon they could hear the excited voices of people bidding loved ones farewell and the cry of seabirds. The blare of the ships horn screamed loud as the ship began to move in the water. Juliette took a deep broken breath, and Selene placed an arm around her.

"We're going to be alright. It's a sad thing not to be able to see your home, but you will get used to it in time," she said.

Juliette gave a wistful smile.

"Thank you, Selene."

Juliette waited until everyone was gone and went to sweep up the broken dishes. She was done crying. It was time to prepare for a new chapter in their lives. She chuckled ruefully wondering what the days ahead would bring. The room shook again and Juliette braced herself between the table and the wall.

When the shaking ceased, she looked out the cottage window to see Colovere calming his herd. Most of the unicorns were lying on the ground looking around in confusion. She ran down the stairs and through the meadow. They were startled, but everyone was fine. She suggested they move within the walls of the cottage grounds so they wouldn't move far when the world shifted. It wouldn't be safe when they were standing, but if they lay down they would be all right, and there was plenty of hay to feed them. Selene and Juliette increased the size of the stable following Tolor's direction. Apparently not all berans were born with claws instead of fingers, and he had learned while helping family and friends build houses.

132

"I'll let you know when the mirror is mounted again," Juliette said, when they finished.

"Thank you," Colovere said.

Exhausted Juliette nodded, and went back into the cottage.

Chapter 25

"I cannot be awake for nothing looks to me as it did before, or else I am awake for the first time, and all before has been a mean sleep." Walt Whitman.

The Mirror World, 1849

While the mirror traveled, the inhabitants in Juliette's world were subdued. Still saddened by her own recent losses, Juliette stayed indoors most of the time reading and penning her story. Although no one would ever believe it, she decided to write it anyway to ensure she never forgot the world she came from. In the real world, women writers weren't honored, but that was changing. Juliette had even read recently in a newspaper that women could get a divorce now, and keep the money they earned. Divorce wasn't a common thing, but it was still a tremendous change. She considered herself fortunate. If her parents had thought to change the will when they disowned her they would have left her nothing. *They probably thought they had time.*

Colovere and his herd weren't as playful as usual, because no one knew when the ground would start moving. Tolor didn't try to use his portal for fear of landing in water, and Juliette hadn't seen any wild animals since the voyage began. Selene and Tolor spent more time at home, but they spent some days with Juliette and Colovere, staying in the stable with the herd.

Juliette smiled when Colovere neighed outside, and ran out to meet him.

"Tolor found and killed a deer. He is cooking dinner for you while Selene puts something vegetarian together for me. Will you come?"

"Of course. Now?"

"It's always good to visit first."

Juliette smiled. Usually Colovere would carry her but not this time. It would take longer than usual to get there, but with the ground sometimes moving without warning Juliette was safer on her feet. She followed him into the woods down an old trail.

Leaves rustled and Juliette's step faltered. A lion snarled and a wolf barked and growled.

"Stay here," Colovere said.

Juliette followed.

The site was a mess, blood splattered on leaves and trees and four dead wolves lay bloody on the forest floor. Nearby an injured wolf lay on its side, its body trembling, and breaths shallow. Another ran in an anomalous pattern, seemingly trying to divert the lion's attention. A wolf yelped and screamed, as the lion thrust its paw at its chest, sharp claws slicing through skin and fur like butter. Blood streamed and the wolf fell. A wolf pup whined shrilly and Juliette's heart became a lump in her throat. The lion lunged for the last wolf, snatched it up with its teeth, and bit into its neck. The wolf yelped and became silent. Colovere ran into the fray, deadly hooves striking at the lion. The lion lunged for Colovere, but the unicorn dodged and lashed out with his hooves, knocking it away.

Juliette turned at the sound of hooves, as Tolor and Selene ran through bushes to Colovere's aid. Blood covered his gleaming white coat. Selene struck the lion hard in the throat with her hooves, and Tolor's teeth elongated. He moved so fast Juliette couldn't follow him, lashing out with teeth and claws, using the weight of his body. Selene pushed herself back, wide-eyed, placing herself between the unicorn and the fight. The lion's movement began to slow. Juliette grabbed Colovere's tail as Selene pushed him back.

"Easy, Colovere. I don't want to see you or Tolor hurt because he's distracted by you," Selene said.

Colovere's chest heaved with long breaths. His nostrils flared and he snorted, but he obeyed Selene's guidance, watching closely.

Juliette checked for wounds on his body where the blood was thickest. Colovere shook his head and sidled.

"There's nothing wrong with me. Let me be."

Juliette backed away, the lion snarled, and she turned to see him fall to the ground as its belly split open on Tolor's claws. Except for the sound of heavy breathing, everything went silent.

"Is he dead?" she asked.

Tolor panted, his chest heaving for air. Long fangs receded slightly, and blood covered his clawed hands. His eyes were cold, his voice slurred. "I...don't know."

Juliette moved toward the lion, and Selene and Colovere stepped in front of her.

"Tolor will check him," Selene said.

Tolor grabbed the lion by the throat. "Dead." With the heavy lion in his arms, he ran into the forest.

Juliette started to follow but Selene grabbed her arm.

"He needs to be alone."

Juliette grimaced. "But—"

"He's in blood lust. It shatters reality and he struggles to keep his rational mind. He could kill you before he realizes what he is doing," Selene snapped. "Leave him." She turned to Colovere. "I think we need to cancel dinner. You will keep your herd out of the forest?"

"Of course."

Selene went into the woods, going the opposite direction from Tolor.

A pup whined and Juliette turned toward the sound. All the wolves from the pack were dead. She moved slowly around them and, following the sound, found the den. She peered inside, two baby wolves growled and yipped at her. One jumped clumsily and barked. Juliette laughed. The other pup bit its tail, and it turned around jumping and growling.

"You put your arm in there you're liable to get bit," Colovere said.

"They're just babies, Colovere." She grabbed the closest by the tail and pulled.

The baby wolf yelped. Juliette lifted it to her chest, cuddling it. "I'm sorry. It was the only way I could get a hold of you."

The pup licked her cheek. Juliette grinned, and Colovere whinnied.

"I think I'll call you..." The little wolf bit Juliette's nose. She squealed, and laughed.

"Storm, since you move so fast, and you're all over the place." Juliette looked at the other pup, sitting at attention, watching without making a sound. Juliette picked it up, and heard a little sigh. Juliette smiled. "I'll call you Whisper." Whisper lay down on her neck, and sniffling, cuddled its way into her hair.

136

"How will you feed them?"

"Tolor throws away meat we can't store all the time. They can eat that. They might be too small for food, but I have to try Colovere. If I don't they'll die."

"You need to understand that if either of them grows up and attacks my herd, I will kill them."

Juliette pulled Storm under her chin. "They won't. I'll make sure of it. Why did you help them if you feel that way, Colovere?"

"The wolves rarely bother us because they fear the prick of our horns, and it would have been wrong to watch them die to a common enemy."

Juliette put the pups down. They whined trying to climb up her legs

"I want to get these two back to the cottage before the world starts shaking again," she said. "They need to get used to their new home."

When the first full moon came, Juliette sat in front of the mirror. She couldn't see past the linen that covered it to know what was on the other side. She didn't know anything about ships, but it certainly wouldn't be good to land in the water. She couldn't hear any of the crew, but she didn't normally hear much unless someone was close or the sound was extremely loud. She bit her lower lip pondering. *I've never been on a boat before. I want to see the other side!*

She reached out and pushed at the linen. It was wrapped tight. *I'm not going to be able to get past that.* She grinned and jogged to the kitchen, picking up a knife lying on the counter. Thrusting the knife into the fabric, Juliette cut two long lines through, then cut across at the top. The opening was large enough for her body, but she only put her head through. No one was there. She pushed her way to the other side.

She found herself somewhere on the bottom of the ship. There were boxes and a vanity. *That must have cost a lot to ship, Jonathan said it was expensive.* A couple of carriages were parked toward the back of the ship, but there were no horses attached to them. She wondered how they would pull them when they arrived in America. Maybe they'll have horses waiting for them. She saw a flight of stairs and headed for them.

One flight up she found herself on the main deck and shivered in the biting wind. Water sloshed the sides of the boat and the movement of the vessel was stronger. She found a rail at the edge and held on to the side. Moonlight sparkled on the open sea, and the stars seemed so close that she felt she could reach out and grab them. Footsteps clunked on the deck and Juliette hid in the shadow of the stairs. A man strolled by with a slender woman under his arm. They stopped where she had stood moments ago, and gazed out over the ocean. Juliette tiptoed back to the mirror, and sat until they were gone. Then she spent the evening on deck watching the water until she could no longer stand the cold.

Chapter 26

"I am prepared for the worst, but hope for the best." Benjamin Disraeli.

San Francisco, California

Two more full moons passed before Juliette and Tolor were able to cross through to the real world. Their own world shook and jostled most of that time. Juliette had heard passengers complaining about the length of the voyage.

They arrived in San Francisco on the third full moon. They couldn't spend much time on deck because there were people there most of the night, but they snuck up there for a few minutes and stared in amazement at a harbor filled with ships of all sizes. There were voices in the night, the sound of sloshing water, the low deep rumble of foghorns, and the cry of seabirds. When heels clunked on the wooden deck they ran down to the mirror and slid back into their home.

The Mirror World

When they were back on dry land, Juliette and Tolor decided to discover the new world together the first time for safety sake.

"Tolor, why don't we ever use your portal?" Juliette asked.

Tolor's face reddened, and he looked away. "Blood lust," he murmured.

"I don't understand. Selene said that twice. What does it mean?"

Tolor sighed, and met her eyes. "I'm half bear, Juliette. There are times when I crave raw meat. And part of that is the hunt. My world is part of your world, but it isn't like yours. It's not friendly, and even I might be a danger to you."

"But you don't have that problem here."

"Going out once a month enables me to keep it under control. The day of the lion attack, you must have seen my teeth."

Juliette nodded, and Tolor studied his furry feet.

139

"Are you afraid of me now?"

"No, I'm not. Are you ready to go?"

He reached out and touched her arm. Juliette jumped, and Tolor smiled. "When I know you're safe, I'll need to leave you for a short time."

"Alright."

Juliette stepped into the mirror, with Tolor behind her.

San Francisco, California

Juliette wished she had paid more attention to the new home the mirror was hung in, but she could only see as far as the mirror showed her. They found themselves in a room in what appeared to be a boarding house. The walls were covered in pink wall paper with flowers flowing down strips of ivory. There was a big enough bed for two, and colorful rugs were spread on the wooden floor. The room was lit by candles on brass wall sconces, and a lamp on a nightstand by the bed. Tolor scrunched his nose at the thick floral scent in the air. They snuck out the door nodding to the people they passed in the long hallway. Hurrying down a flight of steps they found a door to the street and slipped out into cool wind and the salty scent of the ocean.

Juliette glanced at Tolor and stifled a laugh. Everyone they passed turned to look at him. He had to be the tallest and most muscular man the people had ever seen in his tight breeches and a pink shirt Selene had made for him. It was open in the front in the centaur style, baring his chiseled chest. She was certain he was the hairiest man they'd seen. He glanced at her with a questioning eye.

"What?"

Juliette looked down to avoid his gaze. "I think my dress is out of style," she said under her breath.

"Then we'll need to find you a new one."

"How? I'm certain we'll need to change my money into the local currency somewhere, if it's even acceptable here."

"I doubt we'll have the ability to do that, but I've been told by my brothers that shops and vendors here will accept gold coins."

"I didn't bring coins."

"If we can't buy it, we'll have to steal it."

Juliette gasped.

"Do you have a better suggestion?"

"No." She grimaced.

Closing her eyes, Juliette relished the sound of people, laughing and talking. She could hear music in the distance. *How long has it been since I heard a concerto?* The music here was louder, and faster, but it was still music. Her heart leapt. *Maybe we can steal a violin too, if we're going to steal something anyway.* Before long, Juliette thought she heard water. Tolor touched her arm, and motioned for her to follow.

They found a small boutique with women's dresses, hats and accessories that was abandoned for the night. Tolor walked around the building, and then joined Juliette.

"No one is around."

"Tolor... I don't know—"

"It won't take long." He tried the door. It was locked.

I could have told him the doors would be locked. He tried all the windows, until he found one toward the back that slid open with a forceful shove. He motioned for Juliette and lifted her inside, then waited for her to unlock the back door.

"Choose two or three of them. We don't know how long it will take us to work out finances, and I won't be able to come with you every full moon. I must hunt on the nights I am able to go out."

Tolor opened and closed drawers while Juliette looked for dresses. She decided to go with the simpler styles. She was glad Tolor couldn't see how pink her cheeks were turning. Some of the new styles had V-necklines that almost reached a girl's breast. Juliette tried on a floor length blue dress, with long sleeves and a gathered bodice. She couldn't see how the colors benefited her skin tone, but the dress itself looked pretty, and it fit perfectly. She found a pink dress with big puffy short sleeves, and an ivory shawl to wear over it, and a blue one, similar to the first with yellow dots and the bodice more gathered. Then she chose one more that fell just below her knees, a little immodest, but she liked it. The dresses made her feel pretty. *I haven't felt pretty for so long.* Her eyes stung with tears. *Now I'm just being silly.* She wiped

141

the tears away before Tolor saw them and looked around to see if they might have any perfumes.

"Here," Tolor said, placing bills and coins in Juliette's hand.

"We really shouldn't do this, Tolor. We aren't thieves." *I wish my desires and my conscience agreed with each other.*

Tolor squeezed her hand. "I know, and I'm sorry. When we find out how to change your money, or come back with gold coins, we'll leave money on the counter to replace what we've taken. There isn't another way now and I need to take you back."

"Take me back? But I don't want to go back."

"I have to hunt," he murmured.

"Can't I wait for you?"

"I don't know if that's safe. We don't know anybody here."

"I'm a grown woman, Tolor. Not a child."

"All right. I saw a bench you can sit at a short way back. I'll meet you there. I don't want to be near you when the blood lust begins to grow. It's too hard to control and my mind doesn't always think clearly. Go now."

Juliette grabbed a bottle of perfume and went out the door.

Sitting on a bench in the darkness, Juliette enjoyed the lights and sounds of the city, even though the smell was less than desirable with the dung left by horses used for transportation. She heard footsteps and saw a man with curly brown hair carrying a ladder walking towards her. He wore tan breeches with boots and a brown jacket that clung to his slim form. She could barely see the white shirt underneath. He stopped by a pole, positioned the ladder, climbed it and struck a match. Carefully shielding the flame from the wind, he lit the lantern and clambered back down. He smiled at Juliette.

"A beautiful young lady sitting in the dark by herself on a beautiful moonlit night? This must be my lucky day." He put his hand out, and Juliette cautiously placed hers in it.

"Name's Barnaby."

"Juliette," she said, smiling.

Barnaby bowed. "Pleased to meet you, Juliette." He pointed to the empty side of the bench. "May I sit with you?"

"Of course," Juliette said.

"So why is a lovely lady like you sitting out here in the dark by yourself?"

Because I was cursed by a witch and I live in a mirror with blue wolves, a man who's a bear, a centaur, and a unicorn.

"Just enjoying the moon, and fresh air," she said.

Barnaby pulled a sandwich out of his pocket, and offered Juliette half. Her mouth watered.

"No, thank you."

"I insist. It's safe, see." He took a bite and handed her the other half.

Juliette laughed, and took the sandwich. *Oh, when was the last time I had ham?* She ate slowly and savored each bite. "Thank you, Barnaby. I'm sorry, I didn't get your last name."

Barnaby sat back on the bench, and tugged at his suspenders. "Just Barnaby's fine."

Juliette's cheeks warmed.

There was a rustling in the bushes behind them and they turned around to find Tolor standing behind Juliette with his arms folded over his chest. He nodded at Barnaby.

"Are you ready to go?" he asked.

Juliette flushed, turning to Barnaby. "It was good to meet you, sir."

"Barnaby." He smiled.

Juliette laughed. "I really must go. Thank you, Barnaby."

Tolor nodded awkwardly and tugged Juliette's hand, pulling her away.

His smile was wide. "You can flirt another night. Right now, we have to get you back and me into the building without being seen."

When they were out of Barnaby's sight, Juliette turned to Tolor. "Take off your shirt."

"Take off my shirt? Why would I do that?"

"Because it has blood all over it."

"You would rather explain the fur on my chest?"

"It's not too bright in there. Everyone will think it's hair."

Tolor groaned, but he pulled the shirt over his head, and handed it to Juliette. "Happy now?"

Juliette smiled, and stuffed the shirt in between the new dresses. "Very, but if it ruins my new dresses I'll kill you."

"Me? You're the one that wanted me to undress!"

143

Minutes later they strolled into the sitting room of the boarding house. They were almost up the stairs when they heard a voice behind them.

"Excuse me." And then a more emphatic, "Excuse me!"

They turned around to find a tall woman in a long blue dress, with a white apron and dark hair twisted into a bun pointing as she approached them.

"Are you speaking to us?" Juliette asked.

"Who else would I be speaking to? What room are you staying in, please?"

Juliette looked at Tolor and the woman didn't give them time to think of an answer.

"That's what I thought. You two, come with me."

Chapter 27

"Knowledge slowly builds up what ignorance in an hour pulls down." George Eliot.

San Francisco, California

Juliette and Tolor sat in a locked room that looked much the same as Amy Rose and Frederick's accommodations, but in a smaller space. They were presumably waiting for the police to arrive, but Juliette intended to do no such thing. She not only had stolen money and goods in her possession, but what reason were they going to give for the fur on Tolor's body and the bloody shirt tucked in the folds of her dresses? At least they had no way of knowing the dresses were stolen.

Tolor rose, approached the door, and listened. "The woman doesn't seem to be out there. I don't hear her and I don't plan to await her return. Come over here."

Juliette got up and stood behind him. Tolor clutched the doorknob and pushed until the wood split and the door crackled open. Then he grabbed Juliette so fast she screamed as he slung her over his shoulder and ran for the stairs. The dark haired woman ran toward them.

"Stop right there. Stop, I tell you. The police will be here any minute now."

Someone pounded on the front door. The woman ran to open it, and the police joined the chase.

"Which room, which room?" Tolor muttered in irritation.

Upside down, Juliette pointed. "That one."

Tolor flipped around to see where she was pointing. Juliette screamed as her chest flung into the air with his movement. She clutched the dresses with white knuckles.

"What's wrong with you, Tolor? Put me down!" She tried to kick him but her feet only met air.

Tolor ignored her and ran for the door.

"Stop. Police!"

Tolor shut the door behind him. "I run faster than you do," he hissed, as he flipped Juliette to her feet. They stood in a small parlor. Two people were in the bedroom talking. Juliette couldn't make out what they were saying, but their voices were rising in volume. Tolor gestured towards the adjacent room. With a headache from being jostled upside down, Juliette peeked inside. Frederick and Amy Rose stood arguing, arms flailing to emphasize their point.

"This is your fault," Juliette Rose demanded, pointing at Frederick. "You're the one that wanted to come here."

"Because nothing I ever did was ever good enough for you. I'm sorry, I'm not as rich as your daddy." Frederick's face was red, and his fists balled at his sides.

"You had plenty of money. You gave it up to come to this terrible place, and for what? What gold have you found? We would have inherited my father's estate if you had allowed me to take the children as well as your part of the factory."

Juliette recoiled, and backed into Tolor. He pulled her against the wall. Someone banged on the door.

They flattened themselves, and Tolor motioned toward the vacated room. "The mirror is in there."

Juliette frowned. Amy Rose stormed out of the bedroom into the parlor with Frederick close behind her. Looking straight ahead, she didn't see Juliette and Tolor flattened against the wall. She flung the door open and Juliette and Tolor ran for the mirror. Amy Rose and Frederick screamed when they saw them run past.

"Hey, there!" The proprietor yelled. The police, Amy Rose, Frederick, and the woman with dark hair followed them.

"Jump," Tolor screamed, as he leaped for the mirror.

Juliette jumped beside him and crashed into Tolor on the floor of her bedchamber. Panting, they watched their pursuers look under the bed, beneath the roll top desk, behind chairs and even in the corners of the room for them. Juliette laughed with relief.

"It's odd how people don't believe what they see. Every one of them watched us jump through the mirror." She shrugged trying to loosen the knots in her shoulders. "I don't ever want to do that again," she said, her hand on her flushed cheek.

"Me either."

She handed him his bloody shirt, and sat by the mirror. Tolor rose to go downstairs.

"Aren't you coming?" Tolor asked.

"No, I'm going to wait until they are sleeping, and return to see if they have coffee or tea."

Tolor laughed. "You're crazy."

"I'll only do it if I know it's safe."

Storm and Whisper ran into the room, and lunged at Juliette, knocking her over and licking her face. Storm sniffed the air, turned, and Tolor heard a low menacing rumble.

"I'm going, just hold onto your tail," he told the young wolf.

Juliette sat up and pulled Storm into her arms. "He isn't usually like this. He has always loved you."

Tolor headed for the door. "I think it must be the blood. Be careful going back through that mirror and make sure you're back before sunrise."

Juliette stroked her would-be defenders. "I will."

The Mirror World

Juliette sat in her bedchamber eating a bowl of steaming venison stew, with carrots and potatoes for breakfast. Storm and Whisper were lying on the floor gnawing on bones beside her. Storm barked and Juliette shushed him.

"Hello?" Tolor yelled from the front of the cottage. "Juliette?"

"Come in, I'm back here," Juliette called.

Selene, Tolor, and Colovere joined her.

"You are always by this mirror," Selene said, shifting around irritably. "What do you find so interesting?"

Juliette shrugged. "That world affects this one. I like to know the things we're going to have to deal with before they happen."

"And what might that be?" Tolor asked.

"Well, apparently they're moving again."

Tolor's eyes bulged, Selene cringed, Colovere snorted, and Whisper and Storm whined.

Juliette smiled, and began to pet Whisper while she talked. She looked at Tolor. "Remember the last full moon, when we had to run for the mirror?"

Tolor ran a hand through his fur-like hair. "I don't think I'll ever forget that."

"Me either. More specifically, do you remember them fighting?"

"Yes."

"They've been fighting every day since then. Frederick says they have to leave to a place called Clover Springs. Amy Rose says they don't. She's refused to go, but it sounds like Frederick has put his foot down, telling her she's either going, or she can stay in the city alone. Amy Rose gave in."

"Please tell me we aren't crossing the ocean again. I would love to go home… but the constant earth quaking, and jostling. I was sea sick and I've never even been on water," Colovere complained.

"No, we aren't going home." Juliette tilted her head, "We're moving to gold rush territory. We'll be leaving as soon as their rent runs out. I've no idea when that is. I hope we get one more trip to the city though. The tea I found was so nice. I would like to have more."

"I liked it too," Selene said.

Tolor rubbed Selene's shoulders. "Then we will both go. It would be nice to pick up some supplies. Maybe that friend you made can tell us where to buy them, or even where to exchange foreign money."

"Barnaby is hardly a friend. I only met the gentleman one time."

"He wanted to be more than acquaintances, so let us assume you are friends."

Juliette frowned. It didn't seem proper to pretend like that, but supplies always made their lives easier when they could come by them, and she did want more coffee and tea. And if she was being honest with herself, she did enjoy the lamplighter's company. "All right."

San Francisco, California

148

While she waited for the next full moon, Juliette ground her teeth with impatience as she watched Amy Rose pack. They were going to be cutting it close, and they needed to leave as quickly as the moon rose. There were only two more days, but it seemed as though their luck held. They were still in San Francisco, and two hours later, Amy Rose had drunk herself to sleep.

It also turned out to be one of the rare occasions when the moon rose during daylight. For the first time in years, Juliette would be able to enjoy the sun in her own world. She had grown fond of their red one, but she still missed the brilliant golden rays she grew up with. Tolor was going with her again and this time they disguised themselves. He wore a pair of brown trousers and a white shirt that completely covered him to his neck. He looked much more human that way. Selene made him a pair of gloves to make his claws look like fingers too, but someone had to help him put them on. Juliette wore a long yellow dress with a big brown hat she owned before she was cursed, hoping it wasn't too outside the current fashion. Amy Rose was sleeping and Frederick wasn't home when they left.

Juliette laughed, twirling a new dress she bought in the sunlight. Tolor crossed his arms on his chest, and shook his head, but Juliette could tell he was in a lighter mood too. She wondered if he thought her pretty in the pink dress with big sleeves and yellow bows. He did smile when she came out of the dressing room. *I shouldn't even think like that, Tolor is like a brother to me. Is it improper for a man to think his sister is pretty?*

They saw a woman buy something to eat from a vendor on the street, and a tangy smell made Juliette's mouth water and Tolor's stomach growl. They both stopped without even discussing it. Juliette approached a heavyset man beside a red cart and pointed to the woman walking away.

"We'll have two of those, please."

The vendor handed the strange sandwiches to them, Juliette intercepting Tolor's because of his claws. She put them on a bench, and turned back to the man.

"That'll be fifty cents."

Juliette handed him some coins.

149

"That's too much. Here." He returned two dimes and a nickel.

Juliette grinned. "What do you call these?"

The man chuckled. "You're not from here are ya? Those are hot dogs."

Juliette's smile disappeared, her cheeks reddened, and she almost dropped the sandwiches. "Dogs? You eat dogs here?"

The man shook his head. "Those aren't made with dogs. That's just what they're called. Here, take some napkins."

Juliette nodded wondering why he called it a dog if it wasn't, while Tolor found a place amongst some trees where they could relax to eat them. He didn't feel comfortable in the new city, and preferred to avoid as many people as possible. He growled in frustration when he couldn't pick up the hotdog. Juliette enjoyed hers so much she wanted to eat his too, but she laughed, and fed it to him in pieces instead, dropping half of it down his shirt.

Strolling down the hilly roads and soaking in the sun rays Juliette tried to see everything she could. Green grass in front of wooden houses painted in bright colors, and horses and oxen pulling carts. Flowers of red, yellow, and blue swayed in the breeze in manicured beds. Ladies strolled in beautiful full length dresses, some with suitors, and others with baby carriages.

Tolor found a store that had everything they wanted. They bought oranges and berries, and a prickly vegetable they had never seen before. They also found coffee and tea, and they were delighted when they found hot dogs.

"How many would you like?" The butcher asked.

"Is twenty too many?" Juliette asked.

The butcher shifted legs. "They're sold in pounds. How many pounds would you like?"

Pounds? So I tell him how much I want to spend? She glanced at Tolor, and shrugged.

"Okay then, is two pounds too much?"

"Of course not."

Juliette watched him package the hot dogs. Two pounds bought less than she anticipated, but it was enough since they would need to eat them before they went bad.

They picked up a few more items, including a couple of oil lamps, and went to pay the lady in front.

"That will be five dollars," the woman told her.

150

Juliette handed her pounds.

The woman shook her head. "Sorry. We only take American money."

Juliette motioned toward the meat counter. "But the man said two pounds," she said indignantly.

"Not funny. American money."

Juliette handed the woman a bill.

"Come on, I need five of these."

Juliette gave her more bills. The woman handed her a few back.

"Thank you. Have a good day now."

"Can you tell me where I can go to see if I can change this to American money?"

"There's a bank down the street. With all these men flooding the city on their way to look for gold I've heard some of the banks do take money and trade it. Gold pieces too, if you have any of those." The clerk shrugged.

Juliette nodded and thanked the woman.

The bank only exchanged her coins and it was dark when they finished. Juliette frowned. *Worthless. I might as well throw it away. I'll keep it tucked away for now, just in case Amy Rose manages to talk Frederick into going home.*

Tolor led Juliette to the bench she used last time. "I need to go for a short time." He took a deep breath and looked away. "I'll meet you here when I'm done."

Juliette frowned as he disappeared into the night. She didn't care what Tolor was. He was her friend. She just wished he didn't feel ashamed of it. *If he lived amongst his own people he probably wouldn't.* She sighed, *another one of Zylphia's cruelties.* Juliette sat back on the bench and waited for Barnaby.

Barnaby arrived with his lamplighter pole and had set up his ladder before he saw her. He lit the lamp, jumped to the ground, and smiled as he shook Juliette's hand. "Well if it isn't the pretty lady that never gave me her name."

She blushed, and cleared her throat. "Juliette."

"It's good to see you again, Juliette. I haven't seen you lately. What brings you out on an evening like this?"

"The full moon, of course."

151

Barnaby smiled. "Of course." He pulled out his sandwich and gave her half. "Share my lunch?"

Juliette smiled, took what he offered, and thanked him. Once again it was ham.

When Barnaby finished eating he wiped his hands down his breeches, and ran an arm across his mouth. "Well, Juliette, I hope to see you again soon, but for now I must go. Thank you for sharing my sandwich with me."

She grinned, and Barnaby gathered his tools and moved on.

The night grew darker and Juliette couldn't keep herself from yawning. Tired from the day's events she found herself falling asleep. Someone shook her shoulders.

"Juliette... Juliette."

Her eyes flew open and she screamed. Tolor covered her mouth as much as he could.

"No. It's only me."

She held her chest, breathing heavy. "You shouldn't scare me like that!"

"Sorry, that wasn't my intention. Are you ready to go?"

She yawned, stood up, and picked up their things.

As they walked toward the boarding house they could barely make out a wagon in front. They might have missed it if they hadn't seen the oil lamp burning on the sidewalk. Juliette looked closer.

"Oh no. But they weren't supposed to leave for two more days," Tolor stammered. "No!" He started running.

Juliette followed Tolor, confused, until the wagon pulled out and the moonlight reflected off the mirror wedged to the side. "Oh, my God."

They ran as long as they could, knowing Tolor could catch it, but he wouldn't leave Juliette behind. She touched his arm and shook her head, then bent to catch her breath.

"They're getting away," Tolor stammered.

"We can't get through the mirror anyway, with it wedged like that."

"Maybe we could have held on or something until we could get through."

"Don't yell at me. You were the one that was late!"

Tolor took a deep breath. "You're right. I don't know what happens now. Do you have any idea?"

Juliette shook her head. "The last time I didn't make it back before dawn I woke up the next day with the wolves chasing me."

Tolor ran a hand through his hair. Juliette heard a growl in his throat. "All we can do is hope. Come on, let's find someplace to sleep."

They made their way back to the place where they had eaten their lunch, and huddled together until morning.

Chapter 28

"The worst loneliness is not to be comfortable with yourself." Mark Twain.

The Mirror World, 1850

Something pierced Juliette's leg. She screamed and thrashed as her eyes flew open. The curse had returned her to the pond in front of the cottage. She slipped and fell under the water's surface. Ivory fish swam frenzied around her, darting forward, and slicing with razor sharp teeth. A fish lunged for her face, its mouth open, and teeth glistening. She came up choking and splashing. Tolor roared beside her, fangs extended. Biting at his attackers, he pulled himself out of the pond and onto the grass. Blood streamed from angry wounds. Juliette cried out and flailed at the endless assault, unable to crawl out of the water. Tolor grabbed hold of her dress, and pulled.

She landed on grass, coughing. Her chest heaved as she fought to catch her breath, then she clenched her teeth and whimpered at the stinging of her arms and legs. *Do we always have to return to something attacking us?* She threw her hands in the air in frustration. "Ugh! I have cuts all over and my new dress is ruined."

"I guess we know what happens now," Tolor said with a rueful smile. "We wake up behind the mirror."

Juliette sat up. "In random places too. It was part of the curse Zylphia placed on me. Don't you usually wake up here the next morning? We'll be unable to leave for a year now."

"I wake up near my home, but your year of punishment doesn't apply to me. It used to, but it isn't wise for the witch not to allow me outings. She is well aware of that. Zylphia studies every creature in her collection before she takes them from their homes and family to bring them here." He said it matter of factly, but he didn't meet Juliette's eyes.

Selene and Colovere joined them.

"Whisper and Storm heard the commotion out here and tried to claw the door down, barking. Where have you two been?

154

The ground has been moving since last night. We've been so worried." Selene grabbed Tolor's wrists and pulled him up moving backward using the strength of her centauran legs.

Tolor winced and leaned against her. "Sorry, when we returned to the mirror it had been moved onto a wagon. Even if we had caught it, we couldn't have entered the mirror. We found a place to sleep, and awoke here only minutes ago."

"You should have come back earlier," Selene said.

"I had to hunt," he whispered.

Selene nodded. Juliette guessed that she was in the most danger of his blood lust attacks since she lived with him.

Juliette noticed the light of the mirror increase in the room, and sat with her back against the wall. Amy Rose had placed the tin she had taken from Jonathan's home and placed it on a closet shelf, then filled it with a colorful array of dresses. Then she mumbled something about being glad she was finished cleaning, and setting her home in order.

Juliette watched as she stormed in, and threw herself on her bed, crying. Frederick stumbled in a drunken swagger.

"What... do you want... from me?" he slurred.

"Nothing, I don't want anything from you."

"Good."

Amy Rose jumped off the bed. "All you ever do is drink!"

"If you weren't always nagging, I wouldn't... need to drink."

"Blame it on me. It's always me, isn't it?"

"Do you see me nagging? No. I can't ever do... anything to make you happy... not... a... thing."

"Then get a job. We can't live like this."

"There are no jobs. You get a job. I'm going." He belched. "To fine... gold! An' lots of it!"

"I want to go home," she screamed.

Frederick was quiet for a full minute. "Then go." Frederick left the room.

Juliette heard a door slam. Amy Rose started throwing her things in a bag, then she stopped, put her hand on her forehead, and curled up on the bed like a fetus.

"Hello? Juliette?"

Juliette startled at Tolor's voice.

155

"In here."

She sat staring at Amy Rose. Tolor leaned against the door, and glanced at the mirror.

"Why do you sit in front of that mirror, day after day? It makes you unhappy, and yet you still do it. What can you change by watching them?"

Juliette shook her head, and then turned to look at him.

"It helps me feel like I'm still a part of that world. It's changed so much, Tolor. If we were able to leave here tomorrow, where would I go? What could I do?" Tears stung her eyes, but she held them back. "Sometimes I feel like my life is over."

"The world isn't so different. You're watching them too much. All they do is fight, and it's beginning to wear on you."

Juliette took a deep breath. "You could be right." But she didn't believe he was. *The world has changed.*

"Are you ready to go?"

"Go where?"

"It's Selene's turn to cook."

Juliette laughed. "And you're probably thanking the stars for it."

Tolor chuckled. "It's a tradeoff. Since Selene doesn't eat meat she doesn't spice things up. But she doesn't burn it like you do either."

"Sorry. I'll work on that."

Juliette lit a candle, and followed Tolor outside.

"We had dinner at your home last time. Why are we not having it in mine now?" She folded her arms over her chest in irritation.

He turned around so fast, Juliette stumbled back. "Because you don't do anything besides watch that stupid mirror anymore," he yelled. His arms moved forcefully to emphasize his point. Juliette's breath caught, and she stared at him.

"Okay." Her voice was quiet.

She followed him the rest of the way without disturbing the silence. Selene smiled and hugged Juliette warmly.

"We've missed you these last few days. It's been so cold that Colovere and his herd have been staying here. It's a little crowded, but we all fit just fine."

156

Juliette looked around. "Where are they now?"

"Colovere insists he doesn't want to impose so he only brings them at night."

"That sounds just like him."

"Uh, is dinner almost ready?" Tolor asked.

"Hold on. It'll be ready in just a few minutes." Selene looked back at Juliette. "Please don't let his irritation get to you. He's not himself lately."

Juliette nodded. *What have I done for him to act this way?*

Tolor looked at them not blinking. "Dinner, Selene!"

Selene began spooning stew into the set of bowls Juliette had given her when she inherited her parents' things.

Colovere clutched a stick with his teeth, dipped his head and tried to delicately place it on a pile of twigs. The stack fell over.

Selene and Juliette laughed and screamed. "Secret or sing!"

Colovere gave them a big unicorn sigh, and began singing a song in his own language, neighing high, then low, with a few snorts here and there. Selene doubled over laughing, while Juliette held her stomach. Tolor froze, his eyes dilated, looking over Juliette's shoulder. Juliette noticed first.

"Tolor? Tolor, what's wrong?"

Tolor's nostrils flared, long fangs protruded from his mouth, and he cried out in mournful frustration.

"Move away slowly, Juliette," Selene said. Her voice was quiet and calm.

Juliette couldn't move until Colovere pricked her with his horn.

"Tolor?" Selene said. "Your friends are here, Tolor. I know its hard love, but you must fight it. You can do this."

Tolor snarled and launched at Selene. She screamed, trying to move her equine body away from him but she had been in a lying position when he attacked.

She couldn't stand. "Tolor, no. Stop." She cried out, putting all her energy into dodging his teeth and keeping her throat out of his reach while Tolor bit and slashed, the smell of the blood inciting him. Tiny glowing lights began flying around Tolor's head, taking his attention away from Selene, and placing it on

157

them instead. He swatted and bit, but the little lights always eluded him.

Juliette stood staring opened mouthed. Startling out of the stupor, she looked around frantically for any kind of weapon. *Oh, God. Help me do this.* The bottom of the twigs had thicker branches. She grabbed one, but this was Tolor. *He might kill Selene if I don't stop him.* She bit her lower lip and swung. When Tolor didn't stop, she swung harder.

Colovere neighed, frustration lacing his voice. Tolor roared, and turned on Juliette. Colovere reared, hitting Tolor in the chest hard with one of his hooves. The lights still flew around his head, he swatted and growled with frustration, until he backed away, and ran into the darkened forest and the lights dispersed and disappeared. Selene started weeping. Her entire body shook. She was lying on her side, blood pouring from bites and slashes from Tolor's claws. Juliette ran to her.

"Selene. Selene, tell me what to do."

"There's ointment inside on the shelf. He hurt me, oh gods. Tolor." She wept like a widow in mourning.

"What else do I need to do?" Trembling, Juliette carefully shook her shoulder. "Selene, I need your knowledge. Please."

Selene ignored her. Juliette ran into the stable-like house, grabbed the ointment off the shelf, and tried to think.

"I need a clean cloth and water, Colovere."

"You'll have to find it yourself. I need to stand ready for Tolor's return. Don't forget that some part of him knows this is his home."

Juliette found the supplies she needed, and began to cleanse the wounds. "W-why? Why did he do… how could he do such a thing?" Juliette asked.

"He's half bear. He can't control his natural instincts indefinitely. Sometimes he needs to hunt more than once a month." Colovere said.

When Juliette finished cleaning wounds and applying ointment, she stroked Selene's back.

Colovere wouldn't allow Juliette to go home that night, and his herd must have known to stay away, because they never arrived at the stable. Selene lay quiet on a makeshift feather mattress she'd made for herself and Tolor to sleep on.

A few hours later the bushes rustled and Tolor met Colovere at the entrance of his home. He raised his clawed hands in surrender, eyes wide with fear. "I'm okay, Colovere. I'm in control now. I need to see Selene."

Colovere moved aside and Tolor ran for the stable.

"Oh, gods." Tolor dropped to the ground by Selene and sobbed. "I'm so sorry." He said it again and again until Juliette was crying too.

Juliette curled on a bed that Selene kept ready for her, and tried to sleep.

Juliette climbed off Colovere's back, exhausted. "Thanks for bringing me home, Colovere."

"You are welcome."

"Colovere, do you think Selene and Tolor will be alright?"

"She always knew the risks. Whatever happens, hopefully they will be fine. But you must always remember what he is, young maiden, and never forget this night. Tolor has great self-control, but he is meant to be wild and free and sometimes when his beran instincts take hold of him, he loses the battle. He should have left us before he lost control. His shame and revulsion of what he is will consume him in the days ahead. This will be difficult for him to overcome, and also for Selene's heart to heal. They both know he could have killed her."

Juliette nodded. Yawning, she decided to go to bed. She stepped into her room and heard a door slam against the wall.

"I did it, Amy Rose. I got the job." Frederick was all smiles. "Amy? Amy Rose?" He looked around, his eyes stopping on the closet, then he turned to the chest of drawers. The top drawer was open. He checked the rest, and they were all empty. He sat on the bed, rubbing his eyes.

"She's gone."

Chapter 29

"The smallest act of kindness is worth more than the grandest intention."
Oscar Wilde.

The Mirror World

Juliette pulled weeds from the garden in the morning light. The sunshine burned her skin quickly in this place, but she rarely spent much time outdoors when she wasn't gardening, or working on projects with her friends. That took most of her days, since they still had to prepare for the winter months.

A month had passed since Tolor attacked Selene. Juliette hadn't seen them since. Colovere had told her they were fine, but she wanted to see for herself. Her lower lip began to tremble, and she bit down on it. *What did I do that they don't want to be friends anymore? Was Tolor's bloodlust because of something I did? We were excited and loud and he had been in an awful mood that day. Maybe we should have skipped games or even dinner.* She didn't want to think about it. It was time to go inside.

She heated some leftover porridge, and went to see what Frederick was doing. He was home, and drunk like always. *This isn't any better than thinking about Selene and Tolor.* She watched him anyway. At least she knew his issues weren't because of anything she'd done. Amy Rose didn't return, so Juliette guessed she'd gone home to England. She hoped she would find the happiness she sought there. It was possible. *How much has London changed?*

Frederick swayed and left his bedroom. Juliette heard a door slam, and assumed he was gone. She heard hooves in the courtyard, and went to greet Colovere. She froze when she saw that it wasn't Colovere, it was Tolor. He seemed to be looking at everything but her. She took a deep breath.

"Tolor?" she stammered. "I thought I heard Colovere."

"He walked with me, but he's gone now." He stood with his hands in his pockets, and met her eyes for an instant, then looked away.

"I'm sorry, Juliette. I... I don't know what to say. I never meant for you to ever see me like that."

"Well, that's ridiculous."

"What?"

"I know you're half bear. Do you think I didn't know what a bear looks like?" Except for pictures she hadn't known what bears looked like. *Irrelevant.* "I know what wild animals do. I'm not that naïve." *Well, I kind of am, I didn't really know.* "And then you ignore me, like we were barely even friends in the first place."

She threw her hands in the air.

Tolor flinched. "It wasn't like that."

"Wasn't like that?" she yelled. "Then what was it like? I haven't seen you or Selene since the night you attacked her. I thought it was my fault for hitting you with the stick, or maybe something I didn't know about. Maybe I did something to cause your bloodlust."

Tolor paled. "No, of course you didn't."

"How could you just stop talking to me as if I were nothing to you?" Juliette shook with the fear over the loss of her friends and the heart wrenching frustration of not knowing why. She balled her hands into fists in her hair. "I only know—"

"All right, all right." Tolor stretched his hands out in a defensive gesture. "I understand you're mad, but I don't normally attack those I care about. You should know that, and—"

"I do know that," Juliette said, through clenched teeth. "So stop acting like it was a big secret."

"Okay, I will," he spat back.

"Good then."

"Fine!" Tolor shook his head and chuckled, and then he put his arms around her. "I'm sorry."

"Me too." She waited until he released her. "Come in, and I'll make you some tea."

"How is Selene doing?"

Tolor's shoulders slouched, his brown eyes looked old. Juliette realized she had never asked how old he was.

"She's okay. Her body's healing." He twisted his hands in his lap and his eyes became glassy. "I broke her heart." His voice cracked. "And I don't know what to do to fix that. She's

161

everything to me and now she's terrified of me." He ran the back of his hand across his nose. "I don't know how to make things right."

Juliette ran one hand across his shoulders. "Give her time. There is a question I've wanted to ask though."

Tolor looked up. "Yes?"

"Why her? You could have gone after anybody that night, but you didn't."

"There are a few reasons. The first is the kind of thing every couple deals with, but more stressful since we're different species. We had been arguing a lot at the time so we both had pent up anger toward each other. Another reason is that centaurs are prey to berans, they love the challenge of bringing them down. I don't think I would have killed her, but the need to bring her down was all consuming. I don't know how to explain what it feels like. The joy of the hunt, the craving for meat and blood... even the cry of the animal you bring down fills you with anticipation for more. The third reason was what tipped the scale. When she protected you, making you move and talking soft to me, I took it as a challenge."

Juliette shivered. That could have been me. She never believed that before, but now she knew it was true. It made no difference. Without Tolor's help she would have been dead long ago. Over and over he had shown his worth. He was the greatest friend she ever had, and always would be. She nodded slightly and stood, reaching for his cup. "Would you like more tea?" She could see the relief in Tolor's eyes as she took his cup.

"I might have killed her if it wasn't for you and Colovere, and Lilac and Breeze," Tolor said.

"Lilac and Breeze?"

"The button fairies. Didn't you see them?"

Juliette shook her head. "The only thing I saw were the little lights, Colovere made to distract you."

"Those weren't lights made by Colovere. It was Lilac and Breeze's, cluster."

"I don't understand," Juliette said.

"Lilac and Breeze, are button fairies. Zylphia brought them here thinking she could drain their power and keep it for herself. She tried removing their life force, but all she managed to do was make them ill. In frustration, she poisoned them. But their life

162

force simply disappeared, and Zylphia thought they were dead. She threw them out of the cottage door and left to your world.

After Zylphia left, Colovere heard a wail as sad as a siren's song. He came to the cottage and found Lilac and Breeze in the grass. Lilac was weeping. If Zylphia had killed them any other way, Colovere wouldn't have been able to save them. He removed the poison with his horn.

The fairies were not able to pass through the portal to their own world, so they remained here. They live in the woods, and rarely come out except at night.

Juliette placed the steaming cup back in front of him, and he nodded his thanks.

"Why have I never seen them before?" Juliette asked.

"You have, but you probably don't remember it. The first time, was the day you were attacked by the wolves. Without Lilac and Breeze calling for help, we might not have known you were in trouble and been able to save you. They tried to help with the lion attack as well.

"Why haven't I met them?"

Tolor shook his head. "Maybe someday, but the cluster usually keep to themselves. They are shy, and they don't trust humans."

Juliette sighed, and they sat in silence for awhile.

"Not to change the subject, but it's almost the full moon," Tolor said, sipping his tea.

Juliette was always amazed at how well he had learned to use his hands; since the claws presented a challenge.

"Yes, I'm aware of that."

"I want to go together again. We're in a new neighborhood."

Juliette shook her head. "You haven't seen your own people for a year. You should take your own portal."

"That's just it. With the land shifting the way it has we don't know where any of the portals lead, except for the room the mirror is in. And we don't know what's behind that door, or if something more than a bad marriage made Amy Rose run away. I would rather you don't go by yourself. The portals should all still lead to the destinations they were designed for, but there's no way to tell until I try to use them. That can wait for now."

"Tolor… when you hunt in my world, do you hunt…" Juliette looked away.

"What are you asking?" His eyes widened. "No. How can you think that? I get as far away from people as I can when I hunt. I've never attacked a human… until now," he whispered. "The one common thing Selene and I share is we're both half human.

"I'm sorry, I didn't mean anything, I just—"

Tolor raised a hand to stop her. "It's alright. After what I did to Selene your question has merit." He covered his face, rubbing his nose and eyes. "I know you must have questions, but could we not talk about this anymore? Just for now." He wiped his face with his hands again, and then stared at the wall. "Please."

Juliette nodded. "Okay."

Tolor rose to leave. "I'll see you in a couple of days. Selene wants you to have dinner with us when we come back."

"But it's my turn. You're supposed to dine over here."

"She's almost healed, but she's still stiff. She would have been horribly scarred if you weren't there to tend to her wounds. The trip over might be hard on her right now."

"Of course, I'll come then." She smiled. "We never finished our game of Secret or Sing."

Tolor chuckled, and shuffled out the door.

Clover Springs, California

Tolor met with Juliette at the cottage early the night of the full moon.

"Has Frederick given you any idea of what this place is like?" he asked.

Juliette shrugged. "He mumbles and slurs. He's already asleep."

"Let's hope he stays that way."

They stepped through the mirror. Juliette looked around. The wallpaper had an interesting red swirly design, and there was a wooden coat stand. The living room had a rose colored couch, more wallpaper, with bottles and trash strewn everywhere. *Well, he hasn't hired any servants. I should have known that.*

Going down what looked like either the main road, or the only road through the town of Clover Springs, they tried to remain inconspicuous. But people turned to look at them as they passed by. *Maybe because of Tolor's height?* Tolor wore breeches Selene crafted that made him look like a fat man with hairy feet, until he put on his boots and his gloves. His trousers had been ruined by the fish in the pond. Juliette wore one of the dresses they stole from San Francisco.

They could hear music coming from a nearby saloon. Juliette scowled; it was too loud for her taste. The sound of a gun went off, and Juliette jumped. A man carried a bottle, swaying worse than Frederick when he walked. Juliette's back and shoulders stiffened. Tolor put his arm around her. *How does he know?* She sighed. *This time we need to try to find shoes. I hope someone is open, because it won't be easy breaking into anyplace here. There are too many people.*

Most of the merchants were indeed closed, but a few remained open and one was a general store. Juliette climbed the creaky wooden steps with Tolor looming behind her. The store was a treasure trove, with new varieties of garden seeds, spun wool for Selene, and trousers for Tolor made of a blue canvas called jeans.

"They're from a new company in San Francisco," the clerk called. "The miners love them."

They nodded politely and selected two pair for Tolor, surprised to find a size he could wear, and a smaller pair for Juliette. Ladies in the natural world might not wear them but Juliette found men's clothing more comfortable for gardening and chores.

After making their most important selections they browsed, breathing in the musty wood and dust with the fresh scent of new clothes and the bulk tobacco Juliette assumed he carried for the miners. She decided to buy a book for herself and another with rhymes to read to Colovere. She knew he would like that. She grabbed a newspaper and sighed. It was outdated, but only by a month.

The only shoes they were able to find were thick leather boots. They worked for Tolor, but not Juliette. She frowned.

"There is nothing in the way of clothing for a lady here."

165

Tolor returned the cotton shirt he held. "Maybe a tailor will be open. It looked like some lamps were lit down the road."

Juliette sighed and approached the brown haired clerk with hazel eyes who had been watching them curiously. She ordered their bulk supplies of coffee and tea, as well as sugar, beans and flour.

"Is there a merchant that sells women's clothing nearby?" she asked, while the gentleman wrapped their purchases in brown paper and tied them shut with string.

"Sam Moore, two doors down. He's the only tailor in town. He might have something you'll like."

"Thank you very much," she said, paying for their goods.

Tolor picked up their purchases and followed her out the door.

A man wearing an old brown suit with matching shoes and a black cravat was locking his doors when Juliette and Tolor arrived.

"Excuse me sir," Juliette called. "Are you Sam Moore?"

He tipped his hat. "Yes ma'am."

"I'm sorry, we've been travelling, and arrived late in town. But you were highly recommended for women's clothing by the clerk in the general store. Would you be willing to open for just one more customer? We would be so grateful."

Sam unlocked the door, and relit the lamp with a warm smile. "Since you asked so nicely I suppose one more won't be much problem."

Juliette returned his smile. "Thank you, Sir. I promise we'll be quick."

Juliette looked at the dresses. *He doesn't have much.* The shop wasn't as nice as the general store but since Sam was a tailor, most of his goods were clothing, and those mostly for men. There were black and brown suits. Women's stockings in bright colors no respectable woman would be seen in, and the opposite side of the store had trousers and more of the jeans the miners were wearing. The back wall displayed women's dresses. She smiled when she saw the selection of shoes beside them.

Awhile later, Juliette bought two pair of brown leather shoes, a long pink dress that accentuated her trim waist and actually showed her neck and arms. They thanked Sam for his time, and stood in the street, wondering where to go next.

"I don't feel comfortable leaving you alone here. We need to take you back."

"Don't be silly. I'll be fine. We simply have to find a place for me to wait is all."

Tolor eyed her sideways, but didn't argue.

"I would like to see more of the area," Juliette said. "Maybe see what this gold situation is about."

"Okay, it sounds like it's done in water. There's a river that way." Tolor pointed past the buildings.

"How do you know? I can't hear water."

Tolor grinned. "Bear. I have excellent sight and hearing."

"Oh. Alright then."

Juliette hadn't believed him, so she was surprised when she heard the sound of trickling water.

"Are you sure you'll be alright here?"

Juliette tilted her head. "Of course I will be."

"I would be happy to take you back."

"Go Tolor."

"I'll be back as soon as I can."

Juliette sat on the grass, enjoying the sound of the water, the stars, and the normal white moon. She had never thought it was beautiful before she was trapped in the mirror. She had taken many things for granted back then. The blue moons of her world were beautiful, but they weren't natural. She closed her eyes and breathed in the floral night air.

An odd sound interrupted the tranquility of the moment. Someone grunted, and a woman's screams followed the raucous sound of male laughter. Juliette ran toward it, and stopped at the edge of a camp hiding in the trees. She inched her way forward, the woman still screaming, and the men still laughing. She edged nearer, the woman was crying, and trying to speak. It was a language Juliette didn't understand, but it didn't sound coherent. Closer still and Juliette's breath caught in her throat. A group of men were pushing the woman around like a rag doll.

Juliette clenched her teeth. *How dare those men treat a woman so shamefully! What do I do? I could wait for Tolor. He'll know what to do.* She heard a ripping sound and shot into the clearing.

"Leave that woman alone!"

167

The men stopped and stared. Juliette hid her hands so they wouldn't see them shake. *Like dogs, maybe if I don't show them fear.* She made her voice as fierce as she could. "I said let her go."

This time, they laughed. Juliette cringed. The woman stood shaking, one man still holding her by the arm. Juliette had never seen anyone like her before. Her skin was darker, and her hair was black. She was young and beautiful in the odd furry clothing she wore. She had a necklace with what looked like teeth mixed with wooden beads, and a matching anklet.

A man walked toward Juliette.

"So you want to join this party?" he said, toying with a gun at his side. "The more the merrier. Huh, gentleman?"

The men smirked, two of them shoving the woman between them.

"Let go of me," Juliette said as he grabbed her arm and pulled her close. His trousers and shirt were filthy and his body odor nearly gagged her. His hands were rough and calloused.

He tried to put his mouth on hers. She twisted her neck, and kicked his shin screeching through clenched teeth. She ran, but he caught her, cheered by the hoots and hollers of his friends. His breath stank and Juliette's shrieks filled the air as she fought to dislodge his grip. He spun her around, and long red claws raked across his chest, right before a whirling mass of bear jumped into the group of men.

Juliette's captor fell to the ground but she stood shaking so hard she was unable to move. She watched as the man released the woman's arm, and she ran out of the circle of men, holding her torn clothing together, stumbling and sobbing. He started to chase her down, but Tolor was a whirlwind of vengeance as claws raked the back of his neck. One of the men raised his gun, and Tolor's teeth clamped down on his arm. Dropping the gun the man cried out with pain.

When Tolor flew out of the clearing every one of the men lay bleeding. The man that held Juliette was no longer breathing. Tolor picked her up, and ran. She shrank back from his teeth, crying out with fear. He didn't sound winded, but his words were slurred.

"I can't retract them right now. I'm myself, Juliette, you're safe. I swear you are. Trust me, please." Saliva drooled from the side of his mouth. He smelled musty, like a wild animal and looked feral. But she did trust him. Man or beast, he was her friend, closer than a brother and she loved him as such. She clamped her arms around his neck so he could loosen his hold on her and some of the stiff tension rolled off him.

Juliette heard the loud popping of gunfire behind them. Her blood pumped double time, hot with adrenaline.

"Oh my God. Run faster, Tolor!"

He looked at her like she was crazy. "We're well out of firing range now." He turned a corner and Juliette saw the house. Tolor picked up their things from the grass, and ran for the mirror with Juliette still in his arms.

Frederick slept in a drunken stupor through it all.

Chapter 30

"Looking back, I have this to regret, that too often when I loved, I did not say so," David Grayson.

The Mirror World

Tolor leapt through the mirror, and hit the bedchamber floor still holding Juliette. He wrapped himself around her and rolled. The wolves ran to them yelping and barking. Tolor let Juliette go and they both sat on the floor panting for breath. Whisper sniffed Juliette, then licked her nose. She sputtered, and pushed the young wolf away.

"What were you thinking?" Tolor said. "You could have been killed back there."

"I heard a woman scream. What was I supposed to do? Those animals might have killed her."

"Couldn't you have waited for me?"

"How could I have known that you would be back in time to help her? I only meant to..." *What? What did I think I was going to do against who knows how many men?*

She threw her arms up in surrender. "I don't know. I don't know what I was going to do. I'm sorry."

Tolor leaned over, and put his arm around her pulling her closer to him. At first she held herself rigid with anger, but soon his closeness and warmth became a comfort. Juliette's blood felt like heated wax. How long had it been since anyone had held her? Her father hadn't done so for years before she came to this world. It felt nice, and she relaxed.

"I'm not sorry," he muttered. "I'm just glad you didn't get hurt. We should go through these supplies. If I don't get home soon, Selene will worry."

"Secret or sing!" Juliette and Tolor laughed. Colovere neighed, and Selene's cheeks reddened. She tilted her head in thought.

170

"Oh, alright. Let's see… when I was little, my mam always made me go to bed when the sun went down, and I always wanted to see, and learn how to read the stars." She stopped, and cleared her throat, eyes sparkling. "So when mam and my Sire went to read the stars, I would sneak out of my stable to watch. I never learned anything, but one night I fell asleep there and didn't wake up until morning."

"Awww, that wasn't a good secret," Tolor complained. "You should have sung." He smiled.

Selene kissed him, and set the base of the twigs back up. "Okay, I start this round." She picked up a twig, and placed it across the branches.

Juliette, Colovere, and Tolor followed with more twigs. Colovere picked a twig up with his teeth, and placed it on top. The pile swayed. Wide eyed with excitement, everyone laughed, but it didn't fall. Juliette carefully placed a twig to the opposite side. The pile of wood and kindling fell. Everyone shrieked with delight and yelled, "Secret or sing!"

Juliette giggled. "Okay…" She cleared her throat.

"Little Annie Adams was a servant girl
Who worked and cleaned till all did shine
But at night she danced and spun in a whirl
But at night she danced and spun in a whirl
She curtsied to the gentleman
And he would take her hand
Her feet would dance a merry jig
And she danced and spun in a whirl
She danced and spun in a whirl
As little Annie Adams grew older
Her bones would creak and crack
But still the gentlemen took her hand
And memories would take her back
Then she danced and spun in a whirl
She danced and spun in a whirl
In the moonlight Annie dreamed
Of youth and its demise
And though her spins were slower now
She danced and spun like a girl

171

Colovere stood on his back legs, and made a circle in lieu of a spin. Tolor spun in earnest. Selene danced a jig with her hooves. They laughed until they wiped tears from their eyes. Colovere picked up Juliette's violin, careful not to mar the wood with his teeth, and dropped it gently in Juliette's lap, then he lay down to listen. Juliette chuckled.

"Give the girl a break, Colovere. She played almost all night." Selene prodded him with a hoof.

Colovere leaned away from the pawing, and his mouth made the closest thing Juliette had ever seen to a pout on him. "I just want to hear one more song. What's wrong with that?"

Feeling the need to settle in for the night, Juliette began to play a quiet lullaby. Long sad notes pierced the air as the long bow ran across taut strings, adding just a touch of vibrato. Everyone lay back, and quieted. When Juliette finished, there was silence except for the crackle of wood on searing red flame.

"We should really go," Juliette said, yawning.

"Before you do," Tolor said, "I wanted to talk to you about something I found."

"Something you found?"

Tolor pulled a shiny stone from his pocket, and placed it in her hand. Juliette's eyes narrowed as she studied the golden nugget shaped like a small rock.

"You found gold somewhere? I don't understand." She returned the nugget.

"The night of the full moon, I found this."

Juliette's eyes widened. "You found gold? But everybody was saying there was no more to find. How?"

"I went farther inland to hunt. There was a stream through there too, but of course, there were no men. When I finished my hunt, I went to the river to clean up."

Juliette's eyes narrowed. "All that blood is after you've cleaned up?"

Tolor stiffened, and then shrugged. "Yes, now please listen. I was washing up, and I saw a stone that was brighter than the others in the water. It was strange in the moonlight, because it was dark out. I reached for it and that's what I pulled out. There

172

were others, but I wasn't prepared to carry them." He handed her the nugget. "Feel how heavy it is."

Juliette ran her fingers over the gold in her hand. "Do you know what this means? Why didn't you say something sooner?"

Tolor smiled. "You really need to ask me that? We were running from men that wanted to kill us. The stone in my pocket was the last thing on my mind."

Juliette's cheeks colored. "No, I guess I don't. Sorry." She pursed her lips, and thought for a moment. "Even if the site is worthy of a mine, we live in this world. What could we do with it?"

"I don't plan on staying here forever. We'll need money when we moved back into the real world and we do have to buy supplies," Tolor said. "Mine and Selene's funds are beginning to run short. Yours will too at some point. We have family that helps us, but you don't. What will you do then?"

Juliette frowned. "I—"

Colovere rose. "It's time to go."

"No, Colovere, this is serious. She can't live off the land like you do. She's human."

"It shames me that you even have to ask that question, Tolor. We take care of each other. We always have, and now you're telling Juliette a time will come when she'll be on her own and you won't help if she needs you? You are no friend!" Colovere knelt so Juliette could straddle him. "Good night." He dipped his head to Selene and disappeared into the dark of the surrounding forest.

Opening her eyes, Juliette stared at the ceiling until the sound of angry voices seeped into her slowly awakening mind. *Colovere and Tolor? What in the world are they arguing about on my doorstep?* She slipped into a robe a size too big, and stormed through the front door.

"What is wrong with you two? Why are you arguing on the cottage doorstep? Was there no other place in all the space of this ill-begotton world?"

"I came to apologize," Tolor said.

"You have no business apologizing," Colovere said, snorting. "You made yourself clear last night. After all this time you have no loyalty. Shame on you! Be on your way, bear."

"I didn't mean it the way you took it, and you don't decide who Juliette talks to, and who she doesn't."

"I do now." Colovere put his head down, and aimed his sharp horn at Tolor.

Juliette's mouth opened in shock and her eyes widened.

"Move, bear man." Colovere shot forward.

Tolor ran, and Colovere chased. Juliette screamed, waving her hands.

"Stop it. Truce. Stop! Stop it right now." Juliette yelled, running into their path.

Colovere and Tolor stopped, and stared at her. Tolor panted, while Colovere snorted.

"Stop that," Juliette said.

Colovere pawed the turf with one hoof.

"You are supposed to be friends. You apologize to each other right now."

Both mouths fell open. Tolor pointed at his chest as if to say 'me?' Juliette struggled not to laugh. She nodded.

"If you want to visit again, then you need to apologize to Colovere, right now."

Colovere raised his head high, and whinnied. Juliette, turned her attention to him.

"And if you want to hang out here again, or pick apples together, you'll apologize too."

Colovere's head lowered, with a deep sigh. Both mumbled apologies.

"Good, I'm going to go and have breakfast."

"But… "

She slammed the wooden door as hard as she could behind her. Storm cried out.

"Oh! I'm sorry."

She opened the door a crack releasing the wolf's tail and held him while she inspected it. Smooth skin, It looked like it would be okay, but Juliette growled with frustration, and petted the wolf. *This is all Colovere and Tolor's fault!*

174

"Where are you, you cheating bag of horse manure?"

Juliette startled. *What was that?* She had thought she heard a slamming door a moment ago. She looked at the mirror and saw two men with guns quietly moving through Frederick's room.

"Juliette?" Tolor called from the door. She heard him coming toward her room.

"Are you dressed? We need to talk about last night."

"Quiet," she hissed.

Tolor entered the room, tilted his head, and folded his arms. Juliette ignored him, watching the two men in the mirror. One held a finger to his lips and motioned to the other one outside the room. Juliette's eyebrows narrowed.

"What are they doing?" Tolor said.

Juliette raised a hand. "Shh."

She watched as Frederick sat up on the opposite side of the bed, as a man ran into the room. Frederick shook his head. He looked more sober than she had seen him for months.

"Thought you was gonna come back with the money you owe me." The gunman said. "Twenty American dollars."

"I don't have it. But I will. I can have it for you when the bank opens tomorrow morning."

"You think we're so stupid? You would be long gone by morning. No. I want the money you owe me now."

"I don't keep that kind of money."

The gun went off. Frederick grunted. The other man stood in the door.

"That was a warnin.' Last chance."

"I—"

Before Frederick could say another word the gunman shot him through the chest, and Frederick fell bleeding, to the floor. The man turned to his friend.

"He won't be cheatin' anyone else. Let's go." The men grabbed Frederick's wallet and went out the bedroom door.

Juliette stood in front of the mirror, hands over her mouth. She didn't remember standing up.

Tolor too, stared at the man who lay bleeding on the floor.

"What do we do, Tolor? We have to help him."

"I don't think we could, even if we were able. That second bullet went through his heart. I think he's gone."

Juliette shook her head fiercely. "No. I can't sleep in this room with him lying there like that. Looking at a dead man every time I come and go." She ran to the window, and vomited outside.

Chapter 31

The Mirror World

Juliette stared at Frederick's body, unmoving and lifeless. A shiver ran the length of her body causing her to tremble. *It's been two days, is anyone ever going to notice he's gone?* She reached for a clean dress and chose a long yellow one. It spoke sunshine, and vibrancy, a contrast to the dead man lying on the floor. She placed it in a basket and went to find Colovere, who was waiting outside the cottage when she closed the door. Yips and barks filled the air behind her.

"How long will you do this?" Colovere said.

Juliette stopped. "Would you sleep in a room with a dead man?"

"You are not in the same room."

"It feels like I am," Juliette muttered.

"The wolves cry when you leave, and they cry until you return."

"Maybe I should take them with me."

Colovere laughed and snorted. "Selene will enjoy that." He knelt. "Let us go then, young maiden."

Juliette sent Whisper and Storm into the cottage grounds, and when she left the pond merged into a moat behind her.

Selene poured a steaming cup of coffee and placed it on the wooden table in front of Juliette. "Tolor wants to join you again tonight."

"What? What are you talking about?" Juliette asked, sipping the hot coffee.

Selene's eyebrows rose. "You haven't been paying attention lately. It's the full moon tonight."

Juliette shook her head. "I am not going through that mirror."

Selene watched her unblinking, silence growing between them. "Good, it's time for Tolor to deal with our business anyway, and not yours."

Not knowing what to say, Juliette nodded as Selene started washing her dishes.

An hour later Tolor entered the room and latched his arm around Juliette, pulling her out of the chair. "Let's go."

She pulled away from him. "Go where?"

"You know where. This is the night we buy supplies, and I want to show you the gold I found."

"What do we need with gold?" Juliette snapped. "I'm not going."

Tolor moved so fast Juliette didn't know what was happening until she hung upside down over his shoulder, her face smashing into his butt.

"Yes, you are. We can do it this way, or you can walk on your own two feet."

Juliette pounded him with her fists clenched tight. "Put me down you overgrown bear!"

"Very well," Tolor said. He ran through the door and into the forest carrying Juliette. When they reached the cottage and he finally put her down, she puked. Her head felt like needles stabbed at it.

"What do you care, Tolor? Selene said you had business of your own to take care of." She meant to sound fierce, but her voice was so muddled she just sounded pathetic.

"Because you can't hide forever. People die, Juliette. And because collecting some of that gold will give us some security for our futures."

Juliette laughed. "We live in a mirror."

Tolor got in her face. "But we won't always."

"You don't know that," Juliette whispered.

Tolor sighed. "You have the same choice as before, over my shoulder or your own two feet. But you are going."

Juliette went to the kitchen to get water. Tolor followed.

"You don't need to follow me around."

"Don't think you're going to be able to hide to keep from going tonight."

178

Juliette gargled, spit and went to her bedchamber. She wanted away from him. She had been staying with Tolor and Selene and missed being at the cottage, but who would want to stay in a room with a dead man seemingly steps away? Movement in the mirror caught her attention; two men picked up Frederick's body and carried him out of the house.

"Tolor," she yelled.

Tolor ran into the room, his fangs showing and nose twitching as he tried to scent the danger. "Are you okay?"

Juliette pointed to the mirror. Tolor smiled as the men shuffled out the door. "It looks like you can move back into your cottage now."

"But what if someone we aren't familiar with comes into the house? You don't think there's any way they can get past the mirror do you?"

"Where is this coming from? You've never been afraid to be alone before, Juliette."

"I'm not afraid. But two days ago I watched a man get murdered in his own home. A lady should be able to know she's safe." *And there were men with guns. It seems like everybody wears guns there.*

Tolor placed a strong hand on her shoulder. "You're safe. Nothing's going to come or go through that mirror except us. The portal should open soon. Have you fed Whisper and Storm? I don't want two full grown wolves to try and make dinner out of me when we return."

"Maybe you should take a second shirt then," Juliette said.

"Why?"

"Blood. They'll smell it on you."

"Good point. I don't have time to go home though. I'll throw this one away when we're done."

The portal opened, and they stepped through.

Clover Springs, California

Moving outside as fast as she could, Juliette peered around the side of the house. No one was there, but in the back they found a fresh burial mound with a cross made of branches. Juliette sniffed at the smell of freshly turned dirt and flowers she couldn't see. She bent and plucked a few dandelions, then placed them on the grave. *Life was rough for him. I hope things are better wherever his soul is now.*

She glanced up, and saw the chestnut unicorn standing in a meadow across from them. Her breath caught. It was difficult to see in the moonlight but the mare's horn sparkled with the evening breeze and soft light.

"How did she get here?" Juliette murmured.

Tolor followed her stare. "Petaire must have told her."

"How would he know?"

"You act as though you've never been around a magical creature before. What is wrong with you?"

Juliette shrugged. "It isn't as if you've taught me about magical creatures."

"We have to buy our supplies before you two reminisce." He made a rumbling sound in his throat that seemed like he was communicating. The chestnut dipped her head.

"She's going to wait for us. Come on." Tolor took Juliette's hand and she followed him, like a beast and a wraith flittering into the night.

They bought oil for their lamps, herbs for Selene, oats for Colovere's herd, cheese, flour and other staples, and a new shirt for Tolor to wear on his way back through the mirror. He bought blue, thinking Storm and Whisper would find it more comforting since it was the color of their own coats. Juliette bought some candies made with milk chocolate and fry bread made by the local women, and then added little chocolate cakes to their purchase when they were on their way out. Tolor's eyebrow rose.

"Sweet tooth?"

Juliette bit into one of the cakes, moaned in contentment, and smiled.

Tolor shook his head. "And you didn't want to come. Is there anything else you need?"

"No. I just wish we could spend a day here," Juliette said.

"Me too."

A dark haired man with a salt and pepper beard came out of the saloon and unwound the reins from the hitching post his horse was tethered to. Tolor approached him.

"Sir, would you be willing to sell us your horse? Or could we pay for the privilege to use him for the night?"

180

The man scowled. "You couldn't pay me enough to sell my horse. Horses are hard to come by out here."

"Then may we pay to use him for the night? I assure you he will be returned to you in the same condition that we take him."

"No."

"I'll pay you ten dollars, up front. He'll be returned to you, tired but every bit as healthy, by sunset."

"Deal."

Tolor paid the man, and they rode back to the house to drop off their purchases and meet the chestnut.

"I can't believe you did that," Juliette said. "Ten dollars?"

"Why not? Where do I have to spend it? Besides, we can afford it."

"You mean I can afford it."

Tolor nodded and smiled.

The chestnut mare was waiting where they had left her. Juliette ran her hand along her long sleek body. "How did you get here?" Juliette asked.

"Yours is not the only magical portal, young maiden."

"But, what about Zylphia?"

The chestnut snorted, shifting her hooves. "I have not seen the witch for many years. If she calls, I will come. Until then, I will cherish my freedom."

"Why would you return to her?"

"She has something that is important to me."

The rented horse reared and neighed when Tolor tried to climb on him again, until the chestnut snorted and light encompassed the auburn stallion. The horse quieted. Tolor mounted and the chestnut mare knelt for Juliette. Following Tolor's lead, they galloped over the hills, away from town.

"Where are we going?" Juliette yelled. "I can't hunt with you."

"I'll hunt later. Our destination isn't much farther."

They slowed to a canter, and then to a walk. When Tolor dismounted the chestnut stopped too.

Juliette had spent enough time with Colovere to be able to jump down without fear. She followed Tolor to the water. He pulled something out, and handed it to her.

181

"A heavy rock?"

Tolor tilted his head and shook it. "Not just a rock. Look closer."

Juliette twisted it around. The moonlight glinted off the smooth surface. "It's gold," she muttered.

"Yes, it is the gold we talked about, and it's ours."

Juliette laughed. "What are we going to do with it?"

"We'll worry about that later. Someday we'll find a way to turn it into money. For now, we collect and store it."

Juliette smiled. "I think you're crazy, but alright."

They spent time looking for nuggets together until Tolor apologized and excused himself to hunt.

"You don't ever have to apologize for that, Tolor. It's a part of who you are."

Tolor nodded his thanks, relief apparent in his features, and disappeared over the hillside while Juliette continued to look for gold.

Tolor was back earlier than usual, and Juliette showed him the collection she had amassed. Tolor smiled, pulling his shirt off.

"Good."

"If you don't mind, I think I'm going to head back while you clean up," Juliette said.

"Okay," Tolor said wading into the cool water.

The stallion's eyes were wide, whining sounds erupting from its throat. The chestnut sighed. "I will take the beran home. There is no way he will get near that poor stallion now. Horses are so wimpy."

Juliette bit down on her lip to keep from laughing.

"Okay," she told the chestnut. "I'm leaving the gold for you to carry."

"Alright," Tolor yelled, running his claws through his wet furry hair.

Juliette mounted the red horse, nodded to the chestnut and kicked with her heels. The horse took off.

A short time later, she stopped the stallion near a group of men in front of the saloon, looking for the man it belonged to.

"That's them," the dark haired man shouted. "That's one of 'em anyway. They took my horse." Extending his arm, he pointed at Juliette. "She's still on it," he shrieked.

Juliette's heart beat hard against her chest and she looked around confused. People surrounded her. Two men with ropes in their hands came toward her. The stallion reared when one of the men grabbed its bridle. Juliette fell hard to the ground, landing on her back. The other man took her arm roughly and pulled her up. She winced at the pain in her back and the fingers that dug into her flesh.

"Where's your friend?" the man demanded.

Her entire body shaking, Juliette shook her head. "We didn't steal the horse. We borrowed it."

The men laughed.

"We paid this man ten dollars to use it till sunrise."

"Whoa, anyone would have given ya a horse with that kind of money."

"The penalty for stealin' a horse is hangin'," a man shouted from the back.

Juliette gasped, her eyes wide. "But we didn't steal it. I swear we didn't. Why would I return a stolen horse?" She tried to pull away from the man clenching her arm. "Take your hands off me. He's lying."

The man holding her shook his head. "You're a pretty little thing, but there ain't nothin' worse than a lyin' wench."

There were people everywhere, all screaming and yelling at the same time.

"No," Juliette tried to yell, but the tremble in her throat allowed her no volume. Her body trembled as the man half dragged her to a tree with a rope hanging from one of its massive limbs. *Oh God, They're going to kill me. Help me Tolor.* But if Tolor came they would kill him too. Juliette wept as calloused hands forced her onto a chair and placed the coarse noose around her neck.

"No, please, we didn't, I swear we didn't." Over and over she yelled but no one listened. *Why is he doing this to me? Who will take care of Whisper and Storm? Oh God.* She sobbed, and saw Emily in her mind, trying to break free from the governess. Whining, sobbing, begging, and looking with horror at the thick leather with three long flexible straps. "No, please." Her sobs grew

183

louder in Juliette's head until she couldn't tell Emily's cries from her own. The last thing she saw was a huge man with a silver star on his shirt, kicking the chair out from under her. The sound of screeching wood split the air as pain shot through her neck and everything went silent.

Climbing the hillside carrying the gold and the heavy beran, the chestnut stopped. Tolor's eyebrows furrowed.

"What are you—"

"Quiet, beran."

Tolor bit his tongue.

"Can you not hear the humans?"

He listened.

"Juliette is dead," the mare said.

Tolor froze. "Run! We need to get back as quick as we can." His voice was high pitched with fear.

"She's gone Beran. Now they lie in wait for you. You can't help her. You'll only get yourself killed. We need to go around, you can then sneak into the house and back to your world."

"No. I can't just leave her."

"As much as I despise your kind, your death would serve no purpose."

"She needs a proper burial at least."

"And how can you give her that after they hang you? I'll do what can be done for her, if anything can be," the mare said.

The chestnut skirted the town and let Tolor dismount near the backdoor of Frederick's home. He bit into his lower lip, his fangs drawing blood, and hesitated gazing toward the town. "Juliette. I can't leave without her."

The chestnut's horn lit. The mare bent her head and shoved it toward him. "Go back to your friends and the centaur woman! There is nothing you can do here."

Tolor grimaced with pain. Tears fell from his eyes as he turned away from the chestnut, and entered the house through the mirror to Juliette's bedchamber. Whisper and Storm sat panting and waiting for her.

He landed on the other side and roared. A mournful noise, again and again until Whisper and Storm howled beside him. Colovere and Selene ran into the room and stood watching him until his throat was so sore he could roar no more. Juliette, his dearest friend, outside of Selene, was gone.

Chapter 32

"The firmest of friendships have been formed in mutual adversity, as iron is most strongly united by the fiercest flame." Charles Caleb Colton.

The Mirror World

Juliette opened her eyes to wolves howling, and an animal growling. Exhaustion filled her and her neck throbbed. *My neck!* Her hand flew to her throat, eyes opened wide. *I'm alive?* She stumbled to her feet, looked around, and ran through the meadow towards the cottage.

Halfway there, she realized the howls and growls were sounds of mourning coming from the cottage. Her muscles burning, she ran faster through an open door to find Colovere lying with his head on the floor, dirt clinging to his hair as if he had rolled in it, and Tolor weeping in Selene's arms. The wolves ran yipping to greet her, tails wagging. With the exception of the wolves, everything in the room stopped. Her friends stared. Tears stung Juliette's eyes.

Tolor's eyes lit up and he laughed as he moved away from Selene. "How?" he asked, running callous fingers over her cheek. "Juliette, I'm…" He hung his head.

Juliette smiled moving into his arms. "It wasn't your fault. There was nothing you could have done."

"How?" Tolor shook his head.

"I don't know," Juliette said. "I only remember the mob, the noose and the pain, then waking up here."

"It's a part of the curse," Colovere said. His voice gruff from grieving. "It has to be. I suspect it's because you didn't return at the allotted time." He nudged Juliette's hand with his nose and she giggled.

"Are you saying we can't die?" she said, petting the unicorn.

"I think that must be the case. Look at how many years you've lived, but you haven't aged a day since you've been here. I suspect you only age during the time you spend in the real world.

186

This realm exists outside of time. You could probably die here though."

Caught up in thought, Juliette stopped petting and Colovere nudged her again. She wrinkled her nose.

"No offense Colovere, but what have you been doing? You need a bath."

Colovere snorted. "This is how we grieve."

"By rolling in the dirt?"

"If we can't find manure, then yes."

Juliette wrinkled her nose and turned her head away. "Oh!" She pointed toward the door. "Bath, now!"

Colovere huffed and left. Juliette looked toward Tolor, and saw that Selene was gone.

"Juliette... "

She put her hand against his lips. "Let's not talk about it?"

Tolor scowled. "Your hand stinks!"

Juliette laughed. Tolor gently kissed the stinking hand and she backed away. Neither of them looked at the other. She saw the bag that carried the gold and supplies.

"You managed to bring back our things. How did you avoid them? I wouldn't tell them anything." Her eyes became misty, and she choked on her words. "But they meant to try to ambush you."

"The chestnut heard the shouting and chaos before we arrived, otherwise we would have walked right into it. I was going to go after you anyway, but she insisted you were already dead, and encouraged me to sneak back into the house, and through the mirror. I should have gone back, but I knew I wouldn't stand a chance with so many."

"Well, it would have just meant your death too. There was no point in your dying for nothing."

Tolor's eyes flashed. "I hardly think it would have been for nothing."

Eager to change the subject, Juliette opened the bag and dumped out the gold nuggets. "What are we going to do with this?"

Tolor shrugged. "For now, we'll hide it away. Then we'll watch for an opportunity to sell it for a little less than its worth."

"Is Selene alright?" Juliette petted Whisper, staring at her thick silky fur, and bear-like face.

187

"She'll be fine."

"She didn't seem happy to see me." Juliette tried not to care, but her heart hurt. "Did she prefer...? She's always so angry, but I would never think she would want me gone." Juliette shook her head, and stood up. "I think I want to lie down."

"Of course. You're probably exhausted." Tolor put a hand on her shoulder. "Don't worry about Selene, She didn't mean anything. I'll take care of her."

"She resents the time I spend with you. She gets very jealous." Tears tickled down Juliette's cheeks.

Tolor placed his hand on her shoulder. "I'm glad you're back, and so is she." He wiped away a tear, then turned and left.

Clover Springs, California

When it came time to go for supplies again, Juliette and the chestnut mare waited at the house while Tolor bought them. Once supplies were purchased, they went to Tolor's secret stream and looked for more gold. As the years went by, Clover Springs became less populated. Juliette ventured out alone again, and often rode the chestnut mare into town. She dismounted and entered the general store. There were no more fresh candies and cakes that they used to have available. Now they mostly offered staples that any kitchen would need. Juliette approached the store-keeper.

"I would like two five pound bags of flour and a five pound bag of sugar please."

The gentleman looked at her sideways. Juliette didn't care. She figured most people didn't buy in large quantities. She would have bought more, but she didn't want to draw attention to herself. She picked up one of the bags, and walked outside to find the chestnut backing away from a man.

"Excuse me, sir. What do you think you're doing?" *He won't be doing it long if he sees the horn directed at his chest.*

The man put his hands in the air as the chestnut reared.

"I was just trying to tie her up for ya, that's all. So she don't run off. It isn't good to leave an un-tethered horse out here."

Juliette placed the flour in a bag hanging on the chestnut's side. "I'll remember that next time I'm in town."

188

Ignoring the man from that point on, Juliette finished loading her things and mounted the mare, who had allowed Juliette to saddle her with a saddle they found at an abandoned house, for appearances in town. It also made it easier to carry supplies.

Two women walked by chattering amongst themselves, green and blue dresses swaying as they walked. Juliette admired their matching hats. She missed wearing them, they always made her feel pretty. Juliette listened as they talked, remembering walks with her mother in their prettiest dresses and the most fashionable hats.

"—And the Bowers left town just yesterday morning," the woman in blue said. The thud of their shoes on the wooden planks made it difficult to hear them. Juliette listened harder.

"I declare, this town will be empty before long. I don't know why my James is insisting we stay out here," the woman in yellow said. She straightened her hat. Juliette bit her lower lip.

"Well, the gold rush has gone bust. These men are fools to hold on if you ask me. I for one can't wait to get back to a respectable city."

They moved out of Juliette's range of hearing.

"Let's get rid of these supplies," Juliette told the chestnut. *How much time before the general store closes up if people are leaving that fast? Maybe I should have bought more sugar and flour, and oil for the lamps too. But people might wonder about such a large purchase. Next time, I'll have Tolor buy too. What will happen to the mirror? It wouldn't be stealing if somebody took it. Nobody owns it now.* She shuddered at the thought of their home belonging to a complete stranger, but someday it could.

After telling her friends about what she learned in the town, Tolor decided to go with her to make purchases until the general store was closed. Colovere and Selene would be there so they could drop off supplies and go back out, while Whisper and Storm watched. When they were finished, Tolor turned to Juliette.

"Are you ready to go back out?"

Juliette smiled and nodded.

189

Juliette walked along the water, looking for gold while Tolor hunted, then they followed his nose to a huge patch of berries, one of Tolor's favorite foods. Juliette slapped his hands away the second time she caught him eating them. She had learned how to make jam, cookies, and pies.

On the way home, they stopped at abandoned houses stripping the gardens of corn, beans, and watermelons, as well as pots and pans, dishes, and even a dress. In one of the houses, they found a few gold nuggets left behind.

"The man must have forgotten where he put them," Tolor mused. "No one would have left them behind otherwise." He placed them in his pocket and they moved on. They even found clean bed linens and quilts.

When they were finished, Juliette walked around a potbelly stove, opening and closing the chamber door and running her hand over its smooth surface.

"What are you thinking?" Tolor said.

Juliette shut the chamber door, and stood up straight. "I want this, Tolor."

Tolor looked at the size of it and placed his hands on his hips. "Are you crazy? How would we even get it back?"

"You can carry it," Juliette pouted.

Eyes wide, Tolor pointed. "Are you...What do you think I am? A pack mule? A pack mule couldn't carry that by the way." He folded his arms over his chest.

"No, but you can."

"Open the door." It was the Chestnut's, voice. Tolor let her in.

"You two are going to wake up the neighborhood." She walked to where Juliette stood. "Is this what you want?"

Juliette nodded.

The chestnut touched her horn to the stove. Light surrounded it and it disappeared. Juliette hugged her, enjoying the silky feel of her hair against her cheek.

"Thank you."

They returned to the house and handed more supplies through the mirror. Tolor took out a berry and popped it in his mouth, smiling at Juliette. He opened the container to do it again, and Juliette lunged at him.

190

"Give those to me," she demanded, stretching her arm but unable to reach. Juliette was on tiptoes and still couldn't get it, Tolor laughed.

They heard the sound of boots on the steps, and two dirty men in jeans and brown leather boots, entered the room. One with dirty brown hair, and a scar across his chest pressed a gun into Tolor's back, moving him into a corner. Fury covered Tolor's face and his eyes darkened.

Juliette screamed when the other man grabbed a fist full of her hair, pulling her against him.

"Well, ain't you a pretty thing," he said.

His breath stank with half rotted teeth, and Juliette fought to break his grip, her heart pumping wildly. Trembling, she began to sob, until two blue comets flew out of the mirror, teeth fully bared and snarling.

Chapter 33

"The firmest of friendships have been formed in mutual adversity, as iron is most strongly united by the fiercest flame." Charles Caleb Colton.

Clover Springs, California

"Whisper… Storm, No!"

Whisper landed on one of the men and Storm on the other. Their throats were ripped out before the men had a chance to react. Two snarling masses of muscle, teeth, and fur stood over their dead bodies, daring any further threat.

Everything went quiet, save for Juliette's breathing. Whining, Whisper and Storm sniffed at her and licked her face. Cringing at the blood, she hugged and petted them.

"It wasn't your fault," she said. "Thank you."

The wolves lay down and cuddled against her.

Tolor stood to brush himself off and Whisper and Storm snarled.

"Okay, you two. Stop it now. You know Tolor."

Tolor stood still until the wolves quit snarling, and Juliette pushed them back through the mirror.

"Do you think Zylphia will try to harm them for leaving her precious world? Juliette asked.

"When is the last time you saw her?"

Juliette shook her head. "I haven't seen her since she left me in my parents' house looking for a way back to the mirror." Her hands fisted at her sides. "But I won't allow her to hurt Whisper or Storm."

"I doubt she'll ever know," Tolor said.

"We have to clean this mess up before we go back." She swayed, even the coppery smell of the room suddenly overwhelming. She put a hand over her mouth, feeling nauseous.

Tolor sighed. "I'll take care of the men. It's just a little bit of blood." He pulled the first body outside, and returned for the second man not long after.

"That was fast. They were lucky you didn't go into bloodlust," Juliette said.

Tolor laughed. "I'm not sure they would agree with you. I buried them together. Damned if I'll dig two holes for them. A decent burial is more than they deserved. I found linens to wipe the blood up. We need to burn them."

"Why? It isn't as if anyone will know where they are from."

"I think it's best to leave no trace of ourselves," Tolor said. "We don't want anyone watching the house."

"Okay, we'll burn them tonight at home then. We have to finish if we're going to beat the sun."

"I handed the rest of our things through while you were burying the men."

"We're ready to go then. As these cowboys would say, after you, ma'am."

Juliette laughed, and leaped into the mirror.

The wolves were pacing and anxious when Juliette landed in the room. Colovere waited in the corner.

"Where's Selene?" Juliette asked.

"She wasn't feeling well. She left after the men were killed."

"I hope she's alright."

Juliette turned to see Tolor staring at the floor, Colovere glared at him. He pushed the pot belly stove into a corner.

"Let's get this stuff divided," Tolor said.

Chapter 34

"Virtue is the fount whence honor springs." Christopher Marlowe.

Clover Springs, California, 2013

The months that followed turned into years, and soon the town was almost empty. Juliette found it strange seeing the general store and Sam the tailor's shops boarded up and abandoned. The saloon had been left open, its door hanging haphazardly, and warped by the elements. She would never forget the town in its heyday, the music that spilled out of those doors, or the ladies with their colorful dresses and silken stockings and large black feathers adorning big hats. She wouldn't miss the men and lawless atmosphere, though.

Juliette and Tolor continued collecting gold, although Juliette could never figure out what on earth for. There was nowhere to change it or use it, although they had managed to sell some before everyone was gone and that had brought them a bit of prosperity.

Juliette readied herself to go to town, throwing a knitted black shawl over her shoulders. One of the women had left it behind what felt like a lifetime ago. Eventually, Tolor stopped joining Juliette on her forays through the mirror, unless there was reason to. She had rarely even seen him and Selene over the years since then, and when she did see them, she was barely civil. Juliette pressed her lips into a tight line. *I'm just going to ask her what she's upset about next time I see her. This is enough.* Her chin held high, she stepped through the mirror.

Recently, the town had begun to rebuild. Someone had bought and renovated the old general store, and Juliette wanted to visit soon. There were other places of business, some she understood, like the seamstress, and others she knew nothing about, like the place she saw people eat at that weren't taverns, and a place that sold computers and phones. Most of these places were not close to the house, but Juliette worried that in time they would be.

The house was old now and falling into disrepair. Some of its windows were broken, the curtains were ragged and filthy, and the wooden floor had holes. It made the mirror look out of place. Juliette had long since stripped the place of anything valuable, except for the wood burning stove since she already had one. She walked through, looking things over carefully. It looked like no one had been here since the last full moon. She'd heard visitors long ago talking about the house being haunted since Frederick had been murdered there. The two women that said it tried to remove the mirror but hadn't been able to do so. They obviously weren't afraid of ghosts. She glanced out the window and saw the chestnut mare waiting for her. The unicorn whinnied. Juliette laughed and ran out to greet her.

Juliette's long hair blew in the wind, her ringlets having turned into soft curls. She closed her eyes and tried to envision the countryside by day. It was stunning at night, with the arm of the moon caressing the water, and soft silvery grasses beneath their feet. There were mountains, tall and majestic, surrounding them. She heard voices. The mare slowed, and Juliette opened her eyes, and listened. She saw a campfire by Tolor's secret place. They hid in the trees watching two men smoking pipes.

"What do you think, John?" A tall man said. "Is it a worthy endeavor to try and find the source of the gold?"

John wrinkled his nose, and rubbed it with his hand, his masculine features and brown eyes exposed by the firelight. "I just don't know. Could be?"

"That's not helpful. What do you think I should do?"

"Here's the thing, Walter. This is going to be costly. You need to decide for yourself. But yes, there is a good possibility that it'll pay off. Just like there's a possibility it won't."

Walter remained silent, moving his stick through the fire.

"What are you going to do? I can see you're plannin' something."

Walter smiled. "I'm going to look for the source."

Juliette backed out of the trees, the chestnut mare following behind her. *How does she manage to move without making a sound?* She mounted once more and they moved away quietly, skirting the new roads the town put in.

A car passed by them moving faster than a team of horses. Juliette shook her head like she always did when she saw one.

When they were far enough from the men that they knew they wouldn't be heard, the chestnut sprang into full gallop.

The mare stopped on the top of a hill where it seemed like they could see for miles, if not for the darkness. Thousands of lights dotted the landscape. Juliette dismounted, and moved to the edge of the hilltop while the mare caught her breath.

"Where are the lights coming from?" Juliette asked.

"Men are spreading out again. Not like before, but you should see how large their cities are now. Some of them are as frightening as Clover Springs used to be. I spend little time near them."

Juliette sat down in the soft dirt and the chestnut lay beside her. She absentmindedly ran her fingers through the hair of the mares back.

"Where do you go when it's not the full moon?" Juliette asked. "Surely not back to London."

"No, I have no desire to see London now. I stay here, where it's quiet and sleep under those trees across the road."

"I wish I could do that for just one night."

"You could, but you would be penalized for doing so."

"I would gladly pay the price, if I could but watch the sunrise." Juliette smiled wistfully. She looked at the mare. "It's been over a hundred years, will you truly never tell me your name?"

The mare got up and began to pace. Juliette stood and watched.

"I didn't mean to upset you. I know we had a deal. I'm sorry, I promise I won't ever ask again."

The mare stood to her full height, her head held high and silky mane glistening in the moonlight. Her horn sparkled. She looked over the twinkling lights, and then turned to look Juliette in the eyes.

"My name is Ophelia," she said. "And I am Colovere's mate."

Chapter 35

Each player must accept the cards life deals him or her: but once they are in hand, he or she alone must decide how to play the cards in order to win the game." Voltaire.

Clover Springs, California

Juliette's breath caught in her throat. She stared at Ophelia. "What?" She shook her head. "Why?" The question came out cooler than she meant for it to, but she knew how much Colovere loved his *dead* mate. They had talked about her many times, and now she was alive. She'd always been here unless she was a fraud. *But she can't be, can she? "Only someone related to us could have found us,"* Colovere had told her after Petaire healed him.

"If you don't close your mouth, you might catch a mosquito," Ophelia said.

Juliette shook her head. "This isn't funny."

"I haven't said anything with humorous intent. You have agreed to keep my secret and I expect you to do so."

"But, Colovere loves you. Why would you do this to him? Don't you think he would come for you if he knew you were here?"

"That is why you must continue to keep who I am secret."

"But—"

"No more questions, young maiden. I've honored your request based on our long friendship. I'll say no more. Are you ready to return?"

Unable to speak, Juliette nodded.

The Mirror World

With the berries washed and in a container under her arm, Juliette, Storm, and Whisper left the cottage. The wolves played and chased after mice and colorful butterflies, snapping and biting the air. Juliette laughed. *How do they ever survive in the wild?* Button fairies, barely visible in daylight, landed on their tails and

197

noses and laughed a melodious tone when the wolves chased them. The herd joined the chase without fear. Storm and Whisper were more likely to protect than harm them. Colovere saw Juliette, and trotted towards her.

"Colovere." Juliette nodded, and smiled.

"It's good to see you about, young maiden. Where are you going?"

"To see Selene and Tolor. I'm taking them berries."

"That is not a good idea."

Juliette tried not to frown. "Why not? They're my friends. Or has something changed that? Does anyone ever plan on telling me what I've done wrong?"

Colovere sighed. "You've done nothing."

"Then why aren't they talking to me?"

"They have other things to think about."

Juliette shook her head. "No, I don't accept that. There isn't that much to think about in our world besides basic survival, and if there was a problem they should have said something."

"Let them come to you," Colovere said.

Juliette walked toward the forest. *I've had enough!* Colovere followed. "What are you doing?" Juliette asked.

"I'm going with you."

"I can go by myself, I'm a grown woman."

"That's debatable, you haven't aged a day since you arrived."

"Not funny, Colovere." Juliette growled with frustration. "I'm over a hundred years old."

"I still don't think you should walk through the forest alone, there are lions and berans in there."

Juliette opened her mouth to speak, thought better of it, turned on her heels and walked away. "Suit yourself."

"I will, young maiden."

She turned around. "What did you say?"

Colovere cleared his throat. "I will enjoy following you through the forest."

Juliette ignored him the rest of the way there.

The Mirror World

Juliette and Colovere walked into Selene and Tolor's stable-like home as if they belonged there. Juliette sighed, it didn't feel right, but it had always been right before. They even had beds there for nights when they didn't want to walk home. *What changed?* She didn't feel as confident now that she stood in their home. Selene turned, her face flushed red.

"What are you doing here?"

Juliette took a deep breath, trying to regain the confidence she'd lost. "Why shouldn't I be? What have I done that you don't want anything to do with me? We were friends."

"I can't believe you have to ask me that!" Selene reared. "Everything is always about you. I'm tired of it. Tolor can't make my errands, because he has to escort you into town. He can't connect with my family, because he has to show you the gold he found. He can't make my purchases because he is out picking berries with you. When you died, it might as well have been him. He was completely inconsolable. Get out of our lives!"

Juliette frowned, hands curling into fists at her sides. "I never once asked Tolor to do any of those things. He always decided he was going to go with me, and you're blaming me for the way he grieved when he thought I was dead? Have you lost your mind? I had nothing to do with that. All that was a long time ago anyway."

Tolor walked in the door and froze. "What's going on?"

Selene moved between them, her eyes flashing with hatred. Juliette took a step back before she realized it.

"Get your berries from the table you set them on, and get out of our stable."

"Selene—," Tolor interrupted.

"Get out," Selene screamed, pointing at the door.

Colovere nudged Juliette's arm. "Let's go, young maiden."

Tolor moved around Juliette. "Stop, Selene. You're being rude for no reason."

"No reason. You think I don't have a reason. I've had it with you," she said, her hooves pounding the turf. "You can go too. Get your things and by the stars, I don't ever want to see you again."

"No, Selene. You don't mean that," Tolor said, his eyes wide with innocence. "I've never done anything—"

"Get out!" Selene reared high, just missing his head when her hooves crashed to the floor.

"Get Juliette out of here," Tolor yelled, at Colovere.

Colovere nudged her towards the door with his nose.

"Stop it, Colovere. I'm not leaving until this is settled. Leave me alone!"

"Selene, please," Tolor said.

Selene reared, turned and reared again. Tolor had his hands in front of him to ward off her hooves.

"I've done everything you've asked, Selene. Please don't do this."

"Go, damn you."

She reared again and there was a thumping sound. Juliette and Colovere's heads whipped around to see Tolor lying on the floor, blood trickling from a wound on his head. Selene stared at him, her teeth clenched.

"Oh, God," Juliette murmured. She ran to him using the hem of her dress to wipe the wound.

Selene turned away, lying down in a stall facing the opposite direction.

Juliette glanced at Selene, her voice trembling. "Tolor would do anything for you. How could you hurt him like this?"

Selene ignored her. When Tolor came to, Juliette tried to help him up, but he tried to push her away.

"He can't stay here. Colovere, can he ride on your back?"

"Yes."

"I'm not going anywhere," he mumbled.

"You need to leave until Selene calms down," Juliette said, in almost a whisper.

Tolor's eyes filled with unshed tears. "If I leave with you, she'll never forgive me. Please, Juliette. Just leave."

"I won't leave you like this. You're too hurt to even get up. Right now, you don't have a choice but to leave." Juliette grunted, using her arms and shoulders to roll him onto Colovere's back.

A weeping Selene yelled after them as they went out the door. "Don't come back. You don't belong here. You never belonged here... any of you."

Growling, Tolor tried to shift off Colovere's back. Juliette held him in place. The fact that he wasn't able to fight her off worried her even more.

200

Juliette picked up a cup and placed fresh cut pink and blue meadow flowers into a clear glass vase. A sweet woodsy scent mixed with nectar filled the room. She closed her eyes and grinned. Tolor sat in a corner, his arms crossed, and hands clutching his shoulders. Juliette placed a cup of coffee beside him, and went out to greet Colovere.

Tolor had moved into the cottage and Selene hadn't spoken to him since she kicked him out, almost a year ago. Now he was a miserable creature, but he was still her friend. Juliette didn't know what to do for him. She was sorry she hadn't listened to Colovere, and stayed away.

Without Selene to tell them when the full moon would come, Juliette had to watch the stars and mirror closely. Tolor had gone once to see the land where they searched for gold fenced off with *'No Trespassing'* signs. The rest of the time he took his own portal into a world where Juliette could not follow. Their gold harvesting days were at an end, but they had enough to last multiple lifetimes, and in their world, they mostly lived off the land. Sometimes they picked up gold from other areas, but it was hard to find and nothing more than something constructive to do.

Everyone was miserable. Tolor hardly spoke to Juliette, and Selene was more introverted than before. Juliette felt tired, and wanted to go back to a home she no longer had, to find parents that no longer lived. Some days she felt like her life was over.

Only Colovere was unchanged. The unicorns ran and played in the meadow as they always had, unfazed by the rest of the world as the days passed them by.

Juliette strolled through the yard admiring the lavender, pansies and the columbines she had recently acquired from a trip into town. Walking toward the pond, she stopped at the other side of the wall that enclosed her cottage. Colovere and Meneme were running together. They stopped and stared in each other's eyes and Colovere tilted his head and rubbed his nose against hers. Then he moved his body lightly across hers. Juliette's heart pounded at her chest. *Colovere is loyal. If he becomes Meneme's mate and later finds out Ophelia lives, he'll never forgive himself.*

"No," she muttered. "No, Colovere!" She ran towards them.

Colovere turned and stared. Juliette didn't know if it was because of her tone, or something else, but he said something to Meneme and the mare trotted off.

"What troubles you, young maiden?"

"Uh, nothing. Why do you ask?"

Colovere studied her. "Then why were you upset a moment ago?"

"I wasn't upset. It's just that you already have a mate." Juliette didn't think a unicorn's eyes could widen. She was wrong.

"My mate has been gone for many years. I grow lonely."

Juliette swallowed the lump in her throat. "What was her name, Colovere?" Juliette held her breath awaiting his response.

"Ophelia," he whispered. "Did you mean to rip open an old wound, Juliette? Or is there another reason you're here?"

Juliette shook her head, Colovere had never called her by name before. "I'm sorry, Colovere."

Colovere slowly walked away, his head not far from the ground.

"You just have to put your nose into everything, don't you?"

Juliette whirled around, gasping, one hand held to her throat. "Tolor?"

"Everything. You have to ruin everything, for everyone. I don't know what it is. Is it jealousy because you've always been alone and you always will be? I for one am tired of it." He stormed back to the cottage.

"Tolor!"

Picking up his pace, the beran didn't look back.

Chapter 36

"Life is the flower for which love is the honey." Victor Hugo.

The Mirror World

Juliette sat on her bed eating a peach. Ophelia had given her an entire bucket of them. They were a special treat because it was winter and cold in the mirror world. She hadn't had one since before she'd been cursed, and the sweet fibrous nectar reminded her of days she had snuck away with Emily as children. She wiped the dribbling juice from her chin with the back of her hand. It was strange to think Emily had been gone for so many years. She still missed her.

Tolor hardly spoke to her since the day she found Colovere flirting with Menemee in the meadow. *I couldn't very well let them make the connection. He has a mate even if he doesn't know it.* It had been months since that day, and if Colovere had connected with Meneme, he had been discreet about it. She wondered if Colovere and Ophelia would ever come together again. It didn't seem likely. She still didn't know why Ophelia was in hiding. *And yet she stays as close to him as the situation allows. She loves him.* Juliette frowned, wondering if she would ever know what it was like to be in love.

Tolor was still living in the cottage, but it was awkward. If she owned the cottage, she would have asked him to leave. *That's not true. I would never put him out. But having people go out of their way to avoid you in your own home isn't just rude, it's nerve wracking.*

She saw a flash from the corner of her eye, and moved to the foot of the bed. The mirror had been dark for more than a century, and her only contact with people had been on her outings with Ophelia. The world was continually changing. She found it hard to keep up with only a periodic newspaper. Women wore breeches made for them now, so she didn't have to buy jeans that matched Tolor's anymore. Last time she went shopping the saleswoman had tried to sell her shirts that stopped above her

203

navel. *Who in their right mind buys half a shirt?* She hadn't been able to stop thinking about that.

She heard voices. Two women came through the door and light filled the room. Juliette's breath caught, it was so nice to see the gentle rays of the sun, even if it was just a glare in the mirror.

"There are so many options that are better than this, Mrs. Parker. This is the worst kind of fixer-upper. It should be torn down. Why don't we look at something closer to the river?"

Ignoring the woman, Mrs. Parker sauntered toward the bedroom.

"I'm looking for something with some old fashioned charm. I don't want a mansion by the river. Why, look at this old wooden bed frame, and that pot belly stove, and those handmade curtains over there." She pointed at each item.

"You mean the broken bed frame and the shredded curtains the moths have eaten? We have better ways of heating our homes these days."

Juliette frowned. Tolor had refused to transfer the bed frame. He said she had a nicer one anyway. She wanted it for his room, but he insisted he didn't need one. She had taken her pot belly stove from somewhere else.

"Okay, so they have to be replaced," Mrs. Parker said. "But can't you imagine the people that lived here, and what life might have been like for them?"

I can, Juliette thought dryly, as she rubbed her neck. The women came back into view, and Mrs. Parker ran her hand over the edge of the mirror's frame, then brushed the dust from her hands.

"Look at this. It's absolutely beautiful." She looked around the room. "The bedroom is small... but Brayden can..."

Tolor walked into the room, and handed Juliette a plate of deer steak and vegetables. They may not have been talking, but they still shared food. Juliette was grateful for it since she had no ability to hunt. Some days it brought tears to her eyes that he still thought about her. She missed his friendship.

"Thank you," Juliette said, still watching the ladies in the house.

Tolor glanced at the mirror. "May I sit?" he asked.

Juliette nodded and swallowed the lump that had already formed in her throat. Her heart hurt, but she needed to compose herself. She took a deep breath and turned her attention back to Frederick's broken down house. Mrs. Parker continued meandering around the room, running her hand along the wallpaper and on an old ivory lampshade. The other woman had already gone out.

"Who is she?" Tolor asked.

"I don't know, but she wants to buy the house."

"That would leave you trying to sneak through the house at night again."

"Don't worry. I don't expect you to come with me."

"Juliette…"

"Please don't say anything, Tolor. I don't feel like fighting tonight." The rare times they spoke, it was to argue about something. She would crumble into a mass of tears if they fought right now.

"Juliette, I'm sorry."

"I don't want to hear…" Blinking, she turned her gaze from the mirror to his face. "What did you say?"

Tolor stared at his claws for a moment, then looked up at her. "I've been blaming you for something that wasn't your fault, and I've treated you… worse than poorly. I am so very sorry."

Juliette's eyes widened with surprise. She put her plate on a nightstand and rose. Then hugged him and held him close so he wouldn't see the tears that fell. "I'm sorry too," she murmured. When she let go of Tolor, the ladies were gone.

Days later, Juliette awoke to the grinding chaos of electric drills, saws, and sounds she had no knowledge of. Laborers filled the house replacing windows and wooden flooring. *At least I won't have to worry about falling through the floorboards anymore.* Tolor came in to watch as the men started pulling at the mirror.

"Sit down!" Juliette yelled, as the room jolted when the mirror was lifted off the wall.

"Thanks for the warning," Tolor said picking himself up off the floor. "Maybe a little sooner next time."

Juliette cringed. "Sorry."

Tolor smiled. "Tonight is the full moon. Would you like me to accompany you?"

She shook her head. "I'll be fine."

205

Tolor looked away. "I'm interested. I know I said some terrible things before, but I never meant a word of any of it." He looked in her eyes. "I would protect and rescue you, even if you were covered in the scent of blood."

"What does that mean?"

"Only that I will never let anyone hurt you, even myself."

Juliette nodded, but she never forgot the night he attacked Selene. "Alright, you can come."

Clover Springs, California

Juliette slipped through the mirror with Tolor behind her. The floor didn't creak like the old wood did. They looked around the room. It had been painted black.

"No wonder the mirror is always so dark now. Who in their right mind paints a bedroom black?"

Tolor shrugged, and then muffled a laugh. "My brothers do actually."

Juliette gave him a quirky smile. "You have brothers?"

He placed his hands on his hip. "Of course I do. Don't most people have families?"

"I guess so. I just never thought."

"Exactly. I could marry a human woman and she would never know the difference, as long as I left to hunt on occasion. She might wonder at my height, and I would outlive her by many years, but that hardly makes me a beast."

He pressed his lips together, and Juliette saw the struggle inside him. The desire to grow up, have a family, just to be like everyone else. It was unlikely at best… for any of them. He looked away.

"Let's go."

"No," Juliette said. "I want to see the rest of the house."

They moved into the kitchen to find a new electric stove. Juliette and Tolor didn't know how to use it, so they left it alone. There was another appliance. Juliette opened the door to find prongs and a glass, but nothing else. She closed the door and shrugged. The new floors were hardwood.

"At least the paint is a nice yellow color." She smiled warmly, running her hand down the wall. It reminded her of the sunshine that shone from the mirror into her room only a few days ago.

Tolor laughed.

In the living room, a large brown and green rug lounged over the new wood. There were blinds and curtains hanging over sparkling new windows. Juliette saw Ophelia and smiled.

They opened the front door, and an alarm screeched into the silence. Juliette jumped, and Tolor's fangs protruded. They bolted across the new lawn, running towards the safety of the trees.

"Run, beran," Ophelia demanded. "The danger has triggered your instincts. You are not safe to those around you."

Tolor hesitated, growled, and ran into the darkness.

Ophelia lay down so Juliette could mount, and ran the opposite direction of Tolor, and into a small town.

Juliette dismounted. "Why did you do that, Ophelia? Tolor wasn't harming either of us."

Ophelia's sides heaved as she drew in quick, uneven breaths. "He was fighting off bloodlust so he could stay and protect you. He would not have been able to master his nature for very long. We are safe here. He won't follow our trail until he's satisfied his need." She snorted. "Why do you complain, young maiden? You love to shop."

"Will he be alright?"

Ophelia dipped her head. "Yes. The beran is more able to take care of himself than you realize. For all of his niceties, make no mistake, he is still a creature of the wild. That is why he doesn't use the mirror as a portal very often."

Juliette started walking, and Ophelia followed.

"I know about his bloodlust," Juliette said.

"Then why are you so foolish that you don't feel a need to run from him?"

"Tolor wouldn't hurt me." She kicked a pebble across the road.

"The way he wouldn't hurt the centaur woman he loves?"

Juliette flushed. "That was different."

"Indeed. He would die for her at any other time, and yet he still caused her great pain."

"How did you know about that?"

"There are birds that fly between worlds and Petaire visits on occasion."

"Oh. I didn't know that."

"Come, if you wish to make any purchases, your time grows short."

Ophelia had ran much farther than usual in her haste to flee Tolor, and as Juliette browsed the store, she noticed she had many more options than she was used to. She found batteries for some small lamps she had bought, and chose a few dresses, two pairs of the newer jeans, even though they seemed more risqué than usual, and a number of t-shirts and frilly knit tops. When the lights dimmed in the store, she joined Ophelia once again.

"I couldn't find any groceries."

"In most places, groceries and other items are sold in different stores now."

"Oh, I need to make another stop for staples and a newspaper then."

"As you wish."

Without Tolor, Juliette was limited to what she could carry so she only bought what they needed most. But she was pleased to see this store carried almost everything. They even had a meat shop.

"Do you think it's safe to find Tolor now?" Juliette asked.

"I would be surprised if he was not already more than halfway here."

Ophelia was right. Tolor found them about a mile outside of town. He kept pace with Ophelia, running on his hands and feet all the way back to Clover Springs. In the darkness, he looked like a bear. Juliette shivered.

After what felt like only minutes, they hid in the bushes around the house. The alarm still blared.

Tolor sniffed the air. "There's nobody there."

"Maybe the alarm is only meant to scare," Ophelia said.

"I'll go first," Tolor said.

Before anyone could argue with him, he stalked up to the front door, sniffed the air and looked around, then went into the house. Soon, he returned, waving them in.

Ophelia followed Juliette to the door.

Tolor scowled. "I'm ready to knock that alarm off the wall," he yelled over the noise. "It's obviously just meant to scare people."

Juliette took a deep breath. "Regardless, the noise is making the hairs on my back stand up."

Ophelia snorted and Tolor laughed. "You have no hair on your back," Tolor said. "But the noise is bothering me too."

Juliette retrieved her purchases from Ophelia, hugged her, and followed Tolor to the mirror.

Storm growled at the mirror, and Juliette got out of bed and petted the scruff of his tensed neck.

"What is it, Storm?" Shuffling on the other side of the mirror caught her attention.

"But the camera caught them," Mrs. Parker said.

Juliette jumped. Storm barked and Whisper came running. "Quiet, both of you," Juliette said.

Mrs. Parker continued. "The last place they were seen was in this room. There was some sort of light, and then they were gone. Where did the light even come from? The electricity isn't even wired yet."

"I don't know what happened, Ma'am. But we'll start watchin' this place more often. Don't you worry," a police officer said.

"I'm not worried. I have no idea where you got that idea from. If you can't keep this place safe, I'll hire people who can." Mrs. Parker left the room, and another lawman entered.

"She didn't look happy," a policeman said.

"No, and she's crazy. But her husband owns most of this town now." He chuckled and shook his head. "A bright light, in a house with no electricity. She's a crazy old bat."

"Not so old and she has the alarm connected to a battery system." the second lawman said. "That's one fine woman, and she has the intruders on film."

The first lawman laughed. "She's still crazy if you ask me. Who would want to break into this house? But who cares about crazy when you got a trophy like that under your arm? Money can buy anything, including a picture. The electrician should be here soon. Let's go."

209

Leaving Storm to watch the mirror, Juliette went to tell Tolor. *It's good to know they couldn't see us entering the mirror. They didn't seem to know we were in the house earlier either. It only caught our return. A malfunction? Or is the camera activated by the door?*

Juliette found Tolor staring out the window. She called, but he didn't seem to hear. She tried again. He glanced her way, and then ignored her. Juliette moved to where he stood and looked out the window to see the meadow dusted in snow. Selene galloped her way across with Colovere's herd, her dark hair blowing in the wind.

"It's been more than a year since I've seen her do that." He leaned against the wall and studied the floor. "It gladdens my heart to see her run freely and with such joy. And yet it tears me apart to know that it means she's moved on without me." His fists curled tight at his sides, claws digging into tender flesh. "And yet maybe Colovere can find a mate that will love her. Like you, she is a maiden." He glanced out the window once more, and went to his room.

Juliette leaned against the window sill and watched Selene gallop, laugh, and rear in a mock fight with the unicorns. She looked toward the cottage, then went back to her games. Juliette frowned and went to make lunch.

Chapter 37

"Life's tragedy is that we get old too soon and wise too late." Benjamin
Franklin.

San Francisco, California

Brayden adjusted the lights in the room and focused his
camera on the actors. "Good, that's good, now slap him hard."

Sarah laughed. Brayden stopped the camera, shifted his feet,
and stared at her.

"Come on, Sarah. How many times are we going to have to
shoot this thing? You know better than that."

"I couldn't help it." Her lower lip turned into a pout.
"You're funny."

Brayden put the camera down. "You know what? Forget it.
I'll shoot it with Ashley tomorrow."

Sarah's eyes started watering.

Brayden shook his head, lips pressed together. "Don't go
there. I am not dealing with that shit."

"What shit?"

"If you're going to cry, go home."

Sarah's mouth dropped open, but she said nothing.

*Well, that was the desired effect. I never would have thought she could
turn so red.* He tried not to laugh.

Sarah stopped crying. "You're such an asshole."

"Yep. Deal with it."

Sarah sighed, dejectedly.

Battle over. I win.

She picked up her things and stormed out the door.

Cory shook his head. "I can't believe you just did that.
That's cold, dude."

Brayden shrugged. "Why?"

Cory chuckled. "You really are an asshole."

"I need to get home," Brayden said, picking up his camera
and coat. "We'll shoot the scene with Ash tomorrow."

211

Slamming the door behind him, Brayden unlocked his BMW Roadster and got in.

Disabling the alarm to his home, Brayden entered the house and threw his things on the couch.

"You shouldn't throw your things around like that, Brayden. Pick that stuff up and move it to your room. I would think you'd treat your camera better than that," his mom said.

"Carolyn will put it away," Brayden said, throwing his coat on top of the pile.

"No, she won't. You pick your things up right now and take them upstairs or you're grounded."

Brayden scowled, grabbed his stuff, and headed upstairs. He went to his room, put the camera on his bed, and threw the rest on the floor for Carolyn to deal with. Then went back downstairs to talk to his mom. He found her brushing her long dark hair.

"How was your day?" she asked.

He sat on the sofa. "It was good. I've been filming a new short story I want to submit to the Film Festival. It's turning out awesome! It's about a man that—"

"I'm sorry, honey, your dad asked me to take care of some business for him. Maybe I can hear your story another time." She put the brush on an end table, kissed Brayden on the cheek, then grabbed her keys, and ran out the door.

"Yeah, it was good to see you too." He stood to go upstairs when he saw his father coming down.

"Hey, Brayden."

"Hey, Dad."

"What're you up to tonight?"

"I'm going to hang out, I have some—"

His dad walked into the kitchen.

"Has anyone ever told you how rude it is to walk away from someone when they're talking?" Brayden yelled. "I don't want to friggin talk to you either."

His dad put his head out the door. "I'm sorry, son. Did you just say something? I thought you were done and I need to rush."

"Nothing, I didn't say anything. But I was hoping we could talk about my new project. Maybe over dinner?"

His dad shook his head. "I'm sorry. I can't hang out tonight, Brayden. I just bought acreage in Clover Springs. I have workers getting ready to drill a mine so I have to go. The man I bought the property from already started the digging, but he ran out of money. I want to be there to get things started. People work better when you're watching them. Sal said dinner will be ready in a few minutes if you're hungry."

Where the hell is Clover Springs? "Yeah, thanks," he said, his lips twisted with irritation.

"I'll catch up with you a little later," his dad said, going out the door.

Later, it's always later. Brayden's blood felt hot. He went to the liquor cabinet and pulled out a bottle of scotch. He filled a small glass to the rim, held his breath, and drank it down. Then he went to the kitchen to find out if his dinner was ready.

Brayden listened to the sound of slamming lockers as he walked through the hallway of the high school. The chatter was a mild roar. He strained for any other sounds he might hear. Coughing, laughing, shoes clanging on the cheap linoleum floor. This was a game he liked to play when he was alone so he knew how to make things sound realistic in his films. He even scored a juicy piece of gossip on occasion.

He stopped and twisted the lock on his locker. Right forty-two, left twenty-three, eighteen to the right. A small click and the door sprang open. He reached to the back of his locker, pulled out a flask, and placed it in his pocket. Then shut the door, and startled when he noticed Sarah standing beside him. She wrapped her arms around his waist, twisting around to place her lips against his. Brayden didn't respond.

"Come on, Brayden, I was just having fun. Is filming all you ever think about?"

"Of course not. I think about and plan projects for the future, and then there's this whole education thing. I've gotta go." He left Sarah standing alone. She wasn't worth being late.

The bell rang just as he walked into the photography classroom. Before class started, he stopped in a corner to drink the rest of his flask.

Chapter 38

"Cleverness is not wisdom." Euripides.

San Francisco, California

Brayden placed his camera on an end table in his studio. "Good job, Ashley. We're finished."

Ashley pouted. "That's my only part? You're kidding."

"That was all I needed. Your death saves the heroine."

"Can't you re-film it or something? I'll make a far better lead than Sarah."

Brayden had no doubt about that. He wished he had realized it sooner. As it stood, he had changed the end so he didn't have to deal with any more of Sarah's off camera dramatics. Ashley did a great job with the new part.

"I can't believe you'd think I would recast an entire film for you. You're not that good, and I don't have the time. I'm moving on with sound." *Where I don't have to deal with girls that whine every time they don't get what they want.* They would never get what they wanted because this was his film.

He wrapped his arms around Ashley, and kissed her. She swooned when he released her, and tried to draw him closer. He pulled away with a flirtatious smile, but his words were cold. "You need to go, Ash. We're done here, and I have things to do."

He might have pursued an intimate moment, but his parents were home, and he didn't want to lose his privacy or studio if they caught him. It was unlikely they even knew he was in the house, but just in case. Ashley didn't move, but Brayden had dealt with girls before. Acting like she was no longer there, he picked up his phone and went to the pool house to call Peter.

Peter didn't answer. Brayden turned to face Ashley, who had followed him through the door. "What are you doing roaming through my house?" he asked.

"I wasn't roaming, I followed you."

Before Brayden could say another word, she pressed her body against his, and kissed him. Brayden started to pull away,

214

but he had a few minutes since he was going to have to find Peter anyway. He wrapped his arms around her, deepened the kiss, and forgot about time.

The door opened and Brayden looked up to see Sarah. He didn't move away from Ashley.

Sarah stared at them wide eyed. Brayden waited.

"Well, say something," Brayden said. "You look like a frog, staring like that."

Sarah's cheeks flushed. "What are you doing?"

Brayden shrugged. Ashley grinned.

"I never said we were exclusive. If that's what you thought, I'm sorry." He wasn't sorry at all. Sarah had always been presumptuous, and he hadn't done anything to correct her. She knew better now.

He cleared his throat.

"Both of you need to go. I have things to get done, and I really don't have time for this."

Sarah's mouth dropped open. Brayden laughed.

"You did think we were exclusive, didn't you?"

He pushed Ashley toward the door and brushed her lips to say goodbye. She grinned and left. Sarah lunged at him, but he was ready. He caught her arms and held her until she stopped fighting, and burst into tears.

"Are you ready to go home now?" Brayden asked.

Sarah tried to pull away from him, but he held her fast.

"If I let you go, you are going to turn around, and go directly out that door, without another word. If you don't, I will grasp your elbow and drag you to your car, passing my parents, the maid, and the chef in the process. Do you understand?"

Sarah nodded. Brayden let her go and she ran out the door. Brayden sighed, he wouldn't have been so mean if she hadn't attacked him. He had never hit a girl, but he didn't allow them to beat on him either. Even if Sarah wasn't done with him, he was done with her.

Irritated, he speed dialed Peter again, and his phone vibrated with an incoming call. He glanced at the caller ID. *I guess my parents aren't home.* He answered the phone. He learned the day after they bought it that if he didn't answer their calls, they took away his phone privileges. There was no three strikes rule. Once, and you were out.

"Hey Braid," his mom said. "I need you to pick up your father's dry cleaning for me. I'm not going to be able to get there before they close."

"Can't it wait till tomorrow? I'm working on sound, and I need to get this done."

"You can do that anytime. Get off your ass and go get them."

"I'm on a time schedule."

"I don't give a damn what you're on. Don't forget who bought that pretty camera and those fancy lenses."

A veiled threat. Brayden threw one of the lenses; it crashed into the purple wall of his studio, fell to the floor, and rolled almost all the way back to him. He clenched his teeth.

"Fine. Do you have the ticket for it?"

"No, just give them your name. I need to go now. Don't forget to get those suits."

Brayden picked up the lens, and inspected it. "About those lenses, I accidently broke one. It was an accident, sort of."

"We'll talk about it later."

"Why can't Carolyn pick it up?" Brayden asked.

"Because it's her day off."

"Like it would hurt her to do something on her day off?"

"Get the suits."

Mrs. Parker hung up before Brayden could say another word.

Brayden put the phone down, wishing he hadn't ticked off Sarah. She would have picked up the dry cleaning for him. *It doesn't matter now. The sooner I get this done, the faster I can get back to work.*

He went to the liquor cabinet, and pulled a bottle of scotch. He frowned, there was a bottle of Cuervo Gold tequila behind it unopened. *I wonder if they would think one of them opened it.* He went to his bedroom and grabbed a second flask, filled one of them with scotch, and the other with tequila. *This will help me wind down when I'm done.* He pulled his keys from his pocket, locked up the studio, and went to his car.

216

As Brayden came out of the dry cleaner's, his phone vibrated. Reaching in his pocket, he dropped the suits on the pavement. Scowling, he answered the phone.

"Peter, where have you been?" Brayden demanded. "I've been trying to get ahold of you for a couple of hours."

"Sorry. Hey, Heather is having a party tomorrow night. She wants you to come."

Of course she does. "Sorry. I'm not going to that party and neither are you."

Peter scoffed. "Dude, Heather is popular. The hottest babes in school will be at this party."

"Doesn't matter. We have work to do."

"We'll jam on it the next day, we can work all night."

Brayden sighed. "Okay, one night won't destroy everything. But not just the night after, I want the night after that, and the night after that."

"What about my parents?" Peter said.

"What about them? Yours don't give a damn any more than mine do." The phone line was silent. Brayden hung up.

He looked at the suits laying on the oily blacktop, pulled the plastic up, and dragged them through oil and dirt all the way to the car.

Chapter 39

"It is the nature of the wise to resist pleasures, but the foolish to be a slave to them." Epictetus.

San Francisco, California

Brayden's mom jogged down the stairs. "Did you pick up those suits, Brayden? If you didn't you're grounded. And that means no filming or making music. Do you hear me?"

"Lighten up, they're in your closet."

"They better be, that's all I'm saying."

Brayden sighed and went to find the dinner Chef Sal had left for him. *Hmm, Spinach enchiladas with a tangy sauce.* He grabbed a glass of milk, and headed upstairs to his bedroom to wait for Peter.

"Brayden? Brayden!"

He was half-way up the stairs when his mom stormed out of her room, holding the oil stained suits. The plastic was mangled. "What the hell did you do?"

"Nothing." Brayden looked away to hide the smile tugging at his lips.

His mom glared as if her eyes could sear him with fire.

"Okay, I dropped them."

"You dropped them?"

"What? It isn't like I did it on purpose or anything."

His mom huffed, went back in her room, and slammed the door. Brayden chuckled. *She can't prove it.*

Brayden stared unseeing at the floor, listening. He shook his head as if to clear it. "Play it again."

Peter clicked the mouse and dragged the cursor, moving the play head back to the beginning of the clip they were listening to.

The door opened and Brayden glared at the blonde haired, blue eyed maid who entered the room. "You know better than to walk in here without knocking."

Carolyn's eyes narrowed slightly. "And would you have heard it?" She waited, and handed Brayden an envelope when he didn't answer. "I didn't think so," she said, as she turned and left the room.

Irritated, Brayden opened the letter. His eyes bugged wide, and he screamed a cry of victory. "Yes!" He tore his headphones off and jumped around, reaching for the ceiling, and dancing. He kissed the back of Peter's hair.

Peter bounded away from him. "Ewww, get away from me, perv. That was gross."

Brayden laughed.

Peter wiped at the back of his head. "What's wrong with you?"

He handed him the letter.

Peter read under his breath. "Dear Mr. Parker." He sighed. "Blah blah blah. We are pleased to inform you that your internship has been accepted." His eyes widened as he slammed the letter down in his lap. "Shane Bradford? You got an internship with Bradford Productions? Whoa, dude!" They high fived, hands slapping so hard it stung. "We should go out," Peter said. "Seriously, it's time to celebrate."

"Okay, let me just grab something." Brayden opened a cabinet and pulled out a bottle of scotch. "They'll never even miss it."

Peter smiled wickedly. "Let's go."

"Where am I supposed to park?" Brayden asked emptying his flask.

Peter drank out of the bottle.

"Dude! I don't want your germs, man. That's nasty."

Peter laughed. Brayden grabbed the bottle, and handed Peter the flask, at the same time he parked the car. It didn't fit in the space he was trying to wedge into so the front of the car remained in the road. *It's a good thing this car is small.* He cut the engine and turned back to Peter.

"Here," Brayden said. His head swayed a little, and he laughed. "Hold this still. I don't want it in my car." Brayden poured part of the scotch into his flask.

219

He chuckled and raised one of the flasks, while Peter lifted the other.

"To Shane Bradford Productions," Brayden said.

"Shane Bradford Productions," Peter parroted. The flasks clanked and they drank. Peter turned his upside down and frowned. "Mine's empty."

"There'll be more inside. Let's go."

Brayden locked the car and they hiked up the small hill. Loud music filled the night air, and the sound of chatter and laughter caused them to walk a little faster. They walked through the open door, and were greeted by friends on their way through the house. Brayden saw Sarah and looked away. She approached him anyway. He took a deep breath.

She placed her hand lightly on his arm. "Brayden, could we talk?"

"Now you want to talk? Yesterday you were trying to beat me up."

Her cheeks reddened. "I'm sorry, I shouldn't have done that. Please, just talk to me for a minute."

"Let me grab a beer first."

Sarah folded her arms and waited. When he returned, she pulled him to a corner of the pool area. She chewed her lower lip while Brayden waited for her to drum up the courage for whatever she wanted to say. He wasn't going to wait much longer. There were drinks, the pool, pretty girls, and dancing. The music was making him antsy to be on the move.

"Well?"

"I'm just going to say it outright," she said, wiping a tear from the corner of her eye. "I love you, and I don't want us to be done."

"I told you I wasn't looking for any attachments when we first started seeing each other, Sarah." He sighed and placed his hand on the wall behind her.

"I know that, but I can't help what I feel."

Brayden's face flushed. *I don't need this.* "Sure you can. You should have backed off the moment you started having those kinds of thoughts. I won't be tied down to anyone. We're done."

"You're such a bastard."

"And yet you love me. What does that say about you?"

Sarah stormed off. Exactly the effect he wanted. Ashley joined him, watching Sarah go. Brayden shook his head.

"Not tonight, Ash. You and Sarah have been battling over me for awhile now. Not anymore."

Ashley's mouth dropped open. "But—"

"No." Brayden walked away. He would have a grand time with the girls tonight. This was his celebration, but he wasn't going to allow Ashley to smear a victory in Sarah's face. Even he had his limits for cruelty. Sarah was a good girl. She just wanted something different than he did.

Peter lounged in another corner feeling up a girl Brayden had never seen before. *Maybe she'll have a sister. Damn, now I'm almost sober.* He slammed down his beer and went to find something stronger to drink. By the time he encountered Peter again, he was on his way out the door, the girl wrapped in his arm. Brayden stripped naked and went for a swim, the chill of the water revitalizing him. He closed his eyes enjoying the moment. Familiar hands ran over him. Startled and aroused he opened his eyes.

"Sarah—" *This is not a good idea.*

She placed a hand over his mouth. "Just once more."

Brayden closed his eyes, the sensations of her free hand arousing him further. He sighed, swallowed, kissed her, and then whispered in her ear. "I'll meet you outside the front door."

He found the alcohol and refilled the flask with cheap vodka, drank the rest of the bottle, and walked Sarah to his car.

He dropped Sarah off at home, riddled with guilt. She ran her hand over his cheek, but he turned the other way. Tonight was a mutual thing, and Sarah understood it changed nothing. But he had lied, he wanted out because he was starting to have feelings for her, and he didn't want them. He had to break it off before those emotions screwed up his plans. He watched her walk to the door, pulled the flask and took another drink. He had to stop drinking. He could hardly control the car as it was. He would finish the flask at home. He turned up the radio, and Nicki Minaj blared from the speakers. He pulled out of her driveway onto the road.

Damn, this music is good tonight. Wow, I can't believe I got the internship. He flung his head back and laughed. The car swerved. He turned the wheel back and swung right and left over the lines. *That was awesome.*

He passed the party. It was over now and kids chatted in the streets. Brayden threw his fist in the air, screamed a cat call, and the car veered toward people on the right side of the road. He pulled the wheel back hard, overcorrected, and flung it to the right. The tires screeched on the blacktop. People screamed and scrambled. He hit a car and the driver jumped out screaming obscenities he couldn't hear. The back end of his car fishtailed back, and stopped. Two girls stood with their hands covering their heads, screaming.

Blood dripped down the corner of Brayden's mouth where teeth broke and cut into his tongue and jaw. People pulled the screaming girls away. Someone yelled, "Call nine-one-one." Brayden got out of the car and ran to see why the girls were so hysterical.

Brayden's limbs turned to jello. *Oh God!* His mouth dropped open and he stared without blinking. Peter lay without moving under the back end of Brayden's car. The girl he had been with was sitting up, crying, a gash spilling blood from the side of her head. Brayden pulled off his shirt and threw it to her.

"The wound, apply pressure to the wound." His voice was pleading, unfamiliar to him.

Sirens sounded in the background, becoming louder. Grimacing, Brayden carefully nudged Peter.

"Peter? Peter, wake up. Please wake up." Brayden's heartbeat slammed at his chest, his breathing shallow. He raked shaking hands through his hair, and then clumsily checked for a pulse. It was there. "He's alive. Thank God, he's alive. I'm so sorry. Peter. Please wake up."

Brayden held Peter's hand, sat on the pavement, and wept.

Chapter 40

"Knowledge is of no value unless you put it into practice." Anton Chekhov.

San Francisco, California

Brayden sat in the back seat of his father's black Lexus. In the half hour since they'd left the jail, neither had spoken. A clenched fist covered his mouth, and Brayden cleared his throat. "How's Peter?" It didn't work, his voice still cracked.

His dad said nothing. He didn't even look at him through the rear view mirror, like he usually did when he was angry.

Brayden tried to swallow the lump in his throat. "So what? You're not talking to me now? *It was an accident.*"

His dad looked at him through the mirror with the coldest eyes Brayden had ever seen. Involuntarily, he flinched. *Screw him if he's going to be like that.* He wiped the tear that fell from his eye before his Dad could see it. Then took a deep breath and held it until he had control of himself again.

His dad parked the car in the garage, and they got out. Brayden shut his door and stopped. His father was waiting for him. He wiped at his nose.

"You're grounded."

Brayden almost laughed. "Like I didn't already know that?"

His father's eyes flashed with anger and he turned and stalked away.

Brayden turned the knob on his studio door. It was locked. He pulled out his key. It didn't work. After shimmying and twisting the key every way it would move, Carolyn walked by.

"Any idea why my key doesn't work, Carolyn?"

"Your father changed the locks."

Brayden chuckled. "I can easily pick this lock."

Carolyn glanced up at a new deadbolt. "I don't think you'll pick that too easily. It's also boarded from the other side."

"There are no windows except the two facing us. It can't be boarded."

Carolyn placed a hand on her hip. "It's amazing what you can accomplish with enough money. They went underground, and cut a hole in the floor to get out."

Brayden grimaced with shock. "They what?"

Carolyn ignored the outburst and walked away. *They put a hole in my floor?* Brayden strode through the house and up the stairs to his father's room, storming in unannounced. No one was there. He checked the pool house. It was locked too. The library, his game room, everything locked. He found Carolyn dusting the living room.

"Where the hell is he?"

"Where is who?"

"My father, who do you think?"

"Your father has never checked in or out with me. I have no idea why you think he would start now."

Brayden clenched his teeth. *Where's my phone?* He had it in the car the night of the accident. His parents must have put it in his room. He went to look, but it wasn't there. Neither was his tablet or computer. *How am I supposed to do school work without my computer? What the hell is going on? I need a drink.* He found a new liquor cabinet, it was locked. He punched the wood with his fist.

"Damn it!"

With nothing else to do, he showered, then laid down for a nap.

The Mirror World

Tolor held a bowl under Juliette's chin, watching her vomit for the fourth time this morning. *She can't possibly have anything left in her stomach.* Looking away, he crinkled his nose and tried to snort inconspicuously. *That girl eats too much fish.* The retching stopped. Tolor handed her a glass of water. Juliette scowled.

"Rinse, and spit it out."

Juliette groaned, but did what she was told. Tolor put the glass by the bowl, and pushed her back against the wall.

"You're burning up." He shook his head. "You can't go out tonight."

224

"But I need some things," Juliette pouted.

Tolor smirked. "Then I'll pick them up for you. You're staying home."

She squinted at the bright light sneaking in through the window, and Tolor covered it with a thick curtain.

"Try to get some sleep," he said, turning back to see that she already was. *That's a good sign. She's barely slept in days.* He covered her with a light blanket, and left the room to see if Colovere had returned.

Colovere stood on the turf outside the cottage, shuffling his feet beside an irritated-looking Selene. Tolor's breath caught and his heart stuttered in his chest. *She is beautiful even when she's angry.*

Selene handed him a vial of blue liquid and a container of chicken soup. Tolor took it, and opened his mouth to speak.

"Say nothing, Tolor." Selene's voice was firm and commanding.

Tolor's eyes filled with tears. He fought them back. Even after all this time, he loved her no less than before. He held up the vial. "What is it?" He looked away when his voice cracked.

"It's a medicine we give to young colts when they are ill. I don't know if it will help her. She needs human medicine, which I assume you will acquire for her tonight."

Tolor nodded. "Thank you."

Selene dug her hoof in the turf, the smell of dirt calming both of them. "We were friends once. No thanks is necessary."

"Selene."

Selene turned, and galloped away.

San Francisco, California

When Brayden opened his eyes again, the room was dark. He glanced at the lighted display on his clock. *Nine, I slept the entire day.* That wasn't surprising. He had hardly gotten any rest at all in jail. He laid back, snuggled into his soft down comforter and stared at the ceiling, worried about Peter and the girl. There was a shuffling sound in the hallway. *Maybe dad's home and I can get my phone.* He turned on the light and dressed without looking at the mirror, not wanting to see the bruises that covered his body.

He went down the stairs to find his dad at the table.

225

"Where is Mom?"

His Dad looked up from his tablet. "She's figuring out what she wants to do with some of the properties I recently purchased." A smile tugged at his dad's lips. Brayden always thought his parents had a strange relationship. They spent a lot of time apart, but there was no infidelity that he knew of, and they were as close as if they'd never parted. That spelled divorce in most of his friends' families that lived like that.

"Do you know where my phone is? I can't find it."

"Yes I do." Mr. Parker forked more pasta and bit into his garlic bread.

"Can I have it? I need to make some calls. I need to contact Bradford Productions as soon as possible. They accepted me for an internship." He searched for any sign that his dad was proud of him for such a great achievement, but there was nothing. He took a deep breath. "And I need to get ahold of Peter. I haven't heard from him, I need to know he's okay." He was rambling, but he couldn't stop without crying. "And I need to check on—"

His Dad never even looked at him.

"Dad!"

Mr. Parker turned and glared. He swallowed, drank some of his wine, and wiped his mouth before pushing his plate away. Brayden fought the urge to move back. He tried to brace himself for anything.

"You don't need to call Bradford Productions. I've done that for you. And I'm not returning your phone, or the camera, or your computer."

Brayden's breathing became labored. He paled, shocked.

"Or your studio," his father said.

"Those things are mine! You have no right to take them away from me."

"I bought them so I think I do."

"Fine, then give me the keys to my car."

Mr. Parker shook his head. "I sold the car."

Brayden's mouth dropped open. "You sold my car?"

"Is there a reason I should shoulder all of the loss when I get sued because of you?" His dad asked, voice matter of fact.

"That car was mine!" Brayden slapped his hand down on the wooden table. His father didn't flinch.

"It was in my name."

226

"Everything is in your name." Brayden raked his hand through his hair, and froze. "Wait, what did you tell Bradford Productions?"

"I gave them your apologies, and explained that you were going to have to decline the internship."

"You what?"

"You heard me. You can't accept the internship unless you can get yourself to and from the studios. You have no way to do that because you, or we, just settled a multi-million dollar lawsuit out of court. The rest of the multi-million has been taken out of your trust account. It didn't leave you with much."

"The insurance will pay that."

"You don't think this is going to cost me? When the insurance reimburses me we'll talk about it." Mr. Parker stood and picked up his plate from the table. Coming into the room, Carolyn took them from him. He mumbled his thanks.

"Can I at least have my phone?" Brayden stammered.

"There's a phone on the kitchen wall. You can use that."

Mr. Parker left the room. Brayden caught him when he reached the stairs.

"You can't do this. You're taking away everything I own. You have no right!"

Mr. Parker turned to face him. "You don't work yet. Everything you owned, except for a few lenses, was mine. Would you like to have those lenses?"

"Stop being an asshole."

"Goodnight, Brayden." He ambled up the stairs. "And don't forget, you're grounded."

"That makes no difference, I have nothing left to lose."

His Dad smiled and shrugged. "Then I guess those things you thought so important aren't important enough to earn back. Suit yourself, Brayden. But understand this because I will only say it once. I will not be picking you up from juvenile hall again. If you land there, you will remain there. Am I understood?"

Brayden couldn't hold back the hot angry tears anymore. "This is just wrong!

"Am I understood?"

Brayden hit the wall with his fist. His father ignored him.

"Yes," Brayden shouted.

"Good." His Dad moved his head towards the damaged wall. "That will be coming out of your trust fund too." He entered his room and shut the door. Brayden melted to the floor, crying.

Clover Springs, California

"You have to see Brayden's room," Mrs. Parker said, giddy with excitement.

Juliette opened her eyes to see Mrs. Parker pulling her husband into the room with the mirror.

"Isn't this awesome? I just love it," she said.

Looking around, Mr. Parker looked less than impressed. He took his wife into his arms. "As long as you like it, it'll be perfect," he said, smiling. "But wouldn't you like something larger?"

"No. Now come see the kitchen," she said, almost dancing across the room.

Chuckling, Mr. Parker followed.

All Juliette could hear was mumbling after that, until Mr. Parker was close to the door again.

"We need to talk, Pix."

Everything was quiet for a moment. Mrs. Parker pulled him by the hand back into the room. They sat on the new bed that had been delivered that morning. Mrs. Parker had covered it with an ivory comforter that looked soft as pillows. They also delivered a cherry wood dresser, a small desk, and night stands to match. It was an interesting contrast to the dark walls.

"Brayden had an accident after you left."

Mrs. Parker jumped off the bed, her hands against her heart. "What?"

"He's okay. Please, sit down."

"What happened?"

"He was drinking, he lost control of the car, and hit a couple of teenagers at a party. Peter was one of them. I talked to his father the day after the accident. He's okay."

"Oh, my God."

228

"The girl Peter was with had a head wound. She's fine too, but she's seeing a psychiatrist. Her parents were going to sue. Hicks contacted them and settled out of court."

"I'm glad she's alright."

Juliette's eyes were wide. She sat in front of the mirror with her hand resting on it. She didn't remember leaving her bed.

"You haven't told me how Brayden is." Mrs. Parker began to tremble, her face ashen.

Mr. Parker kissed her forehead. "Brayden is fine. He received credit for the two weeks he spent in jail, and he has to go to classes for drunk driving. They took away his license for a year, and he has a probation officer for the next three years."

Mrs. Parker reddened, rose, and paced the floor. "What are we going to do with him," she stammered, her arms flying in the air as if she were making her own sign language.

"I've been thinking about that," Mr. Parker said.

"He's getting worse and worse. I can't even keep a bottle of scotch in the house anymore."

"Calm down Pix. I changed the locks. But this is why I keep asking you if this house is really what you want."

"What the hell does the house have to do with our son?"

"I think we should pull him out of school, and hire a tutor. I've already taken away his camera equipment and his studio until he earns the privilege of getting them back."

"The equipment belongs to him. We have no right to take it away."

"Oh, yes we do. I bought it. The father giveth, and he taketh away."

Mrs. Parker stared at him, lips pressed together.

He shook his head. "He's almost an adult. We can't put him over our knee, and send him to his room. We have to hit him where it hurts to get control of him before he kills somebody, and ruins his life."

Mrs. Parker nodded. "How soon are we moving?"

"If you're satisfied with this place, I'll pull him out of school tomorrow. If you want something larger, you need to decide now."

"I know you don't like this house. We can build a bigger house beside it, and if Brayden doesn't want to use it when he's eighteen, I'll use it for my office, or a guest house. But I would like to live here for a while."

Mr. Parker sighed. "All right. It's time Brayden learned that the sun doesn't shine just for him anyway. Life is about people, family and relationships, not his next allowance, and comfort. We'll stay here. Part of this is our fault. We haven't spent much time with Brayden the last couple of years. Maybe this is the time to get back to family values. He's seventeen, so this is our last chance."

Pixie sat on his lap with her arms around his neck. "I love you."

Mr. Parker chuckled and kissed her. "That's why we're moving into this tiny house. Even trying to teach Brayden a lesson, I would have chosen something bigger. He'll be in shock."

Chapter 41

"But friendship is precious, not only in the shade, but in the sunshine of life, and thanks to a benevolent arrangement the greater part of life is sunshine." Thomas Jefferson.

The Mirror World

"Selene's tonic didn't seem to make a difference," Tolor said, walking toward the cottage with Colovere.

Colovere snorted. "I thought that might be the case. You will be getting human medicine for her tonight?"

"I'm going to try."

Colovere turned towards the meadow, while Tolor continued into the cottage.

"Let me know if I can help with anything," Colovere called back.

Tolor smiled. *We're like a family now.* The smile faded. *And the most important person in the world to me is missing.*

He turned toward Juliette's room and froze when he saw her lying on the floor in front of the mirror.

"Juliette!" Hurrying into the room he picked her up and placed her on the bed.

Her eyelids fluttered open and Tolor sighed in relief.

"What were you doing on the floor?"

"I was watching the new people that are going to live there," she muttered. "I'm so tired, need to sleep so I can go with you tonight."

"Oh, no. That won't happen. Colovere will sit on you first."

Juliette's eyes narrowed. "You can't tell me I can't go. I might not be able to get past those people next time I want to go out."

"Go to sleep. We'll work that out later." Tolor would have laughed if he wasn't so scared for her. He had never seen her give in to anything so quickly. She was already breathing the long heavy breaths of slumber.

231

Come nightfall, Juliette still slept with Colovere watching over her. Tolor checked the mirror, saw nothing, and stepped through. There was a light on somewhere. He waited and listened, but no one appeared to be home. He cautiously entered the hall and headed for the door. Slipping outside, he found Ophelia waiting across the street. He crossed to meet her. She threw her head high.

"Where is Juliette?"

Tolor sighed under his breath. "Look chestnut, whatever your name is. I don't have time for the attitude. As you've pointed out yourself on numerous occasions, I need to hunt, and I have other things I need to take care of tonight."

Ophelia snorted loudly. "Enough of your superiority. Where is she, Beran?"

"She is in her bed in the cottage, and very ill. I need to find her human medicine."

"What's wrong with her?"

Tolor frowned, and rubbed his nose. "I don't know."

Ophelia kicked at the dirt. "I know of a witch not far from here that might be able to help. She's very young, but she could purchase what we need. Put the money to pay for it in my teeth, and I will go ask her to buy it for us. You may hunt while I do this, freeing up the rest of the evening for other purchases, or activities."

"I may, what?" Tolor put a hand in the air. This was about Juliette. He could swallow his pride for the night. "Never mind." He had no idea what it would cost so he placed a one hundred dollar bill between her teeth.

Ophelia bit down, and ran into the darkness. Tolor ran the other direction.

Ophelia slowed to a walk at the home of the young witch and silently found the girl's bedroom window. She placed her horn on the glass, and called to Shayla's dreams. The girl stirred, and pushed the pane open, clinging to a little doll with big blue eyes and curly red hair.

232

"Ophelia, it's nice to see you." Shayla rubbed Ophelia's head.

"I need your help, young witch."

"Is something wrong?"

"Yes, but except for a small amount of help, it need not worry you."

"What do you want me to do?"

Ophelia knew the child would help her. "A friend of mine is sick. She needs human medicine, and I do not know what she needs, or how to obtain it."

"What's wrong with her?"

"She vomits, and sleeps, and she has trouble breathing. The beran says she snorts a lot."

"She snor..." Shayla giggled. "You mean she sneezes?"

"Sneezes, yes, I think so."

"Okay. Let me get dressed. I need to ward the room so my mom and dad won't hear me leave." She put her doll in the bed and lovingly covered her, then raised her arms and spoke words that Ophelia wasn't familiar with. Ophelia moved back as sparkles of light came together creating a solid wall around the room. It was open only on the side that faced the window. When Shayla was finished, she smiled.

"Don't be afraid, 'Phelia. The magic won't hurt you. It's just a sound barrier so no one can hear us come or go." She climbed out the window. "I'm ready."

Ophelia lay on the grass, and Shayla climbed on.

"Where do we need to go?"

"Any store that has food has cold medicine."

"But she is not cold." Ophelia tried to remember what the beran had told her. *No, he didn't say cold.*

Shayla laughed. "Cold medicine isn't because she's cold, silly. It's because she has a cold."

Ophelia slowed. "How does a human store cold?"

"Never mind. You're just going to have to trust me on this."

"I will trust you to do your best, young one."

Ophelia found a store that was open, and screeched when Shayla jumped down, pulling hair from her mane out in the process. Shayla reddened and apologized.

"We will need something we can place around my neck to carry the medicine back," Ophelia said.

233

"They'll put it in a bag for us. Don't worry."

Half an hour later, Shayla returned, and tied a bag full of medicine around Ophelia's neck. Ophelia took her home, thanked her, and returned to wait for Tolor.

Tolor pulled off his bloody shirt, threw it in a dumpster, and put a clean one on. Feeling satisfied, he walked down an almost abandoned street through the old town, and stopped at a new bicycle shop. It had been a long time since he and Juliette had a bike. The door was locked, but there was still someone inside. He knocked.

"We're closed," came the tired voice of the man inside.

"I'm sorry. I am aware of that, but if you will open for only a short time, I would purchase two of your bicycles."

The man looked at him with a wary eye, then opened the door and let Tolor inside. Tolor nodded his thanks.

"What do you have for a lady to ride in the dirt? I want it to be as comfortable as possible."

The man walked to the back row of bikes, and rolled a white one with thick tires, and a black seat around. He began to give him all the details of the bike.

"Do you have anything like the old baskets people used to use?" Tolor interrupted. "She likes to collect things on her rides."

The man walked behind the counter, and pulled out something canvas. It opened into two, basket-like cubbyholes that mounted onto the back of the bike. The man showed him how to put it on and take it off.

Tolor smiled. The man recoiled, and Tolor shut his mouth. He had forgotten his fangs were still showing. "Excellent," he said. "Now, what do you have for a man in the same environment? Nothing small, this one is for me."

The man's eyes widened. "You're really going to purchase two bikes?"

"Yes, sir."

The man thought for a moment, held a finger in the air, then turned toward the bikes again. He returned rolling a bicycle almost twice the size of Juliette's.

Tolor nodded in satisfaction. "I'll take them both."

"But, don't you want to try them first?" the shopkeeper asked.

"There is no need. Thank you."

"I noticed you were walking. How were you going to get these home?"

I didn't think about that. "Maybe I could tie one on the back of the other bike?"

"That won't work. It would be too heavy. Tell you what, I'll drop you off on my way home."

"That would be wonderful. Thank you." Tolor's heart raced with excitement. He had never been in a car before.

The man rang the purchases up, and Tolor paid with a credit card his brother had acquired for him the last time he saw him. The man wouldn't allow him inside so he sat in the back of the truck. He laughed as the wind blew through his hair. It reminded him of running when he was on the hunt, or with Selene through a meadow that no one else knew about except the two of them. His heart thumped hard against his chest at the memory of Selene. The man pulled the truck over where he pointed, and Tolor got out with his bikes. He thanked the man, then watched until the truck was gone, and went to find Ophelia.

Tolor thanked Ophelia and tried to carry the bikes into the house as quiet as he could. The alarm went off. "They live in the middle of nowhere. What is it about humans and their alarms?"

He listened, but heard nothing else. Not even footsteps. He ran toward the mirror, and stepped through. Nobody tried to stop him, but he still needed to bring the second bike across. Juliette was still sleeping. He placed the bag of medicines on the nightstand, then stepped back into the house. He pushed the second bike through, and the portal closed behind it. The grey silhouette of first light shone through the window. Two policemen ran in the house, guns in their hands.

"Stop right there!" one of them shouted.

Tolor ran out the back door and dropped to his hands and feet to run faster. The men chased. Guns fired behind him. He ran until he could run no more. He'd been taking care of Juliette for days and had little sleep. After hunting, he was exhausted. His chest heaved for air. He wanted to go home. Trembling, he hunched down in some bushes near a field and awaited the light of morning.

Chapter 42

"One word frees us of all the weight and pain of life: That word is love."
Sophocles.

The Mirror world

Juliette watched the Parkers look at pictures as she stared at the mirror. A chill ran through her when she realized she hadn't seen Tolor since last night's foray. *But if he didn't return, where did the bicycles and medicines come from?* She was feeling a little better, but not good enough to try to go find him, and she couldn't pass through the mirror.

The sound of hooves clattered through the hallway. She blew her nose, and then closed her eyes against the headache that was forming. In moments, Colovere stood in her bedroom door. She greeted him.

"How are you feeling, young maiden?"

"I'm fine," she said in a thin voice. "Where is Tolor?"

"I was hoping you would be able to answer that question. I suppose he'll be showing up somewhere here in just a few minutes."

"What if something happened to him?"

"You should know the answer to that better than anyone. You were hung, and you returned to us."

Juliette touched her hand to her neck without thinking. That memory didn't make her feel any better. She looked away. The sun was already up. "All we can do is wait."

Clover Springs, California

Tolor awakened from a night of broken sleep. He was never comfortable sleeping in this part of the world. In the mountainous area where he grew up, there was always somebody standing watch for anyone that might stray in. It kept his people safe from predators, and discovery. It was almost light now, and soon he would be sent home.

He heard a car park on the dirt, its door slamming shut, and voices. People moved through the meadow as if they were looking for something. A man in uniform saw him.

"There he is. Look, right there."

Another man raised his gun. Tolor ran, but not fast enough. Even a beran couldn't outrun a bullet. There was a stinging sensation in his leg, and then his back. He fell, face first to the ground, and rolled to find people running toward him. Everything went dark until his scream pierced the air, and he found himself in the meadow near the cottage. He tried to stand and a cry tore from his lips. Consumed by exhaustion and pain, he fainted.

San Francisco, California

Brayden threw the book he was reading on the bed. It was written for ten year olds. He hadn't bought a book in years. *Who even reads them anymore?* His father entered the room.

"What the hell? You don't know how to knock anymore?"

His father's face darkened. He pointed at Brayden's chest. "You watch yourself with me, boy. I'll put you in a school for boys so far away from civilization that you'll beg to spend a day at home. You have no privacy, and no privileges."

"Don't you think you're going a little overboard with this? You've already taken everything I own away from me."

"And I'll take more if you don't pull your shit together."

Brayden took a step back. His father's face was cold as stone.

"Pack your things, we'll be leaving in an hour."

Brayden's breathing became heavy, his face ashen. "But you just gave me the warning. You can't just ship me off like that. Where's mom?"

"First, you need to understand that not only can I ship you off, I will ship you off if I decide to do so. Until you're eighteen, I own you, longer if you stay under my roof. Second, you need to understand that your mother is not going to stop me. You're not a child anymore. Stop acting like one. Pack your bags. We're leaving in an hour whether you're ready to go or not."

The door slammed, Brayden flinched, and then he looked around. *After everything he's taken from me I don't even need an hour to pack.* He ran a hand through his hair. Even this was a punishment. Usually Carolyn would pack for him.

He took a deep breath and went to find his dad who was in the living room on a phone call, calm but pacing. Brayden knew better than to interrupt him. He wouldn't have done that even if his dad wasn't pissed off. He sat down on the couch and waited, wondering if his dad would just ignore him. He never had before, but he'd never seen him this angry. His father hung up the phone and looked at him.

Brayden cleared his throat. "Can I ask where we're going?"

"No."

"Are we going to be gone long?"

"We're not coming back."

Brayden stared. *Calm, I need to stay calm.* The best he could hope for was the possibility of getting some of his things back. "Can I have my camera?"

His father shook his head.

"My computer?"

Again, he shook his head.

"Can I have my TV?"

"You're going to be eighteen next year Brayden. You need to learn responsibility for your actions now. You're not getting your things back."

"Having my things back doesn't equal drunk driving."

"You're damn right about that."

"But I have nothing to do. I'm so bored I could pull out my hair."

"You need a haircut anyway." His father's lip twitched.

Brayden sighed. His father looked at him until he began fidgeting.

"I'm not going to give you those things back, Brayden. You have to earn them. But since you've been civil, we'll stop at a bookstore. You can choose a few books, a jigsaw puzzle, or a game."

Brayden's blood warmed, but he stayed calm. "Can I at least have my phone?"

"No. Go get ready. I have more calls to make."

239

Brayden went to pack. At least his dad was calmer now. He managed not to cry.

The Mirror World

Colovere couldn't stand there doing nothing. He snorted his impatience.

"I'm going to go look for him. You never landed in the same place when the curse returned you to this place. Maybe he is out there, but he hasn't awoken yet."

Juliette threw the blanket off and bolted out of bed so fast she swayed. Colovere moved as close to her as he could to keep her from falling.

"Hold onto my horn so we can move you slowly back to the bed."

"I'm not going back to bed. I'm going with you to look for Tolor." She coughed.

"You are not."

"You can't keep me here Colovere. So please stop arguing. I don't feel good."

Colovere snorted again.

"And stop snorting!"

Colovere neighed. Juliette sighed.

"Let's go."

Meneme ran toward the cottage door. Colovere wouldn't have thought anything of it, but when she spoke, it was in their native tongue. She glanced at Juliette and turned her attention back to him.

"You shouldn't hate, Meneme," Colovere said, in their own language. He didn't like encouraging such rude behavior but he didn't want the maiden to hear that.

"If it were not for her, you would be mine," Meneme pouted.

Colovere rubbed his body against hers. "Juliette was right. I belong to another. What did you come to tell me?"

Meneme looked away. "I saw the beran. He lies in the field as if sleeping."

240

"Show me."

Meneme ran, Colovere followed, and Juliette lagged behind them. Colovere didn't want to move slowly, and Juliette might not have been able to hold on.

Tolor lay on his belly not far from the cottage door, in a place where the grasses were exceptionally tall. There was blood all over him. Colovere needed to get Juliette and Meneme as far away as possible. That wasn't likely where Juliette was concerned, but he feared when Tolor woke up, he would need blood.

"Juliette, do you have any meat? Not dried or frozen, but fresh?" That was not likely.

"Yes actually. Tolor hunted yesterday so he could make a broth with fresh meat before he left."

"Go get it." *It just might work.* "Meneme, go check to see that everything is well with the herd."

"I won't leave you. Do you think I don't know what you're doing? He can kill her, but I'll not allow him to harm you."

Colovere's whinny was sad. "That alone is reason enough for us not to be mated. I would not stand by, and allow a friend of yours to die."

Meneme backed away.

"Go Meneme. I don't wish to share this difficult moment with you."

Meneme's whinny was high and loud. She bolted. Colovere turned his attention to Tolor.

Tolor tried to push himself upright. A low growl rumbled from his chest. His speech was almost unintelligible with his fangs extended.

"I smell you, Colovere. Run! Run from me while you can." Tears fell down his cheeks.

"If I leave, you will bleed to death. I will not allow a dear friend to die in such a way. Juliette comes with meat. I will stay."

"Go!" Tolor threw his head back and bellowed a blood curdling roar.

Shaking and barely able to breathe, Juliette ran toward them.

"Throw it Juliette. As hard as you can."

Juliette hurtled the meat. Tolor had it in his claws before it hit the ground.

While Tolor chewed, Colovere touched his horn to the wound. Tolor screamed as the bullet fell out of the wound in his

241

chest. Colovere had already jumped back when Tolor lashed out with his claws. Colovere slowly moved forward and touched Tolor's leg. Again Tolor screamed and lashed out, just catching Colovere's chest. Colovere neighed, and trembling, turned to Juliette.

"I cannot do what needs to be done, young maiden. The bullets were like poison. My horn removes poison, but I have no hands to wrap his wounds and stop the bleeding."

Juliette tore off large pieces of her gown, wrapping the first around Tolor's leg.

"I need you to sit up Tolor," Juliette said.

Tolor didn't move.

"Please, you'll die if you don't." Juliette's voice was broken.

Tolor clung to what was left of the meat, and sat up with a low growl.

Juliette wrapped the cloth around his chest. Tolor was finished with the meat before Juliette finished, but he was no longer trembling, and the growling had ceased. Juliette finished tying the knot, and sat down. Tolor laid his head in her lap and wept. Running her fingers through his hair, Juliette cried too.

Colovere stretched his neck to relieve the tension in his muscles, then looked up and saw Selene standing at the edge of the meadow. Her lips were in a tight line, and eyes as angry as fire. She turned and ran back into the woods, but Colovere couldn't deal with petty jealousies right now, he would talk to her later.

Chapter 43

"You gain strength, courage, and confidence by every experience in which you really stop to look fear in the face. You must do the thing which you think you cannot do." Eleanor Roosevelt.

The Mirror World

Juliette laid in bed writing the events of the past two weeks in her journal. Putting her pen and paper on the nightstand, she sat back and watched Tolor sleep on the opposite side of the room. It wasn't as if he had never been hurt before, but somehow his helplessness and the gun had unnerved him, and he didn't want to be alone. He had lain on his side watching her for a long time before falling asleep.

"The world isn't the same anymore. My brothers and sisters have even had to move deeper into the woods as society infiltrates their homes. Some of them live a dangerous double life in human dwellings and towns, but if the blood lust came on them..."

Tolor closed his eyes, and Juliette shivered. His fear unsettled her, his words chilled her. The room was silent so long that Juliette thought he had fallen asleep, but then he whispered and his voice cracked.

"Why didn't I come back whole, like you did?"

"Colovere said he thought it was because you're here by magic, imprisoned for Zylphia's pleasure. I'm imprisoned by a curse. He thinks I'll live until the curse is broken. He doesn't think that's true for you." She cleared her throat. "Or Selene."

Tears fell down Tolor's cheeks, and Juliette looked away.

"Selene. It's been more than a year since she told me to leave. I thought... I thought she loved me."

"She does love you."

"She has an odd way of showing it. Even when my life is threatened, she was not there. Even a simple acknowledgment would have shown more kindness. I cannot believe that things will work out any longer."

243

Juliette got up, and sat on the floor by Tolor's cot, running her hand through his hair. He opened his eyes, swollen, and red.

"I could have killed you."

"But you didn't."

"But I could have."

Juliette nodded.

"Do you think we'll ever be able to leave this place?" Tolor asked.

"I'm not sure what to think anymore, Tolor. We have to take things at face value and find a way to make our lives good. Wanting to go home," She frowned, her chest heavy. "I had to stop wishing. It was destroying me."

"Would you leave if you could? What's left for us out there?"

"I don't know, Tolor." She picked up an aspirin and a sleeping pill from the nightstand, and gave them to him with a glass of water.

Tolor managed to swallow them, lying down. Juliette went back to bed more exhausted than she had been in the two days since she started taking the cold medicines. *Tolor wouldn't have been there if I wasn't in need of medicine.*

She turned off the lamp, laid down, and slept until morning.

A door slammed and something large thumped to the floor. Juliette turned to the mirror and stared at a tall young man with dark long hair and wavy curls. His skin was golden as if he were kissed by the sun. She squinted, trying to see his face better, heart pulsing with excitement. Her hand skimmed the mirror as she lowered herself to the floor.

Sitting with her legs folded, she watched the young man look around the room. *That must be Brayden. Why isn't he doing anything? Putting his things away, or exploring his room?*

Mrs. Parker entered the bedroom doorway. Juliette remembered her own mother in the doorway of her room, multiple lifetimes ago. She frowned. The young man turned and stared at his mother. Mrs. Parker looked at him, pursing her lips, and ran her fingers along his cheek.

"You've had a rough time lately."

Thrusting his hands in his pockets, he studied the floor and closed his eyes. Juliette's breath caught as a sense of despair ran through her. *A young man moves in that has hair prettier than mine, and I'm fawning over him like a lovesick pup. What is wrong with me?* She looked to see if Tolor still slept, and was relieved that he did. She turned back in time to see the young man open his eyes again. Smoky grey, with the faintest tinge of blue, wells of devastation.

"Are we really going to live here?"

His mother nodded.

"Why? What is this going to prove? I pissed you off so we're moving into a hut? What do you want to accomplish with this?"

Mrs. Parker ran her fingers through his hair, the young man recoiled, and Mrs. Parker sighed.

"I want my son back. That sweet young boy that was happy, and as lovable as a teddy bear, and nice enough to help Carolyn's predecessor when she cleaned the house."

"We pay Carolyn to clean the house. There's no reason I should help her."

Mrs. Parker shook her head. "You don't pay her Brayden, we do, and your dad's decided that the new maid is not required to clean your room."

Brayden laughed. "Then it won't ever be cleaned."

"That's fine. Then you won't be getting your things back. You can leave when you're eighteen, and work to replace your equipment. That's the worst scenario, but we will be here as long as it takes to bring you back to humanity."

"Don't you think I've already learned my lesson? I've lost most of my stuff, Peter won't talk to me. You've even screwed up my future by cancelling my internship."

"No, you haven't learned your lesson because we aren't the ones that ruined your life. You have a chance to get it back. Just be grateful that you didn't kill anyone in that accident because your life would have been ruined, and theirs would have been lost." Mrs. Parker's shoulders dropped and she took a deep breath. "You haven't learned a thing yet."

She left the room frowning regretfully. Juliette didn't think she was near as calm as she looked. Brayden picked up the heavy bag on the floor, screamed with frustration, and threw it.

Juliette cried out and hurled herself out of the way as the bag smashed into the mirror where she had been sitting. The mirror shattered and thunder, crackling and sizzling, encompassed Juliette's world. The sun disappeared and everything went dark. A silver wall stood where the mirror had once been. Juliette covered her ears, her face to the floor, trembling. Soon the sun returned and the sizzle and thunder stopped.

Whisper and Storm barked at the air. Juliette stood up, stunned.

"Are you alright?" Tolor asked.

Grabbing her heart, Juliette flung herself around. She had forgotten Tolor was there. "Yes," she nodded. "I'm fine."

"The boy did what none of us could do. We should have thought of finding someone to smash the mirror years ago. The witch's power is strong though, because shattering the mirror didn't work. I only hope she doesn't blame one of us for it."

Juliette shivered, remembering Zylphia trying to kill Colovere all those years ago when she thought he was trying to escape. What would the boy's outburst cost them now if the witch didn't believe their story?

Tolor caught Juliette's eyes and frowned. He shuddered as if he had heard her thoughts. "All we can do is wait and see," he said. Then he rolled over and went back to sleep.

Juliette woke the next morning to Whisper and Storm panting and whining at the mirror. She got out of bed, and joined them, Tolor right behind her.

"You shouldn't be up," she insisted.

He smiled. "I'm getting a little stir crazy now. Thank you for tolerating my outbursts these last few days. It was just so... shocking to imagine they would hurt an innocent creature running away."

Juliette didn't know what to say. The world beyond the mirror frightened her too. Whisper whined, her tail thumping against Juliette's leg. She turned to see the Parkers staring at the mirror. They hadn't even heard them talking.

"Honey, you've been through a lot of stress," Mrs. Parker said, placing her arm around Brayden.

He shrugged her off. "I know what happened. Do you really think I don't know what a broken mirror looks like?"

"Of course you do, but—"

"There is no but! I broke the mirror last night. Shattered it to pieces, and now it's not broken. This house is creepy."

"Maybe I should call and see if Joe can see you. You haven't talked to anybody about the accident. That can't be healthy."

"I don't need to see a psychiatrist. I'm fine. You know what, never mind. I'm sure I imagined the whole thing. I'm sorry I bothered you. Thanks for your time."

Mrs. Parker huffed, and left the room. Frustrated, Brayden threw himself on the bed.

Juliette looked at Tolor, and shrugged. "Now we know what happens when the mirror shatters."

Tolor chuckled. "That we do."

Clover Springs, California

Brayden sat in his room trying to force a puzzle piece into a place it didn't belong. After the mirror scenario, he didn't bother his parents again. Sometimes the mirror shocked him when he touched it, and sometimes Brayden imagined if he looked hard enough, he could see right through it, to something scary or magical. Normally that would have creeped him out, but he started having dreams of a hot girl with dark hair, and big brown eyes, long lashes, and big blue wolves that followed her around. They roamed through a meadow, and laughed with a herd of unicorns. Other times she was in a home of some sort, eating with the tallest man he had ever seen. It was crazy, but it wasn't scary. Every time Brayden dreamed of her, his heart beat faster, and his blood warmed.

He rubbed some of the tension from his neck. *Maybe mom's right. Maybe I should see Joe.* He frowned, he was a jerk, and a terrible person. He'd never felt as hurt, and alone as this moment, but he was not crazy. Brayden sat back and sighed, staring into space.

Someone knocked. He knew it was his mother and opened the door for her like his father would have done. She handed him his phone. Brayden looked at her quizzically.

"You've been trying hard to pull things together the last few weeks. I still think it would be good for you to see Joe."

"Mom—"

Mrs. Parker raised her hand. "I didn't come to fight with you. Your father and I felt like you've earned your phone back."

Brayden closed his hand around it.

"Thanks." He kissed her on the cheek. "Would you ask dad if I could have my computer back too? Please..."

She shook her head. "You have to earn that too."

There was no point in arguing. "All right."

His mom left shutting the door behind her. At least with his phone he had some music to listen to, and movies to watch. He looked at the display and touched his finger to the video button. It was empty. He tried the music button. That was empty too. He smiled. *I still have internet service.* He went to his settings, and told the phone to connect. It wouldn't connect to anything. His arm went lax, the phone still clutched in his hand. He sat down at his desk and looked at his contacts. They were still there. He called Peter, but went to voicemail.

"Peter, its Braid. I'm sorry about what happened. Please, call me."

He decided to call Sarah. She answered with an unfriendly, "Hello Brayden."

"How are you?" he asked. The phone remained quiet. "Look, I made some mistakes. I never meant to hurt you. I thought... I don't know what I was thinking, but I'm really sorry."

"Give it a rest Brayden. My parents heard about the accident. I can't see you anymore."

"But I'm trying to change. I'm not even drinking now."

Sarah's voice was frigid. "It doesn't matter."

He hung up, put the phone on the desk and stared at his reflection in the mirror. For the first time in his life, he didn't like the person looking back at him.

The Mirror World

Juliette studied the face that seemed to be staring at her, and shivered. Tolor called her for dinner. When she didn't join him, he came to find her.

"You really like him, don't you?"

"Like him? I don't know what you mean?"

"Oh, I think you do." He took her hand and helped her up.

Juliette's cheeks warmed, and she turned to see if Brayden had seen her move, but he hadn't. He was still staring at the same place in the mirror. She had wanted to believe he could see her. That someone in the real world knew she was there, *but then I would want him to care. No one's going to rescue you now Juliette Barrows. This is your home, so stop acting like a foolish girl.* She followed Tolor into the kitchen, to a lovely spread of slow roasted deer and vegetables.

The Mirror World

Juliette put on a long summer dress for her trip to the other side of the mirror. She was confident she could get past Brayden. He seemed to sleep through anything. Tolor insisted he should come, but she saw the fear in his eyes as he spoke.

"You've always been brave, Tolor. You go and hunt. I'll be alright. I promise."

Tolor's smile was weak. "There's no way you could know that. Something might have changed. Who is to say that if you were hurt, you wouldn't return like I did?"

"You can't keep me hostage, Tolor. I need to walk in my world just like you need to hunt in yours, even if it is only for one night. If anything goes wrong you can send Whisper and Storm after me." She was sorry as soon as she said it. "Maybe that's not a good idea. We know without doubt that I'll be here tomorrow. So stop worrying."

"Stubborn woman." Tolor turned and strode away muttering to himself.

Juliette felt bad, but there was no way she was going to miss going out tonight. This was the first night she would be able to see Brayden face to face, even if his face was sleeping soundly. She clipped on a pair of earrings, and entered the mirror.

Clover Springs, California

It took a moment for Juliette to adjust to the change in light. Brayden's room was dark, and hers was well lit with battery operated lamps and scented candles. Luxuries of the new generation. Juliette wished they could share other modern conveniences, such as electricity, but she didn't know how. Not that she wasn't grateful for what she had.

The room was quiet, except for Brayden's steady breaths. A surge of excitement filled her. She moved forward.

Brayden lay on his side facing Juliette. His hair was still wet from the shower he'd taken before bed. He smelled of something woodsy, but whatever it was, Juliette wasn't familiar with it, except for a lingering scent of pear. She breathed deeply. *I could spend the entire night here watching him, but Ophelia is probably outside waiting, and I have things to do.* She turned to leave. A hand grabbed her arm, she fought, but it held her with a vice grip. Another hand covered her mouth stifling her scream. Slowly the hand moved away, and warm breath tickled her ear.

"Promise you won't scream, and I won't cover your mouth."

Juliette's eyes widened. The voice was Brayden's.

Chapter 44

Clover Springs, California

Struggling wildly and stomping on his toes, Juliette pulled away from Brayden. "How dare you grab a lady like that?"

Brayden bobbed up and down wincing at the pain in his foot. He pointed at his chest. "Me? You're in my bedroom."

Juliette's cheeks warmed, and she grimaced. *I'm in a young man's private quarters.* She cringed looking at the black walls. *Really, what would men do without women?* "That's not the point," she said. "A gentleman never handles a lady in such a fashion. Shame on you, Brayden Parker!" She lifted her chin. *There, let's see how he likes being disrespected. I bet he's never had a lady use his first name before.* Jonathan was different, they had been friends.

Brayden crossed his arms, and backed to the bed without taking his eyes off her. He sat down. "You know my name. You've been spying on me."

Juliette gasped. The color in her cheeks deepened. "I've done no such thing." But her voice faltered. She had been spying on him.

Brayden laughed. "That's what I thought. The question is how are you spying?"

"I don't have to answer your questions. You have no sense of decency." Juliette turned for the exit.

"I have no sense of decency? I'm not the one spying."

She turned around. *He's goading me!* She huffed and strode to the door.

"You won't get past the alarm." His voice was low, matter of fact. The bugger sounded like he didn't care.

With one hand on the doorknob, Juliette stiffened. *He's right.* When her breathing was back to normal she faced him. "I don't have a lot of time, Mr. Parker. What do you want?"

Brayden looked at her curiously. Standing up straight, Juliette fought not to fidget. *Mother always said to meet every challenge standing tall with good posture.* So that's what she did. *Like it or not he has the ability to make my life difficult.*

He picked up his jacket, handed it to her, and grabbed another from the closet. "It's cold outside."

Juliette clutched the jacket frowning. *Ladies don't wear men's clothes... and yet he's right, I had forgotten it was winter here.* It wasn't the first time she had forgotten. It wasn't the first time she had worn men's clothing either.

Brayden waited.

"What?" Juliette stammered.

"Put the jacket on. I'm going with you."

"I've extended no invitation."

"You forfeited that privilege when you broke into my room. If you want past the alarm, I'm going with you."

Juliette heard a low growl, and groaned. "Stay," she commanded, facing the mirror.

"What's that?" Brayden asked, suspiciously. "And I've already told you I'm *not* staying."

"Let's just go," Juliette said, storming out the door.

Brayden punched some numbers into a pad, then motioned Juliette forward, and followed her into the chill night air.

"If you would explain to me how to do what you just did, I could be on my way and you would not have to join me."

Brayden gave her an ornery smile. "I don't think so. This is the most excitement I've had in weeks. Where are we going?" he asked.

Juliette bit her lower lip. *So he's bored and I'm the amusement.* Whatever she was hoping for, that was not it. *What did I want? It isn't like he has the ability to court me.* Her heart thumped uncomfortably against her chest and tears sprang to her eyes. She took a deep breath. *You foolish, foolish, girl.* "I need to pick up supplies if I can. I wasn't able to... I've been ill. I haven't been able to get out as much lately."

Brayden looked at her sideways. Why did he look at her so strangely? *I suppose it isn't everyday a girl comes out of your mirror.* He *must think I'm some kind of freak.* "Where did you plan on shopping? All the stores are closed."

Juliette spotted Ophelia, backing away. It looked like tonight she was on her own. "A friend usually meets me here. It would seem she isn't going to make it tonight."

Brayden scratched his head and smiled.

"What?" she asked.

"Why do I feel like you're not being honest with me?"

"Maybe you're the one that should answer that question. I don't have to answer to you."

"Another untrue statement. You're a terrible liar. We both know you're going to need me to get back into my room and I would like to know the reason behind that."

Juliette chuckled. "I don't think you want to go back into that room without me right now."

Brayden frowned. "Is that some kind of threat?"

"It's a warning, Mr. Parker."

He sighed. "We got off to a bad start. Can we maybe start over? I seriously want to know where you're coming from, what you're doing, and why you're in my room, and..." he bit off the rest.

Juliette's eyes narrowed. "You want to start over. You want me to explain my private life to you. And yet you stand there and in the same sentence, withhold the information I most need? I don't think so. You're an insufferable pretty boy."

Brayden smiled. Juliette raised her eyebrows. "What?"

"Pretty boy, huh?"

Juliette's face turned hot with embarrassment.

Brayden laughed. "There's a restaurant that's open late downtown. Let's go get something to eat."

A restaurant. The closest she had ever been to a restaurant was the hot dog stand in San Francisco. *How do they work?*

"If I go get the car, will you be here when I get back?"

"The car? I heard your father tell your mother you can't drive for a year.

Brayden crossed his arms. "So, you've been spying on my parents too?"

"I haven't been spying on anyone. Why don't we just walk?"

"That would take an hour."

"I can't get my supplies so what else is there to do? Is the restaurant too far for you to walk?"

Brayden grimaced. "You know what? Let's just go."

Juliette sat in a booth looking at the menu, wondering what everything was. The light was bright and the place was noisy. She loved the windows that made up the top half of the wall beside them, imagining the sun shining through them by day. She read the menu after Brayden explained she was supposed to choose something from the list, grateful for the hundredth time that she had been taught to read. What was a hamburger? Or a patty melt? *And who in their right mind eats chicken fingers?* Even Tolor didn't eat those. At least she didn't think he did.

The servant came back to the table for the third time, and she looked irritated. She wasn't wearing the usual black and white, but a pair of jeans with a green t-shirt that said, *The Depot,* on the back. Her apron was green and long, and it had large pockets. One of them held a small tablet. Juliette had never seen such a thing. Brayden sent the woman away.

"Someone should talk to that girl," Juliette said.

Brayden frowned in surprise. "Why?"

"I've never seen a servant act like that. She rolled her eyes at me."

"You mean a server."

"Is that what you call your servants in America?"

Brayden laughed. "Where did you come from? America doesn't have servants. Your accent sounds English, but they don't have servants either."

What does he mean the English don't have servants? Of course we do. Who would do the cooking or cleaning otherwise? The waitress returned and Brayden touched Juliette's hand. Warmth went through her.

"Do you like beef?"

Juliette nodded, afraid to speak.

"Let me order for you."

Of course he would order for her. That's what a gentleman did, wasn't it?

"We'll have two kobe burgers. Medium, and I do mean pink in the middle. With fries, and two vanilla shakes."

Juliette's smile was uncertain. She had no idea what any of that was, but she did like beef far better than the deer meat she was now accustomed to eating.

"So… why were you in my room? And why am I dreaming of you?

Juliette blinked. *He's having dreams of me?* She struggled not to smile but it filled her with pleasure to know that while she watched him, he saw her in his way too. *What a strange thing.* She didn't want to talk anymore, she wanted to just enjoy this moment.

"I don't think we should discuss this, Mr. Parker. I don't think you would believe me, and if you did… you couldn't possibly understand." *How does one explain that they were so terrible and cruel, they were cursed to be taught a lesson.* For the first time in years, her heart ached over her sentence, and tears sprang to her eyes. She looked away.

Brayden watched her, his gaze softening. "My name is Brayden. Try me," he said, softly.

Juliette thought for a moment. He was finally being a gentleman, allowing her to think. The server came and put a plate in front of each of them. The steam from the meat smelled divine. Juliette stared at it, and frowned.

Brayden apparently saw her confusion because he grinned. "Watch." He picked up the lettuce and tomato with his fingers and placed it on the meat, then he picked up the knife and spread something pale pink on the fluffy muffin. After he put the top of the fluffy muffin on top of the meat, he took a bite, without using a knife and fork.

Juliette copied him. She chewed twice, and moaned with delight. Even the shame of not using a knife and fork was wonderful. She took another bite and something dribbled down her chin. Her eyes widened and she covered her face as Brayden pulled a napkin from a metal holder and handed it to her.

"That's how you know it's a good burger," he said, letting mustard dribble down his own chin.

Juliette giggled, shyly. She picked up her knife and cut off a piece of the hamburger, then popped it into her mouth. Brayden reached over and snatched away her silverware. She gasped, but good naturedly.

255

"That's not how you eat a hamburger," he said. "Here." He picked up her straw and put it in her shake. "Try this."

She had watched him drink through the straw. She sucked on it. Her cheeks caved, but nothing came out.

Brayden laughed. "You should see your eyes." He returned her spoon.

Juliette dipped it in the ice cream, closed her eyes and savored the sweet and creamy goodness. When she was finished, Brayden pushed what was left of his shake in front of her. Juliette lit up like a young girl.

"So where have you been all your life? Hiding in my closet? And where are your parents?"

Juliette pretended not to hear him. When they were done, Brayden sat back with a look of satisfaction and ordered two coffees.

"You were about to explain why you were in my bedroom."

He isn't going to let this be. She sighed.

"You can start with your name."

"Miss Barrows. But you may call me Juliette," She said, blushing. "I suppose being in your room does call for an explanation." She took a deep breath and started from the beginning, telling him almost everything; about Emily and how dreadfully she treated her, Zylphia's curse, learning how to live on her own with her new friends and how frightened she was when the mirror travelled to America. She told him about watching Emily die, but left out Frederick's murder. No one wanted to know that someone died in their room. And she didn't tell him how lonely and hopeless the world had been for her all the years she had lived in the mirror with only her friends, knowing all her family and friends outside were gone. When she finished, she studied the table, embarrassed. She barely breathed, waiting for him to mock her.

"So I'll be seeing you once a month," he said, sipping his coffee. "Because you can't get out without going past me."

Juliette met his eyes, her mouth open. "You believe me?" she breathed.

"I broke a mirror and the next day it wasn't broken anymore. And I've had dreams of the world you described. I have to admit I probably wouldn't have believed in the beran or the unicorns if I hadn't seen them in my dreams, but I have, and you would gain nothing by lying. You didn't mention the wolves though. Are those real too?"

Juliette's eyes danced and she nodded. "Whisper and Storm. A lion killed their mother when they were pups. I'm their mother now."

"So, if I don't let you back in tonight, you'll be trapped for a year?"

Juliette stiffened.

Brayden's smile was warm. "Relax, of course I'll let you back in. I might even be able to help with some of the supplies you need since the stores are closed. How have you been getting supplies this late anyway?

Juliette frowned. She hadn't told him about Ophelia. "The friend that usually meets me takes me to places where I am able to shop."

"Will I be meeting this friend?"

She shook her head. "I don't know, Mr. Parker."

"Brayden."

She swallowed. "Brayden," she said, shyly.

Brayden didn't push the issue but Ophelia's secrets were not hers to share.

Are you ready to go?" he asked.

Juliette nodded as they stood, and screeched as a tall man with long hair crashed into her.

"Watch where you're going." The man slurred. "Didn't your mama teach you any manners?"

Juliette scoffed. "You know nothing of my mother, and how I was raised is none of your business."

"Don't get smart with me girl."

Juliette cringed at the smell of alcohol. *Why do men always seem to drink?*

"What, you too good for people like us?" he asked, motioning at a friend who had kept walking when he stopped. He grabbed the top of her dress and pulled her toward him. Buttons fell to the floor and it ripped off of Juliette's shoulder.

Brayden moved Juliette away with one arm, grabbed the man by the collar, and punched. The man fell to the floor, staggered his way up, and tried to ram into Brayden. He moved at the last second, and the man fell into a table, knocking it over and landed on the floor.

Brayden threw down a twenty, and placed the jacket he loaned Juliette on her shoulders. "Let's go."

They moved to the door and into the street. They went only a few blocks before Brayden yelled. "Run!" He grabbed her hand.

Juliette heard a siren coming closer. She ran behind Brayden. He stopped.

"I'm sorry," he said, winded.

Juliette opened her mouth to ask why, and grunted when Brayden knocked the air out of her, shoving her into a ditch. Red and blue lights seemed to be everywhere. A police car stopped. Juliette watched from the ditch, shaking and remembering the feel of the coarse rope around her neck.

"Put your hands on your head."

Brayden did, and the policeman pushed him to the ground and put handcuffs on his wrists saying something about rights. *What should I do?* She whimpered.

The policeman pulled Brayden up and escorted him to the back seat of the car, then looked around. Juliette recoiled deeper into the ditch, and waited. The policeman got into the car and drove off. When the car turned the corner, Juliette ran for the house, hoping she would make it back to the mirror in time. She had to find a way to get back in on her own. *If only Brayden would have given me those numbers.*

Juliette stood under a tree, bruised, dirty, and tired. She couldn't stop trembling. *How do I get into the house?* She wanted to scream with frustration. This was the first time she had ever shared her story. It was the first time she had ever been on a date. *Was it a date? I suppose not, but it was exactly what I thought a date would be like.* It was the first time she went to a restaurant and it was a night she dreamed of from the first moment she saw him.

Tears fell down her cheeks. Would Brayden return? Or would they kill him like they did her? *People don't carry guns the way they used to. Maybe he'll be alright. Even if he does come home I won't see him for another year if I don't get back in the mirror soon.* He was the first human friend she had made since the day she entered the mirror, she wanted to see him again, and hoped with all her heart she would.

How do I get in? She cried harder. *Calm yourself. You need to think. He pushed buttons when we left. Do you have to push the buttons every time?* It didn't matter. The only way she knew to get in was through the door. The windows would surely be locked. She moved to the door quietly as she could manage, and turned the knob. It was unlocked. She held her breath and waited. There was no sound. She walked toward Brayden's room as fast as she could, stopping when a loud noise pierced the air. *It's just someone snoring.* Her hand on her chest, she waited until her breathing slowed.

She continued toward the bedroom. Two steps away from the door, music sounded. Juliette's eyes opened wide. She whimpered and covered her mouth.

"Hello. Yes, I am Brayden Parker's father. He what?"

Juliette jumped for the door to find Storm waiting on the other side, and a large puddle beside Brayden's bed.

She sighed. This wasn't going to be fun to come home to. "You like him too, don't you? But you can't go around marking people," she whispered harshly. Storm whined. Juliette grabbed a towel from the floor, wiped the mess and threw it into a corner. Then she petted Storm, his bottom wagging in a dance with his tail.

Juliette turned to the door and frowned. *I hope you're alright, Brayden. I'm so sorry about what happened.* Facing the mirror once more she ran, one hand over the wolf's back. "Come on Storm, we have to hurry." Together they leapt into the mirror.

Chapter 45

"To expect the unexpected shows a thoroughly modern intellect." Oscar
Wilde.

Clover Springs, California

Brayden sat in the backseat of his parents' car pondering the
chain of events of the evening. They weren't talking to him. They
always waited until they got home so no one had an opportunity
to hear the Parkers' dirty laundry. Like anyone cared. It didn't
matter. Right now silence suited him. He wanted to be alone with
his thoughts, wondering if he'd been a fool to believe Juliette. But
he did have the dreams, and why else would she have been in his
room?

He rubbed the knot on his head. He had escaped injury at
the restaurant to be thrown down on the blacktop by a cop. His
face and arms stung with bruises. He closed his eyes, and
swallowed hard. He could still see the disbelief on Juliette's face
when he knocked her into the ditch.

Brayden frowned as regret filled him. He felt protective of
Juliette. He didn't know why, and didn't know what being taken
to the police station and getting booked would mean to her, but
he wasn't taking any chances with her safety. She might have
been terrified. She would have been alone. There was no one for
her to call. *Would she have woken up in another world like she said she
would, disappearing from the jail cell?*

This was crazy. Nothing about Juliette made sense. His
response to her was even more curious. When had he ever been
protective of a woman? His dad was the ladies man of the family,
opening doors and buying roses. You would think his parents
were newlyweds.

His father pulled into the garage and Brayden winced as he
moved to get out of the car. Once in the house his parents
followed him to his room.

"What has gotten into you, Brayden?" his father asked. "This just gets more and more interesting. Do you want to go to jail?"

"Of course not," Brayden said. *Figures, they never even asked me what happened.* He looked away.

"Why don't you tell us what happened?"

Brayden gaped. "You're asking me for my side of the story? When did you ever care about my side? You never even asked what my story was after the accident. You're going to start now?"

"You were so intoxicated that night I doubt you remember anything about what happened."

Brayden's breathing quickened. His eyes stung with tears. He wasn't going to give them the satisfaction. "I remember every moment of that night, including the accident," he said quietly. "Every moment." He swallowed hard remembering Peter lying on the pavement like he was dead. "Can I just go to bed?"

Ignoring him, his father folded his arms. "They said this fight was over a girl?"

"It wasn't over a girl." He raked his fingers through his hair, and flinched at the pain in his shoulders. "Well, not exactly… Okay, it was over a girl. But not in the way you think."

Mr. Parker's laugh held no humor. "Explain."

"I was with a girl, and a drunk staggered through the restaurant and nearly knocked her down." Even now his blood heated at the way he grabbed Juliette. "What would you have done?"

Mr. Parker didn't answer.

"If it was mom? Tell me, what would you have done?" It was a rare victory for sure, but he could see it in his father's eyes. This round, he had won.

Mr. Parker sighed, and glanced at his mother. "Was there anything you wanted to add?"

She shook her head.

"Then let's all get some sleep."

"Why did you come and get me," Brayden asked, as his father reached the door. "You said next time you would leave me there." Brayden couldn't help it. His voice cracked and he swallowed audibly. His father didn't even turn to look at him.

"Because of your mother." He left the room without another word.

261

Juliette sat in front of the mirror watching Brayden's parents leave the room. He had defended her honor. No one had ever done that before. Her skin tingled every time she thought about it. She had fun until that awful man slammed into her. She cringed remembering the moment, and how terrible he reeked. His breath smelled of stale alcohol and cigarettes. Whisper and Storm lay down beside her.

Her breath caught and her heart beat faster when Brayden approached the mirror. He sat down in front of her looking so defeated. She knew he couldn't see her. No one ever had. He placed his hand on the mirror, and Juliette timidly laid her own hand against his. The mirror sent a rush of warmth through her. Brayden's eyes widened, but he didn't move his hand.

"Did you feel that?" he murmured. Juliette heard him clearly.

She wished he could hear her. More than any other time in her life, she wanted him to know she was there. "Yes," she replied, closing her eyes.

"I'm sorry I pushed you. If you're there, and you can hear me, I was afraid for you. I didn't know what would happen if they caught you." He hung his head, and chuckled. "I can't believe I'm talking to a mirror. Am I going crazy?"

Juliette shook her head and placed her other hand on the mirror. Unexpectedly, the heat increased.

Brayden looked at the mirror in wonder. "I don't know what it means, but I dream of you and your two blue wolves every night. I have to go to bed. You never told me the supplies you need. I'll make a care package and set it here tomorrow if you're able to retrieve it."

He moved his hand from the mirror, and Juliette shivered with cold. "Good night, Juliette."

"Goodnight, Brayden."

Removing her hand, Juliette jumped when she turned and found Tolor watching. His eyes communicated an understanding that she had never seen before. She knew he understood what it was to be alone, to feel unloved, and to need someone. He bowed his head and left the room. Juliette kicked off her slippers, and climbed into bed.

Clover Springs, California

When Brayden woke up the next morning his parents were already gone. He went to the kitchen, found a few cloth bags, and started filling them with anything he thought Juliette might need or want. Salt, pepper, bacon, eggs, butter and bread, Doritos, potato chips, Snickers and Butterfingers. He added popcorn and the Lorna Doones his mother liked to dip into her coffee as an afterthought. These were the things he would want if he was trapped on a deserted island, except for the Lorna Doones. He threw in a soda for good measure wondering if she had ever had one. When he was done, three overflowing bags sat on the floor, and the pantry was nearly empty. *I left the milk behind. They would eventually have had to go shopping anyway.* He imagined his mother's face when she saw the kitchen, and laughed. He would just tell her he was hungry. *What's she going to say? I'm not allowed to eat anymore?* He took the bags to his room.

Brayden stood at the mirror trying to see through it. *There has to be a way.* He needed to see her, to know she was alright. He had never laid hands on a woman before, not with the intent of knocking her down. What if he hurt her? *Maybe if I look hard enough.* He stared at the mirror as minutes ticked by, but nothing happened. He placed his hand on the mirror. It was cold. She wasn't there.

The mirror warmed. Brayden's breath caught and he smiled.

"I brought supplies for you. I wasn't sure what you needed." Brayden looked at the floor. "I'm standing here, talking to a mirror, with grocery bags by my feet. I've gone crazy." But he didn't believe that. The mirror began to vibrate. Fear and excitement jolted through him. He backed away as the movement increased. Something flew out of the mirror so fast it was a blur. Brayden had no chance to react. The next moment he was lying on the floor, staring in the eyes of the huge blue wolf standing over him.

Juliette bounced on her toes, eyes wide, arms flying everywhere.

263

"Storm! You get back here right now! Oh God. Storm!"

He had gone through the mirror like a bolt of lightning. There was nothing she could have done to stop him, and then Whisper went right after him. *Oh God, what if they hurt him? What if they kill him? No!*

"Whisper, Storm. Get over here now!" They ignored her.

Juliette watched in horror as Storm's muzzle moved toward Brayden's face.

"Oh God. No!"

Tolor ran into the room.

"What is wrong with you?"

Juliette pointed.

"Oh no," Tolor said.

Tolor put an arm around Juliette, holding her close as they cringed awaiting the obvious outcome of the attack.

Brayden's arms began to flail. He closed his lips in a tight line, moving his head back and forth.

Shocked, Juliette pushed away from Tolor. They both laughed.

"Get off me," Brayden yelled. Storm was busy licking his face, while Whisper sniffed at the bags.

"Hey!" A lashing tongue caught his lips. He sputtered. "Ew."

Whisper pulled out a loaf of bread.

"Hey you, put that back!"

He finally managed to get Storm off him, and started to take the bread from Whisper. She growled.

Juliette yelled. "Whisper, no!"

Whisper dropped the bread, laid down by the bed, and pouted. Brayden held the mutilated loaf in the air. He threw it to Whisper.

"You might as well finish it."

With Juliette yelling at her, Whisper didn't touch it. Storm snatched it up, laid down where he peed the night before, and finished the loaf in a flash.

"That was you that peed on my bed!" Brayden accused.

Juliette shifted. "You peed on his bed too?"

Storm's panting looked like a smile. Brayden slowly approached him. Storm rested his head on his paws. Brayden sat down, and began to rub his fur. Groaning, Storm offered him his belly.

An hour later, the wolves were delivering supplies in bags tied to their necks, to the opposite side of the mirror.

Chapter 46

"Life consists not in holding good cards but in playing those you hold well."
Josh Billings.

The Mirror World

Juliette cast a fishing line into the lake and wedged the rod between heavy rocks. When she finished, she placed smaller stones on top for added support. She sat down, closed her eyes, and dug her toes in the warm sand enjoying the scent of the salty air. It would be winter soon, and end of season preparations were under way. Storm splashed in the water not far down the beach, leaving Juliette to wonder if the wolf wasn't chasing off the fish.

Juliette smiled; she had become used to the rays of the odd red ball of light tinting the land pink the latter part of the day. Other than color, it was no different than sunshine in Brayden's world.

"A fish tugs at your line, fair maiden."

Juliette yelped in surprise, and fell to the sand, her arms flailing. One hand landed on her rapidly beating heart.

"Colovere."

"I'm sorry, fair maiden. I didn't mean to frighten you."

"I wasn't frightened. Only startled."

Colovere's whinny sounded suspiciously like laughter. Juliette looked at him sideways, eyes narrowed. Stones tumbled as the fishing line broke free. Juliette stood in water to her waist before she caught it. Colovere snorted and looked away. *Teeth? Is he showing teeth? He's laughing at me.*

"If you hadn't scared me, this would not have happened."

"You said I didn't frighten you. So I don't know what you mean."

Juliette sighed. *At least I saved the fish.* She fixed the fishing pole that had come loose and sat back down.

"How do things go with your young stallion, fair maiden?"

Juliette's mouth fell open. "My what?"

"The young stallion. What would you call him? He is no longer a boy, and yet he's not a man. He is at that age where the colt becomes a stallion, and challenges his leader."

Juliette tried to envision what Brayden's genteel face would look like if he knew he was being compared to a unicorn. She laughed. "It seems like he's doing fine. Storm spends more time with him than he does with me these days. Did I tell you he marked his bed while we were gone?"

Colovere's laugh was obvious this time.

"Colovere, how is it that Whisper and Storm can pass through the mirror whenever they please?"

"The wolves were born here. Why would you not expect them to have the ability to come and go as they please?"

"Because no one else can," she said, wistfully.

"There you are wrong. Have you forgotten Petaire? And the birds that sometimes fly between the worlds? We are here by magic, they are not. So they are able to come and go as they wish."

Juliette pondered, and then grinned. "I suppose that makes sense. They don't listen well while they are on the other side of the mirror though."

Colovere snorted. "No, I suppose they don't. They are wolves. Why are you fishing by yourself?"

"It's the end of the season. I wanted to add to our store of fish before the lake freezes."

"And Tolor?"

"He is stripping the garden and plowing the soil so it will be ready next summer."

"Ah, good. Did you save anything for me?"

"Tolor said he was going to. I'm sure he'll seek you out later."

Colovere lay down on the sand beside her. Juliette put her arm around his neck, resting her head against him.

"Do you think we'll ever be able to go home?" she asked, staring out at the lake.

"Hmm, for you maybe… I will seek the hand of the gods. I have nothing to return to."

Juliette's heart stumbled at his words. Colovere did have something to return to, or someone, but she had promised secrecy. She wouldn't betray Ophelia's trust.

Tolor was putting away his shovel and hoes when Juliette returned home. Splotches of rich soil covered him all the way to his sandaled feet. He reached out and she handed him the bucket of fish. The tall beran wiped the sweat off his brow with a damp cloth.

"You usually dig with your claws."

"I didn't feel like dealing with getting the dirt out of them later. I expected you would be home earlier than this. Did you forget this is the first night of the full moon?"

"Of course not."

Tolor laughed.

"What are you laughing about?"

"Aye, of course not."

Juliette folded her arms and tried to look cross.

"That young lad you've been flirting with sent something for you. Storm dropped it off this afternoon and left again."

Juliette laughed. "Where is it?"

He tilted his head toward the cottage. "It's on your bed."

She ran inside smiling at Tolor's laughter behind her. *Whisper isn't even here today.* Even as she had the thought, a blur of blue came flying through the mirror. Juliette hugged her wayward wolf. "You're supposed to live with me you know."

Whisper laid down as Juliette picked up something rolled in paper, attached to a strange type of rope. She opened it, careful not to rip it. A small orange package fell out onto the bed. Juliette read the note.

Hey Juliette,

I've made plans for us this evening. It'll be a long night, and we need to start as early as possible. Come as soon as you can.

Juliette looked out the window and saw the rarest of treats. The sun was still out, but so was the moon. Giggling like a girl, she ran to clean up, and get ready.

After tearing into the clothes in her closet, Juliette decided on a pair of jeans and a tunic. She didn't want to appear less pretty than the girls he was used to, but she wasn't going to look like a trollop in the marketplace by wearing a blouse that showed her belly. She looked in the mirror, and frowned at her hair. She had let it grow without cutting it for as long as she could, but her lifestyle made it difficult. She tied it back in a bun, scowled, and let it down again. *It is how ladies wear their hair these days.* She stood up straighter, took a deep breath, and headed for the mirror.

Juliette stepped through the mirror to find Storm dancing a hello, and the light of the real world. It was something she hadn't seen often over the last two hundred years. She wondered where Brayden was. He'd told her to come early. She looked out the window at the pines, and green grasses, but Brayden wasn't out there. The door opened, and she jumped with a yelp. Storm's tail thumped the floor wildly when Brayden walked into the room. He smiled, and Juliette's cheeks warmed.

"Hi."

Juliette didn't trust herself to speak.

"I'm glad you're early. You said you came from a comfortable family in the Regency Era. I thought you might like to feel what it's like for a lady of comfort now."

"How?" Juliette asked.

Brayden smiled. "There isn't a real spa in this little town, but I found the best hairdresser, and make-up artists. Not that you need it. And I paid them to stay open a little bit later than usual."

Juliette's eyes narrowed in thought. "Someone that dresses hair?"

Brayden chuckled. "A hair stylist."

Juliette shook her head. Brayden sighed.

"You'll see. The cab should be here any moment."

"Cab?"

"You don't know anything about the world today, do you?"

Juliette's fingers clenched the hem of her tunic. "I don't see what there is to know."

Brayden took her hand. "Here, come with me."

Juliette trailed after Brayden until his father stopped them in the kitchen. Juliette could see the immediate clench of Brayden's teeth.

"I heard you're heading into Haverville," Mr. Parker said.

"How did you hear about that?"

"Your cab was here. I tipped him, and sent him on his way."

"You what?"

"Don't get your boxers in a bunch, Braid. I'm going that way, and I thought my car would be a more comfortable ride."

"I arranged for the cabbie to come back for us. How are we supposed to get home?"

"Call me. That's not too difficult. Who's this?" He put a hand out to Juliette.

She placed her hand in his and he shook it.

"This is my friend, Juliette. Juliette, my father."

She nodded. "Mr. Parker."

Brayden's father let go of her hand and chuckled. "I didn't know you had any friends, Brayden."

Juliette laughed.

"Come on, dad."

His voice was irritable, but his smile was warm, sending a colony of butterflies to flight in Juliette's belly. Brayden's smile widened. She looked away. *How does he know?* Embarrassment filled her. He put an arm around her, and led her to the car.

Brayden opened the door, and waited for her to climb in. Awkwardly, she slid across the black leather seats. He followed. She clung to the seat, willing herself to remain calm, until Brayden moved so close to her that the warmth of his body and his scent made her unable to think about anything else. She relaxed against his shoulder only a little embarrassed by her lack of propriety.

Clover Springs, California

Mr. Parker dropped them off at a busy shopping center, and Juliette found herself being pulled to a store called Desiree's House of Style. Stores she understood, but this was something else. There were two women cutting, rolling, and holding something that blew air on the hair of the patrons in chairs. The room smelled like flowers. Brayden talked to a woman and pulled Juliette toward a chair. He sat down and opened a book filled with pictures of pretty ladies.

"This is what modern women do to make their hair pretty. Your hair is beautiful the way it is."

Juliette blushed.

"But I thought it might be fun for you to have a modern day of beauty. Or a couple of hours anyway. Do you see a style you like?"

Juliette looked at the pages and chose a style that looked simple.

"Do you want highlights?"

"What?"

"Color streaks like this."

Brayden put his finger on a girl with half of her hair standing on top of her head. Juliette thought it looked like a bird's nest. Brayden laughed. "Not the style, just the colors. Like this." He pointed to a strip of auburn in the woman's hair.

Why does he think I want to look like a colorful skunk? Two women walked by with colors like that in their hair. She calmed herself. It was normal for the ladies of the day to put colors on their hair, and it did look pretty on some of them.

Juliette bounced out of the chair at the salon after a haircut, threaded eyebrows, a pedicure, manicure, and a facial. She laughed shaking her hair. It was light, and her ringlets were perfect. They gave her a shampoo, and a new hairbrush too. Brayden smiled, and kissed the side of her head. Juliette stiffened, and blinked. *What kind of girl does he think I am? This is what you get for being forward in the car. Now he thinks less of you.*

Tears stung the back of her eyes. She fought them back.

Brayden looked at Juliette, tilting his head. "Is something wrong?"

"No, not at all."

He looked like he was going to say something else, but changed the subject instead.

"I thought we would see a movie, and then eat dinner. We have just enough time to catch the late show."

Juliette nodded.

The theater was almost full but they managed to find seats. Juliette couldn't sit still waiting for the movie to start. The story was about vampires that weren't mean. Silly really, but Juliette loved it. She nibbled on popcorn, and drank her first soda, since Tolor drank the one Brayden had sent to them. She laughed when the characters were funny, and almost jumped out of her chair when a man turned into a wolf, and it looked like it was going to jump out of the screen.

The couple beside her began moaning. She glanced their way to see they were kissing. *That girl was not raised well. Why, all that man will want her for is a tumble.* She tried to ignore them, but the moaning continued. Juliette scowled when the girl giggled and they almost landed in her lap. Popcorn and soda flew everywhere. Juliette jumped out of her chair.

"What are you doing? This is not a brothel, it's a place to watch movies. How dare you act in such a way in public? Ugh!"

Brayden grabbed her arm, his tug gentle yet firm.

"Let's go. We can do this another time."

"They should leave. Not us."

Brayden rolled his shoulders. "The world's a little different now. Values are not as rigid as they were."

"I've noticed. All sense of propriety has gone out the window."

Brayden ran his hand down her back. Juliette shivered.

"I'm sorry that happened." He wove his fingers with hers. "We'll go to an earlier show next time."

By the time they were done with dinner, Juliette was calm again. Brayden's father picked them up, and drove them back to his home.

Brayden unlocked the door to his bedroom, and opened it to Storm's wagging tail. Juliette hugged her, vigorously scratching the skin below her ear.

"Such a good puppy."

Brayden chuckled, and pointed. "That is not a puppy."

"Sure he is."

"He's bigger than any wolf I've ever seen. His head stops at my chest."

Juliette grinned. "I found him as a baby. He'll always be a baby to me. Okay, Storm, that's enough."

Storm lay down beside the bed. Brayden took Juliette's hands in his. She looked away. She wanted to be close to him, but the fact that they were alone in his bedroom hadn't escaped her. Why hadn't it ever bothered her before? *Because he was never touching more than a hand.* He pulled her closer. She could smell his

272

masculine scent again, mixed with soap. Her breasts rested against his chest. Panic swept through her. He tilted her chin, bent down and kissed her. She wanted to melt in his arms, to stay there, lost in that kiss all night. But this was wrong, unacceptable, and downright disrespectful! She pulled away and swung with all her strength. His head turned with the slap, his cheek an angry red where her hand made contact.

Brayden stared with a look of shock and confusion, his hand rubbing his face. He tried to speak but Juliette paid him no heed.

"How dare you! We go out one time and you think I'm a call girl you can tumble?" Her chest was heaving she was breathing so heavy. "I don't ever want to see you again Brayden Parker. Stay away from me."

She turned toward the mirror. Tolor was standing there.

Brayden grabbed her arm. "Juliette, no. It's not like that."

Juliette spoke through clenched teeth. Storm whined. "Let go of me or he'll kill you." The warning was two parts anger, and one part fear. She didn't want to hurt Brayden but she was leaving.

He loosened his grip. Juliette broke away and jumped through the mirror.

Chapter 47

"The heart asks pleasure first, and then excuse from pain, and then little anodynes that deaden suffering." —*Emily Dickinson*

Clover Springs, California.

Brayden stood with his hand on his stinging cheek, confused. His heart raced and his breathing was shallow. Had he misunderstood her? *She liked me. She cuddled, leaned into my shoulder, and smiled, and even blushed when I put my arms around her. Why did she get so crazy? Should I chase her? Or give her time to chill?* He wanted to go after her, bring her back. He needed to understand her anger, but his mind told him to use sense, and give her time. *That could be a mistake too. What if she really doesn't ever want to see me again?* He ran his hand through his hair wincing when his fingers caught in the tangles.

He went to the mirror and rested his forehead on its surface.

"I'm sorry Juliette. Whatever I did to make you so angry… I didn't mean to."

His hands touched the glassy surface, it was cold.

"I never meant to disrespect you. It was only a kiss… I wasn't trying to make love to you." He wanted to, but he had known better than that. "It was just a kiss," he mumbled.

Storm's head came through the mirror, his long slimy tongue licking Brayden's face. Scratching the fur at the scruff of the wolf's neck he managed a small smile for his furry friend. When Storm was fully through the mirror, Brayden lay down on his bed beside him, glad he wasn't alone.

The Mirror World

Juliette put the last of the canned tomatoes and beans in the pantry, went back to the kitchen to sit and spread apricot jam on her bread. Normally she would slather it with butter first, but that was a treasure that came from the outside world, not her own.

274

She had meant to buy some when she was in town last night. Tears rolled down her cheeks, onto her apron. She put the jam away, tossed the bread, and went to lie down.

A piece of paper rolled around a candy bar rested on her bed. She put the candy bar on the nightstand, and opened the note.

Please talk to me Juliette. I don't know why a kiss would make you so angry, but I'll make it up to you if you let me. I care about you. I thought you liked me too. I've never cared about anyone before… but there's something different about you. Even before we met you haunted my dreams. You still do.

Juliette threw the note by the candy bar, lay down, and cried herself to sleep.

Clover Springs, California

Brayden sat on his bed the first night of the full moon, and waited like he had every month for the last year. This would be the last time. He had sent numerous messages, begged, pleaded, even bribed her. Obviously, he read her wrong. If Juliette felt the same way he did, she would have responded by now. If she came out of the mirror, he could try again. Maybe this time would be different. She would care about him too. He sat all night, watching the mirror, and waiting. Even Storm left him alone. He fell asleep at the first light of dawn, his heart in tattered shreds. Juliette didn't come.

When Brayden woke it was past noon. He rubbed the sleep and unshed tears from his eyes, and went to take a shower. Standing under the flowing water, he closed his eyes and enjoyed the pulse of heat on taut muscles as it trickled down his skin. When he was done washing, he dried his hair and dressed.

He had promised his mother he would take photos she could use to advertise a new club she had joined. Their goal was to plant more trees for a cleaner environment. It was unlikely his mom would do any of the planting, but she had accepted a voluntary position as its treasurer. His father, pleased by his offer to help had taken him out to the back roads on his property, and given him the keys to his truck. It wasn't legal, and he couldn't go far, but Brayden missed driving. Four wheeling in back country would be a great way to get away from his life for the moment. His father even joined him.

Brayden grabbed the camera someone loaned his mother to complete the project. As he shut the drawer there was a tap on the door.

"Come in."

Brayden's eyes widened to see both his parents enter the room. *Something's going down.* He hadn't done anything wrong that he could think of. He put the camera on top of the dresser, frowned, and waited.

His father grinned. "Your mother and I have been talking, Braid. You've been here more than a year now. You're past your eighteenth birthday, and we don't think you're the same young man we brought here." Brayden's heart raced. He swallowed hard. "We're returning your things. I'll take you back home, and unlock your studio when you're ready."

"I was supposed to take pictures today… for mom." He wished his voice didn't sound so weak. His father wasn't a big man, but he was a man of authority, and Brayden always felt that power. He had fought it for years from his waking breath till the moment he slept. It was liberating to realize he wasn't fighting it anymore.

His father chuckled. "After you take care of that."

Brayden smiled. "Thanks."

His father turned to leave the room. "Call me when you're ready to go."

"Could I wait until tomorrow morning?"

His father stopped with a look of surprise. He nodded. "Of course. Tomorrow then."

Biting his lower lip, Brayden glanced at the mirror. Tomorrow he was going home. Tonight he would say goodbye to Juliette.

"Are you ready to go?" his mom asked.

Brayden picked up the camera, and followed her out of the room.

276

Brayden grabbed the boxes from his mother's room and put them in the car, then headed to his own room. She had taken him to a steakhouse for lunch to celebrate after he took the photos they needed. She was going to remain here. His father would commute between the two cities, if this could be called a city.

He dropped a box trying to open the door, and set the rest down. A year ago it would have been beyond him to carry a box into the house. It would be strange to have a chef and maid again. He had even learned to cook for himself. He shut the door, dropped the boxes, and faced the one thing he blocked all day.

"Storm." His voice was quiet, but the wolf would hear. He hadn't sent a note in months, but he had to send one now. He tried to do it last night, but he couldn't. The wolf came and sat at his feet. He wrote a note, fashioned it into an envelope, and dropped a small diamond necklace inside. He had meant to give it to her the night she slapped him, now it was a goodbye gift. He tied the envelope around Storm's neck, hugged and petted his friend with tears in his eyes. "Take care of her for me, Storm. I'm going to miss you." The wolf sniffed at him and whined.

"Brayden, are you ready to go?" his mom called, from the living room.

"I need a few more minutes."

"Okay, I'm going to finish loading the car. Let me know if you need help."

"Alright."

Brayden looked around his room, and took a deep breath, resigned. Not a word from Juliette. Why he expected one after all this time, he didn't know. He placed his hands and forehead on the mirror. It was warm.

"I'm sorry I hurt you. I hope you find everything you're looking for, and everything you want. I won't ever forget you, Juliette."

The mirror turned cold. Juliette was gone. Brayden taped a piece of paper with the numbers to the alarm system on his bedroom door, and joined his mother.

Chapter 48

"Love is a better teacher than duty." Albert Einstein.

The Mirror World

Juliette watched Tolor wrap his hand around a green plum feeling for just the right softness. He pulled it from the branch, and placed it in a bucket. He picked a plump berry from a smaller container and plopped it into his mouth. He moaned at its sweet and tart nature. Juliette folded her arms and smiled.

"Will you stop eating the winter rations?"

Tolor whirled around, and laughed. "No, and if you have a problem, pick your own berries."

"I might have to at the rate you're going."

Tolor grinned. "I'm not that bad."

They turned at the sound of familiar laughter, and Juliette groaned. "Selene."

Tolor tilted his head. "You've always loved Selene. Why do you find her presence oppressive now?"

"I do love her. She's like the sister I never had, and a loyal friend. I just wish… you're always depressed when you see her."

"Kind of like Brayden, when he stood at that mirror, night after night begging you to talk to him?"

Juliette's mouth fell open. "It isn't the same thing."

"Isn't it? What in the name of Orion's stars is different about it? Who cares what the cause is?"

"What are you talking about?"

"That filly holds my heart in her hands, like you hold Brayden's in yours."

"It's not the same thing at all. Selene was jealous, and unrealistic. Brayden disrespected me. If he cared about me, then he should have treated me like a lady."

Tolor shook his head. "You need to take your head out of the sand. The world's moved on, and times have changed. People think and act differently. A beran girl left her companion because he snarled at her, and now she has another. Such things were not

278

even mentioned in our time. Brayden meant to disrespect you no more than I meant to give Selene cause to doubt me." His voice cracked, and he cleared his throat.

Juliette looked away.

"Look at me Juliette."

She looked back at Tolor, trying not to see his tears.

He ran a finger along her cheek. "Brayden was doing what came natural to him."

She stared at Tolor remembering the people in the movie theater, others walking arm in arm, or kissing in the street. Even food was different now. Maybe Brayden didn't mean to shame her, but he didn't want her anymore anyway. He'd stopped sending notes a long time ago, until she found the one that said he was leaving this morning.

"So, you're still going to leave him heartbroken knowing that you were wrong. You judge Selene, but you're just like her."

"He stopped sending notes, Tolor. He doesn't want me anymore."

"Like I don't want Selene? I would get on my knees and beg if I thought she would take me back. Will you make Brayden live like this? There is more involved with Selene and I. Our life together was always difficult. Her brothers hated me. They never understood how hard it was for her to be alone, but they were right. There are things I cannot give her. You'll be sorry one day if you don't stop him. Even if you have to beg for a minute because you've been so cruel, don't allow the man you love to walk out that door."

Juliette turned and ran for the cottage, through the house and into her bedroom. The thought of Brayden being gone forever now filled her with fear. She went to the mirror hoping against hope, and looked for him. She found an empty room. Brayden was gone.

After Juliette had gone Colovere laid down by Tolor.

"You finally said what needed to be said?"

"Yes, but I fear I said it too late."

"The boy is gone?"

"He was leaving today. I don't know if he's left, but Juliette knows by now."

279

"Should we check on her?"

Tolor shook his head. "I think we should give her some time."

Colovere turned toward Selene, galloping with her hair blowing in the wind, her lithesome body the picture of grace. "She's beautiful, isn't she?"

"She always has been."

"Do you still miss her?"

"Do you miss Ophelia?"

"Yes," Colovere whispered. "And yet I'm tired of being alone. Meneme is there, and willing."

"But you're really not interested."

"No," Colovere said. "Unicorns mate for life."

San Francisco, California

Brayden listened to the sound of a commercial he'd shot for a car dealership, grimacing. He never understood why dealerships liked such hokey music. He was glad the commercial was done and it was what they wanted, but Brayden still hated it.

He picked up the screenplay he had been working on and plopped it down on the desk. It wasn't very good. Peter had been his screenwriter, but he never spoke to him again after the accident. Brayden locked the studio and went to watch television. A picture of a woman in Regency regalia filled the screen. He stopped flipping channels and watched, wondering if that was what Juliette wore in her generation. It felt like a fist squeezed his heart, and a stone rested in his belly. He turned the television off. Another night thinking about Juliette. Would it ever go away?

He heard the front door close and Sarah walked in. She kissed him on the cheek, and then sat beside him.

"How's it going?" she asked.

Brayden shrugged. "I'm doing all right. Why are you here, and why didn't you knock?"

"It's good to see you too."

Brayden waited until she made eye contact before he spoke again. He wanted her to know he was serious this time. "I haven't seen you for almost two years. The last time I spoke to you, your parents forbade you to even talk to me. It's been over between us for a long time, Sarah."

280

She climbed into his lap before he thought to stop her. "I know, but can't we be friends?" she pouted.

"I don't think it's a good idea."

"I think we should be more than friends. Kind of like kissing cousins." She lifted herself up and ran her hand along the front of his jeans. "I know it doesn't mean anything."

It's the same old game for her. She doesn't understand I'm different now. There was something between them, or someone, rather. He hung his head. Juliette had made it clear she didn't want him. He closed his eyes tightly as the wound in his heart pulsed through him. *I haven't been with a woman in more than a year. He wanted Sarah. Maybe this is what I need to move on.*

Sarah lowered her head to his, and pressed a kiss on his lips. He opened his eyes, the desire in hers feeding his. She touched her lips against his once more, and Brayden met her kiss, deepening it. The auburn hair he held in his hands was no longer straight, it had curls the color of dark chocolate, her blue eyes became dark and warm, her waist felt smaller. He moaned with desire, needing her. Then he saw his dreams; Juliette, running through a meadow with a centaur, and a herd of unicorns. The dream he had night after night varied little. He saw them like a vision or a movie, and he suddenly understood that if he pursued this moment, the dreams would be gone. Juliette would be lost to him forever. His heart ruptured, his eyes opened, and he gently pushed Sarah away.

"No," he mumbled.

"But, why?"

There were tears in her eyes. Brayden wiped them away and lightly kissed her cheek.

"It isn't you, Sarah. I'm sorry." And he was. They had played each other again and again, and now it was really over.

"Then tell me why," she demanded.

He had hoped she wouldn't do this. He didn't want to hurt her.

"Answer me!"

Brayden looked into her eyes. "Because I'm in love with someone else."

Sarah scowled. "Someone from that awful bumpkin town you moved to?"

"Yes."

281

"You can't be serious." Sarah laughed, trying to goad him, but he wasn't listening anymore.

He needed to go home, to find Juliette, to pursue her until he had her in his arms. They would handle any situation they needed to after that. Maybe he could find a way to break the curse. If anyone had the resources for such an endeavor, it was him. He would ask his father for help if he needed to.

"I have to go," Brayden said. Sarah was still talking. "You need to let yourself out." He pushed her off him and went to find his dad. A moment later, the door slammed behind him.

Mr. Parker sat at the table eating a steak with steamed broccoli and potatoes in a béchamel sauce. Brayden sat down. Mr. Parker's eyebrows rose.

"To what do I owe the honor?"

Brayden smiled. "I eat with you when mom's home."

"Only because I force you by threatening the worst consequences I can think of. Therefore, what do you want?" Mr. Parker grinned.

"I want to go back to Clover Springs, tonight."

"Why? There's really nothing there for you, and what about college? You promised your mother you would enroll."

"I can take classes there as well as here."

"There isn't a college there."

"All I need is the internet. Dad, please, I need to go back."

"Why?"

Brayden took a deep breath. "Because Juliette is there."

Mr. Parker studied Brayden's face. Only years of experiencing that stare kept him from looking away. After what seemed like a lifetime, Mr. Parker put his napkin down, and drank the rest of his wine. "You're too young to be in love, Brayden. Not yet, son."

"It's too late, dad. I can't change the way I feel any more than I can change the size of my shoe." He raked a hand through his hair. You of all people should understand this. Could you turn away from mom? I've tried to. I've been back here for months. But she's all I think about and everything I want. I need to go back."

282

"Okay, I agree. You need to go back, but your mother is already on her way there, and I can't go until the end of the week. You've been gone all this time. Surely a few more days won't be a problem."

"I can't explain, but I have to go tonight. Will you take me to the airport if I can get a flight?"

His dad paused, studying him. Brayden knew the moment he understood. "I can do that."

"Thank you." Brayden hugged his father, and went to pack.

Mrs. Parker only stayed for a couple of days so Brayden soon had the house to himself. All he could do was think. He kept his promise, and enrolled in a screenwriter's program, since that was what he needed at the moment. He spent his nights walking the hills with Whisper and Storm, running, playing, and investigating everything they found. He spent as little time in his room as possible so Juliette wouldn't know he was there. He slept on the couch.

Two days later, the time of the full moon had come. He waited for Juliette sitting against a wall outside his bedroom door.

The door opened just enough for someone to peek out. Brayden waited for it to shut behind her. She began to make her way to the front. Brayden's heart beat so hard he was surprised she couldn't hear it. Butterflies filled his stomach. He almost felt sick with nerves and fear.

"Juliette." The smell of roses filled the hall, Brayden almost groaned.

She froze with her hand on her neck. She turned around trying to see him in the darkness.

"I'm sorry, I didn't mean to startle you. I just had to try one more time." While that was true, he had no idea what he would say next.

He got up from the floor, but he stayed where he was, afraid she might run away from him otherwise. "I didn't mean to hurt you. I had no idea you felt the way you did. I didn't know anything about what the world was like when you grew up, but I've learned a few things since then.

Courting today is not what it was in your generation. Women no longer have to find a man to survive, and they can

283

feel beautiful about who and what they are without labels. I've also learned that more than anything in the world, I don't want to live without you. If you'll give me just one more chance I'll wait until you say it's okay to kiss you. You have my word."

Brayden shuffled his feet. *Why hasn't she said anything?* Juliette started walking toward him, silhouetted by moonlight. She put her arms around him, timid at first, but then relaxed when he slowly wrapped his around her. He breathed in relief as peace flowed through him for the first time in months. Juliette placed her lips on his. She kissed him twice, teasing, irresistible flutters. The third time he pulled her closer and deepened the kiss. Again and again he kissed her. He wanted more of her. He held her close, but loose enough to pull away from him unrestrained if she chose. She didn't, and Brayden's heart began to heal. When they came up for air Juliette whispered in his ear.

"Do you want to go for a hamburger?"

Brayden laughed and pulled her into a tight hug. Juliette giggled. He kissed the top of her head.

"I have a better idea, but can we bring dinner back here?"

"I didn't know you could do that. That would be nice."

Brayden saw her cheeks color even in the moonlight and smiled. "Let's go."

Brayden threw two pillows on the floor for them to sit on, while they ate pizza. They filled each other in on their lives over the months they had been apart. Juliette explained that her world didn't change much.

"I've been thinking about the curse," Brayden said. "Shouldn't it be broken?"

"How do you mean?"

He grinned. "I missed that strange accent of yours. It's so cute."

Juliette laughed.

Brayden finished eating, and wiped his fingers. "You said to break the curse, you had to do something selfless for someone, and they had to do something selfless for you."

"Yes."

"Well, not to sound like a martyr or anything, but it was selfless for me to give up the things I was working on to come back here, right?"

"Right."

"And it was selfless of you to forgive me, and kiss me in a way that made my toes curl."

Juliette laughed, and Brayden kissed her again. He couldn't get enough of her. The only thing that held him back was the fear of her running away again.

"So you were selfless too."

"Not really. Tolor and I talked one day, the day you left, and I forgave you then. When I came to tell you, you were gone."

Brayden stared. "Why didn't you leave me a note?" he asked, running his fingers through her hair. "I would have come back to you. I've visited twice since leaving here."

"I thought your world was better in San Francisco. You had always wanted to go back. I didn't want to ruin that for you. My lifetime, as far as the world is concerned, was over a long time ago. That's not true for you. This is your generation, and you should be a part of it."

"No, my life is with you now. And that was selfless of you so the curse should be broken."

Juliette's eyes widened. "Do you think so?"

"I do. We should celebrate. What have you always wanted to do when you got out of that place? I'll make the arrangements and we'll do it this weekend," Brayden said.

"I'd like to see London again. I have a home. If it's still there."

"That sounds like a trip for at least a week. We'll make the plans tomorrow."

Juliette's laugh was lighter than he had ever heard it before. Her face joyful, and animated. Brayden couldn't think of anything he would have appreciated more.

They heard the sound of a horse neighing outside his window. Juliette got up and ran outdoors.

"Ophelia!"

Brayden followed at a slower pace, and stared unblinking at the huge chestnut unicorn standing by his window with Juliette's arms around its neck. She let go when she heard the swishing of his footsteps in the grass.

"Brayden, this is my friend, Ophelia. Ophelia, this is Brayden."

Ophelia dipped her head.

"A unicorn. That's not possible."

Juliette laughed. "Of course it is."

Brayden had seen them with her in his dreams so he decided it had to be true. He wondered if Bigfoot was about to come out of the mountains too.

When they went back in the house, Juliette prepared to go home.

"No, the curse is broken. We've been apart for so long, stay with me."

Juliette shook her head. "Brayden, I can't. I-I just can't."

Brayden's eyes widened. "That's not what I meant at all. I just thought I could hold you, maybe kiss you, nothing more than that. I'll sleep on top of the covers if you want."

Juliette's response was timid, but eventually she agreed, and Brayden wanted to kick himself for all those promises. He rested his head by hers, so he could breathe in her scent the entire night.

"I'll see you in the morning," he whispered, but Juliette was already asleep.

Brayden woke up to glowing rays of sunlight shining through his window. He felt better than he had in years. Smiling, he stretched. He rolled over, his arm swinging to hold Juliette, to feel her body close to his, this first morning they woke up together. His arm sliced through the air and landed on the bed. Brayden sat up. The curse wasn't broken because Juliette wasn't there.

Chapter 49

"We should be too big to take offense and too noble to give it." —*Abraham Lincoln*

The Mirror World

Tolor woke to the sound of Juliette weeping. He flew out of bed and ran to her room. He found her curled in a fetal position, her words lost in the sounds of her lamentation. He sat beside her and ran his hand along her back. This had to be about Brayden, and that made it at least partly his fault.

He spoke as gently as he could manage. "Shh, it's alright. You're home now."

Juliette cried harder. Colovere entered the room, Selene following close behind. Tolor groaned, wishing he had thought to put a shirt on.

"What's wrong?" Colovere asked.

"I don't know," Tolor said. "I woke up to this."

"Did that boy do something to her?" Colovere asked.

Tolor shook his head and shrugged. Juliette's sobs slowed.

"What did he do, Juliette?" Tolor asked.

"He didn't do anything. He was wonderful."

"Then why are you crying?" Colovere asked.

Juliette sat up. Selene handed Tolor a handkerchief for Juliette. Ignoring the slight, she took it murmured her thanks, and blew her nose.

"There now, that was lady like," Tolor said.

Juliette pushed him and laughed. "We thought we broke the curse."

"Broke the curse? What made you think that?" Tolor asked.

Juliette twisted her hands in her lap. "Zylphia said to break the curse, I had to do a selfless act, and another would have to perform a selfless act for me. And we have. We fell asleep planning our future." She lost her voice when she began breathing heavy, tears falling on the shirt she had worn the night before. "And I woke up here," she said, sobbing.

287

"In your bed? That's never happened before. What do you think Colovere? Should it have broken the curse?" Tolor asked.

"I don't know. Some witches prefer to reverse it themselves. It suits Zylphia's selfish nature."

Juliette lay down on Tolor's knee and he placed an arm around her. "It's alright, the boy loves you, surely he'll wait for you."

"Stop calling him a boy. What kind of relationship would we have together when he can only see me one time a month, and then for only a few hours."

"It'll work out. Give us time to think on it," Tolor said.

"That's easy for you to say. Whether you're together or not makes no difference, Selene is here. Colovere has Ophelia. But Brayden isn't a magical creature. He can't just come here, so I will spend my days alone."

Tolor glanced at Colovere, and froze.

Colovere stood with his head tilted, then moved forward until he was almost standing in Juliette's lap. Forgetting her tears, she peered up at him, horrified.

"What do you know of Ophelia?"

Juliette sat up and moved closer to Tolor. "She's alive," Juliette murmured.

Colovere backed away, his tension causing him to glow with magic. "That's not possible. I have her horn. I used it to help you retrieve your things."

"Zylphia cut it off to deceive you."

Colovere snorted angrily. "The chestnut mare," he breathed. "You've been lying to me almost since the day we met. I trusted you and you betrayed me!"

Juliette shook her head, eyes wide. "No, I didn't. I—"

Colovere turned to Tolor. "Did you know about this too?"

Tolor nodded slightly, but remained silent.

"And neither of you thought enough of me to tell me? Has my mate remained on the other side of the mirror so she could find another? Orion's beard, Tolor! You knew I thought she was dead."

Colovere bucked, and particles of asphalt crumbled when his back hoof kicked through the wall. Selene moved away. Colovere stopped, his body heaving, and stared at Tolor for a long moment. "Out of everyone I have ever known, Tolor. I would never have expected this from you." He whinnied, a moaning, terrible sound of loss and pain, and left the cottage.

Selene stared at Juliette and Tolor, then followed Colovere out the door.

Clover Springs, California

Brayden took a shower, dressed, and sat on the bed raking his hands through his hair. If everything Juliette told him was true, and he had no reason to think that it wasn't, the curse should have been broken. She had forgiven him, and he had forgiven her. They could have a life together, but what kind of life would it be when they only saw each other one night a month. He knew his father could overcome any obstacle, and wondered what he would do in this situation? The answer was immediate. He had to find the witch. He went outside to look for Ophelia.

Where would a unicorn be if she was on the property? Is she still here? What if she only meets with Juliette when the moon is full? He cupped his hands around his mouth, and yelled.

"Ophelia." He waited, turning in a circle to see if she was coming. "Ophelia." There was still no reply. "Ophelia, please."

Brayden turned toward the house, and saw her standing on a hill beside it. Her chestnut coat shone in the sun like silk. The darker hair of her mane sparkled with the breeze. She stood larger than any horse, and more majestic than any stallion. Brayden ran to her.

"Thank you for answering. I need your help."

He told her about his night with Juliette, and how they thought they broke the curse. He choked on the words when he told her she was gone in the morning. When he was done, Ophelia remained quiet for what seemed a long time.

"You need to confirm that she didn't return on her own while you were sleeping."

"She wouldn't have done that."

"Why would she not? It wouldn't be the first time a maiden changed her mind. You were away for months before your recent return. Maybe she feels you will leave her again. We will counsel with Petaire. He might open a portal for you, but I will not help

289

you without Petaire's counsel, and he will know better how to find the witch."

"Who is Petaire?"

"Colovere's brother. Colovere is champion among unicorns. Petaire stands in his place while he is away from this world. We will go to him."

Brayden nodded. He would do whatever it took to free Juliette, whatever the cost. Ophelia lay down, and Brayden climbed on her back.

Ophelia snorted.

Brayden's eyebrows furrowed. "What?"

"You are not a virgin."

Brayden's cheeks colored. "Sorry."

Ophelia sprinted into a gallop.

Ophelia ran swift as the wind and still the trip took hours. She finally stopped in a meadow by a forest. Brayden looked around confused. *There's nothing here.*

"Why are we stopping, Ophelia?"

"The entrance to the world you seek is always found by a reflection. Do you see the forest at the opposite end of the meadow?"

Brayden nodded.

"That is the reflection the witch used to create this part of her world. Juliette's mirror first reflected Zylphia's cottage. The meadow and the forest here reflect a meadow and a forest in Zylphia's world. The reflection is distorted, and sometimes changed, but the portals of entry remain."

Brayden had no idea what she was talking about. Suddenly he felt a chill and shivered in the cool mountain air. He folded his arms over his chest to help preserve warmth.

"Where is Petaire?" Brayden asked.

Ophelia lay down. "Now, we wait."

Brayden scowled. He was hungry and cold. He needed to find Juliette. Picking up a stick, he threw it in the forest. It spun surrounded by a myriad of color, and disappeared before it touched the ground. Brayden's breath caught. It was one thing to know it was there, yet still shocking to see the reality of something that shouldn't exist. He sat down beside Ophelia,

290

running his hand over her soft coat. She moaned and leaned against him.

The Mirror World

Tolor ran through the forest seeking Colovere. Finding him in the clearing he called his own, stamping around, snorting and bucking. His neigh was angry and loud, and every once in awhile a mournful whinny broke through. Afraid to move closer, Tolor waited until Colovere exhausted himself, collapsing to the ground with sorrowful whines, and desperate whinnies.

Tolor moved forward carefully, and sat by his friend.

"Why are you here?" Colovere asked in a hoarse voice. "You are no longer my friend."

Tolor bowed his head. "We didn't know who she was at first, only that she was always there to help when we were in trouble, and she always seemed to remain close to the portals. We never meant to deceive you. She wouldn't tell us her name until we were sworn to secrecy."

"Why?"

"I don't know. I believe she confided in Juliette." Tolor smiled wistfully. "She has been more than a little prejudiced toward me, but she seems to trust Juliette."

Colovere stood, and began to leave the clearing.

"Where are you going, Colovere?"

Colovere stopped, but he didn't look back. "To find my mate."

Clover Springs, California

Petaire arrived shortly after Ophelia lay down. He whickered with affection when he saw her in the meadow, and snorted when he spotted Brayden.

"May we speak, Petaire?" Ophelia asked.

Petaire threw his head up, and Ophelia trotted behind him to the opposite end of the clearing.

Without Ophelia blocking the wind, the air was biting. When Ophelia and Petaire returned, Brayden was running in place to keep warm. Ophelia had warned him not to enter the forest.

"I will take you to the maiden, and if it's her desire to put everyone in danger because of you, we will help you. I will not carry you on my back."

Brayden scoffed. "Wait a minute. I'm not trying to put anyone in danger. I want to find the witch who did this, and ask her to break the curse. No one has to go with me. Just tell me how to find her, and I'll be on my way."

"You will not find her without a magical creature to help you. Come with me." Petaire walked into the woods without looking back.

Brayden followed. A few strides and the landscape seemed to liquefy. Brayden's steps were shorter, more laborious, the world blurred, and the sound of life ceased. He couldn't see Petaire anymore, yet he still moved forward. Juliette waited somewhere on the other side of this entryway. When he stepped out of the forest on the opposite side of the reflection, he collapsed to the ground. Petaire waited while Brayden caught his breath. Every muscle in his body burned.

"Why is it so easy for you? Juliette never looked exhausted or felt pain coming through the mirror."

"I am a magical creature, and Juliette belongs here. You do not. Have you lost the desire to pursue this course of action?"

Brayden's blood heated and he jumped to his feet. "No, I haven't changed my mind, but you're wrong, Juliette belongs with me!"

"Then accept the consequences of your actions without complaint." Petaire continued, murmuring to himself.

Brayden's fists clenched at his sides, but he said nothing. His father had taught him to do what needed to be done, and he always had. He knew how to work for things, and that the end was always in sight, even if he couldn't see it. None of his friends were offered an internship right out of high school, but he worked for it. This was no different.

Brayden could see a cottage in the distance.

"Is that where we're going?"

"Juliette resides there."

Brayden ran.

Juliette swept the kitchen and hallway, and tossed the dirt and dust outside. If she had stayed in bed, she might never have gotten up. There had been no word from Brayden this morning, but surely he knew where she was. When she looked into his room, the bed was empty, and Brayden was gone. It was as if the bed mocked her. Tears fell, and dried as she worked, wondering if Brayden had given up on her.

She placed the last of the dishes in the cupboard, poured a cup of coffee, then walked to the pond and sat down. She needed to see Colovere, to know he was okay, but just like Brayden, he wasn't there. For the first time since entering Zylphia's world, she felt the number of her years. She'd had her friends, and they were enough for most of that time… until Brayden came. Now he was gone, and she didn't have her friends either, at least not all of them. Biting her lower lip to fight off the onslaught of tears, she dragged one foot in the dirt, and then heard his voice on the wind. She looked up to see Petaire trotting toward her, with Brayden running at his side.

"Juliette." He waved his hands above his head.

A cry of shock split the air as Juliette plowed into Brayden's arms.

Chapter 50

"Forgiveness is the fragrance that the violet sheds on the heel that has crushed it." —Mark Twain

The Mirror World

Brayden closed his eyes for an instant, enjoying Juliette's unbridled affection. He was used to her being far more restrained. He brushed her lips with his, and grinned.

"Thought you were going to get away from me, huh?"

"It doesn't look like its working. How did you find Petaire?"

"Ophelia took—"

A streak of white hurtled across the meadow slamming into Petaire. He reared and screamed, blood darkening the hair of his rump and running down his leg. Juliette cried out and Tolor ran out of the forest. Petaire tried to back away. Colovere bucked and kicked his back legs into Petaire's flank again and again.

Petaire's cries were sharp and desperate. "Why?"

Colovere wasn't listening.

Tolor pushed Juliette and Brayden toward the cottage. "Get inside and don't come out!"

They didn't go all the way to the cottage, so Selene ran to them, pushed them back, and stood like a sentry as Tolor transformed into an enormous bear. Selene trembled, murmuring a prayer to Orion.

Tolor moved on Colovere, raking long sharp claws into both sides of his rump. Petaire lay on the ground. His entire body trembled, constricting and expanding with every breath. Juliette ran to help him. She screamed and fought as Selene caught her, pushing her back to the cottage with the mass of her long sleek body.

Colovere stood with his head down and his long sharp horn facing Tolor. Tolor backed away and Colovere charged. The beran spun, long claws making furrows the entire length of Colovere's body. The unicorn screamed and stormed forward. His horn nicked Tolor's throat. Tolor roared and bit down on

294

Colovere's neck. The unicorn reared and squealed, unable to break the beran's grip. Selene turned to Juliette and Brayden.

"Swear to me you will not move from here until I call you." Juliette lifted her chin.

"You will swear right now or I will make you unable to move from here. Do you hear me? Someone will die if you don't listen."

Brayden put his arms around Juliette. She nodded, and Selene ran to the fight.

Juliette moved closer.

"You said you would stay," Brayden demanded.

"I am. These are my friends and this is my fault. I need to hear."

"It's over Tolor," Selene said pointing to the woods. "Go now!"

The beran snarled and growled, and Colovere shook with Tolor's teeth sunk deep into his neck. Selene moved closer, holding her ground. Juliette knew what the effort must cost her, remembering those long sharp teeth tearing into her own flesh. If Selene wasn't successful... Juliette shivered at the thought of losing her friends in such a way. Tolor's breathing slowed.

"Release him, Tolor. You are a man, not a beast. You must fight your blood lust. You only wanted to end this and you have."

Colovere whinnied in pain. Tolor released him, hesitated an instant, and ran into the woods. Colovere fell to the ground by his brother.

Juliette ran to him while Selene looked at Petaire's wounds. Ashen faced, Brayden watched. Juliette turned to him.

"In the kitchen, there are jars of red colored salve. Bring them with warm water and towels."

"Where—"

"On one of the shelves against the back wall, please hurry."

Brayden ran, returning with the requested items in minutes. Juliette wept as she and Selene comforted Colovere, and Petaire. They began cleaning and applying the salve to their wounds, glancing uneasily at the forest where Tolor had disappeared. It wasn't long before he returned from the woods, a man in blood soaked clothes.

"Why, Colovere?" Petaire breathed. "What had I done for you to hurt me in such a way?"

A heartrending whinny tore from Colovere's throat. "You took my Ophelia away. You knew she was not dead and you watched me grieve for her." Colovere neighed so sharply, Juliette recoiled. "You are no longer my brother. You are not even kin."

Petaire's voice broke. "I didn't, brother. The witch made her choose. Your life, or her freedom. Ophelia chose you."

"Why would you not tell me?" Colovere demanded, wincing and snorting at the effort.

"You would have come for her, and the witch would have killed both of you. She saved your life again when your magic began to consume you. It was Ophelia who brought Juliette to me."

Colovere laid down, a series of chilling sounds splitting the air around them. Tolor lay down beside him, laying his head on his flank. He wept too.

For the next two days Juliette and Brayden didn't see Colovere or Petaire. Selene had taken them home with her to continue nursing their injuries. Usually the magic in the salve healed wounded flesh immediately, but both of the unicorns' wounds went deep and some of the deepest weren't physical.

Juliette's days were bittersweet. She had Brayden, but she mourned the loss of a friend, as did Tolor. The beran kept to himself, doing only what had to be done. He responded to Juliette when she spoke. Juliette, Whisper, and Storm spent their time walking around the lake with Brayden, and showing him the den the wolves still shared sometimes.

The nights were heaven if there was such a place. Brayden wrapped himself around her, enabling her to believe he could do what he said. She prepared to let go of the girl who had been a victim for more than a century, and to become a woman that had control over her life. She hoped that would be someone Brayden would be proud of. There was still Colovere to deal with, but that would come later. She would do what was necessary to restore the faith of her friend.

On the third day a nearly healed Petaire came for Brayden.

Brayden stood in the doorway of the cottage with Juliette, while Petaire waited at the edge of the meadow.

"It is time to complete your task if you are able to do so, young one."

Brayden raised his eyebrows, wondering about the change in the way Petaire addressed him. He pulled Juliette close, and spoke in her ear. "I will do everything I can, and anything that needs to be done to free you."

Juliette's breathing hitched, and Brayden pulled back to wipe away her tears. He brushed his lips against hers. "We'll be together again. You have to trust me."

Juliette nodded.

"We must go, boy."

Brayden chuckled, glad things were back to normal. Who would have thought he would ever find being called 'boy' refreshing? He kissed Juliette one last time, and ran to join Petaire. If he didn't force himself to leave now, he wouldn't be able to.

When they were almost out of sight, he turned around to see Tolor with his arm around Juliette. He smiled and waved. *One thing is certain. I don't need to worry about her safety.* Whisper and Storm ran and played in the meadow.

The last thing Brayden saw before they crossed the meadow into the forest was Colovere standing with Meneme at the opposite edge of the forest.

"You should not treat Ophelia in such a way," Petaire said, without raising his voice.

Colovere neighed, angry, loud, and clear. Brayden was convinced Colovere heard his brother.

Journey to the Portal

Ophelia paced in the meadow when Petaire and Brayden re-entered the natural world. Ophelia whinnied and trotted over to them. Petaire waited.

"Colovere knows you live."

Ophelia backed away and her breathing quickened. She looked at Brayden, then back to Petaire.

297

"It was not the boy's doing," Petaire said. "You have a choice to make, Ophelia. Will you take a chance and go to him? Or will you continue to live the way you have all these years?"

Ophelia hung her head. "If he wanted me, he would have come the moment he knew I lived. Nothing has changed. I will not allow his death while I can prevent it."

"And yet you will risk everything for the boy and the maiden? You know she is the only other person who knew your secret."

Ophelia whinnied a mournful sound. Brayden looked away.

"The maiden would not have done so lightly and she is important to Colovere."

"Colovere stands with another, Ophelia."

"His choice is irrelevant. The maiden is loyal, and Colovere will always be my mate."

"Very well then. The last place the witch was seen was in London, but she may have another alternate world in which she lives. She frequents a tavern called The Dancing Frog. This is not much information, and it places you and the boy in more danger with the number of witches and warlocks that frequent the place, but it may be that someone at the tavern will speak to the boy."

"You aren't going with us?"

"No, I have wounds that must heal before I may use such a portal."

Ophelia hung her head.

"I made my own decisions, Ophelia. This is not your responsibility. Go now."

Ophelia lay down on the ground and Brayden climbed onto her back.

"Hold tight to Ophelia going through the portal, young one. It will devastate the maiden if you do not return."

Brayden nodded wondering why the warning was necessary. Going through the portal was strange, but it wasn't that bad.

Ophelia stood, placed her horn against Petaire's, turned away, and began the journey to the portal.

London, England

They traveled most of that day, ending their trek at a small cliff over the sea. Without warning Ophelia jumped. Brayden clung to her, resting low on her back, and screamed.

The water didn't touch them but everything blurred, and the atmosphere held no sound. Brayden couldn't see Ophelia. He bent and clung to her neck, careful not to cut off her air flow. His heart thumped against his chest so hard it hurt. He held his breath, but this time they didn't come out the other side. The portal went on and on, and Ophelia seemed to move in slow motion. Brayden shivered with cold.

They were in the portal for hours before Ophelia stumbled onto solid ground. Brayden sighed with relief, and cried out when Ophelia began struggling to stay upright. She recovered, but her legs were trembling when he climbed off her back. Her voice was hoarse.

"I need to rest. I will be hiding between the buildings."

Brayden swallowed hard, nodded, and turned to face the tavern.

The outside of the building was brown brick with small windows, foursquare on each side of the door, painted green to match the dancing frog on the brown sign. Brayden tried, but he could see nothing through the windows. He had come all this way. He wasn't going to stop now. This was for Juliette. His heart fluttered at the thought of being with her. *The only way that's going to happen is to go through that door.* He swallowed hard, and entered the tavern.

The room stilled the moment Brayden walked in and heads turned from every direction to see him. *So this is what the magical community looks like.* It was like going back in time. The tavern had small windows, a wooden bar, floor, tables and chairs. People were dressed in clothing going back as far as the Georgian Era. There was even a bard playing a harp in one corner, or he had been playing until Brayden walked in.

Brayden approached the bar swallowing the lump in his throat and sat by a tall man with brown hair, wearing an old brown suit, and a man wearing all black sat beside him. *I need to look confident.* Brayden nodded and turned to see the bartender in front of him.

"I'll have a coke, and bring another round for these gentlemen."

The man in black nodded without cracking a smile. The other man ignored him. Brayden tapped him on the back.

"Excuse me, sir."

He looked over his shoulder at Brayden, and turned back around. Brayden tapped again.

"I'm sorry, but I need to ask some questions. I wonder if you could direct me."

The man turned around, sat back in his chair and stared at Brayden. "Direct you where? Did you come in here to ask for directions?"

"No, and yes."

The man sighed irritably. "What do you want, kid?"

Why is everyone calling me a kid today?

"I'm looking for someone, and I was hoping you might be able to tell me where to find her."

The man laughed. "Do you know how big this city is kid? This used to be a country tavern until the whole bloomin' city built itself around it."

"This woman frequents this bar and she has a unique name. Zylphia, do you know her?"

Both men stared at him. *So you do.*

"Zylphia hasn't frequented this bar in more than a hundred years," the man in dark clothing said.

"How do you know? Maybe you just missed her. Do you know where I can look for her?"

"You won't find Zylphia around."

"Why not? I have to find her."

The man tilted his head. "Because I killed her."

It was Brayden's turn to stare. "You what?"

"More than a hundred years before you were born."

"Then shouldn't the curse have been lifted?"

"What curse?"

"My girlfriend. She was cursed to live in a world Zylphia created. But we've met the terms of Zylphia's curse. Shouldn't it have broken the day she died?"

Both men laughed. "You've been watching too much TV kid. Of course it's not broken. Her death bound the curse. It's stronger than ever now. That was quite the display of power creating that little world," the man in black said.

Brayden ran his hand through his hair. "Please, just tell me what I have to do to break the curse."

"You're really into this girl, aren't you?"

"Yes, will you help me?"

Brayden heard a screamed neigh and ran for the door.

A heavyset man in filthy jeans and a grimy white T-shirt had white chains made out of magical fire wrapped around Ophelia's stomach and neck. Ophelia reared. The man pulled. Instead of the chains pulling her closer, they tightened. Brayden grimaced as Ophelia screamed. He ran to tackle the man. The man raised his hand palm forward, and electricity burned through Brayden's chest. He fell to the ground panting for air. The wizard laughed.

"Don't worry, I'm just borrowing her. It's her mate I'm after, she don't mean nothing."

Colovere. Brayden shuddered, and struggled to rise, but the pain in his chest pinned him to the ground. The thief flipped his hand, yelling in a language Brayden didn't understand, a blinding light, and Ophelia was gone. The man wearing black lifted Brayden from the ground.

"You'll be alright in a few minutes. Stupid fool you were to attack a wizard mantled in power like that." He pulled him to a bench Brayden didn't remember seeing in front of the tavern. He struggled feebly against the wizard's strong arm.

"Okay kid, stop fightin' like a little cub."

"I have to help Ophelia," Brayden panted. "Can't let him get to Colovere."

"Ophelia and Colovere?"

"How does a human know a mystical creature such as these?"

"Ophelia brought me here."

The dark man scowled. "What do you mean 'brought you here?' No boy, nor man, can tame such a creature."

"I didn't tame her. She carried me by choice." Brayden managed to get to his feet. His legs shook in protest but after a minute he was solid enough to move again. His face contorted and he ran both hands through his hair. "I don't know what to do. I have to free her. Please, help me. I have money, I can pay for your time."

"Some wizards will take a payoff from a human. I'm not for sale."

301

Brayden covered his face. "Then tell me how to get her back. I'll do anything."

"You would do that for a creature you can never own?"

"I don't need to own her. Yes."

The dark man looked at Brayden until he squirmed. "The name is Drist. I'll help you."

The Journey Back Home

Three hours later Brayden and Drist were on a plane to San Francisco.

"I can't believe you don't know where the portal is," demanded Brayden. "This will take forever."

"Sorry little cub, I didn't create this world you're talking about so show those claws to somebody else."

Brayden huffed, closed his eyes, and sat back in his seat. *This is going to be a long flight.*

Chapter 51

"Our enemies have found we can reason like men, so now let us show them we can fight like men also." —*Thomas Jefferson*

San Francisco, California

Twelve hours later, the aircraft pulled up to the terminal door. Drist murmured a spell when the door opened and the crowd moved aside so they could depart.

Brayden smiled ruefully. "You're finally being useful."

Drist eyed him sidelong. "Watch it, little cub. I can still go home."

"I am not a little cub!"

"You show a rough tongue and display claws. So what are you? Certainly not a full grown cat," Drist said, as they approached a car rental counter.

Brayden asked the clerk for a sports car, forgetting he had no license. Sighing heavily, Drist pulled out his I.D, and obtained the keys to a mustang.

After a four hour drive, they pulled up to Brayden's home and entered the house.

"I don't understand why we came here," Drist said.

"It's the only way I know to get to the portal. We're going to have to find a way over the mountains behind us."

"I've had enough of traveling, little cub. I can feel the power in this house." Drist moved Brayden out of his way with one arm, and walked directly to the bedroom.

He smiled, running one hand across the mirror's surface. "Ingenious beauty," he murmured.

"What? Is he crazy? It's just a damn mirror."

Drist looked at him. "This is *not* just a damn mirror. And if you want my help, stop calling me crazy, little cub."

Brayden's cheeks heated. He hadn't realized he'd spoken out loud.

Drist placed his hand on the mirror, closed his eyes, and sputtered when a long slick tongue wiped across his face. Brayden laughed.

"What was that?"

"That was a Storm in wolf's clothing. It's a wonder she likes you."

Drist wiped his face, narrowing his eyes. "Animals like me because I protect them," he said. Then he turned back to the mirror, and closed them again. In moments the surface melted to a silvery fluid. Drist held out his hand.

"Come."

Brayden placed his hand in Drist's, and they stepped into the mirror.

Juliette was not in her room. His urgency restored, Brayden called for her, and ran outside.

"Ophelia has been kidnapped," Brayden yelled.

Drist held back, looking at the world around him. The unicorns came running toward them from the meadow, and Tolor and Juliette came from the opposite direction. Brayden caught his breath.

"Ophelia. A wizard kidnapped her when we were at The Dancing Frog in London." His face twisted. "I couldn't save her."

Colovere reared to his full height, and everyone backed away. Without a word, he set off in a gallop.

"No!" Brayden cried. "It's a trap, Colovere. The wizard wants you." There was no way the unicorn could hear him.

"Do you think he knows that?" Tolor snarled. "Maybe you should have said something before barreling out here and screaming like that."

Drist stepped in front of Brayden. "The boy did not know what would happen, and he has been distraught. Move away beran."

Distraught? Okay, maybe a little bit. Familiar arms wrapped around him from behind. Brayden closed his eyes and brought Juliette's fingers to his lips. Some of the tension melted away from his knotted muscles. He pulled her beside him.

Colovere's scream split the air, and all except Drist ran toward the sound.

Brayden tried to pull Juliette back. She shrugged him off.
"This thief is a wizard," Brayden yelled. "He could kill you."
"If he does, I've lived more years than a human is allotted.
Colovere would do anything to save me. I'll do no less for him."
Brayden followed. *I won't lose her.*
At the end of the meadow Ophelia laid, unmoving.
Tolor saw Selene, and roared. Brayden's mouth dropped
open. A bear stood upright in his place. He had the look of a man
with long glistening teeth, and he was huge. His words slurred.
"This is no place for you, Selene. If we can't subdue the wizard
you may be next."
Her hands curled into fists at her sides and her face
reddened. "I will not run away like a coward."
"I have no time for this!" Tolor snarled. She took a step
back, but held her ground. Tolor's teeth gleamed. He moved fast
and without warning, and bit her rump.
Selene yelped. "How dare you!"
"I said go."
"I will." she yelled, grabbing for a bite on her rump she
couldn't reach.
"Now!"
He bit her twice more. "Stop, Tolor." He lunged again and
she ran, stopping at the edge of the meadow.
Tolor had already turned to the thief. He circled the wizard
whose attention was split between Meneme's slashing hooves and
an attempt at controlling Colovere.
Colovere bucked, reared, and thrust his head. His horn
stabbed in the thief's direction whenever he tried to throw a bolt
at them. The wizard cursed, dodging as he pulled on the ropes of
fire wrapped securely around the unicorn champion's belly. The
smell of burnt hair permeated the air and Colovere shrieked. He
lurched for the wizard, but slammed into Tolor.
Tolor lunged for the wizard's leg, but the thief used
Colovere's distraction to throw a ball of blue fire at the beran.
Tolor roared a horrible sound and fell to the ground. Selene
screamed.
Juliette ran forward, grabbing the magical rope. The air
sizzled with electricity and she fell to the ground. Brayden ran for

305

her, pulling her to safety. She trembled in his arms, her face ashen.

"We have to do something, Brayden. Can't let him have…Colovere."

Scanning the meadow frantically, Brayden called for Whisper and Storm. *Where the hell are they? And where is Drist?*

He turned to see that the pond had closed blocking the wolves and Drist on the opposite side. The wolves barked and yelped with frustration, until they ran through the water without stopping and came out dripping blood on the other side. Baring their teeth to the wizard, they surrounded Juliette. It was a momentary distraction for the thief. Brayden saw movement from the corner of his eye and glanced toward it. Drist held a ball of fire in his hands. The thief saw it too. Brayden rammed into him as he shot a blast of power so fast, Drist barely managed to block it. Brayden rolled and saw it hit an invisible shield. A surge of fire sprayed, erupting into sparkles blackening the grass below them. The wizard pulled tighter on Colovere's rope. Shrieking, Colovere's body convulsed. Drist's face distorted and he fell to his knees in the grass.

A black streak flew from behind the wizard like lightning. The thief dropped the rope holding Colovere captive. Terrible screams curdled Brayden's blood. The line of power made a popping sound and dissipated. The fire stopped, and Drist's shield disappeared.

Petaire stood tall with the thief's body impaled on his horn. A neigh of victory split the air, and Colovere fell to the ground. Juliette crawled to him and Brayden ran to Ophelia.

Drist joined Brayden, and looked her over. "She's only asleep, little cub."

"Thank God," Brayden said, running his hand through her mane. "Will you please stop calling me that?"

Drist smiled. "You were brave to come to the tavern, and try to fight a wizard… or maybe just stupid. All right, I won't call you little cub anymore, boy."

Brayden clenched his teeth, and then sighed. It was preferable to little cub.

Colovere pulled his way across the grass, and laid his head on Ophelia's neck. Meneme disappeared into the trees.

A week after the fight, Brayden sat on the porch with Drist while Juliette and Tolor fixed breakfast. Meneme had left with Petaire that morning. Colovere and Ophelia jumped and played alone in the meadow, while his majestic herd threw their heads, played and danced with joy at their mistress' return.

Brayden hadn't seen Selene since the fight, but Juliette had told him she was sore, angry, and farther away from the beran that loved her than ever before. Tolor, quieter than usual, kept to himself. Brayden turned to Drist.

"The reason I sought the tavern putting everyone in danger was to find Zylphia, and break the curse on Juliette. Now we know that the magical creatures can leave, but Juliette remains caged. Please Drist, I'll do whatever you want in payment if you'll free her."

Drist shook his head. "I can't free her, Brayden."

His name was a slap in his face. Brayden stood to face him. "But why? She's met the conditions of the curse."

"I didn't say I won't free her boy. I said I can't."

Brayden swallowed hard. "Then tell me who can, or what I need to do."

"No one can free her."

Brayden looked at him, unblinking.

"Only a wizard stronger than the wizard or witch that placed the curse can break it."

Brayden sat down and stared at the pond that surrounded the cottage. He was beaten. There was nothing, but hot searing despair. "Thank you, Drist. You've been very kind in helping us save Colovere, and helping us to set things in order."

"What has everyone decided to do?" Drist asked.

"The wolves stay with Juliette of course. Colovere has decided that after all this time, this is his home. Tolor has decided the same. He says the world went on without him, and the only thing he desires is forever out of his reach. Meneme is going to rule as Petaire's mistress," Brayden said.

Drist looked at him confused. "But I thought she was in love with Colovere."

"It turns out that she just wanted a mate, and Petaire has always found her pleasant. His words, not mine."

"After breakfast we'll need to go," Drist said. "I need to get back to my own world. There are many animals that trust in me for their protection. I won't leave them unguarded."

Brayden nodded, and wiped at a tear he hoped Drist didn't see. "I understand."

Brayden helped Juliette with the dishes. Her smile was radiant as she hung the dish towel, and kissed him lightly on the cheek. She looked in his eyes as if she were searching for something. Her smile disappeared and she took a step back.

"What's wrong?"

"Can we go sit down and—"

"No. If you have something to say, you can do it right here."

She thinks I'm dumping her. I'm not, so why does it feel the same. He blurted the words before he couldn't speak. "I couldn't break the curse." He breathed. His heart broke. He had failed her. "It isn't possible."

Juliette studied him. Tears flowed down his cheeks.

"This is goodbye," Juliette said, pressing her lips into a tight line.

"It's not over. We still have the moonlit nights. I'll wait for you, and keep looking for a way to free you."

Juliette shook her head, and ran her hand down his jawline. "That's no life for you. I won't tie you down to a woman that isn't there."

Juliette went to her room and didn't speak to him again, even when they left. She looked at him with a tear-stained face, and ran from the room. Drist took his hand, and Brayden had no choice but to follow him through the mirror.

Chapter 52

"Love is a canvas furnished by nature and embroidered by imagination." — *Voltaire*

The Mirror World

Tolor watched as Selene put her bag of belongings down, and draped a black cloak around her head and shoulders. It fanned her body, covering even her rump. It was as if she had stuck a knife in his heart. She glanced at him. The knife twisted. His eyes filled with tears, but he didn't allow them to spill. Not yet. He wanted this to be easy for her. Perhaps it would have been better if he hadn't come, but this was his way of saying goodbye. He watched as she passed through the portal where he knew her brothers waited for her. He closed his eyes against a pain he hoped never to experience, and yet it was the dream of what he had always wanted for her. Selene was going home. After today, he wouldn't see her ever again.

He didn't have the energy to return to the cottage. He sat on a boulder near an outcropping, remembering the little mare that held his heart from the moment he saw her, alone and afraid in a world she didn't understand. Zylphia would not have been able to abduct an older, more skilled centaur for the centaurs had magic of their own. Selene had been young and untrained. Still, for all their outrage, they were unable to get her back.

Gone, his little Seley was gone. If she ever remembered him, he hoped it would be with fondness.

Selene walked between her brothers solemnly. All she had wanted for years was to go home, to be with her family, see her mam. Now she only felt numb, cold, alone. *Who would have thought one could be so lonely in a crowd of centaurs,* she mused. But she was. Seeing Tolor... she shivered at the look on his face, her heart swelled like a toothache. She had been a fool, he never wanted Juliette. She always thought Juliette could give him more, things every male wanted. She might have even given him a child, something Selene would never be able to do. But Juliette had never wanted him either, and now there was Brayden.

Tonight she had walked out of Tolor's life forever. Did he know that she loved him? She should have told him before she left. The last couple of years had been full of so much anger and loneliness. Jealousy had been her bed partner. Her blood heated remembering his bite the day of the fight. She hadn't forgiven him for that yet.

"Mam and pap have worked hard at finding you a mate," her brother Gordone said. They had thought Bengir would have you, the way he followed you around when you were a filly, but he is betrothed to another. If they cannot find you a mate you will have to join Peden, or Craul's herd."

Selene shivered. "Why must I have a mate so soon? I'm only just coming home after more than a century of confinement."

Confinement? It hadn't felt like confinement, not when Tolor was with her. She was whole, vibrant, even happy. Why had she always wanted to go home? Centaurs were old fashioned, and mares were second class citizens unless they found a stallion that loved them enough to take a mate instead of a herd. Tolor had never treated her second rate. She could still see the pain in his eyes, tears pricked at her own in response.

"You're past the age of mating, Selene. If we wait, none of the stallions will want you."

"Won't want me? What if I don't want them?"

"That's enough. You aren't a filly anymore. It's time for you to take your place. A mate or a herd are your options."

Gordone continued to chatter beside her. Ignoring him, she chewed her lower lip. With a mate she would be more trapped than in Zylphia's world. A herd was worse than the old human harems and degrading. It was a place for the mares no stallion wanted. She imagined initiation and cringed. She didn't want anyone in such a way, except Tolor, but she couldn't have that with him. It didn't matter, she had no need of babies. Her heart pounded, her breathing became ragged. This was the biggest mistake of her life, and it would seal her fate for eternity. *Eternity without Tolor is not an option.* It was time to be humble. She turned around and galloped for the portal.

310

Tolor wiped the tears from his eyes. He didn't know how long he sat weeping on the boulder, but crying would accomplish nothing. He had watched his heart walk out the door. It was time to go home and accept the new life he had never been willing to acknowledge. It was over. He turned toward the cottage. Hoof falls that had to be tearing the soil beneath them caught his attention a moment before she landed in front of him. He startled, stood up straight, and smiled in spite of the pounding in his chest.

"You were always able to stop on a silver," he said.

Selene grinned at his praise, and then her smile was gone. Tolor wanted to reach up, and put it back.

"Don't be sad Seley. This is your day."

Selene shook her head and, biting her trembling lower lip, looked at the grass. "Not if you aren't in it."

"What did you say?"

"Tolor, I—"

Tolor moved the hair from her face, cupping her cheeks in his hands.

"I'm—"

He wrapped his arms around her, years of emotion pouring into his kiss. When he pulled back, he whispered in her ear.

"We'll talk about it later," he said, brushing his lips against her cheek. "Let's go home."

Chapter 53

Clover Springs, California

The month went by, and Brayden waited for the full moon. He sat by the mirror in a candle lit room. He had chocolates, and the largest strawberries he had ever seen, and a box of supplies for Juliette to take home. She never came.

Eyes swollen from tears and a lack of sleep, Brayden went to take a shower. As he undressed, his cell phone rang. He didn't know the number, but he answered anyway.

"This is Shane Bradford calling for Brayden Parker."

"I'm Brayden Parker."

"Shane Bradford Productions here. The intern that replaced you has had a family emergency, and had to leave us. Before I call the next victim in line to replace him, I thought I would see if you might have changed your mind. You can start as soon as you're able to get here. We're in the middle of filming right now."

Brayden closed his eyes. "I'm sorry Mr. Bradford. I can't." He disconnected the call, sat on the floor, and stared at the wall.

Brayden went through the closet looking for his duffle bag. He didn't know where he was going, only that he couldn't stay. He wiped what he swore would be the last tears from his eye, and climbed onto a chair to reach the back of the shelf. He scanned it and sighed, no duffle bag, but there was a tin sitting in the back corner. It wasn't his. He pulled it out, threw it on the bed and jumped off the chair. Frustrated over the duffel bag, he sat on the bed and stared at the mirror. Then he picked up the tin.

It was a small box, plain in appearance with a few rust spots. He tugged at the lid and it slid open with a grating sound. An old pin with a faded yellow bow fell to the bed, along with four very

312

old photos, and a piece of paper that looked like a folded letter. He carefully opened the yellowed paper.

Dearest Juliette,

I lay on my death bed, and all I can think about is you.

I hope you can forgive me for what I've done. I didn't have anything To do with putting you in that place, but I was the one who sealed your fate.

I couldn't let my children grow up and be like her. So I did the only thing I knew to do to stop her. I paid a wizard to kill her.

Zylphia is dead. She will never trouble you again, but there is no one to release you from that awful place she created. Even if you hate me for this, I hope you'll understand why I had to do it. I never hated you, Juliette. For me, you were always, and forever will be the girl I ran with on the beach. May all your days be filled with such joy.

Yours Always,

Emily Walsh

He read the letter numerous times, his heart beating faster. He raked his hand through his hair. It was one thing to hear she was from another era, and something else to see it. A trembling hand reached for one of the photos.

A young girl, not more than ten years old held the hand of her mother, while a tall man with short dark hair and a long moustache rested his hand on the girl's shoulder. He read the back, then turned to the front and stared, with his mouth open in shock, at a picture of Juliette as a little girl. The back had said, '*I found these in your things when I packed your room. You were such an adorable child.*'

Brayden picked up another photo. This one was of a little girl wearing a white bonnet, with a black dress and white apron. '*This one is of me the day I started working at the Barrows home. Even the bonnet couldn't hide my scruffy hair.*'

The next photo made his breath catch. He ran his fingers over a teenage girl, with tight ringlet curls clinging to her cheeks. He couldn't tell the color of the dress she wore because the photos were black and white, but it was long, and it held her breasts high. The sleeves were short and puffed up, and pearl earrings clung to her ears. He kissed the photo and held it to his heart. His Juliette. The curls were softer, but nothing else had changed. *'This is you dressed for your sixteenth birthday party.'*

The last photo was of a family Brayden wasn't familiar with. *'Here I am with Jonathan and our children. I wasn't at all sure you would want this one, but I wanted you to have it if you did. If not, would you leave it on the mantle for Jonathan on a moonlit night. He has others, but this is our favorite.'*

Brayden broke his rule. He wept again. But this time the tears were not for his own loss. They were for Juliette's. What must she have gone through being forced away from her family for all those years, and then when everyone was gone? *Oh Juliette.*

He put the letter and the photos back in the tin, lingering on the old yellow bow. It had to have been cheap even by the standards of the age, but it was cute. He wondered what made it important enough for Emily to throw it in there. He put the tin on a table. He would leave it on the bed with an apology for opening it when he left. He was sure that at some point she would come through the mirror again. He wondered. *When she does will she find me an old man? Grown, like Emily was when she wrote that letter?* One thing he learned from Juliette and her world, nothing was impossible. He would continue to seek a way out for Juliette.

He found a suitcase in his mother's room and borrowed it to pack after breakfast.

When his stomach rumbled a complaint, Brayden realized he hadn't eaten since yesterday. He got in the shower. He would have breakfast in town when he was done.

His phone rang again. This time, Brayden ignored it. There was nobody that he wanted to talk to. But the phone kept ringing long after it should have gone to voice mail. He got out of the shower, and dried off with a towel, then he curiously answered.

It was as if he had placed the call. The phone began to ring. He scowled, and determined to hang up just as a gentleman answered.

"How long does it take to answer a phone, boy?"

Brayden's eyes narrowed. "Drist?"

"Yes. Next time don't keep me waiting or I'll not wait for your answer."

No, of course he wouldn't. Drist had been helpful and he was nice enough, but he was his own man. He did what he felt

314

like and nothing more. Still, Brayden found himself oddly glad to hear from the wizard. His lips curved into a wistful smile.

"Sorry, Drist."

"I've thought of a way for you and Juliette to be together, but it requires a sacrifice on your part."

"I'll do anything," Brayden stammered. "You found a way to break the curse?"

Drist ignored him. "If you're sure, I'll be there tomorrow."

Brayden smiled in earnest. "I've never been more sure of anything in my life."

"Then hold that thought. Until tomorrow," Drist said.

He disconnected the call. Brayden dressed and went to breakfast.

The Mirror World

Brayden opened his eyes, and laughed. He let out a shout of victory louder than he ever had before. He got up from the meadow, brushed the grass off his knees, and hollered.

"You did it Drist!"

He heard a voice behind him. "You don't have to yell. I can hear you."

Brayden laughed. Drist smiled. Brayden couldn't remember a time when the man in black smiled at him. Not that it brightened his features any. He was still cloaked in shadow.

"Go." Drist gestured forward with his arm, and Brayden ran to find Juliette.

Juliette sat on the porch sharing bread with Whisper and Storm. It hadn't been easy keeping them from Brayden's room, but she wanted him to have a clean break. It was the least she could do for him. Tears fell from her eyes. *I'm so tired of crying.* She wiped them away and heard somebody yelling her name. *Tolor must be back earlier than planned.* Whisper and Storm ran to greet him. Juliette sheltered her eyes in time to see them plow into Brayden and roll on the ground with him. She cried out with wonder, and ran.

315

By the time she reached him, he was back on his feet.
Juliette didn't think twice. She landed in his arms, and found
herself lost in the most passionate kiss she had ever dreamed of.
Every ounce of love inside her met with his. They knelt on the
grass, where he kissed her again, and again.

Juliette pushed him away just enough to ask. "How?"

Brayden brushed her face with his finger, grazing it light as a
feather across her lips. Juliette's blood warmed, and her stomach
clenched. Desire filled her. She wanted more of him. She wanted
him to be hers. If she could have this one thing, she would never
ask for anything else. A lifetime with the only man she had ever
loved.

"Drist cursed me."

Juliette sat up. Brayden smiled.

"Calm down. It was the only way to be with you. How is it
any different if I chose to be with you in our world? Does it
matter? We'll have each other, we'll live comfortable enough, and
we'll enjoy the world together under the light of the full moon
and a canopy of stars." He kissed her lightly, and took her hand.
"Will you have me? Boyfriend, husband, lover or friend. I'll take
whatever you're willing to give."

Juliette's cheeks felt warm. Her heart fluttered like a
butterfly. She pushed him back on the green, and straddled him.
"How about all of those things?"

Brayden pulled her down into his arms. "I was hoping you'd
say th—"

They sputtered as Whisper sniffed and licked them. They
laughed. Brayden ran his arm across his face. Juliette had a
permanent smile. "We'll lock them out of our room at night."

Brayden laughed, wrapped his body around her and kissed
her again.

Juliette picked up the tin Brayden had brought her. She
recognized it after all these years. Amy Rose had taken the small
box from the mirror. Juliette hadn't known what it was back then.
She wondered what became of her, and then sat down and held
the tin to her chest, wondering what was in it. She placed the tin
on the bed with trembling hands and tugged hard on the lid. It
popped off too fast and the tin dumped its contents on the bed.

Juliette looked through the photos, her heart pumping with excitement. Priceless pictures of the people she had loved, her family. *Emily was ill when she put this together, what must it have cost her?* She picked up the last photo, and stared at the little yellow ribbon, still dirty as the day Emily had given it to her when they were girls. *'Sorry it's not new.'* Juliette smiled as tears sprang to her eyes, she could still hear Emily's voice. She looked at the photos for a long time, returned them to the tin, and set them on the nightstand. They would be best protected there. Then she smiled, wiped the tears from her eyes, and went to join Brayden.

Epilogue

"Life is thickly sown with thorns, and I know no other remedy than to pass quickly through them. The longer we dwell on our misfortunes, the greater is their power to harm us." —Voltaire

The Mirror World

Juliette sat by the pond watching Tolor race Whisper and Storm on his bike. Storm nipped at his heels as he pedaled along. Tolor might have outrun them, but the bike turned out to be too small for him. Selene laughed as he fought Storm off with one furry foot. He finally got off the bike, threw it aside, and ran like the wind, the wolves barking behind him. Selene set off at a gallop to join them.

Colovere reared and played with Ophelia in the meadow. They stopped on occasion to groom each other, until someone got nipped and they were playing again.

Juliette tingled with excitement when she heard Brayden's footsteps in the grass behind her. He sat down and handed her a plate. *Who would have thought men could learn to cook lunch.* She picked up a piece of chicken, bit into it, and scowled. *Well, I guess you can't have everything.* She placed the plate beside her and waited for Whisper to come and save her from the foul tasting poultry. Brayden took a bite of his own and set his plate beside hers.

Tonight was the full moon and they were going to visit Brayden's parents. The Parkers were working with Drist to arrange solar panels for the cottage. Plumbing had already been installed, complete with a sink, shower, and bath for Juliette's pleasure, but no hot water.

Brayden laid his head in her lap and gazed at the rays of the red sunshine. Juliette ran her fingers through his soft hair. The world may have gone on without her, and she might have been forgotten by anyone who lived. But that didn't matter anymore. Her world had changed too. Even in Juliette's world, everything changes.

www.ingramcontent.com/pod-product-compliance
Lightning Source LLC
Chambersburg PA
CBHW061538170626
46811CB00001B/26

9780991167715